THE ARMOUR OF CONTEMPT

IN THE WAR-TORN Sabbat Worlds crusade, Commissar Gaunt and the Tanith First-and-Only yet again struggle for their lives and souls against the foulest enemies of mankind.

Still haunted by his lengthy mission behind enemy lines on Gereon, Commissar Ibram Gaunt heads back with the Imperial crusade army to liberate the Chaos-held planet. Having made contact with the partisans, Gaunt and the Tanith First-and-Only find that the brutality of the 'liberation' pitches them into opposition with their commanders, who believe victory must be achieved at any price, no matter how cruel.

All bets are off as Gaunt and his men are pitched into direct opposition to his commanders!

A WARHAMMER 40,000 NOVEL

THE ARMOUR OF CONTEMPT

Dan Abnett

For my friend Richard Collins
on the occasion of his fortieth birthday.

A BLACK LIBRARY PUBLICATION

First published in Great Britain in 2006.
Paperback edition published in 2007 by BL Publishing,
Games Workshop Ltd.,
Willow Road, Nottingham,
NG7 2WS, UK.

10 9 8 7 6 5 4 3 2 1

Cover illustration by Cos Koniotis.

A CIP record for this book is available from the British Library.

ISBN 13: 978 1 84416 402 8
ISBN 10: 1 84416 402 0

Distributed in the US by Simon & Schuster
1230 Avenue of the Americas, New York, NY 10020, US.

See the Black Library on the Internet at
www.blacklibrary.com

Find out more about Games Workshop
and the world of Warhammer 40,000 at
www.games-workshop.com

IT IS THE 41st millennium. For more than a hundred centuries the Emperor has sat immobile on the Golden Throne of Earth. He is the master of mankind by the will of the gods, and master of a million worlds by the might of his inexhaustible armies. He is a rotting carcass writhing invisibly with power from the Dark Age of Technology. He is the Carrion Lord of the Imperium for whom a thousand souls are sacrificed every day, so that he may never truly die.

YET EVEN IN his deathless state, the Emperor continues his eternal vigilance. Mighty battlefleets cross the daemon-infested miasma of the warp, the only route between distant stars, their way lit by the Astronomican, the psychic manifestation of the Emperor's will. Vast armies give battle in His name on uncounted worlds. Greatest amongst his soldiers are the Adeptus Astartes, the Space Marines, bio-engineered super-warriors. Their comrades in arms are legion: the Imperial Guard and countless planetary defence forces, the ever-vigilant Inquisition and the tech-priests of the Adeptus Mechanicus to name only a few. But for all their multitudes, they are barely enough to hold off the ever-present threat from aliens, heretics, mutants – and worse.

TO BE A man in such times is to be one amongst untold billions. It is to live in the cruellest and most bloody regime imaginable. These are the tales of those times. Forget the power of technology and science, for so much has been forgotten, never to be re-learned. Forget the promise of progress and understanding, for in the grim dark future there is only war. There is no peace amongst the stars, only an eternity of carnage and slaughter, and the laughter of thirsting gods.

Chaos claims the unwary or the incomplete.
A true man may flinch away its embrace,
if he is stalwart, and he girds his soul
with the armour of contempt.

– Gideon Ravenor,
The Spheres of Longing

'THE TWENTY-SECOND year of the Sabbat Worlds Crusade saw a period of renewed fortune for Warmaster Macaroth's main battle groups. Flush from swift and decisive victories at Cabal Alpha, Gerlinde and Zadok, the Warmaster's forces made a vigorous advance into the disputed Carcaradon Cluster, and threw the principal hosts of the archenemy overlord ('Archon'), Urlock Gaur, into hasty retreat. Macaroth's intention was to scatter and destroy the Archon's musters before they could form a cohesive line of resistance in the Erinyes Group.

'To Macaroth's coreward flank, and increasingly left behind, the Crusade's secondary battle-groups – the Fifth, Eighth and Ninth Crusade Armies – maintained their efforts to drive the forces of Magister Anakwanar Sek, Gaur's most capable lieutenant, from the margins of the Khan Group.

'Weakened by problems of morale and logistics, and the fact that the bulk of its manpower came from new and recently founded regiments (the majority of experienced and veteran Guard units had been routed to the main line), the second front had begun to stagnate by the start of 777.M41.

'To compound the problems, the armies of the second front often found themselves outclassed by the highly proficient ground forces fielded by Sek. It is likely many of the second front commanders would have incurred Macaroth's severe displeasure, had the Warmaster not been so singularly occupied with his own objectives. However, General Van Voytz of the Fifth made strenuous efforts to rally the second front, in particular by promoting a series of uncompromising actions to liberate certain worlds previously regarded as 'lost causes'.

'Van Voytz dubbed his strategy "Crush and Burn", and its purpose was to restore pride to the second front through the systematic purging of worlds that had, until then, seemed incontrovertibly the possessions of the archenemy.

"Crush and Burn" had the desired effect, though the vast expenditure of resources necessitated by the policy was later questioned by the Munitorum. Confidential position papers also reveal that, in one particular case, there was an altogether different motive behind these costly liberation efforts.'

– from *A History of the Later Imperial Crusades*

WALKING GLORY ROAD

I

RIP WAS AN acronym, and it happened in the Basement. There were two hundred and forty-three scalps in the detail, the majority of them there for the 'P' part of the name. On the first day, Criid didn't know anybody, and stood alone, hands in pockets. That earned a few words of elucidation from the instructor, Driller Kexie.

'No bloody Guardsman, not even a wet-fart scalp like you, parks their hands in their pockets!' Kexie opined. Kexie was two-twenty tall, and looked as if he had been woven out of meat jerky. He spoke in a slow measure, as if he had all the time in the world to wither and abuse, and the words came out of his dry, lipless mouth like tracer-shot: hot, bright and burning. If he shouted at night, you'd see his words stitch up the dark like phosphor tears.

Driller Kexie had a stick. For reasons no one in the detail ever fathomed, he called it 'Saroo'. It was a thick spar of turned hardwood, forty centimetres long, and resembled both an officer's baton and the leg of a chair. Kexie liked to reinforce certain words and phrases with Saroo. At 'wet-fart scalp', Kexie stroked Saroo against Criid's left hand, which was still in its pocket. A flash flood of acute pain flared across the knuckles of Criid's fist. On 'like you', Saroo visited Criid's right hand. The words 'parks hands' brought Saroo right up between Criid's legs. Criid dropped onto the metal decking, sucking air.

'Upright, hands at your sides. No other posture is acceptable to the God-Emperor, to me, or to Saroo. Are we clear?'

'Yes, driller.'

'Ech,' Kexie said, tilting his head on one side. He had, they would discover, a habit of punctuating his speech with that particular sound. 'Ech, call that a clean loader?' 'Ech, what a shit-soft attempt!' 'That the best you offer, ech?'

'Ech,' he said, 'I don't believe that Saroo can hear you, scalp?'

'Yes, driller!' Criid shouted. 'We are clear, driller!'

'Get up,' Kexie sniffed, and turned back to the others.

Some of the others were greatly amused. The first day was scarcely ten minutes old, and already one of their number was prone on the deck with pain-wet eyes.

They were an ugly lot, most of them the flotsam of various regiments. Criid had already put a name to three or four of the most prominent. A nickname, at least. There was Fourbox, who was a tall, heavy-set joker from the 33rd Kolstec. He was on RIP, he had proudly declared to them as they gathered, for being 'rubbish at everything'. Lovely was a female tanker from the Hauberkan. She was on her third repeat of RIP, though this was her first taste of Driller Kexie. 'I don't like orders,' she had replied when Fourbox asked her what her reason for being there was, and left it at that. Lovely had a real edge to her. Dark haired and tanned, she seemed as risky as an unsheathed knife in a kitbag.

Boulder, as was often the case with Guard nicknames, belonged to a youth who didn't deserve it. Boulder was small and scrawny, a stick-thin go-nowhere, another Kolstec like Fourbox. Criid supposed the sledgehammer irony of the Imperial Guard had stuck Boulder with his handle. Though he was small, and looked picked-on, it was hard to empathise with him. He had a shrill cackle, and used it to signal his delight at the pain of others. Boulder had been sent on RIP by his commanding officer 'for fixing a bayonet to a rocket launcher, haw-haw-haw.'

In Criid's opinion, less than ten minutes old, Wash was the real poison in the detail. Wash reminded Criid of Major Rawne: tall, dark, handsome and venomous. He knew he looked good, even in the faded RIP issue fatigues, and he regarded all of them with a dismissive silence. When, as they first assembled, Fourbox had asked him 'what he was in for', Wash simply hooded his eyes and turned his back.

'Oooh, hard man, haw-haw-haw!' Boulder had sniggered, and Fourbox and some of the others had laughed along.

Wash had turned, extended the index finger of his left hand, and inserted it into Boulder's mouth, pushing the fingertip up over the front teeth until it wedged, painfully, in the roof of the gum, tenting the lip and philtrum against Boulder's nostrils. Boulder had snorted in distress but, like a fish on a hook, had been unable to pull free.

'I am not "hard man",' Wash had said. 'I am not your bloody friend. You want me, you ask for Wash. And you never, ever want me.'

With that, he let Boulder's lip go. Everyone was suitably respectful of Wash from that point.

'Tanith takes a dive!' Fourbox chortled when Driller Kexie put Criid on the deck. 'First and only, they say. First and only to get a smack!'

'Tanith's tearing up,' Boulder joined. 'Look, look! Like a little girl! Boo hoo! Haw-haw-haw!'

'Go home to mama, little Tanith!' Fourbox sang out.

'She'll wipe your eyes and make it all nice again,' Lovely sniggered. 'Mwah! Mwah!' she added, pantomiming kisses. 'All better now!'

'My mother...' Criid began, getting up. 'My mother would gut you fethers...'

'Oh, *I'm* so bloody scared!' announced Boulder. 'So scared, I wet myself haw-haw-haw!'

'I know your mama,' Fourbox called. 'She wriggled a bit, but she was all right. She still writes to me. "Oh, Boxy, when can we be together again? I long for your hot–"'

'Enough!' Driller Kexie tracered. 'Staple your lips, you wet-farts. Ech, I've seen some details in my time, but you take the brass arse. Muscle up, in a line! Come on, come on! Get up and get in it, Criid. Drill order. Is that a drill order, shit-wit? Get to it! Six lines, now! Come on!'

Kexie walked the lines, twirling Saroo in his calloused hands.

It was cold in the echoing vault of the Basement. Their breath made smoke in the air. Like all bilge spaces, the Basement was unheated and raw. Its walls were a ferruginous stain of rust and metallic gangrene, and the air smelled of the stale urine and solvents that had leaked down-hull.

'All right, ladies and ladies,' said Kexie. 'I'm assuming that's the best you can do. Frig, I've seen foundees dress a better rank. You are *shit*, you hear me? The lowest of the low. You are RIP, and making your life a misery is my purpose, given to me expressly by the God-Emperor of Mankind himself. Ech, I have to turn you into proper bloody Guardsmen. You come to me as wet-farts, and I send you back as real soldiers. Or… you die.'

He paused and ran his gaze along their silent rank.

'Anyone got anything funny to say about that? Come on, now. Speak openly.'

'Well, you can try,' Lovely suggested.

Saroo struck her in the throat, and then across the back of the head as she went down.

Lovely lay on the decking, choking. Criid moved to help her.

'No one bloody move. No one! Let her soak it up. Anyone else got a comment? No? *No*?'

Kexie stopped pacing and stood facing them. 'Welcome, you sons and daughters of bitches, to RIP detail. Let us be sure we understand what those letters stand for. "R" is... I'm waiting?'

'Retraining, driller,' they murmured.

Kexie smacked Saroo into his palm. 'I don't believe Saroo can hear you...'

'Retraining!' they yelled.

'And the "I" is for...?'

'Indoctrination, driller!'

'Getting there. Good. And the "P"? You all know what that means?'

'Punishment, driller!'

Kexie nodded. 'Good and good. Ech. So let me do a head count. I'm guessing most of you scalps are here for "P" purposes. Show of hands.'

Most of the detail, including Boulder, Wash and Lovely, raised their hands.

Kexie nodded again. 'And who's in for "R"?'

A handful, including Fourbox.

Kexie swung Saroo in his hands. 'Imagine my surprise if any of you are here for "I". Anyone?'

Eight hands rose. Criid was one of them.

'Shit,' said Kexie. '*Eight* of you? All right, you eight. Front and centre.'

Criid came forward alongside the other seven. They looked like boys, all of them, with that long-limbed, round-shouldered, malnourished air of puberty.

'Look and learn, you wet-farts,' Kexie told the rest of them. 'These eight are virgins. Cherry bloody scalps. Never seen a day of hot war. Never fired in anger. You'd bloody well better make sure none of them do better than you, or I will personally take a bolt pistol to the sides of your heads and grin when I twitch the trigger.'

Kexie regarded the eight 'I' candidates.

'Deck-thrusts, fifty reps,' he said. 'Now.'

AFTER AN HOUR of reps, the detail ran ropes for three hours or so, and then did circuits of the Basement with weight loads. By the time five hours were done, they were numb and mindless with fatigue.

'Switch, ropes!' Kexie yelled.

Fourbox, sweaty and flushed, could no longer haul himself up the knotted ropes to the Basement's roof.

'Anyone fails, the whole detail repeats!' Kexie informed them.

'Spit on your palms,' Criid whispered across to Fourbox. 'Spit on your palms and you get a better grip.'

Fourbox did so, and began to ascend.

'Who taught you that?' he grunted.

'My father,' said Criid, several metres higher and going strong.

'What's his name?'

'Which one?' asked Criid.

II

THE LIGHTS DOWN the roof of the Basement began to switch off, each bank dying with a loud *rr-chunk*. The members of the detail were scattered like battlefield dead on the practice mats, panting and moaning. Their sweat-soaked fatigues stuck to their bodies. They lay on their backs, holding their hands out like faith healers, away from any contact. Fat with friction blisters, their palms were too inflamed to bear touching anything.

'Right here, tomorrow, at oh six hundred,' Driller Kexie told them. 'Not a minute later, or Saroo will want to know why. Assemble and salute me.'

Drill Instructor Kexie stood, slapping Saroo against his right thigh, as the RIP detail slowly got to its feet and formed ranks.

'Six weeks,' Kexie said. 'Six weeks walking Glory Road to planet-fall. God-Emperor, I'll have turned some of you into fighting bloody Guardsman by then. Today was a disgrace. Tomorrow, you'll do better. Dismissed.'

Kexie wandered over to Criid as the detail broke up.

'Sorry about the hard whacks, Criid,' he whispered. 'I didn't realise you were here on indoctrination.'

Criid nodded. 'That's all right, driller. You weren't to know.'

'No, I wasn't. Shame. Now put the bloody mats away.'

The rush-woven practice mats were heavy, and twelve metres square. Hauling and rolling them into their lockers would have been a significant feat for anyone, let alone a person with brutally blistered hands.

'You're kidding?' said Criid.

'Are you refusing an order, scalp?' Kexie asked.

'No, but–'

Saroo paid Criid a rather more prolonged visit, smacking into places where the bruises wouldn't show.

After Kexie had gone, Criid lay on the deck for a long while, drenched in pain, and then got up and put the mats away. It took a long while. Fourbox, Lovely and half a dozen other members of the RIP detail were lingering by the hatch. They'd all seen what the driller had done. Finally they came over and helped Criid with the mats.

'I can do it,' Criid said.

'Driller really beat on you,' Fourbox said. 'You all right?' The mischief had been robbed from his face. He looked genuinely worried.

'Yes. Look, I can do this.'

'Be quicker if we help,' said one of the others, a thin boy called Zeedon.

'Kexie's a bastard,' Lovely said. 'Think I might stick him good.'

'Yeah, sure you will,' Fourbox said.

'I got a blade,' Lovely snapped. 'I'll stick the bastard, he comes near me with that rod again.'

'Don't,' said Criid.

'Why not?' Lovely asked. 'He's got it coming...'

'Don't be stupid. Attack an officer?' Criid said. 'You''ll be executed. Summary shots behind the ear.'

'Be worth it,' Lovely said, but she no longer sounded so sure.

'Driller's doing his job, don't you get that?' Criid said. 'This is the Imperial Guard. Drill discipline and hard knocks. That's what gets us to the grade and keeps us there. If you expect any different, Throne knows why you ever signed up.'

'You sound like a bloody commissar,' one of the others said.

Criid smiled. 'First compliment I've had today.'

'What's your name?' asked Fourbox.

'Criid.'

'What, like the holy Imperial creed?'

'No. Double "i" not double "e". It's a Verghast name.'

'I'm going to call you "Holy",' said Fourbox, alighting on a nickname in the time-honoured Guard way of zero consideration. 'Yeah, "Holy". Got a good ring to it.'

'Whatever you think best,' said Criid.

'Who's that?' asked Lovely suddenly, pointing. On the far side of the Basement deck, a figure was standing in the shadows of the main entry hatch. A woman, tall and slender, wearing dark combat gear and the pins of a sergeant.

'Feth,' muttered Criid.

'Who is that?' asked Lovely.

'Just my–' Criid began. 'My supervising officer, come to fetch me. Tomorrow, all right?'

'Same time, same pain, Holy!' Fourbox laughed out as Criid hurried away.

'Holy?' the woman asked as Criid joined her.

'I won a nickname.'

'Is that a bruise?' she asked, reaching out to touch Criid's face.

'Don't!' Criid hissed, slapping her hand away.

'Who did that to you?'

'I fell. During an exercise.'

'You're limping.'

'Leave it alone. What are you doing here?'

'I came to see how you'd got on. First day and everything.'

'Well, I wish you hadn't.' Criid pushed past her and limped on down the service way.

'Dalin!' she growled.

Nearly eighteen years old, tall and strong, Dalin Criid was afraid of nothing in the cosmos apart from the sound of her voice. He halted.

'Someone beat you?' she asked.

'The driller was making a point. That there are no favourites in RIP.'

'Bastard. I should kill him,' Tona Criid said. 'Want me to kill him?'

'No,' he replied, 'but if you come here to find me again, ma, I want you to be sure and kill me.'

III

FOOD CYCLE. THE swelter decks were heaving. Grease smoke and steam wallowed out of the mess wells, and rolled along the roof above the milling crowd. The grilles of the vent ducts were matted with ropes of solidified fat. There was a smell of boiled greens, mashed squash and pith oil. Hand bells were ringing. Various vendors called out their bills of fare to the passing tide.

For an issue scrip, a trooper could eat basic heated rations in the Munitorum halls, but the promise of something different drew hundreds of them to the swelter decks at the end of every day cycle. That, and the fact you could get drink here, and indulge other vices, if you knew who to ask.

The swelter decks existed because of the 'followers on the strength'. Every Guard regiment trailed after it an entourage of attendant personnel: wives, children, girlfriends, whores, faith healers, preachers, beggars, tinkers, hucksters, tooth-pullers, contrabandeers, scribes, loan-sharks and a whole panoply of shadowy souls who lived, like parasites, like fleas, on the coat-tails of the military. Hark had been told that some regiments doubled in size when you factored in the hangers-on.

The swelter decks were where they lived and ate, and dealt and traded. He'd once heard a junior commissar suggest the camp followers be purged from the fleet. 'It would reduce Munitorum costs by nearly fifty per cent,' the junior had announced brightly.

'Yes,' Hark had smiled, 'and the following day, every Guardsman in the quadrant would desert.'

As they wandered down through the press of the main gangway, Viktor Hark noted with some satisfaction that his companion showed no signs of voicing any similarly naive comments. Ludd's eyes were wide, for this was Junior Commissar Nahum Ludd's first experience of a carrier's fringe areas. But he was bright and sharp, and Hark could see why his superior had arranged Ludd's formal transfer to the re-formed First-and-Only.

They ducked under a gibbet rack of swinging, salted waterfowls, and then sidestepped to avoid the steam outflow from a rack of broiling vats. Eager voices were raised as dirty hands held out currency to be exchanged for fried meat on wooden sticks and parcels of spiced mince wrapped in cabbage leaves.

'Hungry?' Hark asked.

'I've eaten, sir,' replied Ludd, raising his voice over the din.

'Munitorum basics?' Hark wondered.

'I ate at the early shift. It comes out of our pay, after all.'

'What was it tonight?'

'Ah, some kind of pickled fish, and a starch pudding.'

'Nice?'

'The, ah, fish was piquant, you might say,' Ludd said.

A tender hurried by with a shoulder paddle laden with steaming pies. Ludd turned and watched them go past. Hark could almost see the young man salivate.

Viktor Hark was powerfully built with thick dark hair and a clean-shaven face. His head rose from his thick neck like the tip of a bullet. He had an easy, casual manner about him that Ludd found disquieting, particularly as Ludd knew Hark could be a savage and ruthless disciplinarian. At some point in his life – Ludd had never had the balls to ask about it – Hark had lost his left arm and had received an augmetic replacement.

Hark raised that augmetic now and clicked the fingers. The flick of the mechanical digits sounded like a boltgun being racked.

The tender stopped in his tracks.

'Sir?'

'Two of those,' Hark said, pointing a V-fork of his real fingers.

'Sweet or sour, sir?' the tender asked, sweeping his wooden paddle round to proffer his wares.

'What is it?'

'Spiced fowl, or sugar ploin, sir.'

'Ludd?'

'Ah, ploin, sir?'

'One of each, then,' Hark said, fetching coins from his coat pocket.

They took the hot pies. The tender gave them sheets of grease paper to fold them in.

They began to walk and eat. Ludd was evidently hungry. He was enjoying his pie so much his eyes were watering.

'Thank you, sir,' he said.

Brushing crumbs from his mouth, Hark made a dismissive gesture. 'What are we now, Ludd?' he asked.

Ludd had to hurriedly swallow a hot mouthful to answer. He winced. 'I... ah, I'm not sure I know what you mean, sir.'

'Well, Nahum, what were we before I bought the pies?'

'Ah... two commissars patrolling the rude quarters?'

'Swelter decks, Ludd. That's what the camp followers call them. I know "low quarters" is the official term, but for Throne's sake, it sounds like the start of a barrack room joke.'

'Yes, sir.'

'Eat up.' Hark took another bite of his pie. He had to chew and wait until his mouth was clear enough to continue. 'You're right, anyway. Two commissars, wandering the swelter decks. You're a ne'er-do-well trooper with something to hide. You see the likes of us, you know we're looking. But two commissars, eating pies... and, by the way, getting crumbs and juice down the front of his uniform...'

'Mhm! Sorry!'

'Now what does that say?'

'That we're here for food cycle? And therefore... not on any official duty?'

Hark bowed his head. 'Exactly. A trick of the trade, Nahum. If you can't hide, hide in plain sight.'

There was a sound of music, of reed pipes. Hark looked around with a start. A troupe of entertainers capered past, playing pipes and viols and hand drums. Five acrobats were turning handsprings in their wake along the main aisle. Jugglers ran like skirmishers around the fringes, snatching hats, fruit and other items like spoons and half-eaten skewers from unsuspecting passers-by, and were spinning them in the air once or twice before returning them to their laughing, baffled owners. A small child followed the troupe, her eyes huge in a face smeared lime green with camo-paint, collecting coins in a battered Guardsman's helmet that she held out, like a bucket, by the chinstrap.

Hark drew Ludd back to let them go by. Junior Ecclesiarchy adepts with ink-stained fingers were moving through the crowd, circulating Lectitio Divinitatus texts still damp from the block-presses. Beggars and invalids offered wares of candle stubs and balls of bootblack. At a nearby cook stand, two Guardsmen, one a Kolstec, the other a heavy-set Hauberkan, were arguing over who was next to be served. It looked like a brawl was about to start.

'Ignore it,' Hark said to Ludd. 'Break it up and we show our hand. We're here on other business.'

Ludd nodded, scoffing down the last of his pie. He wiped his mouth on his cuff.

The press around them was getting thicker. Ludd could smell liquor. A scrawny preacher, either half-mad or half-cut, had got up on a handmade pushcart pulpit, and was yelling to any who might care to listen about the 'jubilation of the dying soul'.

Hark wasn't listening. He could still hear the sound of the pipes, fading through the crowd as the troupe moved away. It reminded him of something, in the way that a dream forgotten from the night before sometimes catches up suddenly and becomes memory again. As with such dreams, Hark couldn't define or reconnect the memory. But there was a feeling buried there. Sadness. Regret.

'Sir?'

'What?'

'Sir?' Ludd asked.

Hark blinked. Foolish to be so distracted. That just wouldn't do. Glory Road was always a long walk, and a commissar had the best of his work there. 'Well,' he said, quietly and carefully, 'what did your source say again?'

'Pavver's Place,' Ludd replied. 'It's where Merrt's been seen most. My source says he's over three hundred in the hole.'

'You have to wonder why he keeps going back,' said Hark.

'You do have to wonder,' Ludd said. 'I think there may be more to it than the money.'

Hark nodded. He knew Rhen Merrt of old, one of the original Tanith foundees. War had been cruel to him, and dealt him a bad hand. Seemed like fortune was continuing the spell.

'Are we to execute him?' Ludd asked bluntly.

'What? No!' Hark said. 'Throne, no! You think I'm that hardline, Ludd?'

'I don't know you, sir,' said Ludd. 'I wanted to understand your thinking.'

Hark nodded. 'Sound, then. Decent question. No, I won't shoot him. Unless he gives me real cause. He's one of our own, Ludd, and we've come to save him before he tips over the brink. For the good of Trooper Merrt *and* the regiment. Morale and discipline dance a delicately balanced polka, Ludd. You know what a polka is?'

'Like a… leopard?'

'No. Is that Pavver's Place?'

'Yes, sir.'

'Good. Give me your cap and coat,' Hark said.

'My cap and coat?'

'Come along. Take this.' Hark held out a fold of dirty bills. 'Go and take a look.'

Ludd handed over his cap and coat. Without them, he looked like a junior trooper in his grubby fatigues. He took the fold, tucked it in his hip pocket, and headed towards Pavver's Place.

Pavver's Place liked to think of itself as some kind of 'establishment'. In truth, it wasn't. It lay a few steps down from the deck gangway, a dark, smoky gaming den fashioned into the stanchion holes between hull supports. Most of the roof was a tent made of stolen tarpaulin. There was a charge pending in that alone, Ludd thought.

Music was playing, loud 'pound' music issuing from battered vox-horns wired up in the tent roof. Several lightly clad girls sashayed through the crowd, hoisting trays of drinks, moving their skinny hips in time to the beat. There was no joy in their eyes, nor any bounce in their step. Pavver paid them to swing their bodies to the music as part of their jobs.

Ludd entered, crossed to the makeshift bar, and ordered an amasec.

The barkeep regarded his apparent youthfulness dubiously, until Ludd slapped a bill on the counter. His drink was served in a little, thick-milled, dirty glass.

Without looking around, Ludd had made out Trooper Merrt at a side table, amongst a card school. There was no mistaking him. A round to the mouth on Monthax years ago had blown his jaw out, and he now sported a crude augmetic implant. Merrt had once been a sniper, one of the Tanith's better marksmen, but the injury had put paid to that career speciality. Since the forests of Monthax, Merrt had tried six times to rejoin the sniper cadre. Every time he'd been unsuccessful.

He was scowling as the cards came down, though he always scowled with his face. Around the table with him were four other players: two Kolstec, a Binar and, Ludd noticed, a Belladon. Sipping his drink, Ludd fought to remember the Belladon's name. Maggs. That was it. Recon Trooper Maggs. Bonin spoke highly of him. What the feth was he doing here?

Merrt seemed distracted. The flop clearly hadn't gone his way, but he was raising anyway.

Ludd looked around the place. There, in the corner, was Pavver, with four of his strong-arms. 'Pander' Pavver, lean and nasty, with a thick, crusty fork of beard and a glassy eye. Ex-Guard. In 'the strength', ex-Guard were usually the worst kinds of predator. Pavver and his lackeys were watching Merrt, and talking low. Another loss to the house, another loss Merrt couldn't cover, and they'd skin him.

Ludd reached into his trouser pocket and felt the comfortable grip of his auto-snub. This was going to get ugly. Uglier than Rhen Merrt himself.

He wanted to be ready.

OUTSIDE, VIKTOR HARK thought about another pie. Ludd was taking his time. The heavy-set Hauberkan loomed into his field of vision.

'You Hark?' asked the trooper.

Hark narrowed his eyes. 'I think you'll find I'm referred to as *commissar*, trooper,' he said.

'Yeah, yeah. Commissar Hark, right?'

'What do you want?' Hark asked. 'I'm busy.'

'We've got a problem, Commissar Hark. I think you'll want to deal with it,' the trooper said, ushering Hark on.

Hark sighed and followed. He folded Ludd's coat and hat under his arm. 'What sort of problem?' he asked.

The Hauberkan trooper led Hark down some grille steps behind the mess wells. It was dark and steamy down there. Molten fat dribbled down the walls.

'I said what sort of problem?' Hark demanded.

There were suddenly five Hauberkan troopers around him. One held a knife.

'You're the bastard who executed Gadovin,' said one of them. 'You're gonna pay.'

'Oh, you stupid boys,' Hark said.

IT WAS ABOUT to go off. Finishing his drink, Ludd made a hasty exit onto the gangway. There was no sign of Hark.

'Sir?' he called out. Some of the passing crowd cast him curious looks.

Ludd turned and ran back down into Pavver's place. There was a small pocket of frantic activity that every one else, even the girls, was trying to ignore. Pavver's men were dragging Merrt out through the back door. Merrt had raised on a bet that even the house refused to cover. He was crying out, but his cries, strangulated through that awful augmetic jaw, seemed comical.

What was he saying? 'Sarat'? 'Sabbat'? *Something*.

Patrons in the vicinity were laughing at him. Just some poor old damaged fool, risking too much.

One of the serving girls, a pretty thing with short black hair, was urgently following Merrt out.

'What are you going to do?' she was yelling. 'What are you going to do?'

'Get away and serve!' spat one of the strong-arms, kicking out at her.

Merrt cried out again as he disappeared through the back doors.

Ludd pushed through the crowd. He saw the other men who had been players at Merrt's table. They were on their feet. Wes Maggs, the Belladon, looked like he was about to follow Merrt. When he saw Ludd, he halted, and sat back down sharply.

'Stay there!' Ludd yelled at him, and ran on towards the back doors.

They were still ajar when he reached them. He peered out. Beyond was an undercroft, a dank box of dead space that stank of piss and rotten vegetables. Against the far wall, the strong-arms were already busy beating Merrt to a pulp. Ludd took a deep breath and stepped out.

'That's enough!' he yelled.

The strong-arms stopped hitting Merrt. Glazed and semi-conscious, the Tanith trooper sagged and slid slowly down the wall. The four pieces of muscle turned to regard Ludd with narrow eyes.

'Who the hell are you supposed to be?' one of them asked.

Ludd knew they weren't about to wait for an answer.

IV

THE KNIFE CAME first, a glint of steel.

It was early. If the Hauberkans had been drinking at all, they hadn't been drinking much. They were still sharp, quick, confident. It was also likely they had been planning this ambush for a long while, and were therefore coiled tight like clip-springs.

The knife came first, and Hark simply caught its blade in his augmetic grip. He squeezed. It snapped with a sound like a dull bell.

'Well, that broke,' said Hark. He let go of Ludd's coat and hat, and punched the knife wielder in the

face with his real hand. The man dropped hard. The
impact was satisfyingly dense, even though it hurt his
knuckles.

This again. This was old news. Since Ancreon Sextus, Hark had found himself in three brawls with
Hauberkan troopers, all of whom hated him for his
execution of their incompetent leader, Gadovin.

Well, tough feth to them.

The moment unspooled. They were on fight time
now, that unreal measure of passing moments that
seemed an eternity while it lasted but in reality was
just a handful of seconds. Fight time. Instinct time.
One of the others swung at him. Hark sidestepped
the telegraphed blow, and thumped his augmetic
fist into the man's chest, breaking ribs. The fool
stumbled away, gasping, aspirating blood. The rest
were on his back. Hark used his elbows. He heard
a nose crack, and felt something soft give. He was
released.

Hark rotated on the balls of his feet, the tails of his
leather storm coat floating out. It was a surprisingly
graceful move for someone so solid. He surveyed his
work.

One Hauberkan was on his knees, his hands
clamped to a ruptured nose from which blood was
pouring. The other was on his back, curled up, hands
clamped to his throat gasping. Hark tutted, then
kicked the first one in the head and laid him out on
his back. He looked at the second and decided he'd
done enough there.

The fifth Hauberkan was off to his left. Hark had
presumed the man would bottle and run, seeing as

how all his cronies were down and broken. Mob mentality worked that way.

But it wasn't going to happen, Hark realised. Fight time was still unravelling the moment according to its own curious tempo. The fifth man was wearing a chain fist. It had undoubtedly cost him a great deal on the black trade. He'd bought it to do Hark, and he was going to use it. It started snarling as it swung towards Hark's face.

Hark deflected the strike with his augmetic hand. Drilled chips of steel and black plastek flew off his hand-plant as the buzzing weapon wrenched away.

A knife was one thing, but you didn't fool with a chain fist. It offered no latitude, no second chances. The moment the chain fist appeared, the situation stopped being aggravating and became serious. Fight time spun faster.

The man was saying something. Hark didn't let him start or finish. He kicked the man in the groin, punched him in the mouth, then gripped him around the throat and slammed him back against the filthy wall of the mess well. He kept the grip tight, reinforcing it with his knee and the rest of his body weight. His augmetic arm pinned the chain fist out, helpless.

'Drop it,' Hark instructed.

'Ghhk!' the man choked.

'Now would be good.'

'Gnhh!'

'Two or three more seconds will make the difference between penal service and summary execution. Write your own sentence.'

The man shook the chain fist off his hand. It dropped onto the ground, bounced twice, and lay there, twitching like an insect, eating into the deck.

'Penal service it is,' Hark said. He stepped back and let go. The man staggered forward, regaining his breath.

'One last point,' Hark added. He punched the man in the side of the head with his augmetic. The man tumbled the length of the wall and fell on his face. His skull was probably fractured. A mercy, Hark considered. Thirty years on a penal colony would probably pass a lot easier if you were simple from brain-damage.

Fight time ceased. Breathing hard suddenly, Hark took a step backwards and checked himself. No damage. No wounds. You could take a lot in the unreality of fight time and only learn about it afterwards. He'd been taught that on Herodor. When the loxatl had blown his arm off, he hadn't realised at first.

He looked around at the grunting, coughing bodies around him.

'You stupid bastards,' he said. He reached into his coat pocket and hooked out his vox.

'Hark to Commissariate control.'

'Reading you, commissar.'

'Verify my position via vox-link.'

'Verified, commissar. One eight one oh low quarters.'

'Thank you. Despatch a handling team to that location. Five, repeat five Hauberkan troopers for detention. Zero tolerance. I'll file charges later.'

'Handling team on its way, commissar. Do you require medicae attention?'

'Yes, for them.'

'Also despatched. Will you remain on station, sir?'

Above, at gangway level, the troupe was passing by again. Hark heard the pipes, and the tune got into his head for a second time. Like a dream when–

'Sir, will you remain on station?'

Hark shook himself. He saw the coat and cap lying on the ground.

'Feth… Ludd…'

'Sir?' the vox crackled.

'No, I won't. Deal with this.' He started to run, towards the stairs, up them two at a time. He came up onto the busy gangway, and knocked his way through the capering troupe. The piper stopped playing.

'Hey!' he complained.

'Not now,' Hark warned.

LUDD TOOK HIS auto-snub out of his pocket and aimed it at the strong-arms.

'That's close enough,' he said. He wondered what was wrong with them. He had a gun to them, and they weren't backing down.

The pound music behind him had got louder suddenly.

'We have a problem?' asked a silky voice.

His eye and aim still on the circle of strong-arms, Ludd glanced sideways and saw Pavver beside him. Pavver was calmly standing there, side on to Ludd, looking at the muscle.

'Yes, we have a problem,' Ludd said tightly.

Pavver nodded. 'You, I don't know,' he said, still not looking at Ludd. 'You, you're new to me.'

'Nahum Ludd, Commissariate,' Ludd said.

'Well, they all say that, don't they?' Pavver chuckled. The strong-arms nodded.

Ludd gently took a step or two backwards until he was covering Pavver and the thugs. Pavver turned slowly to face him.

'I am Junior Commissar Nahum Ludd,' Ludd stated.

'Junior commissar, is it?' Pavver nodded. 'That's nice. A nice touch of reality. A nice detail. More credible. *Junior* commissar. Here's a tip. Next time you play the part, get yourself a cap and a coat. Live the role.'

'I'm going to reach for my insignia now,' Ludd said, his left hand straying towards his breast pocket. 'No one do anything stupid.'

Pavver shrugged in a 'take your time' kind of way. 'Only one of us here doing that,' he said.

Ludd flashed his warrant card.

'All right then,' Pavver admitted. 'You're a commissar. I don't want any trouble. I run a decent establishment and–'

'Stop talking,' said Ludd. 'This place persists thanks to the tolerant attitude of this vessel and its Commissariat function. In fact, it's not an "establishment". It's a hole in the wall. It's a den. You so much as cough wrong and we ship you out. You have no rights, no influence, and feth all authority. So stop pretending like you run the finest saloon on Khan Nobilis.'

Pavver nodded. 'I understand my place, *Junior* Commissar Nahum Ludd. I am a little man, and I scrape by. Let us reach an understanding. What is the nature of your problem?'

'Your men were busy killing one of my troopers,' Ludd said.

'That ugly shit?' Pavver shrugged. 'You even care what happens to him? He broke house rules. He staked too high against the bank. My cash hurts me when someone plays rough with it. Yes, my boys were going to kill him. A lesson.'

'You admit it?'

'Where's the point in denying it?'

'You wouldn't get away with it,' Ludd said.

Pavver brought out a lho-stick and lit it. He exhaled smoke. 'You know the turbine halls, *Junior* Commissar Nahum Ludd?'

'By the reactor engines? Yes.'

'Furnace domes down there. Big and hot. Melt skin and bone in a second. We kill a trooper or two who insults my establishment, there's no trace. All gone in a puff of ash. No awkward questions. No come-back. Tidy. This I do to keep the peace.'

'You're admitting to murder?'

Pavver shrugged.

'Why would you do that? To me? I'm a juni– I'm a commissar! I've got you at gun-point. I–'

He hesitated. The strong-arms laughed. Pavver smiled.

'You've got *me*, haven't you?' Ludd asked.

Ludd felt the cold nudge of a pistol's muzzle at the nape of his neck. Pavver hadn't emerged from his den alone. Another of his boys stood behind Ludd, gun aimed at the back of his head.

'One body into the furnace domes? Two? Makes no odds to me. I'm a business man, *Junior* Commissar Nahum Ludd. I've got a hole in the wall to run.'

Pavver pinched the lho-stick between his lips and took out a roll of notes. 'If you'd like to walk away,' he said, edging the words out around his smoke. 'I can make it worth your while. How much does your blind eye cost?'

'If I took your bribe,' Ludd said, 'I could still report you.'

'Ah,' said Pavver, halting his shuffle of cash. 'You've seen the flaw in my argument. You know too much.'

Something odd happened. Time seemed to dilate. Ludd flinched, expecting to feel the hot round scorch through his brain case from behind, and his finger began to squeeze the trigger of his auto-snub. A gunshot rang out, and something hot and wet splashed across the back of Ludd's head and shoulders.

Pavver was yelling. The strong-arms were moving. Ludd fired, and dropped the first of them with a bullet to the chest.

'Balance of power restored,' said a voice. 'Get your hands on your heads, you feth-wipes.'

Viktor Hark stepped into Ludd's field of vision. He was aiming a large combat automatic at Pavver. The muzzle was breathing smoke.

'On your knees!' Hark growled. Pavver and his men obliged quickly. The man Ludd had shot lay on his face in a slick of blood.

'All right, Ludd?' Hark asked.

Ludd nodded. He looked behind him. A body lay on the ground, a pistol in its hand. The headshot had blown most of its cranium away. Ludd realised what was dripping down his back.

'Commissar Hark,' Hark announced, routinely. 'This is the end. Expect no mercy and resign yourselves to a life of misery.'

Pavver started to wail. Hark kicked him in the ribs.

Ludd stepped past the cowering men and reached Merrt. 'We need a medicae,' he said, after a quick inspection. 'Right now.'

Hark nodded and reached for his vox.

Pavver's Place closed forever about fifteen minutes later. It wasn't the first establishment on the swelter decks to come and go so fast, and it wouldn't be the last. As the Commissariate troops led Pavver and the strong-arms away in chains, the girls grabbed their things and fled.

'What about Merrt?' Ludd asked.

'What about you?' Hark answered. 'You sure you're all right?'

'It was weird for a moment,' Ludd confessed. 'Back there, I mean. Thank you, sir. I thought I was dead.'

'These things happen. Weird how?'

'Ah, well… everything seemed to speed up and slow down, all at once.'

Hark nodded. 'Fight time,' he said, as if that explained everything.

V

LARKIN LET THE view through the sniper scope drift and settle until the reticule was framing his target. The young man. A boy really. How old was he? Eighteen standard? The very thought made Larkin feel as old and leaden as a dying sun. He couldn't remember being eighteen himself. *Wouldn't*, actually. Trying to remember being an eighteen year old required him to recall a place and a time, and that place was Tanith, in the deep woods. Larkin didn't like to think about Tanith. After all these years, it was still too bleak and private a loss.

He remembered the boy, though. The kid must've been about ten when he'd come to them. That had been after Vervunhive, after that grinding war, when the First-and-Only's ranks had been swelled by the Verghastite intake. Just a refugee kid, with a baby sister, another two souls dragged along with the followers on the strength. A pair of orphans rescued and protected with maternal fury by a bleach-blonde hiver girl with too many piercings and too many tats.

The hiver girl's name had been Tona Criid. Now she was Sergeant Criid, the regiment's first female officer, a comrade and a friend, her military record outstanding, her worth proved ten times over. Larkin owed her his life, more than once, and had returned the favour, more than once. Seeing her that first time, on the embarkation fields outside Vervunhive, scrawny, dirty, full of rage and spite, dragging two filthy children into the landers with her, Larkin would never have imagined befriending her, or admiring her.

How times changed. He admired her now. For everything she'd done, and everything she was, and every charge she'd led against the Archenemy of Mankind. But most of all, he admired her for being a mother to two kids who weren't hers. For raising them in this squalid, itinerant life.

She'd done a good job. The boy was tall, strong, good looking. Like his father. He had a confidence to him, and smarts, and an easy way with others. And it wasn't just what he was. It was what he represented.

Larkin watched Dalin Criid approaching through his scope for a while longer, then lowered it and pretended to clean it. He had sat himself down outside the main hatch of the barrack hall, his back against the khaki metal of the wall. The excuse was that the uninterrupted length of the concourse outside gave him the chance to test and recalibrate his gunsight.

He took out a patch of vizzy cloth, and began polishing the lenses. His longlas, broken down, lay on the deck beside him in its bag.

People came and went down the echoing concourse. Dalin came up to him.

'Keeping your eye in, Larks?' he asked, coming to a halt over the cross-legged man.

'Never hurts,' Larkin replied.

Dalin nodded. He paused. He didn't expect much, but he thought there might be something. A comment about his first day, perhaps.

'You all right?' Larkin asked looking up.

'Yes. Yeah, I'm fine. You?'

'Golden as the Throne itself,' Larkin said, and returned his attention to his work.

'Well. Good. I'll see you, then,' Dalin said.

Larkin nodded. Dalin waited a second longer and then walked away through the hatch into the barrack hall.

Larkin touched his micro-bead link. 'He's coming,' he said.

'HE'S COMING,' SAID Varl. 'Are you coming?'

Gol Kolea sat on the edge of his cot, turning the pages of an instructional primer on spiritual faith.

'He won't want me there, getting in the way,' Kolea replied.

'Yes, he will,' said Varl, arms folded, leaning on the frame of the billet cage.

'Why?'

Varl shrugged. 'Dunno. Perhaps because you're his father? Stop pretending to read and get off your arse.'

Kolea scowled. 'How do you know I'm pretending to read?'

Arms still folded, Varl very slowly and very gently tilted his upper body over until his head was almost upside down. 'You're holding that book the wrong way up.'

Kolea blinked and stared at the primer in his hands. 'No, I'm not.'

Varl straightened up. 'Yeah, but you had to check. Stop prevaricating and get off your arse.'

Kolea tossed the book aside and got up. 'All right,' he said. 'But only because you used a word like "prevaricating" and now I'm scared to be alone with you.'

'HE'S COMING,' SAID Domor.

'Already?' Caffran replied.

'Larks just voxed.'

'Did you get it?' Caffran asked. He was busy folding the blanket back on the billet cage's cot.

Shoggy Domor's eyes would have twinkled in an avuncular manner if they hadn't been oversized augmetic implants. He reached into his musette bag and slid out the bottle of sacra. The bottle, a re-used water flask, had a handwritten label 'Try Again Finest'.

'The real stuff,' said Domor, tossing it to Caffran. Caffran caught the bottle and smiled at the label.

'Not fresh and burn-your-belly out of Costin's still,' Domor added. 'That's the real thing. Matured. Vintage. Laid down.'

'Laid down?'

'In Obel's foot locker, for "future pleasures", but it's the stuff.'

'It cost?'

Domor shook his head. 'When I told Obel what it was for, he just handed it over. "Wet the baby's head", he said.'

'He's not a baby.'

'He's not.'

'He's *not*.'

'I know he's not.'

'Just so we're clear. How do I look?'

Domor shrugged. 'Like a tight-arse feth? What did you do, starch your uniform?'

Caffran paused. 'Yes,' he confessed.

Domor sniggered. 'Then you have succeeded in looking like a tight-arse feth.'

'Thanks. Why are you my friend again?'

'Pure fething accident,' Domor smiled.

A head poked round the cage door. It was gnarled and ugly, like the protruding head of a startled tortoise.

'Hello, father,' said Domor.

'He's coming!' announced Zweil.

'We know, father. So are we,' Caffran replied.

'Big day,' Zweil added. He looked at Caffran and frowned. 'Tight-arse feth. Was that the look you were shooting for, son?'

'Be quiet,' said Caffran.

BARRACK HALL 22 was a vast enclosure given over to the billets of the Tanith First-and-Only. Across the concourse, the Kolstec 15th were housed in similar conditions. Something over four thousand troopers, packed away for the long voyage, for the long walk down Glory Road.

The billets themselves were metal-framed boxes five storeys deep. Each trooper had a cage-walled cell, like animals in a battery farm. Every cell had a cot and locker, and most troopers improved privacy with strategically arranged ground sheets and camo-cloaks.

It was sweaty-hot and noisy. A fug of smoke hung in the chamber roof from the lho-sticks and pipes. A chemical stench issued from the latrines at the southern end. The Tanith lay around, relaxing, leaning on staircases, playing cards and regicide, basking on folding chairs. In the open space beyond the billet cages, troopers were playing a loud game of kick-ball, stripped to their vests. Tanith, Verghastite, Belladon. Three races now bound together as one fighting unit.

Dalin walked in through the campsite. He felt a vague despondency. No one acknowledged him, not even the men who he regularly chatted to. A few 'hellos', a few nods. No one asked how his day had gone.

That was all right, though. He didn't want a fuss. He had been one of them for a long time, but not one of them. Now, finally, he was turning eighteen, and training for his tags. This had been his aspiration, his whole life. To be one of them, equal, an Imperial Guardsman.

Dalin sometimes wondered if he would have aspired to the Guard if his life had followed a different path. If war hadn't blown out the home-hive he grew up in. He probably would've become a seam miner, like his dad. His real dad. But war had embraced him, and warriors had carried him away, and their calling was all that appealed to him now. To be a Guard. To be a Ghost, more importantly. One of Gaunt's chosen.

To fight and, if necessary, die, in the name of the God-Emperor of Mankind.

He hurt. Damn Kexie and Saroo. He hurt, and all he wanted was to collapse on his cot and sleep the pain off.

He walked around the end of the fifth cage block and into the circulating space where troopers dozed and gamed. He heard a strange sound, staccato, like gun-fire.

It was applause.

To a man and a woman, the Ghosts had risen to their feet all around him, and were clapping wildly. He stopped and blinked.

'Dalin Criid! Dalin Criid! First day in "I", everyone! Dalin Criid!'

Dalin blinked again and looked around at the smiling faces surrounding him. They looked… proud. Connected to him, like they owned him, in the very best way.

Mach Bonin stood on an upper landing, leading the cheer. 'Dalin Criid! Show him we approve!' he was shouting.

'This…' Dalin grinned. 'This is…'

'The way Ghosts welcome one of their own,' said Domor, coming forward. 'Dalin, this is a rare moment, so you'll excuse us if we make the most of it.'

He shook Dalin's hand.

'Your dad's here,' he said, over the clapping.

Dalin looked around, and saw Caffran smiling at him.

'Oh, you mean Caff,' he said.

'All right, then?' Caffran asked, coming forward.

Dalin nodded. 'What did you do to your uniform?' he asked.

'Don't you start. Look, I did a thing. I hope you like it. I set you up with a billet cage, right upstairs, two down from mine. Guard issue, all proper.'

'I'm not Guard yet, Caff.'

'I know, but you will be.'

Dalin smiled and clamped his hands around Caffran's.

Dermon Caffran wasn't old enough to be Dalin's biological father, but, as Tona Criid's partner, he had raised the boy and his sister as his own, as far as Guard life allowed that to be possible. Then complications had set in.

'I got you this,' Caffran said, producing the sacra. 'To toast you.'

'Thanks.'

Dalin turned in a slow circle, acknowledging the applause. He saw all the faces: Obel, Ban Daur, Wheln, Rafflan, Brostin, Lyse, Caober, Nessa Bourah. Larkin was there. Larkin winked. The old dog.

Zweil came forward, holding a psalter and bless-bottle. 'Heavens, Dalin Criid. You're very tall suddenly,' he exclaimed. 'I thought I might bless you, but I fear I won't reach!'

Dalin grinned and bowed.

The crowd hushed as Zweil made the sign of the eagle on Dalin's forehead. 'In the name of the God-Emperor who watches over us, and the Saint whose work we do, I vouchsafe your soul against the horrors of the dark,' Zweil announced. He sprinkled some holy water over Dalin's shoulders.

'The Emperor protects,' he finished. There was more applause.

Tona Criid had appeared at Caffran's side. 'Enjoy this,' she told Dalin. 'The Ghosts don't make a fuss much.'

'They didn't need to make a fuss at all, ma,' Dalin said. She smiled, and touched her fingertips to his cheek briefly. Truth of it was, when the Ghosts gathered like this, it was usually to say goodbye, not hello. To bid farewell to another friend or comrade lost in the grinder. This was an expression of welcome, a salute to the living. Criid's heart was heavier than her smile suggested. They were welcoming her son into the Imperial Guard, into a way of life that had only one conclusion. This, too, was as good as saying goodbye, and she knew it. From this moment on, sooner or later…

'There's someone here who wants to say a few special words,' Varl said, appearing from the crowd.

Varl beckoned. In the shadows behind the cage wall, Kolea stiffened and cleared his throat. Then he pulled back as a tall figure strode past him.

It was Gaunt.

VI

'I wouldn't miss this,' said Ibram Gaunt. Silence had fallen.

'How did you go?' Gaunt asked.

'Good, sir. Good,' Dalin replied. 'Just starting out.'

'You'll be a good trooper,' Gaunt said. 'Is that sacra, Caffran?'

Caffran froze, half-hiding the bottle. 'It might be, sir.'

Gaunt nodded. 'You know there's a charge related to illicit alcohol?'

'I'd heard something of that, sir,' Caffran admitted.

'We'd better drink it before someone sees then, hadn't we?' Gaunt said.

Caffran smiled. 'Yes, sir.'

'Get some glasses, Caff,' Gaunt said. 'By the way, what the feth is going on with your uniform? A starch accident?'

'That might explain it,' Caffran said.

Shot glasses were produced. The bottle emptied as it filled as many cups as it could.

Gaunt raised his. 'To Dalin. First and next.'

They slugged it down. Dalin felt his torso go warm.

'We're walking Glory Road,' Gaunt told him, handing his empty glass to Domor. 'You know where that leads?'

'Well, glory?' said Dalin.

Gaunt nodded. 'I have complete confidence you'll be a trooper by then, Dalin. I'll show you glory, and I'll be proud to have you stand at my side.'

Gaunt looked around. 'I know I'm not wanted here. But I needed to come. That's it done. Carry on.'

He walked away.

The troopers closed around Dalin, shaking his hand and scrubbing his hair.

'Come on!' Varl hissed.

'Not now,' replied Kolea. 'He's happy. I don't want to go walking in there...'

'Gol...'

Kolea turned and walked away.

'VERY CLEVER, SIR, if I might say so,' Beltayn said, following Gaunt through the billet.

'How's that, Bel?'

'Sharing the grog out like that.'

Gaunt nodded. 'Dalin will need a clear head in the morning. Anything awry?'

Beltayn smiled and shook his head. 'Nothing right now, sir.'

'Dismissed then, Bel. Thank you.'

Gaunt had reached the medical tents. Dorden, the regiment's venerable chief medicae, stood in the doorway of the main surgery.

'You don't look happy,' said Gaunt.

'Do we still not know where we're going?' Dorden asked. Gaunt shook his head.

'Then come and look at this.'

Dorden led him into a freight space that was piled high with wrapped boxes from the Munitorum.

'These just arrived,' he said. 'Standing order is to distribute them throughout the regiment, double dose.'

Gaunt picked up a packet and read the label. 'Anti-ague drench?'

Dorden nodded. 'Remind you of anything?'

'I'll assemble an informal,' he said.

VII

SERAPHINE. THE LETTERS were inscribed into the heavy ironwork of the vent duct, and again on the duct beside it, and again on the duct beside that. Eszrah ap Niht traced his fingers across the bas-relief letters. *Seraphine*. It was, he understood, the name of the great boat they flew in. It wore its name on metalwork all about the place, as if acknowledging that it was so vast, a person might forget where he was, and need reminding.

Eszrah had been on a great boat before, but not as great a boat as this. It was so mighty, it was a world within a world. Gaunt had told Eszrah that it was a 'mass conveyance', a carrier ship. Several dozen regiments were being carried in its belly, more people than he'd seen in his whole life before leaving the Untill.

There was no sense they were moving. No soaring sensation of flight. Just a dull vibration in the deck, a harmonic in the heavy iron of the ducts and walls and plating.

He touched the word again, following the letters left to right as Gaunt had taught him. His lips moved.

'S... sera... serap... hine...'

He heard a noise and stopped, withdrawing his hand sharply. He was struggling to master the out-tongue, but it was hard, and he didn't like people seeing how hard he found it.

He was Nihtgane, Sleepwalker, bow-hunter of the Untill. It did not do for people to see his weaknesses.

It was bad enough they had to see him without his wode.

Ludd was approaching down the companionway. Ludd was all right, because Gaunt trusted Ludd, and Ludd and Eszrah had bloodied together in the hollow city.

Nahum Ludd saw Eszrah Night waiting for him as he came up. Gaunt's private quarters lay at the end of Barrack Hall 22, accessible via the narrow companionway flanked by ductwork. Eszrah had taken to guarding this narrow approach, like a warrior-spirit guarding a secret ravine in some ancient myth. In the months since they'd met, Ludd had begun to relax around the towering Nihtgane partisan, although his initial impression that Eszrah was about to kill him in some particularly silent and effective manner was never far away. When he'd first met him, Eszrah had been a fearsome giant of dreadlocks and painted skin. Gaunt had tidied him up, disguising the savage a little. The wode had gone, as had the shaggy mane and beard, and the eye mosaics, but still Eszrah stood out. Unnaturally tall, rake thin, he wore black, Guard-issue fatigues, heavy laced boots and a camo-cloak. His skull was shaved, and had a regal sculpture to it. His skin was gun-metal grey. His eyes were hidden behind a battered old pair of sunshades Varl had once given him.

Everything about Eszrah Niht, in fact, was hidden. Hiding was what the Nihtgane did. They hid themselves and their thoughts, their emotions, their hopes and their fears. Ludd knew Eszrah, but he didn't *know* him at all. He doubted anyone did. Not even Gaunt.

'Histye, soule Eszrah,' Ludd said. With a little tuition from Gaunt, Ludd had been practising the Nihtgane's tongue, just a few phrases. It seemed to Ludd unfair that only Gaunt could converse with him.

Eszrah nodded, faintly amused. Ludd's accent was terrible. The vowels were all too short. Ludd had almost said *histyhi*, the word for swine mash, rather than *histye*, the greeting.

'Histye, soule Ludd,' Eszrah replied.

Ludd grinned. This was almost a proper conversation by Eszrah ap Niht's standards. The over-long vowels of Eszrah's accent amused Ludd, especially the way he made his name sound like 'Lewd'.

'We're gathering for an informal,' Ludd said. 'More people will be coming this way.'

And I'd rather you didn't kill them, was the unspoken end of that sentence. Eszrah considered himself to be Gaunt's property, and for this reason alone had followed the colonel-commissar all the way from the

deep Untill of Gereon. As Ludd understood it, Eszrah
didn't regard himself as a slave. Gaunt owned him as
one might own a good sword or a balanced rifle. As
part of this relationship, Eszrah protected Gaunt's
person and his quarters with what Gaunt's adjutant
Beltayn had described as 'maternal fury'. A few days
earlier, a Belladon NCO had been hurrying down the
companionway to bring an order slip to Gaunt, and
Eszrah had pounced on him from the shadows,
presuming him to be, perhaps, an assassin. It had
taken quite a while before Eszrah could be convinced
of the man's innocence enough to let go of his
throat, and a good deal longer for the NCO's
breathing to return to normal.

Eszrah nodded again. He understood. Ludd was
warning him, decently, that others were coming, giving him time to melt away. He disliked company.

Voices could be heard at the mouth of the companionway. Ludd glanced round. 'That'll be the rest,'
he began, 'so we–'

He turned back. Eszrah ap Niht had vanished, as
surely as if he had never been there.

Ludd sighed, shook his head, and walked on.

THE OTHERS CAME. From the shadows of the ducting,
the Sleepwalker watched them, his reynbow loaded
and aimed. Major Rawne first, walking with Dorden,
the old surgeon. Eszrah didn't know Dorden well,
but he had warmed to him. The Nihtgane respected
the seniors of their tribe, and Eszrah showed the
same courtesy to the elders of the Ghost clan. Rawne
was different. Of the out-worlders who had come to

the Untill, Rawne was one of the most ferocious warriors, and for that alone, he had earned Eszrah's
respect. Gaunt valued Rawne too, and that counted
for a great deal.

But there was a quality to Rawne. A malice. Eszrah's
people had a word – *srahke* – which they used for
people like Rawne. Literally, it meant the keen-ness
of a newly-whetted dagger's edge.

Next came Major Kolea and Major Baskevyl, and
Beltayn, the adjutant. They were chatting convivially.
Kolea, a Verghastite, was a big man, physically
imposing, with an air of reliability and determination about him as heavy and hard as a block of
ouslite. But his weight of personality was leavened
with a good humour. Baskevyl was a Belladon, a
well-made, compact man who, like Kolea, married a
stern reliability with a refreshing brand of confidence. Beltayn, a Tanith man, was small and bright
and so lightly built it seemed soldiering was entirely
the wrong profession for him. But Eszrah had seen
Beltayn fight, and seen him survive the Untill. Along
with Gaunt and Ludd, Beltayn was one of the few
Ghosts Eszrah considered to be friends. Though, in
the Nihtgane tongue, the words for 'friend' simply
meant 'someone I consider to be a trustworthy hunting partner'.

Belladon, Verghastite, Tanith... this was where
things became complicated for Eszrah. Gaunt had
explained it many times, but still it seemed peculiar.
The fighting clan was the Tanith, the Tanith First-and-
Only. At some point in their history, after, so Eszrah
had been told, a mighty battle, the Tanith had agreed

to accept men from another clan into their order. These were the Verghastites, and some of them were females. The two clans had bonded into one. This, in Eszrah's experience, never happened amongst the tribes of the Untill. Unless disease or famine had ravaged one tribe, and breeding partners were needed.

Then had come the matter of the hollow city. Eszrah had been there and seen it, following Gaunt to war. During Gaunt's expedition to Gereon, his fighting clan had been given to another leader, and had bonded to yet a third clan, who were called the Belladon. Following Gaunt's return, and the death in war of the other leader, all three clans had unified under Gaunt, taking the name Tanith First-and-Only.

This, as far as Gaunt and the others seemed to think, had been a good thing.

Eszrah wasn't sure. In the Untill, clans seldom combined successfully. For a start, there was the scent. No clan smelled alike. How could they bond when their bodies gave off such different scents? With his eyes closed, Eszrah could tell them apart quite easily. The resin sap of the Tanith, the mineral dust of the Verghastites, the hard steel of the Belladons. Eyes open, it was even more apparent. Tanith were lean and hard, pale skinned, dark haired. Verghastites were more solid, flat-faced and fairer. Belladons were between the two in their average build, darker-skinned, lighter in voice.

Eszrah didn't understand how such a compact of fighting clans could work. It wasn't even a fact that these could. At the hollow city, they had fought to victory together due to the extremities of circumstance. Genuine bonding had yet to be proven, and that test would happen wherever they were going, wherever the great boat was taking them.

To complicate matters further in Eszrah's mind, Gaunt wasn't Tanith, Verghastite or Belladon. He was other, with a scent of good, oiled hide. So too was Ludd (fire ash and flint), and Hark (bone dust and chemicals). And the old man Zweil too, though as Eszrah understood it, the clan kept Zweil around so they could be amused by a capering madman. Untill chieftains often allowed a simpleton to live for exactly the same purposes. The name for that was *jestyr* or *foole*.

Gaunt, Ludd, Hark. They were Tanith, but not Tanith. It was perplexing. A fighting clan, already intermingled in blood and scent, allowed itself to be led by men from other clan territories.

Eszrah decided he would never understand it, not even if he lived to be forty years old.

Kolea, Beltayn and Baskevyl had passed down the companionway into Gaunt's quarters. After a moment, Gaunt himself went by, alone, striding purposefully.

Eszrah lowered his reynbow. Then he raised it again, quickly, as a final figure passed by.

Mkoll. The master of scouts. The master of hunters. Tanith, so Tanith that his Tanith scent was stronger than any, though Eszrah doubted any could ever track the man's spoor.

Mkoll stopped suddenly, halfway down the companionway, turned and looked directly into the shadows at the place where Eszrah was concealed. He smiled.

'All right, Eszrah?' he asked.

Eszrah froze, then nodded.

'That's good,' Mkoll grinned. 'Carry on.' He walked away into the commander's quarters.

The Nihtgane had a word for people like Mkoll too. It was *sidthe*. It meant ghost.

THE ROOM WAS quite small, just a steel box, with a table in the centre of the floor. Beltayn had, over the days since they'd boarded the carrier, begged, borrowed or robbed a number of seats to furnish the place into some semblance of a briefing room. Pew benches with sagging upholstery, a few stools, a couple of high-backed chairs, both of which were so loose on their spells that they creaked and swayed.

'Hello to all,' Gaunt said, taking off his storm coat. 'Take a seat.'

The officers of the regiment had been standing out of courtesy. Now they took their places. Kolea and Rawne reclined on one pew, Dorden and Hark on another. Baskevyl scooted forward on one of the creaking high-backs, and Mkoll settled himself on its twin. Beltayn perched his backside on a stool. Ludd withdrew to a corner of the room and remained standing.

The room was dark, lit only by the outer light shafting through the door and high window slits. Gaunt nodded to Ludd, and the junior commissar activated the overhead lamps.

Holding his coat up by the collar loop, Gaunt brushed it down as he carried it over towards a row of wall hooks.

'Let's start with basics. Any reports?'

'The men are bedding down well, sir,' Kolea said. 'Good transit discipline.'

'Gol's right,' said Baskevyl. 'No nonsense. Smooth ride.' He leaned forward as he spoke, and his feeble chair let out a screech of wood.

'Eli?' Gaunt asked over his shoulder, hanging his coat up.

Elim Rawne was the regiment's second officer, the senior man in the Tanith-Verghastite-Belladon command pyramid formed by himself, Kolea and Baskevyl.

He stayed reclined, arms folded, and shrugged. 'I've no reason to refute those statements. The Tanith have always conducted themselves perfectly during carrier transits. In my experience, the Verghastites have too. I can't speak for the Belladon.'

That was pointed. Gaunt looked around sharply.

'Eli…'

Baskevyl snorted and sat back. Another terrible groan issued from his chair. He said, 'Major Rawne and I are reaching an understanding. He goads me and mine, sir, and I let his scorn drip off me like rain. Come the zone, the Belladon have agreed to allow Rawne to buff our medals.'

Gaunt sniggered. 'Providing he asks nicely?' he inquired.

'Naturally,' Baskevyl said. His chair complained again.

'I seem to remember,' Gaunt said, 'I asked you to work hard to welcome the Belladon into our company, Eli.'

'This is me working hard,' said Rawne. 'You should see me when I'm being a bastard.'

'We've all seen *that*,' scoffed Mkoll. When he moved in his seat, for some reason his chair, as ailing as Baskevyl's, made no sound at all.

'There is one thing, sir–' Ludd began.

'Not now,' Hark warned.

Ludd shut up and pursed his lips.

'I've time on my hands,' Gaunt said. 'Let's hear it.'

Ludd cleared his throat and took a step forward, producing a sheet of paper from his pocket. 'There was an incident earlier, sir. On the swelter decks… see, as it says?'

He handed the paper to Gaunt. Gaunt read it quickly.

'Merrt?'

'I dealt with it,' Hark said.

'You dealt with it?'

'Yes, Ibram. It's old news.'

Gaunt nodded. He handed the paper back to Ludd. 'That's a shame. A man like him. Get any reasons?'

Hark's eyes were more hooded than ever. 'He's a broken man. Has been since Monthax. Men like that run off the rails.'

'You've set him on charges?'

'Yes,' said Hark. 'Full stretch. All six weeks. I'm assuming this is still a six-week voyage?'

'As far as I know,' Gaunt said.

'Not wishing to gloat,' muttered Gol Kolea, 'but very much wishing to support Baskevyl… may I just say, ho ho, it's a Tanith that steps out of line?'

'You may,' said Gaunt.

Baskevyl grinned so broadly his chair creaked.

'Funny,' said Rawne. 'You Verghastites are as funny as the Belladon and they're, let me tell you, funny.'

Kolea looked sideways at the man on the pew beside him. 'You kill me, Eli. You and your sense of humour. You kill me.'

'Oh, for a dark night and the opportunity,' replied Rawne.

There was general laughter. Smiling, Gaunt reached into the pocket of his hanging storm coat and pulled out a box stamped with the seal of the Departmento Medicae.

He set it down in the centre of the table top so they could all see it.

'This is why I called an informal.'

Rawne, Hark and Kolea leaned forward to inspect the object. So did Baskevyl, with a protest from the spells of his chair. Mkoll nodded.

'Anti-ague?' he asked.

'Anti-ague,' Gaunt replied. 'Inhibitors. Full shots.'

'Double-dose standard,' Dorden said. 'That was my instruction. Double-dose courses for all personnel, starting now.'

'We get ague drench before every planet-drop,' Baskevyl said, looking round at Gaunt with another noise from his chair.

'We do,' Gaunt agreed.

'But not double-dose and not a course,' Dorden said.

'It's like before Gereon,' Mkoll said, leaning forward and picking up the box to examine it. His chair made not a single sound.

'Gereon?' asked Baskevyl. 'Is there a point?'

'Aside from the one on the top of your head?' Rawne asked.

'Yes, there's a point,' Gaunt said. 'When I led a mission team to Gereon, it was full insertion, enemy territory. They dosed us up real good, double shots. They knew we'd need to survive as long as possible on a world lousy with Chaos taint. Now, let's think, your standard infantryman gets a shot in the arm or buttock every few weeks during transit, and never asks why. I know better. I'm asking.'

'You think?' Kolea began.

'Always,' smiled Gaunt. 'I think this means we're being routed to a liberation effort. We're going to be deployed against a Chaos-held world. High Command still hasn't confirmed our destination, but I believe the brass expects us to go in against a hard target.'

'I thought combat policy was to ignore the worlds too tough to break?' Mkoll said.

'I think policy has changed,' said Gaunt. 'I think they want us to break the tough worlds we can't ignore.'

Mkoll sat back and let out a long, plaintive whistle. His chair let out no noise at all.

'What does that mean, practically?' Kolea asked.

'It means double-hard preparation,' Gaunt said. 'It means tight drop training, around the clock. It means, if we can, slipping the hint to other regiments, so they can begin the same.'

'I can do that,' said Hark. 'I know the commissars in the Kolstec and the Binars. We can spread the word.'

'Do you understand the meaning of the word "subtle", Viktor?' Gaunt asked.

'It's my middle name,' Hark smiled. 'Viktor bloody subtle Hark.'

'Bear it in mind,' Gaunt replied. 'I don't want to be accused of starting a scare. There's something else.'

He looked round at his adjutant. 'Bel? Course correction added in, how many hostile-held worlds are there approximately six standard weeks transit rimward of Ancreon Sextus?'

'Two, sir,' replied Beltayn.

'Their names?'

'Lodius, sir. And Gereon.'

Gaunt looked back at his senior staff. 'I fancy, gentlemen, we might be heading back to Gereon. For the liberation they never thought we'd bother to bring.'

'Gereon resists,' Rawne muttered.

'Let's hope so,' said Gaunt. 'Well, that's it. Carry on and be ready. Anything else?'

'I have a question,' Baskevyl said. 'When I move, my chair creaks, but when Mkoll does, there's no sound. What the frig is that about?'

'Scout training,' Mkoll chuckled, getting to his feet and patting Baskevyl on the arm.

The meeting broke up.

'I hear your son's started basic,' Dorden said to Kolea.

'What? Yes. Yes, he has.'

'That's good. He'll do well, I think.'

'I hope so.'

'A father and son in the ranks again,' Dorden mused. 'That's wonderful. Like a new start.'

'I'm not so much his father, doc,' Kolea said. 'His blood father, yes. But then there's Caff. Two fathers and one son, you might say.'

Dorden nodded.

'Dah!' said Kolea suddenly. 'Gak it, that was clumsy of me. I'm sorry, doc.'

'For what?' asked Dorden.

Once there had been a father and son in the Tanith ranks. Dorden, and his son Mikal. Mikal had been killed during the defence of Vervunhive.

'I didn't think...' Kolea began.

Dorden shook his head. 'My son died on Verghast. Coincidentally, that's where your son joined our ranks. Now he's training to be a Ghost. A son lost and a son gained. One father bereft, one... sorry, *two* fathers made proud. I think there's a certain completeness to that, don't you, Gol? A certain symmetry?'

'I hope so,' said Kolea.

'One thing,' Dorden added. 'Gol, in the Emperor's name, look after him.'

THE SENIORS HAD gone. Gaunt sat at the table in one of the terribly creaking chairs, reviewing order papers. Beltayn brought him a cup of caffeine.

'Anything else, sir?' Beltayn asked.

'No, that'll be all, Bel. Thanks.'

Beltayn left. Gaunt worked his way through the papers.

'Geryun?' asked a voice.

Gaunt looked up from his work. Eszrah stood in the doorway.

'Iss...' he said slowly, mangling his words. 'Iss ite true, soule?'

'That we're going to Gereon?' Gaunt replied. 'I'm not sure, Niht. But I think so. You were listening in? Of course you were.'

'Geryun, itte persist longe, foereffer,' Eszrah said.

'Yes,' said Gaunt. 'That's what I've always believed.'

VIII

ANOTHER DAY-CYCLE, another slog, another step along Glory Road, another RIP drill. Eight days since the start of RIP, and something different that morning.

'New body,' said driller Kexie. 'New body. And you are, apart from shit-on-my-toecap ugly?'

'Merrt.'

Kexie looked the newcomer up and down and began the long and ritualistic process of bagging him out in front of the detail. Nothing was taboo. Kexie spent a particularly long time likening Merrt's face to a number of things, a bilge hatch, a grox's rectum, and so on.

Dalin tried not to look or listen. He stared at a fixed point far away on the opposite wall of the Basement, and waited for reps to begin.

'Hey, Holy! One of yours, isn't he?' Fourbox whispered.

'What?'

'Tanith?'

'Yeah.'

'He's in for P?' Fourbox probed. 'What he do?'

'I dunno.'

'I mean, what he do to his face?'

'Got shot,' whispered Dalin. He didn't know much about Merrt's story. Merrt was a loner and didn't mix much. For as long as Dalin could remember, Merrt's face had looked like a bilge hatch.

'Someone yapping?' Kexie asked, turning from Merrt suddenly to regard the rest of the detail. 'Someone yapping there in the file?' He aimed Saroo at them and panned it along the line, as if the baton could sniff out malfeasance like a sentry dog.

'Some wet-fart scalp exercising his lip, ech?' Kexie wondered. Wise to the driller's tricks after eight days of RIP, no one made the mistake of saying 'No, driller'.

'Let's start it, then,' Kexie announced, stroking Saroo in a way that suggested the baton was disappointed not to have doled out clouts. 'Five laps, triple time! Move!'

THREE DAYS LATER, Kexie took the detail up to the range deck, a converted hold in midships. It was a serious space, and made the Basement seem like a foot locker. They trooped in over grille bridges as the previous mob drained out of the place via lower walkways: a river of shaved scalps and laughter down below. Range officers in flak coats and ear protectors issued them with rifles that had been marked with big, white serial codes.

Off to the left, a combat-certified unit was conducting clearance drills in an area of the range that had been faked up into streets and buildings by the use of cargo crates and conveyance pallets. The unit was maintaining its hard-edge frontline readiness, determined not to let the slow days of a long haul make them slack and dull. RIP could hear their back-and-forth shouts, the corner by corner call and return, the bursts of gunfire.

Kexie yelled this and that. RIP milled about, trying to look useful, checking over their weapons, while the range officers led them up to the shooting line in groups of forty. At the line, in a grubby dugout made of flakboard and tarps, they were each handed a live clip, and began rattling away at tar-paper targets at the far end of the sandbox.

The air became thick with heat exhaust and the cracking sounds of multiple discharge. It was a sound like kindling being split, like a hundred greenstick fractures all together, an uneven, brittle racket that rolled up and down the line of shooters.

A buzzer sounded. The shooters gave up their clips and stepped back to make way for the second batch.

So the rotations went for the whole shift.

Dalin took the gun he was issued with great reverence. He'd fired plenty before. You didn't grow up in the middle of the Ghosts and not know one end of a las from the other. But he wasn't in RIP for punishment or retraining, so he hadn't dropped back out of the ranks for this. He'd never formally been issued with a weapon.

It was a loaner for the afternoon, and Dalin was pretty glad of that. It was old, a scabby mark I with a chipped and flaking khaki paint job, a broken bayonet lug, and a folding skeleton stock that had belonged to another weapon in an earlier life. The range officers kept a cache of weapons like it for drill use: scrap weapons or battlefield flotsam that the Munitorum regarded as unfit for service issue.

He went up to the line when his turn came, and popped home the cell the instructor handed him. The las made a noise like a cane switch, and pulled badly to the left. He compensated. The nearest range officer was walking the row, shouting advice at them in turn, but Dalin blocked that out and heard a voice of his own. Caffran, teaching him to shoot, teaching him the basics of rifle drill and firing discipline in a campsite field on Aexe Cardinal, or out on the obsidae of Herodor, or amongst the nodding windflowers on Ancreon Sextus.

The buzzer rang. Dalin ejected the clip, handed it back to the officer, and withdrew to the assembly area. Behind him, a fresh round of gunfire caught up, like the rat-a-tat-tat of a company snare drum.

'Anyone,' Kexie was yelling, striding through the company, 'anyone who scores less than a thirty gets three days of punishment reps.'

There were some groans.

'Anyone got a comment? Ech, address it in writing to me, care of Saroo.'

Dalin went to one side. Now he had some time between shoots, he could take a rag to his weapon. The action was gummed up with dirt and old lube, and that made the trigger pull hard and snatchy. He worked to free it.

'What are you doing, Holy?' Boulder asked, regarding Dalin's industry with some amusement. Boulder and Lovely and a few of the others were using the lull between shoots to rest their arses on the ground and chat.

'Improving my score,' Dalin replied.

'When you get good, do me a favour,' said Lovely. 'Shoot Kexie in the brain.'

'Why wait?' Boulder asked. 'Why not do it now?'

'Because,' said Lovely, 'the driller's brain's so frigging small, you'd have to be a marksman shot to hit it.'

Dalin noticed that Merrt was in their batch. Merrt was the only other scalp apart from Dalin who was tending to his rifle. The older trooper was adjusting the fore- and back-sights, lifting the gun to his shoulder to check between each adjustment.

He spoke to no one, and no one spoke to him.

Dalin remembered, now he came to think of it, that Merrt had been a sniper once. A specialist. He should have no problems with this drill, Dalin thought.

AT THE END of the rotations, Kexie pulled them off the range and stood them in a transit hallway while he called out the score groupings from a data-slate that one of the range officers had handed him. Everyone tensed to hear their name alongside the magic thirty or higher. Thirty was combat standard, the acceptable average grade a man had to make if he wanted to be Guard, like the weight and height and vision requirements.

Either through lack of effort or incompetence, fifteen members of the RIP detail scored under the line, including Boulder. Even he couldn't raise a 'haw haw haw' to that.

Most of the rest got in a band between thirty and thirty-five, with the top five per cent of them hitting fifty and above. Merrt got forty-eight. When Kexie read this out, Merrt seemed to shudder, and he grated some caustic word under his breath.

Kexie peered at Merrt, eyes narrowed, wondering if there was a juicy infringement there to be pounced upon.

'You speak, scalp?'

'No, driller.'

Kexie regarded him for a moment longer, and then carried on with his list. He reached Dalin's name. Dalin had scored sixty-six, twelve points clear of the best of the rest. There were a few whoops and cat-calls when Kexie read the number out, but they quickly simmered down. Kexie went over to Dalin – using that easy, shoulders-back, hip-roll walk he had – and stared him in the face.

'No new body clocks a tally like that.'

Dalin didn't know what to say, so he said nothing and remained staring straight ahead.

'I said, this is a joke. You hear my voice, wet-fart? What'd you do? Bribe a range officer? Switch some numbers?'

'No, driller.'

'No?'

'No, driller.'

'Then how would you explain this, ech?'

Dalin wanted to say he'd fired a weapon before, that he had experience, but the same could be said for every 'R' and 'P' in the detail. He wanted to say he'd been well-taught, and his teachers were the best.

He wanted to say that it was probably less to do with marksmanship skill and more to do with simple weapon discipline and method, and that most of them would be scoring in the fifties if they simply took the time to check, adjust and *listen to* their rifle.

But all he found himself saying was, 'Luck, driller?'

'No such thing as luck,' Kexie said. 'Allow me to prove that particular dictum.'

Kexie cracked Saroo across Dalin's knees, and then rammed the blunt end of the baton into the small of Dalin's back as he folded forward and crumpled. Teeth bared, Kexie whaled the stick down into the boy's ribs, glancing several loud, bony blows off Dalin's forearm as it came up defensively.

Kexie stepped back, planting his left toe-cap in Dalin's gut. Dalin, on his side on the deck, grunted and coiled up like a foetus.

'See?' Kexie crowed, loud and laughing. 'He got the top tally, but he don't look all that bloody lucky now, does he?'

No one responded.

'Does he?'

There was a muted answer. Annoyed, Kexie looked back at Dalin and laid in again.

'That ain't right.'

Kexie stopped and swung about. Merrt, hands at his sides, had stepped out of the pack to face the instructor.

'You what?'

'That... gn... gn... ain't right,' Merrt repeated, his clumsy jaw misfiring a couple of times over the words.

'What?' There was a high, almost querulous tone of disbelief in Kexie's voice. He craned his neck forward and cupped a hand around one ear. 'Bloody *what*?'

'You're too happy with that stick,' Merrt said plainly. 'You deal out the licks when someone needs punishment, that's how it goes, but he don't deserve it. What kind of fool punishes someone for gn... gn... getting it right?'

'The kind of fool that's in charge of your entire bloody life,' Kexie announced, and came forward at Merrt. Everyone else shrank back. They knew that mad-eyed look.

'Maybe, but I still say what's right,' Merrt said. He spread his hands wide, palms open, and tilted his chin back so he was looking at the ceiling. 'Come on, whack me. I spoke out of line, I gotta have something coming, but not him. He didn't do nothing.'

Kexie came up short, and lowered his baton slightly. No one had ever invited Saroo's attention before. That rather took the fun out of it.

Kexie allowed a grin to tear across his mouth like a slow knife-slit. This was going to be interesting.

IX

DURING TRANSIT, THE barrack deck chapels conducted their services at all the devotional hours, according to shipboard timekeeping. The principal act of worship was held immediately after the noon watch bell.

Aboard ship, the noon watch was the axle on which all timings turned. Standing orders were for all horologs and timepieces to be synched with the chime of the watch bell.

The 'bell service' lasted about forty minutes. It was the very least devotion a Guardsman was expected to make, duties permitting. The Ghosts used Drum Chapel, near the aft quarters, a medium-size hold space that had been converted and consecrated. The room was cold and spare, crudely dressed in wood and canvas. Worship was conducted by prefects and celebrants of the Ecclesiarchy using cheap, military issue incense that smelled stale and dusty. There was none of the pomp and regalia of a civilian ceremony, none of the opulence and heady perfume of a high-hive mass. Thin priests in threadbare robes exhorted the congregation to uphold the honour and tradition of the Guard, the glory of the Imperium and the spirit of Man.

Hark listened without hearing any of the content. From his place at the back, he was scanning the rows of kneeling figures, marking faces. No wonder turnout was so regularly poor. It was dreary. Hark's own past had been privileged, and he remembered occasions at temple in the cities where he'd grown up. Glory and splendour: ecclesiarchs in billowing silks carried to the podium on golden-legged walking platforms, the choirs singing hymns into the lofty rafters of the cathedrals, the light bursting radiant white through the colossal splinter windows behind the stalls.

He met up with Ludd outside as the congregation filed away. Ludd had the roll book.

'Many?' Hark asked.

'Mostly the same few,' Ludd replied. He showed Hark the book, turning pages and pointing to several names. 'Repeat absenters.'

Hark read and nodded. 'We'll root out the chief miscreants this afternoon, Ludd. Put a rocket up them.'

Hark looked around and scanned the thinning crowd. 'He wasn't here, was he?'

'No, sir.'

'Some example. Leans on us to boost attendance, and then doesn't bother himself. I didn't miss him, did I?'

Ludd shook his head. 'That's the third day in a row. If he... I mean, if he was anybody else, he'd have a red tick beside his name by now.'

'I should, I think, explain that to him,' Hark said. 'Carry on, Ludd.'

HARK WALKED THE rusting, water-stained half-kilometre of companionway back to the regimental office, a suite of chambers and cabins midship. Most of the staffers were Munitorum officials, or officers from the support battalions and company command. The Commissariat had a presence too. In some of the larger chambers, ranged at folding desks in the low light, commissars and line officers sat written exams on battlefield theory, tactics and discipline, or engaged in simulation tests around chart tables.

He saw faces he recognised around one of the stations. Ban Daur, Kolosim and Obel were working through a tactical problem with a trio of Kolstec officers. They all straightened as he approached. He glanced at the glowing hololithic projection that covered the console top between them.

'Line assault?' he asked.

'Principles and applications of bounding cover,' replied Daur.

'Intermediate level, lesson three,' added Kolosim snidely.

Hark chuckled and nodded. The simulation confronting them was complex and demanding. 'Time sensitive?'

'On a real-time clock,' replied Daur.

'Then I won't spoil your rate any longer. Have you seen the colonel?'

Daur checked his wrist-chron. 'Won't he be coming back from bell service?'

Hark shook his head.

'I saw him about an hour ago in 22,' said Obel. 'I don't know where he was going, but he had his sword with him.'

'Thank you,' said Hark. 'Good luck with that.'

HARK FOUND GAUNT ten minutes later in one of the individual practice rooms. Gaunt had signed the chamber out on the chalkboard outside, and added 'NOT TO BE DISTURBED'.

Hark went inside anyway. Just inside the door there were racks of training blunts and some target dummies. Past that, open and dormant, was a mobile practice cage shaped like a clamshell.

Gaunt was in the main part of the room, duelling with four training drones: multi-legged machines with lashing weapon limbs. They circled him, jabbing and striking. Gaunt was stripped to the waist, sweating hard, ducking and spinning, lashing out with his power-sword. Every clean hit he made to the pressure-sensitive pads on the bellies and heads of the drones shut them down for ten seconds. After each count, they jerked back to life and resumed their attacks.

Four drones. Four at once. That seemed excessive to Hark. He'd always admired Gaunt's blade skill, and knew it took a lot of practice to keep such close-combat skills honed. But four...

He watched for a moment longer. He noticed a mark on Gaunt's back, low down, just left of the spine. A tattoo, or...?

Hark started in surprise. The mark was blood, blood streaming from a deep cut. He realised what he was seeing.

All the drones had untipped blades. Between them, the four machines were engaging Gaunt with sixteen double-edged, half-metre long blades.

'Feth!' Hark breathed. 'Shut down! Shut down!'

The rattling machines continued to mill and strike. All Hark had managed to do was distract Gaunt, who glanced around for a moment and was then forced into a frantic, defensive back-step to avoid a slicing blade-arm.

Hark rushed forward. 'Shut down!' he ordered. 'Vox-control: shut down! Cut! Power out!'

Sensing his movement, the nearest drone broke away from Gaunt and came for him, skittering its metal legs off the practice mat onto the hard metal deck. Its weapon arms rotated and scissored.

'Feth!' Hark said again, backing up quickly. 'What the feth is this? Shut down!'

Gaunt let out a curse. He exhaled as he ducked sharply and turned his body in a low spin under the lunging blades of one of the drones. Then he came up clear and parried the weapons of another aside with his sword. He kicked out savagely and sent the deflected drone stumbling backwards. The third was close on him. Gaunt turned and sliced under its guard, drawing the power sword clean across its torso and out through its head unit in a flurry of sparks. The edges of the sheared metal glowed brightly as the head section fell away.

Gaunt leapt past the dead machine.

The fourth drone was right in Hark's face. Hark drew a plasma pistol from under his coat and raised it to fire.

But Gaunt had reached the cut-off switch on the far wall of the chamber and punched it. The three remaining drones went slack as they made power-down whines.

Hark lowered his pistol, re-engaged the safety and put it away. He looked across the room at Gaunt. The colonel-commissar was breathing hard. He deactivated his power sword as he reached for a towel to mop his face and chest.

'Unsafe weapons and a cancelled voice override?' Hark asked.

'I believe in diligent practice.'

'A trainee must have a second and a medicae present if he intends to make the practice drones capable of actual injury. Standing order–'

'57783-3. I'm aware of the rule.'

'And the punishment?'

Gaunt glared at Hark.

'The voice safety is never to be shut off,' Hark said. 'You could have been killed.'

'That was the point.'

'How was this drill supposed to end, Ibram?'

'When I'd had enough, I'd break free and hit the wall switch. You pre-empted things, Viktor. What do you want?'

'I want you alive to lead the Ghosts when we reach the next zone,' Hark replied.

'I believe in diligent practice,' Gaunt repeated. 'I believe in pushing myself and testing myself.'

'So do I,' Hark said. 'I put time in on the range, run a few sparring sessions and exercise. What you're doing is tantamount to obsessive.'

Gaunt shrugged. He threw the damp towel aside and reached for his shirt. 'Then let's just hope you never have to fight me, Viktor,' he said with a wolfish grin. 'What do you really want?'

'You missed bell service.'

'Did I?'

'Yes. It's regrettable because we're trying to whip the malingerers back into attendance and, frankly, you're not setting an example.'

Gaunt pulled his wrist-chron out of his trouser pocket and looked at it. It was an old, battered thing, the strap long since replaced by a hand-woven bracelet.

'According to this, it's another seventeen minutes to noon watch bell.'

'Then that's slow,' said Hark. 'About sixty-five minutes slow.'

'It kept good enough time on Gereon.'

'It's not keeping good enough time now, Ibram. What? You're smiling.'

Gaunt was strapping the chron to his wrist. 'I've kept this set and wound since we embarked. Fifteen days' transit and I've not synched it to the noon bell.'

'So?'

'Diurnal settings, Viktor.'

Hark frowned. It was standard Guard practice, during long voyages, to adjust the length of shipboard day/night cycles to match those of the destination world, so that over a mid-to-long duration voyage, the troops would become accustomed to a different circadian rhythm. It helped with acclimatisation. The changes weren't made in one fell swoop. Time was shaved off or added incrementally over a period of days. Synching to the noon watch kept everyone in step.

'So you're running on Ancreon Sextus time?'

Gaunt nodded. 'And the ship's set to a daylight cycle that's about an hour shorter.' He walked over to where his coat was hanging from the rail of the practice cage and slid a data-slate out of the pocket. 'I consulted a compendium of sector ephemera to check,' he said as he switched the slate on and scrolled through the data, 'but I was pretty sure anyway. It was familiar.'

He showed Hark the screen. Tight-packed data showed tide charts and seasonal daybreak and sunset tables, grouped into geographic regions, for a number of worlds in the local group. One was highlighted.

'Gereon,' said Hark.

'Pretty much the confirmation we wanted,' Gaunt said, snapping the slate off and putting it away.

'That's why I shut off voice safety, Viktor. We're going back, and I wanted to remind myself what it was like.'

X

THE MEMBERS OF RIP who failed the range grade, and that included Dalin and Merrt, got circuit marches for the next three nights.

A circuit march involved full kit, weighted backpacks and a heavy spar of pig iron as a substitute for a rifle. It involved looping the ship, end to end and back, following outer hull-skin corridors, twenty times. Kexie, who had paced the route, assured RIP that this was the equivalent of fifty kilometres.

Kexie did not march the whole distance with them. He'd go with them a way, and then cross the ship laterally via transit halls while they were toiling round the prow, or slogging through the low ducts over the enginarium, and meet them coming back up the far side.

There was a temptation to shave corners off the route, a temptation that Boulder had all but planned, but Kexie had set up a dozen servitors as checkpoints. Miss any one of these way-markers, fail to let one register your tag as you went by, and you got to spend some quality time with Saroo before repeating the march.

Most of the route wound through scabby metal ducts and long, unpainted, unheated tunnels where few people had any business being. They jogged through the canyons behind the heavy hull skin plates, behind the riveted shield of the dust sheath. They ran through the clear spaces between oily field generators that stank of ozone, and splashed through rusting compartments waterlogged by condensation. They pounded across empty holds where greased chains swung from ceilings invisible in the shadows. They struggled through the stinking chambers of the husbandry and livestock section and the sweaty, marsh-gas fug of hydroponics.

They'd started out quite up-beat, intending to take the march in their stride and let Kexie suck on it. Boulder had even tried to get a round of call and chorus cadences going to keep the rhythm. Before they'd completed even one circuit, those good intentions had soured. Breathlessness, blistered feet, bruised elbows and knees from impacts with bulkhead obstructions, and, most of all, a sick realisation of exactly how far twenty circuits was, had strung them out into a long, toiling line, grinding its way, dead-eyed and hopeless, around the course.

Every time he appeared, grinning, at some point in the route, Kexie would wave them by, and tell each straggler in turn precisely how useless he was. He'd learned some new insults for the march, or else had been saving up some particular favourites for this special occasion.

Dalin didn't complain about his inclusion. He'd grown up understanding there was a basic strand of unfairness running through a soldier's life. Soldiering was about the whole, about the unit, and about the way that unit functioned in terms of discipline and coherence. Once an individual got used to the disappointment of being levelled out whether he was right or wrong, he began to function with the unit, and life got easier.

He also understood the importance of examples.

Kexie had not beaten Merrt after the range drill. Even his attack dog logic had recognised it was unproductive to beat a man who was asking to be beaten. Such an act would also weaken him in the eyes of the detail. Kexie was determined to remain above these affairs, untouched and unscathed by the numbers his charges pulled. It was possible he thought of himself as inscrutable.

Kexie put Merrt on the march. Then he told the others that the ten circuit marches they owed for failing to score above thirty were now going to be twenty circuit marches, thanks to what he called Merrt's 'lip'.

On the third circuit, Dalin dropped into step with Merrt. It was the first time he'd ever spoken to him.

'I wanted to–' he began.

'Skip it,' Merrt replied, without looking round.

'Was it…' Dalin hesitated. 'Was it a Ghost thing?'

That made Merrt glance round, his sunken eyes bright and curious above the awful facial prosthetic. 'A gn… gn… Ghost thing?'

'Because I'm regiment, I mean.'

Merrt shook his head. 'The fether was just wrong. I'd have spoken up no matter who it was.'

'Oh.'

They ran on, through a loading hatch and out across the grille floor of a port stowage bay. The mesh rang with their footfalls.

'How did you end up on RIP?' Dalin asked.

'The traditional way.'

'Yeah, but how?'

Merrt pulled up to a stop and Dalin stopped with him. Bodies clattered past them, slogging onwards.

Merrt stared at Dalin for a moment, right in the face. 'Do I know you?' he asked.

'I–'

'Do you know me?'

'No, but–'

'Then I'll thank you to keep your fething personal questions to yourself. I'm gn… gn… not your friend.'

'Sorry,' said Dalin. He felt himself blushing, and that made it worse. Merrt turned away and started to pace up to a jog again.

Suddenly he stopped and looked back at Dalin. 'If you must know,' he said, 'I raised my head out of gn… gn… cover during a firefight on Monthax.'

'No, I meant–'

'I know what you meant. That's still the answer.' Merrt turned again and began to run.

After a moment, Dalin followed him.

XI

OUT ON THE clear deck beyond the billet cages, a crowd had gathered to watch a team of Ghosts kick a ball with some troopers from the Kolstec barrack hall. There was a lot of good-natured shouting and cursing.

Kolea watched the game from one of the upper landings, his arms leant on the railing. Varl was with him, smoking a hand-rolled lho-stick. Every now and then, they exchanged a few philosophical remarks about the relative skills on display, especially Brostin's reluctance to pass the ball to anyone useful.

'It's like he has a disability.'

'More than the ones we know about.'

'Right.'

Down in the crowd, some of the Belladon had begun to thump out a rat-a-tat-tat on some hand drums to urge the Ghosts on. It was a fast, pacy beat. It sounded like the urgent drum march of an execution detail.

'This place we're going to–' Kolea began.

'No one knows for sure where we're going,' Varl replied.

'Yeah, but if. What's it like?'

Varl had been one of Gaunt's original mission team to the occupied world of Gereon almost three years before. The fact that any of them had come back alive was a major miracle. A garrulous man ordinarily, Varl had seldom spoken of the matter.

'It's a bad place,' he told his friend. 'Bad as can be. And I can't imagine it's got any better since I was last there.'

Kolea nodded.

'I'll be glad to go back, though,' Varl admitted.

'Really? Why?'

'Ven and Doc Curth. We left them both there. Their choice. We all meant to go back for them if we could.'

'Do you think they'll still be alive?'

Varl shrugged. 'The Doc? I dunno. But Ven... you imagine anything in this cosmos having the stones to kill Ven?'

Kolea grinned and shook his head.

Varl pinched the ash off his lho-stick and slipped the extinguished remainder behind his ear. 'I gotta go do something about that game,' he said. 'Shoot Brostin, maybe.'

Kolea had been alone on the landing for a few minutes when Tona Criid came up beside him. He nodded to her, but said nothing for a while.

At last, he said, 'How's the lad doing?'

'He's doing well, 'specially given the mongrel squad he's in.'

'That's good.'

'He's fitter than I've seen him,' Criid added, 'though his feet are hurting him right now. Last few weeks, a lot of circuit marches.'

'Yeah?'

'Punishment.'

Kolea frowned. 'Punishment for what?'

'For being too good. For showing the driller up. He's being made an example of, and he's sucking it up.'

'Maybe this driller needs–' Kolea began.

She shook her head. 'No, no, Gol. It's fine. It's the way Dalin wants it. He knows how the Guard works, and he's toeing every line. The driller's on him because he's never had such a model recruit and he can't shake the feeling that it has to be a trick.'

Down below, there was a sudden whoop and the drums picked up their beat again.

'You could ask him how he's doing yourself,' she said.

'I don't want to get in the way.'

'You're his father.'

'I'm his surviving biological parent,' Kolea replied. 'He's got a father and a mother.'

'You're his father,' Criid repeated. 'There's nothing normal about the lives we lead, so I don't believe it matters how you, me and Caff fit together, so long as we do. Dalin wouldn't mind if you showed an interest.'

'Maybe.'

'I'd go as far as to say he'd like it if you showed an interest.'

Kolea pursed his lips and thought about that. He didn't look at her. His eyes remained fixed on the game below them.

'Do it before it's too late,' Criid suggested.

'Too late?'

'We're walking Glory Road,' she said. 'Sooner or later, we get to the end of that, and you know what's waiting there. Leave it till then, and it could be too late.'

XII

THEY WERE IN the Basement, cleaning kit. Each one of them had their stuff laid out on their ground sheet. Kexie would come by, occasionally kicking a meal-can or a cup the length of the chamber if it wasn't up to regs. Sometimes he'd pick up a tin, toss it lightly into the air as he straightened up, and use Saroo like a bat to swat it into the roof.

Dalin could see the distant figures of several comrades down the far end of the Basement, recovering their launched kit items.

Kexie came up to Dalin. As he arrived, Dalin stood at attention, the ground sheet at his feet.

Find a fault with that, he willed.

He heard Kexie grunt – the slight disappointment of finding nothing to pick on.

'Pack it up. Carry on,' Kexie hissed, moving to inspect the next candidate.

It was the end of the fifth week of RIP detail. At the close of the day's cycle, they would hand in the battered practice kit they'd been caring for over the last three weeks and get issued with service materials. The following day, they would get their weapons. Then, a last three days of tight drill and prep.

It had been getting tougher every step. Kexie had been supplemented by Commissariat officers to hone the mindset alongside the body drill. There was a feeling of order, of discipline. No one played up any more.

Just looking around, Dalin could see how most of the detail had changed. Intense exercise had worn them all lean and tight, even Fourbox. The patched hand-me-down fatigues they were wearing were loose. There wasn't a pick of fat on their frames. Their hands and feet were hard and calloused. Their scalp-cuts were just growing back in, hard-edged. Their minds were wound tight like wire. Off detail, they walked with a swagger and a presence.

In just under four days they would be cycled back into their home regiments to return to duty or, like Dalin, pass out of Basic Indoctrination and become a Guardsman.

Not everyone in RIP would make it. Statistically, Caff had told Dalin, a reasonable chunk of any RIP detail got folded in again for another shakedown. The rate was higher on the Second Front, where the abnormally high percentage of sub-standard troop quality was the Crusade's shame.

Some fethers just never made the grade. That was true of this bunch. There were slackers who couldn't meet the physical grades and idiots who couldn't perform, and there were individuals like Wash who *wouldn't* rather than *couldn't*. Wash had got fit enough, but his attitude still stank. Dalin was fairly confident that Wash was one of thirty or so of them who would fold back.

Sooner or later, the repeat malingerers just got kicked out of the service, which is what most of them wanted, or got executed by the Commissariat, which is what most of them didn't.

Dalin cinched his kitbag and carried it over to the group that had finished packing. Amongst them were Fourbox and Lovely, and Hamir, one of the detail's other 'I' candidates. He and Dalin had bonded particularly well.

Hamir was a tall, olive-skinned youth from Fortis Binary. He'd followed his father and uncles in the Binars off-world after their founding and, like Dalin, had lived amongst the followers on the strength until he was old enough to take the aquila. Hamir had intelligent eyes and a slightly learned manner about him, so Fourbox had dubbed him 'Scholam'.

'No Saroo for you, Holy?' Lovely asked.

'He knows when he's beaten,' Dalin replied, looking across the chamber at Kexie, who was clubbing a candidate's shoulder blades for the incorrect fastening of a bed roll.

'Nearly there,' Hamir said.

'What?' asked Dalin.

Hamir looked up at the lights. 'We're nearly there. Can't you feel it?'

'Where?'

'The end of training. The start of Guard life. Wherever this transport is going. Take your pick.'

'I'm going to miss this,' Fourbox muttered ruefully.

Dalin, Hamir and Lovely stared at him. He beamed. 'That was a joke,' he said.

As THE DETAIL assembled, the last stragglers running to their places pursued by Saroo, Dalin caught sight of Merrt. He hadn't spoken to him since the night on the circuit march weeks before. Not before or since. Merrt had kept himself to himself.

Dalin felt terrible pity for Merrt, which he was sure the older man wouldn't appreciate. The pity came from the fact that the bulk of the RIP were all youngsters. Merrt was an old man in their midst. It seemed cruel to see him forced to repeat the mindless drills of basic 'I', like an adult forced to play along in children's games. He was above it, beyond it. He'd seen real life and felt its lash. He didn't need a refresher course.

Dalin wasn't sure what it was that Merrt needed. Merrt simply got on with RIP duties and never uttered a word of complaint. He hadn't stood up to Kexie over anything again. In Fourbox's opinion, this was because 'with a mouth like that' Merrt hated to have to speak, but Dalin believed it was that Merrt didn't have to. After that day on the range, although he had beaten many of them since, Kexie had never pulled a stunt so vindictive and unfair.

'All right?' Dalin said, stepping up alongside Merrt. Merrt looked around, then nodded.

'Can I ask you a question?' Dalin said.

Merrt shrugged.

'On the range–' Dalin began.

'We've spoken about that,' Merrt said quickly.

'No,' replied Dalin. 'No, not then. I mean since. On the range, you're regularly getting, what, sixty, sixty-two?'

'Yeah,'

'You never seem happy with that.'

'What are you rating, son?'

'Around seventy-one.'

'You gn… gn… gn… happy with that?'

'Feth, yes. Of course.'

Merrt sighed. 'Know what I used to get? On an average day, I mean?'

'No?'

'Ninety-seven,' Merrt said. 'Ninety-seven, without any trouble. It was just in me. Range best was ninety-nine on three occasions.'

A consistent, sustainable ninety-four got a man a marksman's lanyard. Dalin knew specialists the likes of Raess, Banda and Nessa Bourah, even Larks himself, were happy with a steady ninety-five.

'Now I'm scraping sixty-one. You think I'm gn… gn… gn… happy?'

XIII

TONA WOKE WITH such a shock that her hands clawed at the coop-wire of the cage-wall and made it shake and rattle. There were muffled complaints from nearby billets.

It was dark, and there was the heavy body smell of night cycle. Caff was asleep. She went out onto the cage landing. The barrack hall was dim, just deck lighting on, but the overheads were warming up. Day-cycle was close.

She looked at her hands. They were pale in the spare blue light. She couldn't see them shaking, but she knew they were.

SHE WALKED DOWN the companionway towards Gaunt's quarters and heard the sounds of a blade striking another blade. She drew her warknife and stepped forwards cautiously.

Eszrah appeared, magically, from the shadows, and shook his head. She put the knife away again.

At the end of the companionway, in a small open space of deck in front of the hatch into Gaunt's private accommodation, two men were duelling with swords, by lamplight.

Gaunt and Hark, both in breeches and shirts, were swinging sabres. The swordplay was intense, and from the sweat on them, they'd been at it for a while.

Leaning against some ducting, his arms folded, Rawne was watching them.

'What is this?' Criid asked.

Rawne glanced at her. 'Just sparring. They've been doing it just before the start of day-cycle for weeks now.'

'Why?'

Rawne shrugged. 'Practice. Hark said something about improving his blade skills.'

'Has he?'

'Well, if I wanted to take him, I'd choose a gun,' Rawne replied. Tona watched the combatants. Gaunt had always been skilled with a sword, and she reckoned these last few years she'd seen none finer. But Hark, who she'd always thought of as heavy and slow, was holding his own.

'Why are you here?' she asked Rawne.

'I was just watching. You never know. He might slip and kill him.'

'Which one are you talking about?' Tona asked.

Rawne grinned. 'I don't care.'

Gaunt and Hark broke off and saluted one another.

'We've got an audience,' Gaunt remarked. Hark nodded and took a swig of water from a flask on a nearby stand.

'Word is, orders are about to be sent down,' Rawne said. 'I just came to tell you that.'

Gaunt nodded. 'You need something, Criid?'

'A private matter,' she said.

'Give me a moment,' Gaunt said, sheathing his sword and fetching himself a drink.

'Rawne tells me you wanted to improve your blade skill,' Criid said to Hark.

'The colonel-commissar was recently good enough to remind me of the importance of diligent practice, sergeant,' Hark said. 'A little reminder against complacency. He's been good enough to offer some instruction.'

She nodded. Gaunt waved her over and she joined him, while Hark struck up a conversation with Rawne.

'What is it, Tona?' Gaunt asked.

'I feel stupid saying this, but–'

'Just say it.'

'I dreamed you died.'

'I died?'

'Yes.'

'Are you sure it was me?'

She hesitated. 'I think so. It mattered that much.'

'And you told me this because of the dream on Gereon?'

'Yes, sir. I dreamed of Wilder there, and that was true. I wonder if it's something about Gereon.'

'Thank you, Tona. I appreciate that this was an odd thing to confess. Tell you what, though… Gereon didn't kill me the first time. I'm not going to give it a second chance.'

She nodded, faked a smile and realised Gaunt was looking past her. Beltayn had appeared.

'Bel?'

'Just issued, sir,' Beltayn said, saluting and handing a wafer envelope to Gaunt. Gaunt tore it open and pulled out the tissue-thin paper inside.

'It's what we've been waiting for,' he said. 'We'll be translating in ten hours, at which time the ship will be marshalling with others at a designated staging area. All units are to make themselves combat ready and prepare for dispersal.'

'I'll get on it,' Rawne said.

'With you,' Hark said, following him out.

'Is that all?' asked Criid.

'What?'

'You hesitated when you were reading the orders, sir,' she said. 'Was there something else?'

'Just a list of disposition details,' he said. 'Nothing to worry about.'

XIV

THE BRIDGE AND sub-bridge levels were about the only locations aboard the vast spaceship where a man might be afforded a look outside. Most occupants spent the long passages stacked blind, deck after deck, inside the armoured hull, like seeds in a case, but the bridge decks were furnished with cabin ports and windows.

Since translation from warp-space, the ship had been on a steady deceleration, and armoured shutters had been peeled back from those ports like eyelids from waking eyes.

A strange, silvery light shone in from the void outside, a light quite at odds with the hot glow of the instrumentation and decks lamps. As he waited, his cap under his arm, Gaunt crossed to the nearest cabin port and peered out.

He always misremembered the sheer blackness of space. He would think of it as a rich, solid, substantial black, and picture it in his mind's eye, and then when he saw it again, he was always surprised. It was a black like no other, admitting no form or variance, but of impossible depth. The light of stars and other objects, simply sat against it, hard and contained and tiny. Starlight itself ran off the background black like water down a wall.

There was a star nearby, a cone of silver smoke, bright as a flashlight, even through the metre-thick porthole, and Gaunt could feel the faint impulse through the deck as the ship turned in towards it. This was the staging area. They were moving in through a silent shoal-pattern of other ships, all of them sharply lit at their sunwards ends and silhouetted at the others, some of them breathing furnace glows from idling drive systems.

Many of the cathedral-like ships were massive, massive like the carrier on which he stood, some more massive still: manufactory vessels, Munitorum supply ships, bulk conveyances. Great and ancient cruisers and frigates lay off to sunward like fortified broadswords. In places, transport ships and tankers were lashed together in long drifts, like the seed-purses of sea creatures. Small craft – luggers, shuttles, cutters, lighters and tugs – flitted between and around the great warp-going vessels, sometimes bright specks in the sunlight, sometimes trace-glimmers of exhaust in the lee of some cyclopean hull shadow.

Gaunt began to count the ships and lost the tally at seventy-three. Sunflare and the hard lines of shadows made it hard to differentiate shapes. This was a fleet, however. A fleet massed for invasion on a vast scale.

Gaunt wondered which of the basking giants out there contained Van Voytz.

'Sir?'

Gaunt turned from the port and found a junior deck officer waiting for him. The officer, a subordinate of the ship's Master Companion of Vox, offered Gaunt a sheet of message foil and waited politely while he read it. Gaunt balled the foil up in his hand.

'Will there be a reply, sir?' asked the officer.

'No. Just re-send my original request.'

'With respect, sir, that has now been declined three times,' the officer ventured tentatively.

Gaunt was well aware of the two other scrunched up foils in his coat pocket. 'I know, but repeat it, please.'

The officer hesitated. 'The Master Companion has made it known that he will not have all signal bands tied up with traffic during the manoeuvring phase.'

'One more try, please.'

Gaunt waited twenty minutes for the man to come back. During that time, with a series of deep thumps and heavy vibrations, the carrier came to a standstill alongside another ship whose bulk all but occluded the window ports. The dull noise of machine drills and unspooling cables began to echo up from the lower levels, along with the occasional distant rasp of a hazard siren.

The junior officer reappeared, trotting up the wide iron screwstair from the vox hub. The gabbling of the deck crew running post-dock crosschecks filled the sub-bridge air. The officer presented a foil to Gaunt, but the commiserating look on the man's face told Gaunt what to expect.

'Very well,' Gaunt sighed, casting his eyes over the repeated form message: BY ORDER OF THE LORD GENERAL'S OFFICIUM, REQUEST DECLINED.

'Your name is Gaunt, sir?' the man asked.

'Yes. Why?'

'There was a separate message for your attention.' The officer consulted a data-slate. 'A party is en route to meet with you, and requests you wait for them at the aft 7 airgate.'

IT WAS THE first time he had seen Commissar-General Balshin since the Ancreon Sextus campaign. She stood on the extended ramp for a moment until she caught sight of him, and then strode swiftly in his direction. Two men in the dark uniform of the Commissariat flanked her.

The airgate was cold, and stank of fumes and interchange gases. Steam from the pneumatic clamps hung like fog, and billowed occasionally in the sharp gusts of directional vents.

Gaunt bowed his head and made the sign of the aquila across his breast. 'Lady commissar-general.'

'Gaunt,' she replied with a curt nod. Her face was hard and pale, like white marble, and no warmth whatsoever flickered around her thin mouth. Her violet right eye, beady and bright, was utterly unmatched by the augmetic embedded in her left socket.

'I had not expected my remonstrances to draw a personal visit by so august a person as you,' Gaunt said.

'Remonstrances?' she asked.

'Yes, concerning the activation of the reserves.'

Balshin frowned. 'I know nothing of such matters, Gaunt. That's not why I'm here.'

'Ah,' Gaunt murmured. He had suspected as much.

'I'm here to brief you, Gaunt, and supply you with your specific orders. The armada's objective–'

'–is Gereon.'

Balshin allowed herself a tiny, mocking smile. 'Of course. You will have worked that out.'

'Commissar-general, if I hadn't been certain before now, your arrival would have been all the confirmation I needed. You'll have a special objective for the Ghosts, no doubt?'

'Indeed.'

'Due to their skill specialisations, and to my prior knowledge of the target world?'

'Invaluable prior knowledge, Gaunt.'

'You flatter me.'

'Not my intention, sir,' she said. 'Gaunt, you are uniquely placed to perform a great service to the God-Emperor.'

'May He protect us all,' one of the commissars at her side muttered. Gaunt glanced at him and recognised the man as Balshin's efficient but unctuous lackey Faragut.

'May He protect us all indeed,' Gaunt echoed.

'There is a chance here,' Balshin said. 'A chance to make a quick breakthrough. I will not allow that opportunity to be missed. Months of planning, Gaunt. I think it's time you got up to speed.'

She looked around the air gate. 'Is there somewhere private we can discuss this?'

Gaunt nodded. 'If you'd care to follow me?'

Balshin turned and looked over her shoulder. 'This way!' she snarled back at the open side-hatch of the lander.

A figure emerged and came to join them through the thinning steam.

It was Sabbatine Cirk.

* * *

XV

IN FULL BATTLEDRESS, the Ghosts came to order in company blocks. As he walked out to inspect them, setting his cap on his head brim-first, Gaunt could hear Rawne and Hark yelling commands to dress the outer ranks, but such instructions were purely cosmetic. There was a background whine of loading hoists, and muted fanfares and drum-play from the nearby Kolstec barrack hall.

Gaunt came to a halt at the head of the ranks, took a salute from Rawne, and turned on his heel to face the troops. He cleared his throat.

'We've walked the road,' he announced, 'now glory's just another step away.'

There was a robust murmur of approval. Some of the Ghosts beat their hands against the furniture of their rifles.

Gaunt raised his own hand for quiet. 'In two hours and fifty minutes, we will board drop ships for descent. Descent will be five hours' duration. Planetfall will be into a hot zone. You are to expect serious opposition from the moment you disembark. Stay in your company groups after this to receive briefing specifics.'

He ran his gaze along the ranks. Stock still, not a man wavering.

'Target world is Gereon,' he called out. 'I told you I'd show you around one day. Dirtside objective is the market town of Cantible. I won't tell you what I expect of you, because you know what I expect of you.' He paused. 'Soldiers of the Imperium,' he cried, consciously altering a phrase that had once begun 'Men of Tanith…', 'do you want to live forever?'

There was a huge cheer. Gaunt nodded, and made the sign of the aquila. 'The Emperor protects!' he yelled. 'Dismissed!'

The ranks broke up into company groups for discrete briefings. Gaunt saw some of the section leaders – Obel, Domor, Meryn, Varaine, Daur and Kolosim – drawing their commands into huddles and opening map cases.

Dorden approached him, medical pack slung around his body.

'Doctor?'

'Would you talk to him, please?' Dorden asked, gesturing to Ayatani Zweil. The old priest, in his full regalia, was kneeling down to tie the laces of a pair of oversized – and evidently borrowed – Guard boots. A rood topped with an eagle lay on the deck to his right, a golden censer to his left, its swinging chain slack.

Gaunt nodded. 'Father–' he began.

'Stick it up your arse,' Zweil said.

'I beg your pardon?'

The laces lashed in place, Zweil rose to his feet, hauling his bony self up by the haft of the rood. He shook out the skirts of his blue robes to cover his gnarled knees and scrawny shanks.

'Your suggestion, Gaunt. Up your arse with it.'

'That's very ecumenical of you, father. Now what suggestion would that be?'

'The same one as Dorden made, of course. That I should bless the men and do my "holy, holy" schtick and then wave farewell to you all and stay here.'

'And you don't want to do that?'

Zweil pouted and tugged at his long, white beard. 'Don't want to, don't intend to. Dorden says I'm too old. Says I'm "medically" too old, as if that is a completely different kind of too old. I'm as fit as a Tembarong grox, I am! I'm as fit as a man half my age!'

'Even so,' Dorden put in, 'a man half your age would need to have his food mashed up for him.'

'Shut your fething trap, sawbones,' Zweil returned, and stamped his feet. 'I'm coming with you, that's the up and down of it, and the side to side. I'm coming with you to minister to the needs of the regiment.'

'Father–' Gaunt tried to interject.

'I've got boots, if that's what you're worried about,' Zweil said, raising his skirts to prove it.

'It wasn't,' said Gaunt.

'I'm coming with you,' Zweil hissed, seizing Gaunt's sleeve with his claw-like fingers. 'That place we're headed for, that poor place… it's been unholy for too long. Perhaps it's past redemption, but I have to try. I happen to think it needs a man of the cloth like me more than it needs a soldier like you, Ibram, but I accept there are gunfire issues to consider.'

Gaunt held his stare for a few seconds. Then he looked at Dorden. 'Ayatani Zweil will be accompanying us.'

Dorden shrugged and rolled his eyes skywards.

'Sir?'

Hark had joined them. Criid and Caffran were with him. Their eyes were hard, hurt. Gaunt breathed deeply. He had been dreading this moment.

'Can they have a word?' Hark asked.

'Of course. Carry on, doctor. You too, father.'

Gaunt led Criid and Caffran away to the edge of the assembly area.

'Is it true?' Criid asked.

'About the reserve activation, you mean?' Gaunt asked. 'Yes, I'm afraid it is true.'

'Is there anything we can do?' Caffran asked.

Gaunt shook his head. 'I've been trying to fix it myself, but I'm not getting any joy.'

'It's not right,' said Criid. Gaunt had never seen her quite so brittle.

'No, it's not, but reserve activation is standard military practice. It's one of the Warmaster's regular tactics when manpower is needed, and Throne knows it's needed here. Departmento Tacticae and the Commissariat both approve. I will keep trying, until the moment we make the drop. After that too, if necessary. But you've got to accept right now that the Guard is a huge and grinding mechanism, and it rolls blindly on over individual requests and objections. It loves expediency and mass effect and hates exceptions. What I'm saying is, we may not be able to affect this decision.'

'It's not right, Criid said again.

'He should have been a Ghost,' said Caffran.

'Yes,' said Gaunt. 'He should.'

XVI

HE FELT AS IF he had been hit somewhere between the head and gut with the flat edge of Saroo. He was numb, almost dazed. His eyes were hot. He looked around and saw the same hurt and surprise in the faces of others.

Strange. He had been so sure today was going to be the best day of his life: passing out of Basic Indoctrination, becoming a Guardsman, taking ownership of his rifle from the armourer. Getting his trooper pin, his aquila, his sew-on patches…

…becoming a Ghost.

The gun in his hands felt like a dead weight. No thrill of pride came from gripping it.

'What's going to become of us, Holy?' Fourbox asked.

Wash and some of the others were voicing their disbelief. Candidates like Dalin had at least expected, and wanted, to see active service after RIP. Wash and his kind had done all they could to dodge activation for another cycle. This was devastating news to them.

A sour-looking, middle-aged commissar named Sobile had come to share the news with them just before they'd been issued with their kit and weapons. He stood up before them under the Basement's lights, and took half an age to unfold the notice.

'Hereby order given this day of 777.M41 that to meet the imperative drive for able troops in the coming theatre, High Command has committed to the activation of all reserve units, including punishment details, whereby they are to retain formation, be given designation, and be fielded as battlefield regulars. No individual currently on reserve status, be it for reasons of punishment, retraining or indoctrination, is to return to, or join, any other tactical element. For the present purposes, this detail will be afforded the name Activated Tactical 137, that is AT 137. Section details will follow. May the God-Emperor protect you. That is all.'

'GOL?'

Gol Kolea didn't look up.

'Gol? Shift your arse, the buzzer's gone.' Varl came down the walkway between the empty billet cages. Down below, the assembled Ghosts were emptying out of the barrack hall like water draining from a tank.

'Gol? Hark'll have your knackers if you don't move,' Varl said. Both men were bulked up with full webbing and battlegear, packs on their backs, helmets slung from their belts. Both carried their rifles in their right hands.

'I'm coming,' Kolea said. 'I was going to give him this. I meant to give it to him before, but today seemed like the right day.'

He looked at Varl, and held out his left hand. A Tanith cap badge, deliberately dulled with soot, lay cupped in the palm.

'Come on,' Varl said.

Kolea nodded. He slipped the cap badge into his breast pocket.

'It's like Tona warned me,' he said. 'I left it too late.'

PLANETFALL

I

THEY DIDN'T WAIT for daybreak. They didn't wait for clement weather, or a favourable turn in the tides. They didn't wait because they were greater than the weather and more powerful than the tides. They were brighter than the daybreak.

Along the west coast, down the line of seaboard towns and cities that had been linked and fortified into one long snake of battlements called K'ethdrac, or K'ethdrac'att Shet Magir, the sky went white. It was off-white, a sour white, and the whiteness pressed down on the high roofs and machicolations. Hot, dry clouds rolled in off the sea, and pooled wire-rough fog in the lower parts of K'ethdrac, as if the ocean were evaporating.

There was no wind, and everything was hushed. Visible static charges gathered like ivy around the raised barrels of the weapon assemblies standing ready all along the seventy-kilometre long fortress.

A door opened out to the west, out over the ocean, and cool air rushed in. In seconds, it had grown into a gale, a blistering, eastward-rushing belt of wind that lashed across the ramparts of the city-fort, and blew soldiers off the battlements, bent the stands of coastal trees into trembling right-angles, and stacked the sea up, white-top wave upon white-top wave, before driving it at the rockcrete footings of K'ethdrac.

As the huge wind reared up over the coast, the earth below shook, as if a terrible iron weight had been dropped upon it, and there was a noise, the loudest noise any man has ever heard and it not kill him. It was the sound of the atmosphere caving in as billions of tonnes of metal fell into it like rocks into a pool.

Less than a minute later, the first strikes seared into K'ethdrac'att Shet Magir. They were not pretty things, not the lusty, romantic blooms of fire a man might see delineated on a triumphal fresco; they produced no halo of purifying light, no magnificence to back-light a noble hero-saint of the Imperium.

The first strikes were like rods of molten glass, blue-hot, there and gone again in a nano-second. The cloud cover they came through was left wounded and suppurating light. Where they touched, the ground vapourised into craters thirty metres wide. Bulwarks, armoured towers, thick barriers of metal and stone all vanished, and with them, the gun batteries and crews that had been stationed there. Nothing was left but fused glass, lignite ash and deep cups of rock so hot they glowed pink. Each strike was accompanied by a vicious atmospheric decompression that sucked in debris like a bomb-blast running backwards.

The strikes came from the batteries of giant warships hanging above the tropopause. Their ornate hulls glowed gold and bronze in the pearly light of the climbing sun, and their great crimson prows parted the wispy tulle of the high, cold clouds, so that they resembled fleets of sea galleys from the myths of legend. So thin and peaceful was that realm of high altitude, their massive weapons systems blinked out the rods of visible heat with barely an audible gasp.

Other vessels, bulk carriers, had emptied themselves into the sky, like swollen insectoid queens birthing millions of eggs. Their offspring fell in blizzards from the scorched and punctured clouds, and were picked up and carried by the hurricane winds slicing in from the sea. Countless assault ships spurted like shoals of dull fish. Clouds of droppods billowed like grain scattered from a sower's hand.

The defenders of K'ethdrac began to fire, although their efforts were merely feeble spits of light against the deluge. Then heavier emplacements woke up, and sprawling air-burst detonations went off above the coast. At last, substantial orange flames began to splash the sky, twisted into streamers by the monstrous gales. Bars of black smoke streaked the air like a thousand dirty finger marks.

To its occupants, K'ethdrac had always seemed horizontally inclined: the long parapets and curtain walls running for kilometres, bending and twisting around the curves of the coast, with the flatness of the tidal mud beyond, the hinterlands of marsh and breeze-fluttered grasses and the undulating plane of the grey sea. It was a place of wide angles and vistas, of breadth.

In five minutes, that inclination had changed. It became a vertical place, where that verticality was emphatically inscribed down the sky by the beams and stripes of glaring energy jabbing out of the clouds. The sky became tall and lofty, illuminated by inner fire. The fortified blocks of K'ethdrac were reduced to just a trimming of silhouette at the bottom of the world, as the towering sky lit up above it, like some vision of the ascent to heaven, or the soaring staircase that leads up to the foot of the Golden Throne.

Shafts of light, so pure and white they seemed to own the quality of holiness, shone down from an invisible godhead above the sky, and turned the clouds to polished gilt and the smoke to grey silk.

The blizzard of crenellated assault ships fell upon K'ethdrac's burning lines. They came in droning like plagues of crop-devouring insects, and struck like spread buckshot. Furious scribbles of light and pops of colour lit up the seventy kilometres of wall in an effort to repel them. Thousands of tracer patterns strung the air like necklaces. Sooty rockets whooped up in angry arcs, trailing hot dirt. Rotating cannons drummed and pumped like pistons and turned the sky into a leopard skin of black flak smoke.

In the steep fortress wall, gunports oozed with light like infected wounds as energy weapons recharged and then sprayed out their ribbons of light.

Drop-ships burned in mid-air. Some melted like falling snowflakes in sudden sunlight and some blew out in noisy, brittle flashes and pelted the battlements with metal hail. Some fell into the sea, trailing plaintive smoke, or buried themselves like tracer rounds in the towers and tuberous spires of K'ethdrac. One great tower, at the southern end of the city region, half collapsed after such a collision, and left just a part of itself standing above the billowing dust, a finger of stone with a broadening crest like the trochanters of a giant thigh bone rammed into the ground.

Some drop-ships made it to the ground intact.

II

DALIN CRIID saw nothing of this.

He suffered the awful turbulence of descent, rattled like a bead in the bare-metal casket of the lander. He heard the shrill whine of the engines, like spirits screaming to be freed. He smelled and tasted the fear: acid sweat, rank breath, bile, shit.

Fear made some men weep like babies, and others as silent as marble. The company pardoner, a flat-faced, gone-to-seed fellow called Pinzer, was reciting the Sixtieth Prayer, the *I beseech*. Many of the troopers were saying it along with him, some gabbling fast and loud, as if they were anxious that they wouldn't get to the end before they died, or before they forgot how it went. Others spoke it like they meant it, meant every word with every fibre of their wills;

while others said it like a charm, a superstitious rhyme you recited to bring you luck. They spoke it carelessly, as if the words themselves were meaningless and the act of saying it was all that mattered.

Others just murmured the lines, probably not even knowing what they were saying, just fastening their scalded minds to something other than mad panic.

Criid saw a dead look in Fourbox's eyes, in Hamir's too. It was a sunken look, and it showed how totally hope had left them, and how deeply their personalities had withdrawn to hide in the very kernels of their heads. All around him, there were eyes that looked the same. Criid was sure his own eyes shared that dead look too.

The turbulence was unimaginably violent. There was simply no let-up in the shake and slam, the jump and rattle, and no relief from the howl of the engines. At particularly catastrophic lurches, some of the company would shriek, assuming the sudden death they had been anticipating.

The shrieks made Pinzer forget his words. He kept having to go back and pick up. He didn't seem scared – unlike the scalps of AT 137, he'd done this before. But Criid could tell it was an effort for the pardoner to keep expression from his face. This didn't come easy, no matter how many times you did it.

The shaking and lurching became so intense that Criid could no longer bear it. There was no escape, no exit from it, and he became so desperate that he thought he might rip open the deployment hatch and step out, and let the thundering windshear snatch him away.

A clear voice was speaking the Sixtieth Prayer. 'God-Emperor, in whose grace I persist and in whose light I flourish, I beseech thee to lend me the strength to endure this hour…'

He realised it was his own voice.

Sobile, the commissar, sat silently in his restraint harness, watching the rows of troopers from the end of the cabin. He looked like he was attending a particularly tedious dinner.

Beside the commissar, Kexie – Sergeant Kexie, as he was now – listened to his intercom and then reached up and yanked on the bell-cord vigorously. Kexie was in charge. Major Brundel, their newly appointed CO, was riding in another lander.

'Company, stand up!' Kexie bellowed over the row.

Zeedon, the trooper two seats down from Criid, bowed forward and spewed watery sick onto the steel floor between his boots.

'Ech, I said stand up, not throw up,' Kexie barked.

Criid released his restraint and took hold of his lasrifle.

Thirty seconds.

He saw Commissar Sobile take something out of his pack and lay it, ready, across his lap. It was something he'd never seen Gaunt carry, or even heard of him using.

It was a whip.

III

ZEEDON WAS THE first to die. The first Criid saw, anyway. Fourbox told him later that a Kolstec called Fibrodder had got scragged while they were still in the lander. A piece of white-hot debris, probably a piece off another drop vehicle, had punched through the hull wall two seconds before the hatch opened. Flat, sharp and rotating, the object struck Fibrodder in the back of the head with an effect similar to a circular saw, and opened his skull in a line level with the tops of his ears.

The screaming and retching of the blood-drenched troopers strapped in around Fibrodder's corpse was lost in the tortured hammer blow of landing. The landing was so brutal that Criid felt like his bones were shaking free of their tendons, his teeth flying loose from his gums. His jaw flapped and made him bite his tongue.

His mouth filled with blood, but the pain kept him sharp: the preposterous, tiny, impertinent pain, the indignation. *I've got enough to worry about and now I've bitten my fething tongue?*

Kexie and the other officers were blowing whistles. The air was hot, and it filled entirely with acrid yellow smoke as soon as the hatch opened. Noise blasted in from outside. It was gunfire, mostly; the unrestrained, unstinting chatter of an autocannon mowing at the sky.

Criid got out into cold air, felt grit beneath his boots, solid ground. The smoke was thick, and big, deep thumps of overpressure kept dulling his hearing. Head down, they were all running, weapons across their chests. There was a loud *pock-pock-pock* sound, and the patter of pebbles pinging off nearby metal plating. *Not pebbles, not pebbles...*

Criid didn't know if he was running the right way or not. He didn't know how they could tell which

way to run. The smoke had swallowed both Kexie
and the sound of his whistle. They were in some kind
of rockcrete canyon. Slabby grey-green towers rose up
on either side.

He looked back. The lander lay like the carcass of
an animal kill. In its final few seconds of flight it had
barged through a fortified wall and augured into the
yard behind it. Criid didn't know if this could be
reckoned a good landing or a bad one.

He realised there was an awful lot of things he
didn't know. He was starting to form a list.

He spat out the blood he'd been holding in his
mouth since he'd bitten his tongue. He heard
Sobile's voice, barking about 'cover spread'.

He looked up.

Through a roof of moving smoke, he could see the
sky. It was full of fire, choked with giant feathers of
yellow and amber flame. For as far as he could see,
the sky was blistering with explosions, big and small:
airbursts, shells, tracers, rockets. It seemed random
and bewildering.

There were black dots visible in the sky – other
ships, other aircraft. Two more landers, flying in formation, suddenly swept low overhead, crossing the
fortified wall, and disappeared around the far side of
the towers. The downwash roar of their engines was
painful. Far more painful was the bombardment that
opened up from the top of the towers, and swept
around chasing them.

Soot flakes ambled through the smoke. Criid took
his eyes off the sky and tried to get some sense of the
deployment. Given how many hours they had spent

in the Basement learning the rudiments of unit cohesion, there was precious little sign of it now.

Commissar Sobile appeared from the smoke about a hundred metres away. He was pointing urgently with one hand and cracking his whip with the other. A gaggle of troopers rushed past him, preferring, it seemed to Criid, to dive blindly into the drifting smoke than stay anywhere near his lash.

Criid started to follow them. They were heading towards the base of one of the towers. As he turned, the air shivered and another lander screamed in low overhead. He looked up involuntarily.

The lander was much lower than the previous two. Criid could see the detail of its underside and landing gear. Its tail section was on fire. He looked at it with a sick fascination, knowing exactly what was going to happen, while simultaneously knowing that there was nothing he could do to prevent it.

The lander rushed over him. It was thirty metres up, but it made him duck anyway. It hit the side of the nearest tower, the one he and the other troopers had been running towards.

It hit with annihilating force. One moment there was the moving bulk of the lander and the immobile face of the grey-green tower; then there was a huge and spreading fireball, a bulging fiery cloud that swallowed the lander as if it was drawing it into the tower's interior. Debris – huge pieces of stone, mortar and reinforcement girders – scattered outwards, trailing dribbles of smoke and fire.

The troopers who'd reached the base of the tower ahead of him turned and ran back. He saw the nearest of them clearly. It was Zeedon. There was still a speckle of puke on his chin. He was shouting '*Get back, get back!*'

Huge chunks of masonry and burning sections of the demolished lander – one of them, a whole engine pod, clearly still running – came down in a torrent. The avalanche caught the running troopers and enveloped them in a bow wave of dust.

Zeedon was ten metres from Criid and still running towards him when the stone block landed on him. It was a large block of ouslite, bigger than two men could have lifted between them. One face was still caked in grey-green plaster. Zeedon didn't fall beneath it or even fold up. It simply flattened him in the most total and abrupt way. He was there and then he was gone, and all that was left behind was a block of stone with a man's leg stuck out flat on one side, and another stuck out on the other. The force of violent compression had sent a powerful and curiously directional jet of blood out more than twenty metres. It left a dark red, glittering trail, like gemstones, on the dust for a moment. Then more dust filmed and tarnished the red beads, covering them over.

IV

BEYOND THE TOWERS, that particular sector of the fortress of K'ethdrac'att Shet Magir was a wilderness of fire and rubble. Kexie and Sobile gathered up the squads and managed to link up with some of the company from the second AT 137 lander, which had come down inside the perimeter wall. There was no sign of Major Brundel.

They were closer to some of the area's major gun emplacements, and subjected to the side-effects of their bombardment.

The emplacements, mainly anti-air and long range anti-orbit weapons, were firing at full rate. Their flashing concussions tore the sky overhead, and the ground shook continuously. It overcame the senses. It was too loud for the ears, too bright for the eyes and no voice could penetrate it. Criid tried to find cover. In the open, the bombardment was as crude a sensory experience as having a high power lamp pack pressed against each eye socket and then switched on and off rapidly. Even with his eyes closed, the flashes came through white and traced with capillary threads.

Criid half-jumped, half-fell into a rockcrete drainage trench, a culvert running along the edge of the yard. Rubble littered its dry bed. He passed the body of a Guard trooper, curled up in the culvert as if he was asleep, but not even the deepest sleep relaxed a body that much.

At the end of the culvert, he caught up with a squad led by Ganiel, a Hauberkan who Kexie had made corporal. Boulder was amongst the troopers. They crossed a smoke-washed concourse and came up towards what Criid was certain were the munitions silos for two of the thundering emplacements. Somewhere along the way, Kexie joined them. He took them as far as a low wall, and then got them down into cover.

Criid wasn't sure why at first. Then he saw puffs of stone dust lifting off the top of the wall, and realised that they were under ferocious small-arms fire, the noise of it lost in the bombardment. Lip, a Kolstec girl on RIP for arguing with a superior, was slow getting down. She walloped over onto the ground and lay there with her legs kicking furiously for a few seconds. Then her limbs went slack.

When the firing became sporadic, Kexie led them over the wall. He did this with a simple gesture and a certain look on his face. It seemed clear from both that ignoring him was a more dangerous proposition than breaking cover into a fire zone.

Criid started to run, leading Boulder, Ganiel and a Binar called Brickmaker. Criid felt the movement of air against his face as rounds tore past.

They reached the cover of an upturned slab of rockcrete that a rocket had scooped out of the yard, got down, and started firing. It felt satisfying, somehow, to be firing back at last. His first shots in anger, although he couldn't see where he was shooting.

Kexie got to the cover of a mangle of engine debris five metres away. Socket, Trask and Bugears slithered up behind him. Three others weren't so fortunate. Landslide was cut up messily by lasfire the moment he left cover. His broken body lay on the ground, the jacket on fire. Likely, a diligent little Binar who had been, with Criid and Hamir, one of the few 'I' candidates in RIP, had covered half the distance when he was hit in the knee and went sprawling. He rolled over, clutched his ruined knee, and was immediately shot in the same knee a second time. This shot had to pass through his clutching left hand to do so and blew off three fingers.

Likely screamed in pain. Bardene stopped and turned to help him, and was killed outright by a bolt round to the base of the spine that left him spread-eagled on his face. A second later, cannon fire put Likely out of his torment.

Criid reloaded. Stone dust and fycelene stung his eyes. A horn sounded, deep and long and loud, like a manufactory hooter.

'Ech, look at that,' Kexie bawled.

Criid turned to look. Behind them, the god-machines were moving in.

V

AGAINST A SKY ragged with fire, titans were coming in off the shore to raze K'ethdrac'att Shet Magir. Criid had seen them before – in books and picts, and also for real at several victory parades. He'd once nursed an ambition to be a princeps when he grew up, until the honest aspiration to be a Guardsman took over.

At that second, he could no longer recall why he'd made that choice. If nothing else, being a princeps high up in an armoured thing like that would have been a lot safer.

Criid knew titans were big; he was just utterly unprepared for the scale of their violence. It was the way they strode along, demolishing walls and roofs without effort, and the way their weapon limbs unleashed apocalyptic doom at targets great distances ahead.

There were two assaulting the fortress wall about a kilometre to Criid's left, but his attention was transfixed by the third one, the nearest, coming in through the walls behind him.

It was matt khaki, its flanks inscribed with big white numerals. Its movements were ponderous and arthritic, like a heavy old man shambling after his grandchildren. Its head and torso rocked backwards and forwards gently on its hips as it took each step. There was a sound of gears, of giant hydraulics, of creaking metal. The volcano cannon, its right arm, tracked slowly, fired out salvos of rapid, shrieking shots, and then tracked again and repeated. Criid saw tiny lights high up under the beetle brow, and felt as if he'd glimpsed the thing's soul, even though it was surely only the cockpit lights.

It was on his side, but it terrified him, and it terrified the men around him. It was a war machine, and this was its natural habitat. Criid felt he had no business being anywhere near it. For a start, how would it know that the screaming dots around its feet were loyal soldiers of the Imperium? How could it make that subtle differentiation when each blundering step it made brought curtain walls tumbling down in cascades of bricks or ripped through razorwire fences like they were long grass? Criid believed that if he was a princeps, commanding that power, he would trample over everything in his way and, afterwards, if he was told he'd crushed friends on his way to the foe, he'd say 'But we have a victory, that's what counts.' It was preposterous to think that a titan should be bothered with the details of what lay under its feet. You unleashed it, and then you got out of its way.

The sergeant had clearly arrived at a similar opinion. At the top of his parade ground voice, he was yelling at the squads to move clear, to move right. Small-arms fire was still raining down on them like summer drizzle, but the titan at their backs was approaching like a tidal wave. Another barrier wall came down around its shins, filling the air with the clopping sound of loose blocks tumbling together, filling their nostrils with the fresh, dry stink of masonry dust. The volcano cannon ululated again, shredding the air above them with fizzling javelins of light. Criid felt his skin prickle and the hairs on his arms lift as the close energy blasts altered the ionisation of the air.

He could smell ozone and oil, and hot metal. Steel plates shrieked, dry and unlubricated, as they took another shuddering step forward. A horn blared. The manufactory hooter noise was the thing's voice, its warning, not to the foe but to its own kind. *Out of my way, I'm walking here. Out of my way, or die.*

They started to run, to the right, as Kexie had instructed. The sergeant was running too. Again, Criid felt the stinging breeze of rounds cutting the air beside him. He saw las bolts soar and flicker past. A flying pebble hit him in the leg. He saw a trooper running a few paces ahead twist and fall over. He got down in a shell hole.

The ground trembled with the tread of the titan as it passed. Down in the shell hole, small rocks and sand trickled down with each quiver.

A body fell into the hole on top of him. It was Boulder. He kicked and struggled to get the right way up and dropped his rifle more than once.

'Holy?' he said, realising who he'd fallen in on. That made him laugh, although Criid couldn't hear it above the titan's horn. *Haw-haw-haw*, went Boulder's mouth. He had a cut over one eye, and his left cheek was covered with soot. Criid signed to ask if he was all right, but Boulder didn't understand. Caff had taught Criid how to sign. It was a stealth thing, a Ghost thing.

The reminder made Criid wince. There was nothing heroic or exciting about the situation he found himself him, nothing even remotely sensible or purposeful. It was a mad, ragged scramble, full of fear and shocking glimpses of mutilation, and with no clear purpose. He had dreamed of a Guardsman's life, wanted a Guardsman's life, and if this was it, it was wretched and idiotic. He felt cheated, as if Caff and his ma and Varl and all the others had been lying to him all these years. No one would want this. No one would choose this.

Except, maybe, if he had been going through this as a Ghost, instead of as a member of the arse-wipe detail AT 137, maybe all those qualities would have been there... the excitement, the heroism, the purpose.

'What do we do?' Boulder was yelling, his manner part whining, part sarcastic. 'What do we do? Can we go home now, haw-haw-haw?'

Criid took a look up out of the hole. He looked for Kexie, or the commissar. He saw Ganiel in a ditch nearby with Fourbox, Socket and Brickmaker. He saw a body, out on the open rockcrete, half-turned on its back, leaking blood into the dust. Who was that? Did it matter?

Criid didn't know which way to go, or what to do if he got there. He could discern no value whatsoever in the Imperial Guard's investment in bringing him and his comrades to this place.

'You've been shot,' Boulder shouted.

Criid looked. The calf of his fatigue pants was holed and bloody. It hadn't been a pebble that had bounced off his leg. He'd been shot and hadn't realised it.

The titan passed by fifty paces to their left. Its shadow, cast by the seething fireball of a burning fuel tank, had slid over them. The ground continued to tremble with each step, and the air was still rent with the horn, the shriek of metal plating and the squealing of the cannon.

Criid craned around to see it. It was tearing into the inner yards, passing the munition silos on its advance towards the main emplacements. It was trailing part of an electrified wire fence from one ankle, like a shackle, and the bouncing, jangling wires sparked and fizzled. Criid was suddenly struck by what the titan really reminded him of. The bear.

Years ago, with the followers on the strength of another transport, there had been a dancing bear, a big black ursid from some backwater world that one of the regiments had kept as a mascot. It was shackled to a post by one of its rear feet, and the handler would stab it with a goad to make it rear up and dance to tunes played on a tin whistle. The bear could shuffle about well enough. It reared tall and huge, forearms bent at its sides, rocking from side to side in a manner that amusingly mimicked a man, but it was no biped. As soon as it was able, it would stop pretending to be human and drop back down onto all fours to become a big, simple beast again.

That's what the titan reminded him of: a wild beast, a giant carnivore, taught to roar and shamble on two legs, plodding slowly, uncomfortably, yearning to drop back into its natural stance.

Boulder tugged at his sleeve.

'What?

'See that?' Boulder pointed. Sobile had reappeared, leading twenty members of the company in across the smouldering rubble. There were more troops too. Several dozen figures in brown battledress were clambering into the compound through the gap that the titan had made in the outer wall.

The dozens became hundreds, the hundreds thousands. Criid blinked. He saw regimental banners rise and bugles sound. Androman Regulars, he made out from the gilt thread of one banner, Sixth Regiment. Regular Imperial Guard at battalion strength, swarming in from shore landings. The tide of men flooded the concourse and advanced behind the titan like the train of a cloak. Criid could see the white and yellow tinder strikes of their rifle fire as they aimed up into the blockhouses. Rockets whooped upwards on erratic arches of smoke.

'Get up,' Criid told Boulder. 'Get up. Let's go.'

VI

THEIR CONFIDENCE TEMPORARILY lifted by the company of so many others, AT 137 moved forwards. Commissar Sobile hardly had to use his whip. They surged out onto a vast yard or parade ground beneath the network of emplacements, following the plodding titan.

The enemy guns were still pounding. All down the coast, for kilometres in either direction, the defences of K'ethdrac ripped into the morning sky, pummelling the air with concussion and echoes of concussion. A shroud of fycelene vapour clung like a sea fog.

The sky seemed, to Criid, to be the greatest casualty of all. It was swollen with smoke and the light from massive fires. Great black and orange mushrooms welled up into it. To the north, thick squadrons of attacking aircraft swirled around like flocks of birds gathering to migrate.

One of the more distant titans, visible over the line of burning roofs, took a direct hit from a super-heavy emplacement. The centre of the torso and the head blew up in a vast fireball that rose, writhing and expanding, and finally separated into a crowning ring of flame that wobbled into the sky. Its structure shorn through, the torso plating failed and the heavy weapon limbs, the titan's arms, fell away and tore the folding halves of the body with them. The rest of the machine remained standing: locked, frozen legs and a black iron pelvis gutted by fire.

A great moan of dismay rose from the foot troops at the sight. The Androman Regulars began to charge the emplacements, bugles and drums sounding.

Criid was caught in the surge for a moment and was carried along. Men in brown uniforms were all around him and he couldn't see another shape in the drab grey of his own unit.

'Keep going, boy!' one of the Androman troopers told him. He was a big fellow with sallow skin, as hirsute as the rest of his breed. He grinned at Criid.

'Come on! The Emperor protects!'

Criid wasn't so sure. He was pretty certain he ought to be linked to his own company. He searched for his comrades, but his foot caught on a slab of rubble and he fell.

The Guardsmen charged past him. Some were yelling battle cries. He tried to get up again, but was knocked over twice by barging men. Some cursed him.

Enemy fire began again. It fell like sleet on the Imperial force from gun nests and strongpoints up on the looming emplacements. The spirit that had driven the men forward en masse left them. The advancing flow recoiled.

Criid got up and started to run. A series of mortar shells planted themselves into the rockcrete not far from him and sprouted into cones of fire and grit. Two or three men were thrown bodily into the air and came down heavily like sacks full of rock. Others were cut down as they turned back, smacked into by whining cannon fire. Each shot wailed for a split second before it arrived and made the *thwuck* of impact that brought a man down in a mist of blood.

Criid saw the big Androman who had spoken to him. He was staggering about, sneezing, spitting and aspirating blood through a face that had lost its nose, top lip and upper teeth. The man flailed past him and Criid didn't see what happened to him after that.

Criid ran across the concourse. It was littered with bodies. The Androman Guardsmen were now flooding off to the left, shrinking back from the killing ground below the emplacements. The titan strode on, oblivious to the tidal changes in the infantry around its feet, oblivious to the small-arms fire and mortars pinging off its hull.

Some parts of AT 137 had taken cover in a rock-crete gulley leading to a heavy loading door. The loading door, riveted metal, was shut and had resisted attempts to open it.

Sobile saw Criid approach along with other stragglers, and cracked his whip at them agitatedly.

'Watch the unit and stay together, you worthless morons! Stay together and stay focused! How can we achieve our objectives if we don't have unit cohesion?'

Criid wanted to answer back. He wanted to ask how they were supposed to achieve their objectives if they didn't know what their objectives were. He wanted to ask if Sobile had a fething clue what the objectives were himself. Criid had a long list of questions.

One of Sobile's petulant whip cracks caught him across the right shoulder and the corner of his jaw and he forgot about his questions and his lists. The corded leather sliced right through his jacket and drew blood along his collar bone. It felt like his jaw had been dislocated.

'Get up!' Sobile ordered, generally disinterested in Criid's plight. The pain was so sharp that Criid could barely move. His eyes filled with hot tears.

'Get up!' Sobile snarled and then turned to the others. 'I'll damn well skin the next moron who forgets to focus. Are we clear?' He coiled up his whip and glanced at Sergeant Kexie. Kexie was rubbing a scratch on his gnarled cheek. The troopers were all gathered in the shadow of the gulley, panting, trying to draw breath. Some were sobbing.

'Sergeant?' Sobile said.

'Break into squads, advance that way across the yard,' Kexie said, indicating with his lasrifle. 'Come at the nearest emplacement from the side, see if we can't storm it and shut it down.'

'Instructions are clear, 137,' Sobile thundered. 'Get into position!'

Artillery, a kilometre or so away, was suddenly thumping like the drums of a giant marching band. The skyline lit up with pulsing flashes. Beyond the gulley, the Androman troops were massing for another attempt to get across the parade ground.

Criid got up. Blood was leaking out of the split flesh at the corner of his jaw, and his shoulder throbbed. He could feel the tissue stiffening and swelling. The fingers of his right hand were numb. Getting into position was a joke. Of the two hundred and fifty individuals that made up AT 137, about forty were gathered in that dank gulley. Criid didn't know if that meant the rest of them were dead, or were simply somewhere else, equally bewildered. Another question for his list. This chunk of AT 137 seemed to qualify as the 'main section', because it happened to have both the commissar and the sergeant with it.

There were barely any surviving vestiges of prede-termined fire teams or squads. People just joined up with people they knew into assault teams that had roughly the right number of bodies. Criid got in with Ganiel's mob, along with Bugears, Socket, Trask and Fourbox. He saw Boulder in another gaggle with Cor-poral Carvel. Boulder was looking confused and dazed. The cut over his eye had begun to bleed more freely.

'Where is your weapon? Where is your issued weapon, trooper?' Sobile shouted.

Boulder suddenly realised that the commissar was speaking to him. He looked around and blinked. His hands were empty, and they'd been empty for a long time, and he hadn't noticed. The last time Criid had seen Boulder's rifle, he'd been busy dropping it in the shell hole. It was probably still there.

'I think I dropped it,' Boulder began. He tried to curl his lips into a smile, but the full, trademark laugh wouldn't come.

No, no, no, Criid thought. Boulder had no idea what he was heading for. He wasn't thinking.

You didn't drop your rifle. You didn't lose your rifle. A Guardsman protected the rifle issued to him with his life, and vice versa. It was basic and funda-mental.

'Gross infringement, article 155,' Sobile said and shot Boulder through the head. Boulder jerked as if he'd been told surprising news. It obviously wasn't funny news, because he didn't laugh. He pitched over, slack and heavy, and hit his sagging head against the gulley wall on his way down.

There was a moment when even the artillery seemed silent. It was the first ten-ninety Criid had ever witnessed. He felt sick. In a day filled with waste and hopelessness, this was the most obscene thing yet.

'Anyone else?' Sobile asked holstering his pistol.

Everyone looked away. They didn't want to catch Sobile's eyes, or look at Boulder.

'Ech, you soft-shit scalps!' Kexie snapped. 'You want to be proper bloody Guardsmen, you better show me and the Emperor what you've got. On the whistle…'

The sergeant's whistle blew. They broke from cover and ran, leaving Boulder alone in the shadows with steam gently rising from the wound that had killed him.

VII

CORPORAL GANIEL'S SQUAD reached the western corner of the large emplacement without incident. They were all out of breath from the dash across the open, and wired from the fear of making that dash. Behind them, smoke wreathed the scattered rubble. A noisy, widespread firefight was raging beyond a row of warehouses, spraying tracers and backflash into the lowering sky, and they could see Corporal Carvel's team spread out and running for the building's eastern end. Sporadic, almost tired cannon fire barked lazily from the roof high above, and kicked up dirt around them.

Up close, the building was dead and dark. It was built not from stone but from some synthetic or polymer, faced with pitched wooden boards. Criid could see sections of the chipped resin in places where gunfire had shredded off the wood. On close examination, it looked less like polymer and more like bone or fossilised tissue. There was a smell to it, up close. It was a warm, animal smell, slightly rancid, slightly spicy. It wasn't entirely unpleasant.

The sergeant came up behind them, with another of the squads.

'Move up!' he grunted.

'There's no door, sergeant,' said Ganiel.

A missile squealed overhead and caused a large explosion beyond the ruptured sea wall. Two fighters – Thunderbolts, Criid guessed – swept in past the emplacements at rooftop height and peeled out towards the northern districts of K'ethdrac'att Shet Magir. The cityscape was dense with thousands of columns of smoke like trees in a woodland.

Sobile moved up with another squad. He'd found the pardoner somewhere. The man, unfit and unhealthy, was wheezing as he muttered the words of grace and benediction to a wounded man.

Carvel's squad moved around the eastern end of the emplacement. They'd been gone about thirty seconds when there was a fizzling crump that tore the air like dry paper, and a flash lit up behind the corner where they'd vanished.

Kexie ordered Ganiel's team forward to investigate. They had no man-to-man vox. Either there hadn't been spare micro-bead kit available for issue at AT 137's sudden advancement to active status, or a rattail dreg outfit like AT 137 didn't deserve such costly luxuries. They had a unit vox-officer with a field set, a Kolstec called Moyer, but Criid hadn't seen him since boarding. He was probably dead along with Major Brundel.

Covering each other with jerky, nervous switches of their lasrifles, Ganiel, Criid and Trask reached the eastern corner. Bugears and Fourbox were close behind.

Around the corner, a wide service lane led up to loading shutters built into the back of the emplacements, access for the heavy carts of the ammunition trains coming up from the silos. The area had been hit comprehensively during the first phase strikes. The Navy bombardment had missed the blockhouse gun emplacements but had expertly flattened a row of empty bunkers behind them. The service lane was littered with debris and rubble from the bunkers. It was quiet back there, just some drifting smoke. The heavy weapons within the emplacement had been silent for some minutes.

'Where's Carvel?' Ganiel asked.

One patch of the rockcrete roadway was smoking with particular vigour. The smoke rose from a wide, tarry puddle of debris. It was organic debris. Criid smelled burned meat and took a step back.

'Carvel…' he gagged.

The remains of the five men lay in the dark, smoking scorch mark. They'd been incinerated, although some parts of them were still identifiable: skulls, ribcages, long bones, heat-twisted rifles. The bones were black-wet with sticky meat and cooked blood.

'Get back,' Ganiel said.

'Good idea,' Kexie muttered. He'd arrived behind them to take a look. 'Ech, get running.'

He said something about a tank that Criid didn't hear properly because of the sudden roar of a flamer behind them, and a gust of heat singed the back of his neck as he ran.

He never saw the tank, but he heard and smelt it – the deep, grinding rumble of its engines, the clatter of its treads, the stink of its oil. According to Kexie, it had been hull-down in the ruins of the bunkers, guarding the service lane with its hull-mounted flamer.

They ran from it. Disturbed, it roused from its lair and came after them.

'Back up. Back up. Find cover!' Kexie yelled as they rejoined the others. 'Bandit armour right behind us!'

Sobile started to run. They all started to run, to scatter, but Sobile ran in a way that suggested to Criid that he no longer cared about his duties and responsibilities, and certainly didn't care to risk his skin any longer trying to preserve either unit cohesion or the moronic lives of any of the rejects he'd been lumbered with.

Criid heard the flamer roar again as the tank cleared the emplacement. He looked for cover, any cover, spotted a shell hole in the rockcrete and threw himself into it.

He'd been there before. In the oily seepage at the bottom of the hole lay Boulder's rifle.

VIII

HE STAYED IN the hole for what seemed like a year or two. He wrapped his arms around his head, but they didn't block out the increasing volume of the clattering tracks and the throbbing motor. The gushing roar of the flamer sounded like an ogre's wet snarl.

There were screams. There were a lot of screams. Some lasted longer than a scream should decently last.

He tried to block it all out. All he could see was the blood-red sky above, filmed with driving smoke, and the occasional afterglow of a big flash. He kept expecting it to be blocked out by the black, oiled belly of the tank as it rattled over the top of him.

Rolled up like an unborn child, Dalin Criid felt more mortal than he'd ever felt in his life. All the self-deceiving vitality of youth drained from him and left just a silt of pain behind. His needs reduced to an undignified, simple level, and became the sorts of things that grown men scorned as weaknesses in the mess hall or the bar room, and cried out for shame in extremis. In a hole in the ground, in the path of a tank, for instance.

In that moment, he knew with astonishing clarity that this happened, sooner or later, to every man or woman who became an Imperial Guardsman. It was the moment when a person faced up to the fact that everything he'd bragged about wanting – action, glory, battlescars and reputation – was, without exception, chimerical and of no value or reward, and everything he'd disparaged as weak and soft, and cowardly was all that genuinely mattered.

He wanted the noise to stop. He wanted to be elsewhere too, but the noise was the key thing. It was relentless and he needed it to stop. He wanted the pain in his face and shoulder to go away. He wanted to see his ma. He wanted to be eleven years old again, playing paper boats with his baby sister in the deck gutters of a troop ship.

In that hole in the ground, so like a grave, these things acquired a sudden and resonating value that went far beyond comfort or escape. There was something else he yearned for too, something he couldn't quite resolve. A face, maybe.

He understood that he was experiencing the soldier's universal epiphany, but he didn't know what would happen next. Was it fleeting? Was it a mood that came and went, or was his heart now hollowed out, his courage permanently compromised? Had his fighting mettle perished? Was he of no use as a soldier?

What actually happened next was a loud detonation, fierce and visceral, that sounded like two anvils colliding at supersonic velocities. The metallic impact physically hurt, jarring his bones and making his sinuses ache.

Then there was a second explosion, much richer and throatier with the sound of flames than the first.

Criid heard the sergeant's muffled voice, as if from a long way off. '137! 137, regroup! Regroup!' The whistle blew.

He raised himself up out of the shell hole and saw figures moving through a dense heat-haze. The haze was rippling off a vast bonfire twenty metres away, a huge stack of black material the size of a revel fire, swollen with leaping orange flames.

Criid got out of the hole. He looked at Boulder's rifle and wondered if he should take it with him. In the end, he decided to pop the power cell and take just that.

He walked through the washing heat towards his regrouping unit. There were bodies on the ground, charred and smouldering. One was the trooper Fourbox had given the name Socket. His whole form had been wizened and shrunk by extreme heat, but Criid could tell it was Socket because, mysteriously, Socket's face had remained untouched, like a mask tied to a pitch-black dummy.

Kexie was drawing the unit together. There was no sign of Sobile, which was the only decent thing that had happened since they'd arrived.

'What happened to the tank?' Criid asked Brickmaker.

The Binar nodded to the big bonfire.

'That's it?'

It was, apparently, it. No one could say exactly what had killed the tank, but the best guess was 'a stray shot from something big a long way off'. According to the sergeant; 'This kind of shit happens on the battlefield sometimes.'

Commissar Sobile turned up alive a few minutes later, so that kind of shit happened on a battlefield too apparently. He got busy with his whip, and tore two troopers new exits for losing their helmets.

They moved north, up the line of the emplacements, towards an enormous firefight about a kilometre away. The titan, now long gone, had flattened the emplacements on its way past. Most were burning and broken open to the sky. Some had burst, leaking dark, sticky fluid out in wide lakes around their foundations. It was as if the buildings were bleeding. Kexie warned them not to go near the stuff, but no one had the slightest inclination to anyway, and nobody wanted to take a look inside the ruins.

They reached a main thoroughfare that thrust east up through the gloomy city. A river of Imperial tanks and light armour was flowing inland, heading towards the gourd-shaped super-towers at K'ethdrac's heart. Vs of fighter aircraft skimmed up the line above the tanks. The city district on the far side of the thoroughfare, a region of dark towers and strange, crested structures the colour of tungsten, was being pummelled into extinction by pinpoint orbital fire. The ribbons of light, eye-wateringly bright, jabbed down through the stained cloud cover and, with chest-quaking concussion, reduced habitation blocks to swirling storms of ash.

Back the way they had come, more titans stalked the burning skyline, visible from the waist up behind the roofscape as if they were wading a river. They were booming silhouettes against the amber twilight, their hands flickering luminously with laser discharge.

To Criid, it seemed like the entire city was on fire.

Another wave of drop ships began pouring in overhead.

On the debris-strewn pavements, AT 137 encountered a fast-moving stream of Guardsmen, a Kolstec regiment, pushing inland behind the armour thrust. There were hundreds of Kolstec, all regular troops moving quickly and urgently, with drilled precision and fixed, unruffled faces. Kexie and Sobile spoke briefly to their white-haired commander, who indicated something on a hand chart.

'Listen up!' Sobile shouted as they returned. 'Listen to your sergeant. He speaks with the voice of the Emperor!'

Criid wasn't sure Driller Kexie did speak with the voice of the Emperor. From the look Kexie gave Sobile, Kexie wasn't sold on the idea either.

'Moving in support,' Kexie drawled, pitching his voice above the factory clatter of the tanks. 'The enemy is thick in this district, so we're going in with the Kolstecs to clear it. By squads, now. Watch closely for my signals, and watch the Kolstec officers too. I don't want no soft-shit fraghead mistakes from you morons.'

The sergeant had adopted Sobile's generic term for them which, while unflattering, was one step up from 'scalps', the lowest of the low, the newest of the new, heads fresh shaved by the Munitorum barber.

The sergeant did a time check, and they moved off. Criid was sure his chron was broken, because there was something wrong with the time check, but there was no pause to adjust it. Halfway down the next cross street, gunfire lit up from a towering grey building that was already extensively ablaze. Flames gushed from the upper storey window slits. Multiple cannon fire ripped across the street and mowed down the front ranks of the Kolstec advance. Everybody scrambled for cover. Fire was returned, but too many Kolstecs were caught out in the open, and were simply scythed down like corn.

Criid got into cover as the full force of the street fight got going. The Guard sections opened up with everything they had, and the hidden enemy seemed to increase its rate of fire to match. Criid took a shot or two, but was forced down by a series of close impacts that chopped deep grooves in the stone wall above him. He could feel the fear rising in him again, the trapped, pinned terror that had found him in the shell hole.

It was at that point it started to rain bodies.

It was so horrific, so unreal, he didn't believe it at first. The living bodies of men in full kit were dropping out of the sky and hitting the street or cracking off the faces of buildings. Each impact was shockingly solid: a writhing, living man struck flagstones and instantly became a splattered mass of gore wrapped in split cloth. There were screams, cut short.

Only when Criid understood what he was witnessing did he believe it. An incoming drop ship had been hit by enemy fire and the side of its fuselage torn off. As it shrieked down on its swan dive, the troops inside were wrenched out by the slipstream and showered across the streets.

Criid saw the stricken drop ship for a second before it hit a tower and vapourised. Some of the men falling from it seemed to be jumping.

The bodies rained down, striking like bundles of ripe fruit. Several Kolstecs on the ground were hit and killed by falling bodies. There was an abominable stink of raw meat and excrement. A fog of blood steamed off the street.

It made Criid gag.

He bent low and rubbed at his face, feeling the sharp pain of the whip-cut on his jaw. He began to murmur the *I Beseech* again and took a look at his chron. It wasn't wrong after all. The time check hadn't been wrong at all.

His mind refused to accommodate it, but he'd only been a Guardsman for an hour. It didn't fit. It seemed like days – vile, barbaric days – had passed, but just an hour before, he'd been clean and tidy, riding the platform hoist up through the two metre-thick carrier deck with the rest of AT 137, while the military bands played and the dropships lit their engines.

One hour. One hour of insanity and blood. One hour more savagely extreme than all the other hours of his life added together.

And he hadn't even seen the enemy yet.

ENEMY COUNTRY

I

EVEN AT A distance, they could hear the fetch-hounds baying in the pens inside the town. The dogs could smell them coming. They shivered the pale daylight with their yowling.

'Dogs,' remarked Ludd, crunching across the dry moorland grasses.

'Big dogs,' Varl corrected with an unhappy look. 'Fething big dogs.'

Ludd looked over at Gaunt. 'Have they got our scent, sir?'

'Oh, I'm sure they have,' Gaunt said, 'but it's more than that.' He nodded in the direction of the horizon. Far away, across the rolling moors, there was a tremble of light in the west, a fluttering wash of radiance brighter and whiter than the wan daylight and

147

the overcast sky. It was as if a giant mirror was being waggled just behind the horizon to catch and dance the sun.

It was coming from the coast, four hundred kilometres away. It was coming from a place that Navy Intel had named K'ethdrac'att Shet Magir, one of the eighteen primary objectives earmarked on Gereon.

'That's one feth of a song and dance,' Varl murmured, looking at the light show.

Cantible was not one of the eighteen primary objectives. It wasn't even one of the six hundred and thirty secondary objectives, or one of the five thousand and seventeen second phase objectives. On High Command's complex logistical diagrams, it appeared amongst a list labelled *Tertiary/recon*. Light scout, reconnaissance and intruder regiments were being dropped forward of the main assaults to secure bridgeheads and clear lines of advancement. Cantible, the municipal and administrative hub for an agri-belt province called Lowensa, defended one of the main west-east running corridors between K'ethdrac and the Lectica heartlands.

But even that wasn't the main reason they had been sent there.

Gaunt took a look left and right. The entire strength of the Tanith First was advancing in a wide spread across the rolling grassland from their dropsite higher in the moors. Supporting light armour was chugging to meet them along a pasture route to the south.

There were woods ahead, then broad stretches of farmland, and then the town itself. Gaunt could see the chubby finger of the guildhall tower above the trees.

He'd always vowed to return. He'd always vowed to come back and deliver what the resistance and the people of Gereon had deserved from day one, from the very first Day of Pain. He had no idea what Day of Pain it was now, though he estimated somewhere in the low two thousands. Far too long. Far too late, perhaps.

Gaunt hadn't visited this part of the country on his previous stay, so he couldn't compare directly, but it seemed like everything had fallen into dismal ruin. Everything was spoiled somehow, stained, contaminated. The sky, the ground, the vegetation, the weather. The noxious imprint of the invaders permeated everything.

It was early spring in this part of Gereon, but the sky was hot and frowzy. The moorland grasses were yellow and parched. There was a dull, persistent crackle in the air as if the sun was sizzling. Radiation was spiking. Vox links were wandering and full of squeals and phantom voices.

The woods ahead looked like they consisted of eshel and talix, but they had grown wrong and sickly, sprouting deformed limbs out of true. Leaf cover looked autumnal, in its shades of red and yellow. The seasons of the world had been unravelled.

The farmland was also corrupted. Vile black crops, the product of intensive xenoculture, covered the far side of the valley. Gaunt could smell the maturing fruit. Other patches, overworked and rendered barren by chemicals, lay scorched and brown in the sun.

Rusty pink crusts of nitrate scummed the edges of the blighted acreage. The fallow fields and dead land had a stink to them too.

'Untillable,' Cirk murmured as she gazed at the fields. Her heavy flak coat was pulled in around her. 'They bleed us dry and make it all Untill.'

Gaunt nodded, although he was still not comfortable having her around. He'd told Faragut to keep 'specialist' Cirk with the rear echelons, but both she and Faragut had wandered out to the front of the line the moment the drop ships emptied.

'We'll have to burn it all,' Gaunt told Rawne.

'The farm land?'

'The crops. All of it.'

'Brostin will be pleased. Presumably you want this to happen once we've taken the town? The fields catching fire will be a bit of a giveaway that we're here.'

Gaunt gestured into the breeze, as if he could catch hold of the travelling sound. 'Listen to the dogs, Eli. They know we're here.'

II

So THIS, CAFFRAN thought, is the famous Gereon at last. The site of the one big Ghost operation most of the Ghosts hadn't taken part in. The ones who had gone, and come back alive, had spoken of it afterwards in secretive, reverential tones, as if it was a dark mystery they wished to forget.

It wasn't all that. Just another place that the Arch-enemy had fethed up. Of course, it must have been hard digging in here, hiding with the resistance on an occupied world for all that time. Caffran didn't doubt that. Maybe that was why Rawne, Varl and the rest spoke about it as if it was some exclusive trial or initiation that they had gone through and no one else had managed. The members of the Sturm mission still kept themselves a little bit aloof.

No, Caffran didn't doubt it had been a tough tour, but other things in the cosmos were tough too. Missing Tona for all that time, for example, and friends like Bonin, Varl and Larks. Thinking they were dead and never coming back. Thinking Gaunt was dead. Command had taken the Ghosts apart because of that, and only put them back together again when he returned like a...

'Ghost,' Caffran said aloud, softly. The woodland around him was quiet. Dry leaves rustled in a slight breeze and cold, watery sunlight filtered through the canopy. He held his lasrifle across his chest and stopped walking.

In the distance, he could hear and smell the burning fields. As the wind changed every few minutes, soot and ash blew back through the trees. It was pungent. Something bad was burning.

The advancing troops were almost silent. There was no way to guess the scale of the infantry force closing on Cantible.

This place had a lot to answer for. Things had not been the same since Gaunt and the others had come here the first time, and they hadn't been the same since they had come back. It wasn't just the forced influx of the Belladon leftovers. They were good men and the fit was fine, as good as the fit between the

Tanith and the Verghastites had been after the hive war. In fact, Caffran missed Colonel Wilder, and regretted his loss on Ancreon Sextus.

The differences that really mattered weren't the big things. It was the small stuff. It was months spent getting over Gaunt's death only to find out that he was back. It was like reverse grief. Caffran almost resented it, and he wasn't the only one.

Tona and he hadn't been as close since Gereon. Things had got a little better of late, but it still wasn't the same. She was withdrawn from him, altered. He had wondered at first if it was some kind of Chaos taint, but it wasn't that. She had just changed. She'd seen stuff that he hadn't. He wasn't someone she could talk to any more, not about the things that mattered to her anyway.

Well, that would change, starting from right now. He was going to taste the infamous Gereon for himself. He was going to know it like she knew it, and that would help him lift its shadow off the two of them. They'd exorcise Gereon together, and get back to where they had been.

Caffran knew others had experienced the same thing. Varl and Kolea had been close for ever, and Varl was the biggest mouth in the company, but since Varl had come back, even Kolea hadn't managed to get him to open up about Gereon.

Ghosts moved up past him. Caffran realised he was slowing the line. He started forward through the dappled sunlight.

'All right there, trooper?' Hark asked, moving by.

'Yes, sir,' Caffran said, getting back in the game.

Hark looked at him with an almost sympathetic expression. 'I know what you're thinking about,' he said.

Caffran blinked. He did? About Tona and Gereon and resenting Gaunt and–

'He will be all right,' Hark nodded, and headed on.

Caffran cursed himself, guiltily and silently. Hark had been wrong, because Caffran, so lost in thought, had not had his mind in the right place at all. Not at *all*.

Dalin. *Feth*!

FIFTY METRES AWAY through the woodland, Eszrah ap Niht paused, slowly removed his sunshades and blinked at the light. He touched the fingers of his left hand against the bark of a tree.

Gaunt had told him this was Gereon, that they were going back to Gereon, but this wasn't Gereon. It was a dead place. He could smell the death-stink in it, as surely as a man could smell the death-stink from another man raddled with disease.

If this was Gereon...

Eszrah put his sunshades back on, and loaded his reynbow.

III

'RERVAL?' GAUNT ASKED quietly.

Kolea's adjutant listened to his voxcaster for a moment longer, then slipped the earphones down.

'Whipcord reports they'll be in position in another ten minutes, sir,' he said.

'And when they say position, we can confirm we're both talking about the same place?'

'I'm cross-checking their coordinates now,' Rerval said.

'All right then,' Gaunt nodded. 'Bel?'

Nearby, his vox caster leaning against a gnarled tree bole, Gaunt's own adjutant Beltayn was delicately adjusting the set's dial. Retrofitted with a bulky additional power cell and an S-shaped low frequency transmitter, his vox was decidedly non-standard.

'Beltayn?'

Beltayn shook his head. 'Nothing, sir.'

'Still nothing?'

'I've tried Daystar and Mothlamp. Nothing.'

'Keep trying, please. Stay here and keep trying.'

Beltayn nodded.

Gaunt waved up Captain Meryn of E Company. 'He's your responsibility, Meryn,' Gaunt said. 'Stick a guard around him. Six men at all times.'

'Sir,' said Meryn.

Gaunt turned and walked a few paces to the edge of the clearing. Baskevyl handed him his scope.

'There could be all sorts of reasons why they're not transmitting,' Baskevyl said.

'I know,' Gaunt said, panning the scope round for a good view of the town.

'And not just bad ones,' Baskevyl went on. 'Power failure. Vox breakdown. Atmospherics…'

'I know. We'll pick them up soon enough. Are we set?'

Baskevyl nodded. 'I've had taps from Rawne, Kolea, Daur and Kolosim. Varaine, Kamori, Domor and Obel are on the facing slopes. Arcuda's mob's covering the ford.'

'Mkoll?'

'Since when was Mkoll not in position?'

'A good point.'

The sky south of them was a haze of smoke from the blazing fields. The town, a wide cluster of grey-green blocks and towers behind a wall at the hill crest, was quiet. The dogs had fallen silent.

Ludd and Hark came up through the woodland behind Gaunt and Baskevyl, and stood with them.

'Set?' Hark asked mildly.

'Whipcord's position confirmed,' Rerval called.

Gaunt pursed his lips. *Whipcord* was the operational call-sign for the Dev Hetra light armour supporting them.

'Tell them to load and stand by. They don't fire without a direct order from me.'

'Understood, sir.'

'Make sure they do.'

'Whipcord,' Hark mused. 'You know, Ludd, in some theatres, it is still common for commissars to carry lashes.'

'For purposes of encouragement, sir?' Ludd asked.

'Naturally. What other purpose would there be?'

Ludd shrugged. 'Spiritual mortification?' he suggested.

Hark sniffed. 'You've far too much time for thinking, Ludd.'

Gaunt looked at them both. 'If it's all right by you, can I commence the attack?'

'Of course. Sorry,' Hark said. 'I was just telling the boy. A commissar with a whip–'

'Had better not show up when I'm around,' Gaunt said. 'This isn't the Dark Ages.'

'Oh,' smiled Hark blithely, 'I rather think it is.'

Gaunt thumbed his micro-bead.

'Mkoll?'

'At your service.'

'Go.'

'Gone.'

Gaunt turned and drew his power sword. Activating it was all the signal Baskevyl required. He pointed to Rerval, who immediately sent the code for advance.

Across the tangled field and brush in front of the woods, the first rows of Ghosts got up, weapons aimed, hunched low, and began to scurry towards the town.

IV

THE MOST GHOSTLY of the Ghosts melted through the sunlight towards the foot of the town wall. They made no sound, and their signing was so understated that even their hands were whispering.

Without haste or rush, Mkoll, master of scouts, stepped from one shadow to another, pouring himself out of one dark space and into the next. He had a good view of the wall. Guard post, two guards in sight. He raised his hand, twitched his fingers and spread the information.

Bonin moved forwards five metres to his left. Their skills were identical, but their methods of silence were totally different. It was an odd detail that only real recon experts would pick up, but each Tanith scout had his own 'flavour' of silent movement. Mkoll flowed like liquid, running through the levels of darkness. Bonin had a dry drift to him, like a shadow moving with the sun.

Caober, for his part, seemed always in the periphery of vision, always there until a second before you looked. Caober, who'd been a scout since the Founding, had held the regimental specialty together while Mkoll, Bonin and MkVenner had been away on the Gereon expedition. He'd done a good job, and brought on several newcomers. Mkoll owed him a good deal.

Jajjo was one of those newcomers, elevated to scout operations after Aexe Cardinal, the first Verghastite in the specialty. His hard-learned skills were more industrial and mechanical than those of the Tanith-born. He would never have their instinctive grace, but Jajjo was all concentration. It was as if he stayed silent and unseen by force of will.

What appeared to be market gardens or allotments covered the slopes outside the town wall. The patches had gown wild with weeds and grox-eye daisies. Vermin scurried under the dry nets of foliage. Jajjo ducked under a broken gate, and crossed between a row of wooden lean-tos and an overgrown cultivator. He was low, twenty metres down and right of Mkoll. He spotted, and marked, five more guards on the run of town wall above him. He signed it to Mkoll.

Right of Jajjo's position, there were patches of scrub and a bone-dry paddock littered with the mummified carcasses of livestock. Hwlan, who moved like smoke, took up a spot by the gate and held cover as Maggs and Leyr crossed up the paddock to a woody clump of wintergorse. Leyr was Tanith, and moved as secretly as slow thawing ice.

Wes Maggs was Belladon, one of the Eighty-First's primary recon specialists. Immensely good at what he did, he'd had to learn the rules from scratch to keep up with the Tanith experts. He was still a little in awe of Mkoll, and that respect tended to blind him to his own abilities.

Maggs was short and broad-shouldered, and had a scar that dropped vertically from the corner of his left eye. Off duty, his mouth could give Varl's a decent race. He had his own style too. It was 'try damn hard not to get seen and killed'.

He came up into the gorse on his belly, rolled into a dry dirt cavity around the dead root, and peered out. *Clear*, he signed to Leyr, who relayed that down the line.

Maggs worked his shoulders round for a different look. The town wall was made of stone, dressed in some kind of planking, a grey-green material. There was a door ten metres away from him. Not the main gate or even a minor one, some sort of sluice or storm hatch. Maybe a waste outlet.

Too much to sign. He sent 'minor entry' and its position.

Mkoll nodded this.

Maggs made the dash as soon as the nod came back to him. A second out in the sunlight, and then down in the cool shadow at the foot of the wall, pressed in close to the cold, smelly boards. He edged along. The town was awfully quiet. The place had to be on alert because of what had hit from space that morning.

The hounds had whined, the fields had burned, but the place was quiet.

He arrived at the door. It was a wooden hatch, half-height for a man, badly built into the wall covering. It was bolted shut and the bolt secured with an ancient padlock, but the wood was damp and fibrous. Maggs began to work it with his warknife, levering the bolt away from the soft board.

Back from him, in the gorse, Leyr saw the guard coming. A single enemy trooper in dirty green combat armour strolled through the overgrown ditches around the wall, running a sight-check of culverts and drains.

Leyr tapped his earpiece and Maggs looked up and saw the guard approaching. Recommended practice at that moment would have been for Maggs to curl up and hide where he was and let Leyr nail the guard from behind.

Maggs had other ideas. He rapped the blade of his warknife against the rusty door bolt, clinking it like a little metalwork hammer.

What the feth, Maggs? Leyr blinked, toggling off to make the shot he was certain would be called for.

The guard heard the clinking, and headed right over to the source. As he came down the ditch to the door, Maggs just got to his feet to meet him in one smooth motion and buried the blade through his neck. Maggs caught him in an embrace and pulled his body back down into cover with him. A blink of an eye and they were both out of sight again.

Maggs forced back the bolt and gently flopped the door open. He kept having to prop the guard's limp body up out of the way now they were sharing the same ditch. He peered inside.

It was the soak away of a stream or sewer outflow built to run out under the wall and into the ditch. The door was simply a lid over a much smaller cavity, a sump under the wall base blocked, along its course, by three heavy wrought iron grates. Even without the bars, the soak away was far too small to allow a man to crawl through.

The ground, however, was parched and dry. The soak away had shrivelled and enlarged in the months without rain, and become a dusty, desiccated hole, pulling away from the underpinning of the stone wall like a diseased gum from a tooth. Maggs could easily reach in and wiggled the nearest iron grate free.

He signed to Leyr. *Tell Mkoll. We're in.*

V

TEN MORE MINUTES ticked by. At Baskevyl's instruction, the first wave of Ghosts advanced again, closer to the wall slope, keeping low and using the brittle, dead undergrowth for cover.

One of the wall guards finally noticed them, or at least noticed movement in the lower scarps and terraces below the wall. There was a shout, and then an ancient stubber began spitting slow, desultory shots down the slopes. The shells tore into the brambles and dried leaves, showering up papery fragments. The shots made high pitched buzzing hums as they flicked through the ground cover. In a moment, a second gun had opened up, then a third. Las-locks cracked from the wall platforms. Then the spring-coil *tunk! tunk!* of mortars started up, lobbing shells over from the yards behind the wall. The mortar bombs dropped short into the allotment patches and kicked up hot, gritty spumes of smoke and soil, each one with a rasping fiery heart, each one turning to thready smoke that wafted away down the hill.

The mortar rate increased.

'Permission to engage?' Baskevyl asked Gaunt.

'Granted,' Gaunt said.

The Ghosts fanning out on the slopes below the town began to fire. Las shots rained off the wall tops. The range was bad, but the effort was more to suppress the enemy shooters. The light support teams, bedded in ahead of the woodline, opened up. Seena and Arilla, Surch and Loell, Belker and Finz, Melyr and Caill, gunners and feeders. Their large calibre cannons began their *tukka-tukka-tukka* rattling, like giant sewing machines. the heavy fire festooned the main gate with thousands of little curls of smoke.

'Start making it personal,' Gaunt voxed, moving forwards.

The regiment's marksmen had been waiting for that nod. All were bedded down and all had selected targets. Jessi Banda was watching the heads of the enemy sentries on the wall top through her sniper scope.

'Like tin cans on a stump,' she murmured as she lined one up.

The head popped in a puff of red. Banda blinked to make sure she'd seen it right.

Close by, Nessa Bourah looked up from her long las. 'Like tin cans on a stump,' she grinned, speaking

the words with the slightly nasal flatness of the pro-
foundly deaf.

The snipers set up a steady rate of fire, notching
every figure fool enough to appear on the walls.
Larkin's rate was the highest of all. Five kills in three
minutes. He left one target draped forwards over the
parapet.

Something considerable exploded behind the wall
and the mortars shut up. The scouts were plying their
trade inside.

BEHIND THE WALLS, the old market town was a sick,
dishevelled place. Filth littered the streets, and the
buildings were all in miserable repair, though many,
like the town walls, had been refitted or converted
using a patchwork of unpleasant materials that
weren't immediately identifiable. There was a grey-
green sheeting that was halfway between flakboard
and tin, and odd, resin-like substances. Walls had
been reinforced with struts and beams of iron that
had begun to rust, and many roofs had fallen in.
Civic statues had been smashed and, in places,
stretches of wall were pock-marked from old gunfire.
The occupiers had decorated the place with lurid
scrawlings in their own, hideous script, sickening
graffiti that unsettled the mind.

There was an odour in the air, cloying close and
sickly, and human remains – most of it bone – scattered
everywhere. It was as if, rather than taking the town over
and occupying it, the Arch-enemy had nested in it.

Working in silently from the entry point Maggs had
provided, the scouts set to work. Jajjo and Caober

threaded the shadows in a series of side streets until they emerged at the edge of a wide cobbled yard under the walls, where eight mortars had been set up on flakboard pallets. Tall servants of Chaos were crewing the weapons. They were rancid creatures in grey scale armour, the high brass collars of mechanical speech boxes covering their mouths and noses. Most had implants sutured into their eye sockets. Some were using goads and lashes on a team of half-naked, emaciated human wretches – skin and bone and rags – forcing them to ferry shells from a supply stack to feed the weapons. The wretches were prisoners, captives, grotesquely malnourished and abused, the stigma rune branded on their faces.

Caober signed to Jajjo to draw attention with a little gunfire and get the slaves clear while he moved in with tube-charges to blow the weapons.

Jajjo nodded, and moved forward, skirting some iron scaffolding, into the open yard. Without any hesitation he opened fired, squirting bursts of las fire into the mortar crews. Two of the armoured creatures dropped. The others turned, scattering, reaching for las-locks. Jajjo fired some more and blew another off his feet. The slaves, halfway through their plod between ammo dump and weapons, stopped in their tracks and just stared at the Ghost.

'Come on! Come on!' Jajjo called, firing his lasrifle one-handed from the hip as he gestured wildly with his other hand. 'This way!'

None of them moved. They simply stared, dull-eyed, blank. Some still clutched mortar bombs in their arms like babies.

Caober readied his tube-charges and hurried around to the side. He was concerned that the human captives weren't moving. They were still well inside the blast radius that he was about to lay down.

'Come on!' Jajjo yelled again.

More blank looks.

Cursing, Jajjo moved towards them, firing between a pair of them at one of the crew who had got hold of a las-lock. Grey scales flew up from the being's broken armour as Jajjo's laser bolts sliced through him and knocked him onto his back.

'Come on. Move!'

Two more of the enemy crew had seized weapons and returned fire. One las-lock shot skimmed over Jajjo's head. The other, hasty, struck one of the motionless slaves in the back. The man, elderly it seemed, though the abuse he had suffered may have aged him mercilessly, toppled forwards dead. The mortar bomb he had been clutching rolled free and ran, clinking, across the cobbles.

The slaves remained stationary. They didn't run forwards to his aid, they didn't scatter for cover in fear. They turned their heads slowly and looked blankly at the body for a moment.

Jajjo ran right up amongst them, still snatching off shots at the enemy.

'Come on!' he shouted, pulling at reluctant arms and limp shoulders. 'Move, for gak's sake! Move yourselves!'

This close, he could smell them. The stench made him gag. The filth caking them was unbelievable. He could see the lice and the ticks. Their skin felt like cotton, thin and loose on frames where all body fat had gone.

'Move!'

Another las-lock blast blew out the skull of the woman he was pulling at. Her body had been masking his. As she fell, wordlessly, Jajjo brought his lasrifle up to his shoulder and furiously belted full auto across the mortar stand, raking all the enemy creatures he could see. Two fell back, spread-eagled. One spiralled sideways, knocking an entire mortar off its tripod with a dull clang.

Jajjo backed away, squeezing off more shots. There was no more time. No more time for compassion.

'Do it!' he yelled, desperately.

Caober plucked off the strip of det tape and bowled the bundle of charges over arm into the midst of the weapons. He and Jajjo dived for cover.

When they got up, in the billowing smoke, the mortars were trashed. The slaves were all on the ground, flattened by the blast.

'I w–' Jajjo began. Caober grabbed him and pulled him back. There was no point checking if any were alive. The effort would be as futile as trying to save them in the first place. They had to keep moving.

There was still work to be done.

MKOLL HEARD AND felt the blast that gagged the mortar fire. He was two streets from the yard, with Hwlan, heading for the gate. He'd expected to encounter more resistance inside the town. The place was half-empty. They saw a few of the enemy guardsmen, the scale-armoured spectres that Mkoll had

learned to call excubitors on his last visit to the occupied world, and kept out of their way. The excubitors
were hurrying towards the walls, summoned to face
the external attack that had broken out five minutes
earlier.

There were enemy troopers too, men dressed in
polished green combat armour. They were double-
timing in squads, under the command of excubitors
or sirdar officers. Some rode on battered trucks or
wheezing steam engines. Cantible was mobilising its
defences, but where were the people? Most of the
dwellings and commercial properties the scouts
darted past were empty and abandoned.

It occurred to Mkoll that there were no people
because, like any resource, they had been used up.
He'd seen the process half-done before he left the
first time. The occupation had progressively
exploited and consumed Gereon's raw materials:
manufacturing, minerals, crops, water, flesh. Vast
swathes of the country had been turned over to xenoculture producing gene-altered or warp-tainted crops
that depleted the land by strip-mining the soil of its
nutrients. The crops fed the occupying forces, but
were harvested in such gross abundance that they
could be transported off-world to supply the raven-
ous armies of the Archon. For a few years, until the
process killed its fertility, Gereon would be one of the
Archenemy's breadbasket worlds in this region. Fuel
and metal reserves went the same way. With his own
amazed eyes, Mkoll had witnessed two jehgenesh,
warp beasts deliberately unleashed into Gereon's
water supply by the occupiers. These… *things* drank

lakes, seas and reservoirs, and excreted the water via the warp to distant, arid worlds in the Archenemy's domain. He had helped to kill both of them.

Flesh was just another commodity. Those of Gereon's human population who had not become proselytes and converted to the new faith had been made slaves, robbed of all rights and dignities. More literally, others had been fed to the meat foundries, where the flesh of their bodies had been cut apart to supply the enemy with a source of spare parts and transplants. The dead, the useless and the unviable were fed into the ahenum furnaces which powered much of Gereon's abominable new industries and lit the sky red at dusk. Ultimately, the furnaces awaited everyone.

In the long months and days of pain since he had last been there, Mkoll realised, the human supply, like all finite resources, had begun to dwindle. Gereon was close to exhaustion. As Gaunt had feared, and privately confided to Mkoll, they were bringing liberation far too late.

Mkoll and Hwlan scurried through the dry, dead husks of homes and workplaces. Every room contained a warm, stale atmosphere and a yellowed cast of neglect. Everything had shrivelled and flaked. Window glass, where it still existed, was stained the colour of amasec. Dust mould and a virulent fungus, violet and blotchy, were endemic across walls and ceilings. Heaps of dead blowflies, like handfuls of coal dust, lined every windowsill.

They came up through a tomb-like building that must once have been a butcher's shop. In the workshop, the gouged wooden counters were stained dark brown, and traces of dried meat clung to the iron hooks that swayed slowly on their long black chains.

Hwlan reached the back door and checked outside. *Main gate*, he signed, *sixty metres*.

Mkoll nodded. He pulled the canvas satchel he had been carrying off his shoulder and put it on one of the chopping blocks. One by one he took out the tube-charges, checked each one, and laid them out side by side. Twenty, and one, Rawne had put it, 'for luck'. Major Rawne, who knew about these things thanks to what he described as a 'misspent youth', had built the detonator himself. It had a simple switch, triggered by mercury in a gravity bottle, a glass phial the size of Mkoll's little finger. Dislodged by impact or a change in attitude, the mercury would flow down the phial and make the connection.

Mkoll bound the tubes into a bundle and taped the switch to them, twisting together the wires that ran from the switch to the tubes' detonation caps. Only a little slip of labelled parchment, wedged between the trigger phial and the feeder reservoir full of quick-silver, kept the weapon safe.

The shooting war outside had picked up pace. To Mkoll's experienced ear, they had about ten minutes left before the wild card of a stealth intrusion ceased to have any value. Ten minutes to achieve their goal and prove the tactical worth of the scouts.

'Vehicle,' he said.

Hwlan, down at the back door, looked at him in surprise. It was the first time either of them had spoken aloud in twenty-five minutes.

'We need a vehicle,' Mkoll expanded. He'd been expecting to commandeer a truck, a traction engine or something similar. Now they were there, inside, he saw how limited resources were.

Hwlan moved to the butcher's side door. There was a yard out the back, adjoining several sheds that he presumed had been used for smoking or salting meat. What appeared to be a handcart was visible in one of them.

'Let me check, chief,' he said, and went outside.

Mkoll waited. He heard marching footsteps on the road and ducked down behind the butcher's table. The shadow of a squad of excubitors travelled over the dirt-clouded windows.

The hand cart was useless. It was missing its back wheels. Hefting his lasrifle up under the crook of his right arm like a gamekeeper, Hwlan walked down the sheds and discovered that they backed onto the annexe of a neighbouring property. He crossed the narrow, shadowed yard and stood on tip-toe to look in through the window lights.

Hwlan sighed.

It was a nursery. The place had been ransacked some time before and left to rot in disarray, but he could see small wooden blocks, painted bright colours, scattered over the floor, the tattered remains of dolls, and some rather less identifiable piles of rubbish.

And, on its side, a baby carriage.

He tried the door. The lock had been kicked off a long time before. Inside, there was a terrible, musty smell of enclosed air, of dry rot, of decay.

For the first time he realised, with a strange start, that there were no cobwebs at all. Arachnids, like rats and lice, had accompanied mankind out into the stars and had permeated all his living spaces. What had happened to all the spiders here? Was there something about Chaos that drove them out or – and Hwlan had always had a thing about spiders – was the absence of webs a sign that spiders enjoyed some sort of collusion with the Ruinous Powers? He wouldn't put that past them, filthy little wrigglers.

Contemplating the essential evil of all eight-legged things, Hwlan crossed the room to the overturned carriage. Effortlessly and skilfully, his feet avoided every loose object in his path. He stooped to move aside a pile of rags to get to the baby carriage.

The pile of rags was alive.

IN THE BUTCHER'S, Mkoll froze when he heard the shrill wail echo from the neighbouring building. With smooth, expert calmness, he picked up his satchel and the tied package of tube-charges, and slid them out of sight under the counter. Then he ducked down behind a large galvanised vat.

The back door opened. Two excubitors, alerted by the cry, stepped inside from the roadway and peered around. Down in cover, Mkoll could smell the sweet perfume of the oils and unguents they used to dress their flesh. It was a smell he hadn't known in a while, but he hadn't forgotten it. He closed his grip around his lasrifle.

'Eshet tyed g'har veth?' one of the excubitors said to the other. *What was that sound/noise in here/in this place?* The sounds crackled from the speaker boxes in their brass collars.

'Voi ydereta haspa cloi c'shull myok,' the other replied. *You go join the others/attend to duties while I look/check/search.*

Like Gaunt, and the rest of the Sturm mission team, Mkoll had learned the basic elements of the enemy language as a survival skill.

'Desyek? Seyn voi shet?' *Are you certain/sure/confident?*

'Syekde. Jj'jan fer gath tretek irigaa.' *Go/I'm sure. This is nothing, but I should check nevertheless.*

One of the excubitors turned and went. The other moved into the room, his las-lock aimed from his chest.

Mkoll stood up, leaving his lasrifle out of sight. The excubitor started, turning to aim at him.

'Eletreeta j'den kyh tarejaa fa!' Mkoll said. *Thank goodness you're here! Look here/look at this thing I have!*

'Jabash je kyh tarej?' said the excubitor, taking a step closer. *What thing must I look at/must I inspect for you?*

'Straight silver,' Mkoll said, and plunged his Tanith warknife into the excubitor's forehead. The excubitor dropped his las-lock and reached both hands up to his impaled skull. Mkoll hugged the excubitor down onto a chopping block table top, his left hand cupped behind the thing's scalp, pulling the head deeper onto the knife. Foul, septic blood poured out around the wound over Mkoll's knife hand. The excubitor spasmed and went limp.

Gently, Mkoll lowered the body to the floor rather than let it fall. He jerked the knife out.

The other excubitor reappeared in the doorway.

VI

THE EXCUBITOR FROZE. It saw the fresh blood spilt across the worktop, and the body of its comrade curled on the floor. It began to speak and, at the same time, began to lift its primed las-lock.

Mkoll flicked his wrist and threw the blood-wet dagger. It planted itself, blade-first, in the excubitor's left eye, so deep that the hilt bars were stopped by the rim of the socket. The excubitor swayed for a moment, its head rocked back by the impact. Then it fell on its face.

Mkoll started forwards, dragged the corpse fully indoors, and quietly closed the back door.

THE PILE OF rags was something vaguely human. An old man, an old woman, Hwlan wasn't sure. Something half dead and bone-thin. As he moved it, and it came to life and wailed, he struck out involuntarily, and knocked it aside. It fell, turned and ran away back into the house.

Hwlan followed it knowing, if nothing else, that he had to silence it, but it had vanished, and it wasn't making any more noise. He picked his way back through the shuttered, abandoned rooms to the nursery and the baby carriage.

He was just righting it and checking it over when Mkoll appeared behind him. The master scout's right sleeve was soaked with blood.

'What the feth are you playing at?' Mkoll whispered.

'Vehicle,' Hwlan replied.

HALF A TOWN away, Bonin and Maggs were heading deeper into Cantible, hugging the shadows and not staying anywhere for long. They both turned as they heard the rolling boom of Caober's tube-charges.

'Temple?' Maggs whispered, pointing.

Bonin shook his head. *Iconoclave*, he signed carefully.

'What's that then?' Maggs whispered with a smile.

Do you not know how to sign? Bonin signed angrily.

Yes, Maggs signed back, and to prove it elaborately signed, *You are a total feth-wit.*

Bonin tried not to smile. Maggs was all right, for a non-Tanith. Feth, he was all right for a non-Verghastite.

They ducked into cover as a troop of soldiers rushed past, followed by a long, gawky procession of excubitors, heading towards the gate.

The building Maggs had mistaken for the temple was a long, new structure raised of heavy dressed stone. An iconoclave was where the forces of the enemy pressed citizens into the wholesale destruction of any icon, statue or motif that honoured the Imperium. The town temple was two streets away, a grand but wrecked edifice.

They hurried to it. There was meant to be a sign here, a contact. Navy Intel had said there would be. Maggs and Bonin could find nothing except miserably defaced temple dressings and the sacrilegious handiwork of the enemy. The great mosaic of an aquila in the temple floor tiles had been damaged with hammers.

Maybe there's another temple, Maggs signed. Before Bonin could reply, a las-shot passed between them, narrowly missing both of them. Several more followed, but Maggs and Bonin were already rolling for cover.

Occupation troops in green armour were surging in through the main doors of the derelict temple, firing their weapons. Bonin wondered if this was just an unlucky mischance, or if the enemy had kept the temple under surveillance.

Laser bolts splintered into the old wooden seating and high-backed chairs. Maggs and Bonin, both on the cold floor, raised their rifles and began to fire back. Bonin's first burst dropped the leading trooper, and his second burst killed the two men behind him. The enemy was fanning out around the sides of the fane, taking cover behind pillars and the stone tombs of ancient grandees. Though temporarily protected by the fragile shield of the congregation seating, Maggs and Bonin would shortly find themselves outflanked on both sides. There was no cover for them to drop back to.

'Not good!' Maggs yelled.

'You can say that again,' Bonin replied. He fired another burst that caught an occupation trooper in the neck and the side of the head. The man's frame twisted around violently. A spigot of blood emptied out of his throat as he crashed over into a bench.

Maggs tried to move, but gunfire from the side of the fane chewed at the tiled floor and drove him back. Thick smoke from the weaponsfire began to clog the air and catch the bars of weak sunlight stabbing in from the clerestory windows.

Bonin fired selectively, but there were too many targets to hit, too many targets to drive back.

The situation had just become very lousy indeed.

A FULL-SCALE battle raged beyond the town walls and the main gatehouse. In answer to the Imperial onslaught, the forces occupying Cantible had filled the wall tops with troops and opened up with the heavy weapon nests built into the high towers and gatehouse. Though it had taken the Archenemy a while to properly rouse itself, as if from a cold-blooded torpor, the resistance was now considerable.

Inside the main gate, reinforcement squads of occupation troops clambered out of trucks and hurried up the gatehouse stairs to take position. More troops from the town's garrison were arriving in vehicles that came speeding down the hill from the town hall.

Thirty metres from the gate, Mkoll peered out from an alleyway and looked down the cobbled slope to the gatehouse. He waited while two decrepit army trucks went by, let go of the wooden handle and stepped back into cover beside Hwlan. There was a little scrap of parchment in his hand.

Occupation troops were scrambling down from revving trucks by the gates when the baby carriage appeared. It was rolling free, jiggling over the cobbles, picking up speed as it came down the long slope of the road. A couple of troopers looked at it in frank puzzlement, others called to friends and comrades. The baby carriage rolled right past a few mystified troopers, past a truck, heading for the gates themselves.

One officer, a sirdar, cried out, recognising the sinister subtext to the curious apparition that his men had missed. He shouted for someone to stop the carriage, to grab it, to prevent it from reaching or hitting the gates.

No one moved to obey. Puzzlement was slowing them. So the sirdar leapt from the flatbed of the truck where he was standing and lunged at the carriage as it rolled by.

He stopped it three metres from the gates. He stopped it with a violent jerk. The jerk snapped quicksilver along a glass phial.

There was a click.

VII

THE BLAST HURT, even from a distance. The tarnished moorland air outside the town seemed to snap, as if the day had fractured suddenly. All of the advancing Ghosts felt it deep in the warm cavities of their bodies and the tight knots of their joints.

The main gates of Cantible rose up off their giant iron hinges on a luminous cloud of fire, and spread like great wings as they disintegrated. Only small burning slivers were left to flutter back to the ground. The gate blockhouse vanished in a swift, roiling, rising mass of fire-threaded smoke, and collapsed, spilling outwards in a noisy torrent of loose stone and tiles.

As a downpour of ash, cinders and burning flecks rained across the hill slopes and approaches, a considerable cheer issued from the Imperial forces. The charge began at once.

Heads down, Ghosts began to flock up the main trackway to the burning ruin of the gate, heading in under the billowing swathe of black smoke that climbed above the town and made a broad stain across the pale sky.

They met no resistance at first. All the enemy personnel in the vicinity of the gate had perished in the blast, or had been injured so fearfully that they died in minutes. Others, especially wall defenders further down the curtain from the gate, were knocked down by the shockwave, or hit by debris, or simply stunned into temporary immobility by their sudden misfortune. The Ghosts poured in through the ragged breach unopposed.

Captain Ban Daur's G Company was the first inside, closely followed by Ferdy Kolosim's F Company. Daur's approach was methodical and efficient. He brooked no dallying in the initial advance, but urgently pushed his platoons into the main street network to secure strongpoints before the reeling enemy could recover. Ban Daur was a tall, clean-cut and youthful man of good breeding and polite manners. Meeting him, it was easy to forget he was a veteran of the Vervunhive War and had first-hand expertise in siege warfare and city fighting. Gaunt often thought Daur was the most underestimated of his unit commanders. Daur didn't trail a robust air of soldiering about him like Kolea,

Obel or Varaine, nor did he have the air of a killer like Rawne or Mkoll. It was too easy to mistake him for an affable, well-mannered chap who could run a neat camp but who left war to the grown-ups.

G Company invaded Cantible with well-drilled grace. Daur's principal squad leaders – Mohr, Vivvo, Haller, Vadim, Mkeller and Venar – pushed their troops forwards in overlapping fan formations, securing street corners and likely buildings. Sporadic fighting broke out as the advancing Tanith met pockets of bewildered excubitors.

Within five minutes, Daur's beachhead had opened the way for Kolosim's company to push forwards, followed by Rawne's and Kolea's. The last two were the heavyweight, thoroughbred companies of this new model First, rivalled as warriors only by Mkoll's scout pack and the fighting companies of Obel and Domor. They began to claw into the town where Daur had stabbed.

In their cover position thirty metres from the gate, Mkoll and Hwlan slowly picked themselves up. The shockwave had smashed across the entire area and blown out every window and door. His ears ringing, Mkoll quietly cursed Rawne's 'one for luck'. The two scouts started to move in time to link up with Daur's advance.

'Nice work,' Daur commented as he met Mkoll.

'Let's make the most of it,' Mkoll replied.

Within ten minutes of the blast, the picture had changed a little. Waking up from the explosion that had slapped it into a daze, Cantible began to fight back. The unseen commander of its garrison realised

little mattered except that the enemy was now inside
the walls, and had directed all of his forces through
the town streets to engage and repel. Squads of
green-armoured troops appeared, along with
armoured carrier vehicles and a few light tanks. The
narrow streets of the lower town began to ring and
shake with gunfire and cannon shot. Gaunt, entering
the town himself for the first time, ordered up the
armour support, and the first of the Dev Hetra units
began to roll in across the smashed gateway and clatter up into the town.

THE BLAST TEMPORARILY saved Bonin's life, and Maggs's
too. The enemy troops had been pouring into the temple, surging inside to overwhelm them. Maggs had
taken two las-burns across the left arm, and Bonin had
suffered a hit to the back that had burned a deep gash
in his flesh but which had glanced off the surgical plate
of his old spinal wound.

Both of them knew, without saying it, without con-
ferring – and there was no opportunity to confer in
that hell-fight – that they had two or three minutes
left to live at the most optimistic guess.

Then Rawne's present went off across town. The
ground shook and all the south facing windows of
the temple blew inwards in a cascade of glass. Caught
by the flying shards, several enemy troopers
screamed and fell, lacerated and shredded.

Low, in cover in the heart of the place, Bonin and
Maggs were the best protected. Seeing the momen-
tary confusion, the fleeting advantage, both seized
the initiative.

Maggs rolled to his feet and began a headlong dash towards the heavy wood and stone of the altarpiece at the back of the temple.

Bonin began to sprint towards the base of the nearest screw stair, a stone-cut arch on the far side of the congregation space that led to a narrow twist of steps to the temple gallery.

Collecting their wits and realising their quarry was in flight, the enemy troopers resumed shooting. Las bolts and hard rounds chased Maggs across the floor of the temple, scratching tiles and chipping stones. He threw himself bodily forward into cover, but a shot struck him in the left heel and slammed him against the altarpiece rather than behind it. The heavy frame of inlaid wood and its ouslite base went over with him. He fell, dazed for a second, under the lancet windows of the nave. Three enemy troops rushed forward across the open heart of the temple, their boots scuffing over the desecrated mosaic of the aquila on the floor. They had, for a second, clean kill-shots on the fallen Maggs.

However Mach Bonin had reached the carved stone cover of the stairway. Turning, face set like an angel bringing solemn notice of death, he emptied half of his last power clip in a flurry of shots that blazed across the echoing chamber.

The shots struck – and chopped into – the three troopers like hacking axe blows. One of the enemy troopers was hit in the knee by a shot that severed his leg. Before his toppling body could fall, he had been sliced through the torso twice, and the shoulder, and the neck. The second pitched over as two shots entered his back above the waistline and incinerated his gut and lungs. He fell, foul steam exhaling from his screaming mouth. The third was hit in the ankle and calf of his left leg, the hip and the side of the head, and went over as if run into from the side by a truck.

The rest of the considerable enemy force turned their guns on Bonin, but immediately had to duck and find cover as Maggs rose behind the felled altar-piece and opened fire.

Briefly guarded by Maggs's frantic support, Bonin turned and ran up the narrow stairs onto the gallery. This balcony of stone ran around the upper level of the temple dome, supported by the ring of pillars. As he came up onto the gallery deck, Bonin could feel the heavy pulse of the gunfire below as the enemy turned its attention back to Maggs.

Bonin ran to the edge of the gallery and unloaded the last of his clip down at the gathering enemy. They scattered backwards through the smashed and over-turned seating, leaving several dead, twisted and still, behind them.

Bonin ducked down and ejected his dead clip. There was abrupt slience in the fane as the enemy regrouped. Clattering footsteps and boots crunching over glass and wooden splinters replaced the whine of gunfire.

'Wes!' Bonin voxed from his vantage point. 'I'm out. Chuck me something.'

'Where the hell are you?' Maggs replied.

'Upstairs. Gallery, to your left.'

Down in cover, Maggs took out one of his last clips, weighed it up and hurled it towards the gallery. It

struck the rim and fell back into the main space of
the fane. Several enemy troopers fired at the movement.

'Feth! Do better!' Bonin snarled. He drew his
laspistol. It wouldn't do the job his rifle could, but it
might have to do.

Maggs had two clips left. During the ferocious firefight, he'd been more economical than the Tanith
scout. He kept one for himself and put his back into
launching the other up at the gallery. It flew in over
the balcony's edge and disappeared.

Realising their original advantage had been lost, the
occupation troopers attempted to rush the Imperials
again. Some charged out across the fane floor towards
Maggs's hiding place, firing wildly. Others headed
towards the three sets of stairs up to the gallery.

With one clip left each, Bonin and Maggs met
them. Bonin swung up over the balcony lip and dec-
imated the figures charging Maggs's position.
Simultaneously, Maggs lit up and fired at the hostiles
heading for the stairwells. In ten seconds of sustained
firing, they laid out thirty of the enemy.

Then they were out. They fell back into cover, and
dropped their empty rifles in favour of pistols and
straight silver. The fight had entered its final, most
brutal stage.

During the melee, Bonin had seen something from
the vantage of the gallery as he'd fired down. Something that was more important than his life.

He cued his micro-bead. The enemy was creeping
forward, ready to smother the pair of them with their
numbers. He had seconds left.

'Bonin to Gaunt. Bonin to Gaunt. Urgent. Respond. Respond.'

VIII

RECEPTION WAS POOR. Bonin thought he heard Gaunt's voice replying, but it was hard to tell in the midst of all that crackle. He started to send his message anyway.

The enemy troopers rushed the gallery. They came up one set of stairs to begin with. Later, Bonin could not explain how their first few shots missed him. He could only presume that the enemy's haste to storm the stair head caused their aim to be rushed. He felt the sucking heat of shots passing his face and began to squeeze off bolts in reply with his laspistol.

Cornered, his efforts were desperate and his aim was no better than that of the soldiers trying to kill him. He hit nothing living, but at least managed to wedge the enemy into the cover of the stair head, seriously restricting their field of fire. That was fine... until troops started to emerge from the other staircases.

There was a sudden and unexpected halt in the attack. Firing ceased. The only sounds were the throb of the street fight raging in the town outside, and the slithering bump of the troops inside the fane moving about. Bonin waited. He heard boots crunching on broken glass and boards creaking. His mind envisaged the enemy quietly manoeuvring into place to spring one final, sudden death trap.

Nothing happened.

'Wes?' Bonin voxed a whisper.

'I hear you.'

'Still alive down there?'

'Less alive than I was when we started,' Maggs replied, his breathing short and laboured over the link, 'but, yeah.'

'What's happening?'

'Dunno. I think… I think they just fell back. I think they broke off and made an exit from the building.'

'All of them?'

'I think so. I don't really want to stick my head up to find out.'

That was a sentiment Bonin could sympathise with. Slowly, very slowly, and very quietly, he crawled forwards under the sheltering lip of stonework until he had reached the edge of the gallery. With a muttered prayer to the God-Emperor for protection, Bonin slowly raised his head and peered down.

The temple, already in great disrepair when they first arrived, had been shot to pieces. The stone walls and pillars were chipped, flecked and scorched in a million places, and the wooden seating banks had been pulverised into lacy, punctured shells. The bodies of the occupation troopers they had killed in the frantic gun battle littered the floor, the tumbled-down seating, and the main aisle all the way back to the front doors. Discharge smoke hung like mist in the profaned air.

There was no sign of anything alive.

Bonin was about to call to Maggs when the handles of the temple doors rattled and the doors opened. Bonin dropped down again, pistol raised.

Dark figures with steadied rifles melted in through the doorway. Bonin knew that style at once.

'Straight silver!' he called out.

'Who's there? Mach?' a voice answered.

'Major?'

Flanked by half a dozen Ghosts, Rawne stepped out of the shadows and looked up at the gallery.

'I think we scared them off,' he remarked. 'You boys finished making a mess in here?'

Bonin stood up and holstered his pistol. 'See to Maggs. He's down behind the altar. I think he's hit.'

Rawne gestured two of his men forward.

'I was trying to reach the colonel,' Bonin said. 'I believe I've found what he was looking for.'

'What?' asked Rawne.

Bonin pointed. 'Sir, you're standing on it.'

THE BATTLE OF Cantible didn't so much end as tail off like an unfinished sentence. Three and a half hours after Gaunt had given the 'go' command to Mkoll, the fighting was done, and the principal locations within the hilltop town captured.

The enemy was dead or fleeing. Gaunt had heard such abandonments likened to the frantic exit of rats so often in his career it had become a stale cliché, but the sentiment had never seemed more appropriate. In headlong flight, the occupation troopers and some of the excubitors and higher dignitaries threw open the northern gates of the market town and ran off into the decaying countryside. Some literally ran: troopers discarding weapons and armour in an effort to make themselves more fleet. Their bobbing shapes slowly disappeared into the stands of sickly corn and overgrown fields. Some of the more senior enemy personnel attempted flight in vehicles, tracked machines and motor carriages laden with ransacked spoils and valuables.

Gaunt was not in the best of moods. He felt dispirited and dissatisfied. The last few years of his life had been inextricably linked to Gereon, and its redemption mattered to him a great deal. In the preceding weeks, and that very morning before and during the drop, he had been energised by a driving force of satisfaction: at last, at long last, he was going to contribute to the liberation of a world he cared about with particular intensity.

He hadn't even objected to the low priority site that High Command had selected for his regiment. However, the battle for Cantible – 'battle' was itself a laughable term – had been muzzy and half-hearted. The Ghosts had performed commendably, and particular appreciation was owed to the scouts, but it all seemed so oddly colourless. Liberating Cantible was like putting a sick animal out of its misery.

He walked up through the steep heart of the town. A swarthy belt of smoke was rising off the place and smearing along the white moorland sky. He had just ordered the most mobile Dev Hetra machines and two of his companies to pursue and finish the fleeing enemy stragglers beyond the town.

Gaunt tried to pinpoint the source of his unhappiness. The defence of the town had been second-rate, but no commander should regret an easy, low-cost win. His Guardsmen had done a perfect job. According to Rawne, who seldom exaggerated, Bonin and Maggs had been heroes for a brief, shiny moment, facing down superior numbers in the temple, in a stand-off that wouldn't have shamed any of the battles on the Tanith First's roll of honour.

But where were the people they had come to save? Where was the relief and the release? Where was the point of liberation if a place, emptied of its sordid, inhuman occupiers, was just empty?

Gaunt had heard great things in the early reports from the main theatres. Colossal war, and the endeavour of the Imperial Guard. Less than half a world away, real battles were being fought against real enemies. Real victories were being won.

Not here. There was only death in Cantible. Literal, messy death and a more general, lingering sense of demise. They had come to save a place that was too far gone to save. Gaunt hoped, prayed, that Cantible was not a representative microcosm of Gereon as a whole.

He walked in through idling Hydra carriages and gaggles of relaxing troops, accepting salutes and nodding greetings. There was relief amongst his own, relief of a task less than had been feared, and he had no right to extinguish that. He approached the town's temple, the site of Maggs and Bonin's admirable combat. Rawne was waiting for him.

'Find what we need?' he asked.

'Bonin says so,' said Rawne and looked into the shadows of the temple porch. Bonin, hunched over Maggs's prostrate body with a tending corpsman, saw the look and came over to join them.

'Maggs?' Gaunt asked.

'Shot to the ribs,' Bonin said. 'Nasty. He needs to be seen by Dorden.'

'Dorden's down in the lower town,' Gaunt replied. He looked over his shoulder and yelled, 'Ludd!'

The young commissar ran up obediently. 'Sir?'

'Can you escort Trooper Maggs down to the field hospital?' Gaunt asked.

Ludd nodded. He went over to Maggs and helped him get to his feet. They hobbled off together.

Gaunt looked back at Bonin. 'So?'

'In here, sir,' Bonin replied. He led Gaunt and Rawne into the devastated fane and they picked their way between the enemy dead until they were standing on the wide mosaic of the aquila.

'It's been desecrated,' Bonin said. 'Just beaten up and dirtied. It was only when I was up there that I saw it.' He pointed to the gallery.

'Saw what?' Gaunt asked.

'The aquila,' said Rawne.

Gaunt looked down at the mosaic. Evil, corrupt hands had gleefully defaced the Imperial bird, paying particular attention, and effort of pick-axe, to the twin heads. However, the left-hand head had been repaired. Long after the torrent of abuse, the left-hand head had been quite carefully repaired and re-cemented, sometimes using stray mosaic chips that hadn't been components of the original head.

'The head's been put back together,' Gaunt said.

Bonin nodded. 'It's a signal. It's pointing.'

'To what?'

'There's a section of fresh plasterwork on the wall over there,' Rawne said. 'You follow the way the beak's pointing, that's what you come to. We hacked it off.'

Gaunt walked across to the wall. The removed stretch of plaster lay in dusty pieces on the floor. On the exposed wall, they could see six digits, cut there with a tightly narrowed flamer.

'Six eight one nine seven three,' Gaunt read.

'It's got to be a frequency,' said Rawne.

'Have we tried it?'

'As soon as Beltayn gets here,' Rawne replied.

GAUNT WALKED BACK into the open while they waited for his adjutant to arrive. Cirk and Faragut were approaching, strolling up from the lower town like a couple on an afternoon constitutional.

Gaunt was surprised by how pleased he was to see her. For reasons he had never been able to explain, he could not contain Sabbatine Cirk in his mind. She was dangerous and she was untrustworthy, yet he had learned to trust her completely during his first venture on Gereon. She exuded considerable sexual appeal, and that appeal was contaminated by her aura of damage. No one embodied Gereon in his mind more than Cirk. She was a living victim, the planet personified, beautiful, appealing, but damaged and abused.

Most of the time, he tried not to think about her. Now, he had to and he allowed himself to. He found he felt great kinship with her. She, and she alone, understood the sense of disillusion he felt.

Cirk had done more than anyone to bring about the liberation of Gereon, more than even Gaunt knew. She had been on the brink of tears since the drop ships had launched – first tears of anticipation, and then tears of dismay.

'Colonel-commissar,' she said smartly as she came up to him.

'Are you all right?'

She glanced at him, quizzically, taken aback by his unusual warmth.

'Yes, I'm fine. A little strung out. I hope you've some good news.'

'We may have a link to the resistance. We're about to try raising them.'

'That's good. You'll want me to talk?'

'We'll need your ciphers,' Gaunt said.

'I should be present,' Faragut said. They both looked at him as if he was an intruder.

'My brief was very specific,' Faragut said, smiling to diffuse the hostility.

'Of course,' said Gaunt, softening, knowing the man couldn't be blamed for his masters. 'Of course.'

'We're on the same side,' Faragut said sweetly. 'I mean, that's the point, isn't it?'

'AM I HURTING you?' Ludd asked. They took another shuffling step.

'No,' said Maggs.

'Are you sure?' Ludd cinched his arm up tighter under the scout's armpits. 'You can lean on me more heavily, if you like.'

'I'm fine,' Maggs grunted. They were about ten minutes away from the field hospital and progress was slow.

'Really,' said Ludd. 'I could–'

'With respect,' Maggs said, exhaling with pain, 'could you talk about something else, son? Walking's really hard, even with you propping me up. Can't you take my mind off it?'

'Oh, yes, yes,' Ludd reassured, thinking frantically. He ransacked his memory. He had no stories to tell about battles or girls, certainly not any that a heart-breaker and woundmaker like Wes Maggs would be impressed by. He'd once known a man who'd owned a cat, and the funny thing was... no, no that wouldn't do.

'Merrt,' he said.

'What?'

'Merrt. The Tanith with the fethed-up face. The ex-sniper who–'

'I know who you mean.'

'The day Hark and I busted him on the swelter decks. Dragged his backside out of trouble. You were there. I saw you in that dive.'

'I was there.'

'Coincidence?'

'No, Ludd.'

'Want to tell me about that?'

Maggs groaned. 'Sit. I need to sit,' he said, clutching his bandaged ribs. Ludd helped him over to the doorstep of a derelict hab. Maggs sat down.

'We should get to the field hospital,' Ludd said. He was edgy. He'd never done well at first aid drills and he was worried that Maggs might start toppling over with a swollen blue tongue. Or worse.

'Just give me a moment to catch my breath,' Maggs said, leaning back against the scorched doorpost. 'I'll be fine for another walk once I've caught my breath.'

Ludd nodded and waited. 'So, Merrt?' he asked.

Maggs was leaning back, fingering his blood-heavy bandages. 'Merrt. Right. We look after our own, you know.'

'What?'

'First-and-Only. It might surprise you to hear that, given that I'm Belladon and fresh into the mix, but it's true. When a bunch of soldiers come together and bond – I mean, really bond – they stick tight. The Tanith were lucky to find us Belladon, and we were lucky to find them. I'm not going mushy but shit, we make a good pack. You know what I mean?'

'I think so.'

Maggs nodded. 'Leftovers, dregs, remnants. Tanith, Verghast, Belladon. The bits they couldn't kill. Mix us together, we come from the same place and we stick like glue.'

'That's good to hear,' Ludd said.

Maggs leaned forwards and sighed. 'Merrt. We knew he was in trouble. Gambling. In well over his head. Varl noticed it first, and he got us together. Drew us in. Told us we needed to look out for Merrt. Well, we couldn't clear his debt. Even clubbing up, we didn't have anything like the cash. So – and this was Bask's idea – we drew lots to follow him and keep an eye on him. If he got into shit, one of us would be there to bail him out. We drew up a rota. That night on the swelter decks, it was my turn. I knew something dark was about to happen, and I was going to move when you showed up.'

'What would you have done?' Ludd asked.

'Something stupid, probably,' Maggs replied. 'Something that would have got me up on charges,

even got me a ten-ninety, but I would have done it.
It's that sticking together thing, you see? If we don't
stick up for one another, if we don't stick our necks
out for one another, what's the point? I mean...
what's the fething point? Merrt's one of us, and us is
all that counts.'

Ludd nodded.

'What's up?' Maggs asked. 'You look far away all of
a sudden.'

'I was just thinking,' Ludd said. 'I was just thinking
if I could bottle the regimental spirit you just
expressed, I'd be the best commissar in the history of
the Guard.'

Maggs grinned, and then his smile slowly faded. 'I
hadn't thought of Merrt until just now. Shit. I wonder where he is. That poor ugly bastard.'

FACE-TO-FACE

I

EVERYWHERE, THE DEAD were smiling at him.

Firestorms had scorched through the district of streets and small squares, and left the crisped shells of habs behind. The sky was low and black, and lay like night. Heat radiated from the stones and the rubble, and there was a powerful chemical stink of the burned, the oxidised and the transmuted. Many fires were still burning.

Dalin Criid could feel the warmth of nearby flames against his face, and feel his own sweat trickle through the dirt of his face like tears. He didn't move. He just stood for a while in the jumping shadows of the ruined street, and stared into the flames.

Fire had reduced all of the corpses in the area to scrubby black things made of twigs. They were barely

197

human, barely humanoid, just scorched stumps of driftwood. The only things the fire could not reduce were the eyes and the teeth. Indeed, it magnified both. All eyes became huge, staring sockets of darkness, at once mournful and hating. With the flesh burned away, all teeth became wide, white smiles, part amused, part clenched in pain. From the ground, from doorways, from windows, and from heaps of rubble spoil, they smiled and stared at him as he went past, sometimes several side by side, all smiling at the same joke.

There was something about their smiles. They were rueful, as if so taken aback by the suddenness and ferocity of their demise that there was nothing they could do except put a brave face on it and chuckle. *Look what happened to me in the end, eh? Oh well, what can you do...*

They were so denuded of anything except stares and grins that it was impossible to tell who the dead were. Local people, citizens of the coastal towns, engulfed by the fury of war, or Imperial Guardsmen who had got there some time ahead of AT 137 and found death waiting with a tinderbox?

The other possibility was that these smiles of chagrin and welcome were the smiles of the enemy. Were these his enemy, these blistered black-tar mannequins with their gleaming teeth? If they were, they were the first he'd met.

'Holy.' A word, not even a question. He turned his head. Hamir came close, through the smoke, carrying his rifle across his stomach. Criid fell into step with him and they moved down the street, picking over the smoking rubble.

A quiet had fallen with the darkness. There was the immediate crackle of the flames, the scurry of falling masonry and the distant rumble and thump of something important happening somewhere else. Generally, though, there was a warm quiet, the sound of aftermath.

Criid knew it was no aftermath. He'd become reluctant to check his chron, because the maddeningly slow passage of time was sapping his will, but he knew they'd been down for about five hours. K'ethdrac was an immense target and it could not have fallen yet, even considering the fury of the assault. As with so many great cities and hives, the Imperial ground forces might be picking their way from street fight to street fight for weeks, for months.

For years. That wasn't unheard of. Criid wondered, if he lived that long, whether he would survive mentally. If his body avoided being shot or blown apart or cut into pieces, would his mind withstand a length of time like that here? He doubted it, if the passage of time continued to be so heavy and prolonged. He would end up mad, with a rueful smile on his face.

Hamir gestured ahead of them with a nod. A trio of troopers, Fourbox amongst them, was edging forwards behind a low remnant of wall. On either side, they could make out other members of the company advancing through the rubble and the lazy smoke. In the last, creeping hour, their numbers had grown. Crossing a road bridge into the deeper parts of the city, they had encountered about thirty-five members of the AT 137 drop under the command of Corporal Traben. They'd come off a dropship that had overshot and ended up in some kind of manufactory compound. Wash and Lovely were among the troops. Like Kexie's group, they'd seen nothing of Major Brundel.

A blurt of gunfire rang in from their right. Some of the troopers turned to peer into the smoke.

'Should I find Kexie?' Hamir asked Criid.

'Don't bother,' said another voice from just behind them.

It was Merrt. He'd been with Traben's party too.

'Shouldn't we…?' Criid began.

'In this?' Merrt asked. 'Surrounded by this? You report in every bit of gn… gn… gn… gunfire you hear, Kexie'll be chasing his tail the whole day checking it. Best to keep moving, keep your formation. If it turns out that gunfire needs to involve you, it will.'

It was almost reassuring just to ignore it, to just get on and get through without looking for trouble. There was enough to go around anyway. It did the element more harm jumping at every last thing than it did keeping firm with the deployment.

To prove the point, they went on for another twenty minutes, and the gunfire got personal.

II

THEY HAD ENTERED a part of the fortified city where the air was so black and the smoke so dense that it felt subterranean. Buildings on either hand – some ruined, some intact, and all empty – loomed like the smooth, grey walls of cyclopean caves. It was hot and dank, like the centre of the earth. Moisture dripped out of the noxious smoke. It was not rain or climate damp, but the condensing vapours of warfare: fuel oil, lubricants, accelerants and volatiles. It was sticky and brown like a lho-smoker's phlegm, and the air coughed it out like spittle.

To the west of their position, about five kilometres away, a firestorm blazed through eight or nine city blocks like a communal fire at the centre of the cave. It made the faint light russet and gold. When they stopped to wait and listen, the members of AT 137 resembled gilded statues on a victory arch.

To the south of them, at a similar distance, an emphatic battle was raging, either between armoured forces or duelling batteries of artillery. It was evidently a formidable clash and raised a huge, slightly muffled, noise. They could see nothing of it, however, not even the merest hint of a flash or shell burst.

They had been some time without taking fire, so when the first shots came upon them, they seemed mystifying and unfamiliar. The trooper known as Gyro suddenly fell and rolled violently backwards across the ground as if he had been unrolled briskly out of a carpet. The sergeant yelled everyone to cover, but as they scrambled, Splits, a Kolstec with an unpopular, nasal voice, was also hit.

Unlike Gyro, his wound wasn't fatal. He started to scream, tortured by the pain. His cries became strangulated and high-pitched. Criid had never heard such sounds come out of a person before.

Sergeant Kexie was pinned near the rear of the group, so Commissar Sobile ordered the first men forward. He fired his pistol into the dark and cracked his whip so they could hear it.

'Take out that shooter!' he yelled.

Everyone wondered who he was talking to.

Criid had found cover behind the thick exterior wall of a hab. Ganiel and Fourbox squashed in behind him.

'Can you see it?' Ganiel asked.

Criid couldn't see much of anything. It was all he could do to think of anything apart from the awful screams coming from Splits. Occasionally, a shot whined past the corner of the wall.

'I'll take a look,' Fourbox announced, and peeked around the corner. Almost immediately, he jerked back, banging his head against the bricks in his haste to withdraw.

'Fourbox?'

Fourbox was doing a little stamping dance, his hands to his head.

'Fourbox?'

'How bad is it?' Fourbox asked, turning his head so that they could see his right ear. A hard round had punched it clean off, nicking the rim of his helmet as it deflected. He had a scorch mark burn across the top of his cheek, and a bloody rosebud of tissue and cartliege where his ear had been. Blood streamed down his neck.

'How bad is it?' he asked again. He was in a little discomfort, but didn't seem genuinely distressed.

'Get a dressing on it,' Ganiel said. Fourbox sat down and fumbled with a belt-pack.

Splits was still screaming. Gunfire was coming from several places in the Imperial spread. It sounded like they had half a dozen shooters firing at them.

'Somebody move forwards!' Sobile yelled. 'In the name of the Golden Throne, advance and engage, or by Terra I will flog you all for cowardice!'

Criid started to run. He was running before he'd even realised he'd decided to. He vaguely heard Ganiel, left behind, cry out, 'Criid, no!'

He was out in the open. Several shots hit the ground near his feet like firecrackers, and a las round shrieked over his head. He reached the far side of the street, rolled down behind a flight of stone steps, and started firing. Other figures followed him. He heard running footsteps, hard boots thumping over grit, the sound of voices cursing.

All the while, Splits was in the background, wailing like a child.

Lasfire was coming from directly above him. Looking up at the gloomy face of the building he was cowering against, he saw the sparks and fizzles of muzzle flash from an upper window.

Moving without thought or hesitation, he rose and ran up the steps into the building's entrance. It was hard to tell what the place had originally been. Wall tiles had been chipped away and littered the floor. Rot discoloured the ceilings of the unlit hallways. He moved from doorway to doorway, swinging his aim around, lugging the heavy barrel of the lasrifle from one imagined target to the next. He climbed a flight of creaking, decaying steps, his back sliding against the wall, and then turned a landing onto a second flight.

On the next landing, he finally met the enemy face-to-face.

* * *

III

HE HAD JUST come out of a room, as if breaking from some activity and casually heading off in search of a smoke or a latrine. Afterwards, Criid was able to remember in astounding detail the specifics of the man's clothing and equipment. He was wearing dark green combat armour of an exotic style not worn by any Guard unit Criid had ever seen. The armour was well-finished and well-made, and had once been polished to a good shine, but dust had caked its surfaces badly. It looked light and wearable. It had insignia marked in red and green on the breastplate, and some kind of ornate shoulder braid. The marks were vulgar and alien, and made no sense.

The man's webbing, his boots and most of all his lasrifle, were Imperial issue. His kit closely resembled the equipment Criid was carrying. Criid could even see the little yellow Munitorum stencil, half worn off, on the rifle butt that had denoted the theatre of issue. He had been told, time and again in briefings, and anecdotally by his extended family in the Ghosts, that the enemy frequently used the weapons, uniforms and vehicles they appropriated from the Imperial Guard.

Of course, sometimes they even used the men themselves, if the men could be turned.

They were face to face on that dingy stairhead for less than a second, although the frozen moment embedded itself in Criid's memory forever. Two things broke the hesitation. First, the man began to raise his rifle. Second, the man wasn't a man at all.

He wore no helmet or head covering, except for a padded canvas hood that tied beneath the chin, the sort worn by a tank driver under his wide-bowl helm. With the exception of the insignia, from the neck down, the man might be mistaken in every respect for an Imperial Guardsman. His face, however, was a rancid, distorted mass, so bloated that its original structure was gone. It was as if the hood had been tied in place simply to hold the face together. There was no nose, just a raw socket, and the eyes under the deformed brow were the staring, circular eyes of a large bird. The wet mouth hung open to reveal teeth like quills.

The horror of the face was the last thing about the figure that Criid noticed, as if he was blocking it out and absorbing all the non-disturbing details until he couldn't put it off any longer.

Criid exclaimed in disgust and shot the enemy soldier three times with his lasrifle. The shots lifted the creature off the floor and bounced it off the corridor wall.

Two more equally depraved creatures stormed out of the same room. One had a drooling snout, full of yellow peg teeth, that wouldn't close. The second, draped in a long Guardsman's greatcoat, looked perfectly human except that his left eye socket was shared by two eyes.

The snout had a laspistol and was firing it in a wild, panicky manner. Splinters blew out from the wall behind Criid and from the banister posts in front of him. Yelling, Criid ran up the last few stairs, squeezing the trigger of his lasrifle. The snout with the laspistol was hit so hard that it flew back through the doorway with a sharp jerk, as if someone had yanked it back inside. The other thing, which seemed to have no weapon, turned and ran down the landing, arms wide, greatcoat tails flapping, desperately yelling something in a language that made Criid's brain sizzle. Criid dropped to one knee, the rifle up to his cheek, and fired two aimed shots to bring the fleeing thing down. It fell flat on its face, halfway down the mouldering hall, with an impact that puffed dust up from between the floorboards.

Criid got up slowly. There was a lot of noise down below where others from AT 137 were following him into the building. Around him, on the second floor, sound seemed suspended. Dust, disturbed by the brief but frenzied exchange, wafted in the air. Criid took a few steps forwards gingerly, his heart punching at his ribs, his hands shaking. Everything seemed to be alive around him. Out of the corner of his eyes, shapes seemed to scurry and shuffle behind the grey wallpaper, or fidget and gnaw behind the skirting. Patches of mould and decay seemed to spread while his back was turned. There was a buzzing, like flies. A comb-on-teeth clicking of dusk bugs.

Another step, another. Was that all of them? Where had the thing in the greatcoat been running to? What had it been shouting? Was there anything else in the rooms at the far end of the hallway?

Criid tightened his grip on his rifle and took another few steps along the landing. He was a metre or two short of the place where the corpse in the greatcoat lay, just drawing level with the half open door that all three of the enemy had emerged from.

His attention was fixed on the end of the hallway. Where had the thing in the greatcoat, the thing with the nightmare eye, been running to? The hall ahead – bare dusty boards, stained walls, rot-infested ceiling – led to a foggy, soot-stained exterior window at the far end. Adjacent to that, two doors on opposite sides of the hall were both closed.

Something was in there. In one of the rooms. Criid knew it. His nerves sensed it more acutely with every step he took. Something. Left or right? Left or right? Another step, another. What was that? A movement? Did something just move in the shadows under the right-hand door? Was–

'*Get down,*' Caff said.

Criid obeyed without even thinking about it. He hit the boards prone as the right-hand door flew open and a squealing pig-thing came out.

It was huge, as tall as Criid, but four or five times the body-mass. It wore old, unlaced Guard boots and ragged battledress trousers belted under the girth of its distended belly. It was bare from the waist up, a sagging barrel of hairless pink flesh smeared with dirt and sweat. Its shoulders and arms were massive, massive like old Corbec's used to be. It was carrying a heavy autocannon, greasy and black, like a normal-sized man would carry a combat shotgun. Its head was tiny, a puckered, bald, pink ball with dot eyes and brown tusks. It made a shrill, bleating squeal as it opened fire.

Fed by a long, swinging belt of ammunition, the cannon thundered, its muzzle crackling with fierce flash jags. Each rapid sound was a blend of numbing boom and metallic ping. The hallway behind Criid tore apart under the onslaught.

From the floor, beneath this concussive rain, Criid fired back. He hit the huge, shuddering torso three times, and then his fourth made a definite kill-shot as it struck the thing's squealing face. The pig-thing toppled backwards, the cannon tilting with it, the last of its belt of shots firing blindly into the hall ceiling. The impacts ripped out the centre of the ceiling in a violent flurry of plaster, dust and splintered lathes.

Collapsing, the thing struck the hall-end window and shattered it, but did not fall all the way out. It crashed to the floor, its right arm hooked up on the broken glass of the window. The cannon barrel, sobbing smoke, hit the floorboards like a piece of lead piping. A long gurgling sigh issued from the dead bulk.

Criid slowly regained his feet, still aiming at the pig-thing. The air was dirty with cannon-smoke. Pieces of ceiling kept fluttering down like autumn leaves. He moved towards the pig-thing to make sure that it was dead.

Something slammed into him from behind and drove him against the far wall of the hallway. Criid struck his chin and his cheek against the wall as he fell, and pain flared, but he was more undone by confusion and shock. Something was screaming in his ear. Everything was blurred. Something was on top of him, pinning him to the floor.

He managed to half-roll over. Another enemy trooper, his howling face a diseased wreck, was

astride him, raining fists down on him. This wretch
must have sprung from a side room that Criid hadn't
checked. Criid tried to block the repeated blows.
He'd lost his grip on his rifle, and he couldn't raise
his own arms to defend himself properly. The enemy
was intent on beating him to a pulp.

A las shot cracked out and the enemy trooper
folded up with a judder. The body slumped sideways,
and Criid was able to heave himself out from underneath. Three or four metres back down the hall in the
direction of the stairs was Merrt. The Tanith lowered
his lasrifle.

'All right?' he asked.

Criid's head was swimming. His face throbbed and
he could taste blood and feel it running down his lips.
He nodded to Merrt, and made an attempt to stand.

He was almost on his feet when there was a commotion. Yet another enemy trooper had rushed out
of the side room to grapple with Merrt. They were
struggling face to face, Merrt pressed against the hallway wall, his rifle pinned impotently between his
chest and his aggressor's. With snapping needle
fangs, the trooper was trying to get at Mertt's throat
while its hands tried to wrestle Merrt's weapon off
him.

Dizzy, Criid tried to move. He looked around for
his own weapon, or something else that he could
club Merrt's attacker off with.

At his feet was the sprawled figure of the enemy
that had been beating him. Merrt's shot had punched
clean through its torso, and it was leaking a wide
puddle of stinking black blood across the dusty floor.

It wasn't dead.

Unable to stand, barely able to move, it was hacking out its last few breaths and, with trembling fingers, pulling the pin from a stick grenade.

IV

CRIID THREW HIMSELF at the dying soldier, clawing at its hands to win ownership of the grenade. Lying on its side, the enemy trooper cried out, and blood gushed from its mouth. It struggled with Criid for a moment more, and then suddenly expired.

It had pulled the pin out.

There was no way to put it back. Criid simply snatched the stick grenade out of the dead thing's hands and threw it through the open doorway opposite. There was some vague hope in his head that the wall of the room would take the brunt of the blast.

In the two or three seconds it had taken for Criid to wrestle the bomb away, Merrt had fought with the other soldier. Locked together, grappling face to face, they had struggled frantically until Merrt butted the enemy in the face with his augmetic jaw. The soldier reeled away, finally, by accident, tearing Merrt's rifle out of his hands, and staggered backwards through the doorway a fraction of a second after Criid had hurled the grenade in that direction.

The blast was dull and flat and rough, and filled the air with spinning tatters of debris and clouds of dust.

Coughing hard, Criid rose and looked around. Merrt's attacker was half-visible through the smoke gusting out of the room. He'd taken the force of the mangling blast. The room's door was stoved in. Merrt himself had been thrown back as far as the stairhead.

'Are you all right?' Criid called out, still coughing. Merrt nodded and began to pull himself up.

Voices were calling out from below. 'Clear?' a voice was calling. 'Clear?'

'Clear!' Merrt yelled back.

'Make way! Who's up there?' the voice asked. Merrt and Criid realised it was Sobile. Sobile was on the stairs. He was coming up. His boots were thumping on the steps.

Merrt had no rifle.

Criid looked at Merrt, and then put his foot on his own lasrifle, which was lying on the ground, and slid it as fiercely as he could across the landing to the Tanith.

Merrt grabbed it.

'Report? Who's taken this building?' Sobile demanded as he came up the final flight to join them with his pistol drawn. Criid looked from side to side and snatched up the nearest fallen lasrifle.

'Report!' said Sobile. He looked at Criid. 'You clear this?'

'Yes, commissar.'

'What's above?'

Criid shook his head. Sobile shouted to the gaggle of troopers coming after him to sweep the upper floors. He looked at Criid again. 'Don't just stand there!' he snapped.

THE UNIT WAS moving again in less than half an hour, back into the blackness of the night-afflicted city. A

Krassian division was pushing in left of their position. Their gunfire and flamers lit them up like a river of lava in the darkness. Aircraft swooped in overhead to support them. Criid heard the distant voice of a titan.

They appeared to be fast approaching some kind of inner city wall or second line of defences. Criid glimpsed huge bulwarks dotted with gunports, and flamer towers that periodically dressed the face of the cliff-like wall with curtains of sheet flame. High towers and hab blocks loomed massively behind the inner wall.

'Halt!' Kexie ordered, and made them crouch down along a bombsite street while the area ahead was scoped. From where they were crouched, Criid could see parts of the defence wall above the nearby ruins. The scene was lit up by intense firelight, the ruins in the way just fragile silhouettes.

They waited. Criid dabbed at his bruised face. His whole head, face and collar bones ached and throbbed from the frenzied beating he'd taken. His jaw, mouth and one eye were swollen, and his lips were split and sore. Blood from grazes and abrasions had dried on his skin. It felt as if he'd torn a muscle in his neck in his efforts to twist his face away from the fists.

He replayed the fight in his head several times. Each time he ran through it, he hoped that the faces of the enemy soldiers would diminish in their horror, fading through repetition and familiarity. They refused to. He'd met the enemy at last, and it had scarred his mind.

The squealing pig-thing with the heavy gun was worst of all. If he hadn't dropped to the ground when Caffran gave the warning, he–

Criid thought about that. Caffran wasn't with them. He was hundreds, maybe thousands of kilo-metres away. Yet it had been his voice, clear and distinct.

Hadn't it?

Perhaps it was the blessing of the God-Emperor that allowed Caffran to watch over Criid. Criid didn't object, but he wondered why Caffran? Why not his ma, or his real father?

'Rise up!' Sobile ordered, and the unit got up with a clatter of kit. 'Ready to advance!'

They began moving forwards again. The fight ahead sounded loud, like the loudest fight they'd been drawn into yet. Criid ran his tongue around his teeth. Several felt loose.

'Hey,' said Merrt, falling in step beside him. He held out his lasrifle.

'You gave me yours,' he said.

'Oh,' said Criid. They quickly exchanged weapons. Merrt looked his up and down.

'That *is* yours?' he asked Criid.

'Yeah. What's the matter?'

'Nothing.'

Kexie was shouting. The unit was starting to run forward, clearing the jagged ruins and coming out onto the approaches of the huge defensive bulwark.

It was immense, bigger than Criid had even imag-ined. The flame light was so bright, it was like a grounded sun. Furious blizzards of gunfire billowed in the air under the great wall. The streets and transit ways of the outer districts met the wall, both at ground level, and by way of giant road bridges that crossed the trench in front of the wall, and entered the wall through huge, defended gates. Hundreds of thousands of Imperial Guardsmen were sweeping forwards in fast flowing rivers of bodies along the roads and out across the bridges to assault the wall.

AT 137 went with them.

HUNTERS

I

'WHAT'S THIS ONE called?' Zweil asked.

'Syerte,' Eszrah replied. The old ayatani sniffed, nodded and wrote the word down on his flap of parchment.

'And this one? This one here?'

Eszrah cocked his head and stared. Then he frowned and shrugged.

'Is that a "no" or a "not sure"?' Zweil asked.

Eszrah shrugged again.

'Well, far be it for me to condemn an entire genus of plant to eternal damnation,' said Zweil, 'so I'll play safe for now and describe it under "others".'

Eszrah didn't seem particularly bothered either way. Zweil scratched down a brief description of the dull, unimpressive plant in question, and then moved further along the overgrown ditch.

Tona Criid jogged up the curve of the parched field to join them. Cantible, still exhaling smoke into the glassy sky, lurked on the neighbouring hill. There was a general bustle of activity coming from the town: a distant clatter of armour, the hum of Valkyrie engines, a very occasional gunshot.

Noa Vadim, the Ghost assigned to watch the ayatani out in the open, saluted as she approached. She looked down at the priest in the tangled field trench, the Nihtgane standing over him at the edge of the field, watching him diligently.

'What's he doing?' she asked.

'Don't ask,' replied Vadim. He yawned expansively.

'Tired?' she asked. He shrugged. 'You should have taken the rest while you could,' she said. Some of the regiment had been given a few hours' sleep overnight.

'I slept all right,' Vadim replied. 'Thought I wouldn't, bedding down in a place like that...' Vadim shot a sour look in the direction of Cantible. 'But, no. I slept all right. It was just the dreams.'

Criid nodded. 'The dreams'll get you here, every time. Keep saying your prayers. So... what is he doing?'

'I'm not entirely sure. When I asked, he said something about a "systematic benediction", and left it at that.'

'I've come to get Eszrah.'

Vadim shrugged again. 'You'll have to take it up with him,' he said.

Criid slid down the dusty bank into the weed-choked ditch. It was part of the old field system, an agricultural divider, but the neglect and abuse Gereon's most recent masters had imposed upon the land had allowed it to run wild, and then wither. She picked her way over to where the priest was bending.

'This one?' Zweil called.

'Syerte,' replied Eszrah from the bank.

'Ah, yes. That's come up before, hasn't it. And here, this one, this one down here, this ugly fellow?'

'Unkynde,' the nightwalker said.

'You sure now?' Zweil asked.

'Unkynde.'

'Unkynde… khhaous?'

Eszrah nodded. Zweil scratched down a few words on his long flap of parchment, and then stopped to pull up the offending plant vigorously and toss the scraps up onto the edge of the dead field. The recently pulled remains of other plants already lit tered the field rim.

'Father,' said Criid. 'Your errand here seems rather botanical.'

'This world's been a long time without the ministry of the Throne,' Zweil said. 'It needs a damn good blessing, every last soul and beetle and pebble and wildflower. The tall fellow is acquainting me with the local flora, so that I can be quite specific in my prayers.'

'You're cataloguing the flowers you have to bless?'

'Flowers, plants… we'll get to trees this afternoon, I hope.'

'This afternoon?'

Zweil looked at her. 'You think it might take longer?'

'I think it's possible you haven't undertaken a comprehensive bio-survey of a planet's indigenous plant life before,' she said.

He held up his flap of parchment. 'So, what you're saying is, I'll need a bigger piece of paper?'

'That is what I'm saying,' she replied.

He turned back to the weeds around his legs. 'You see, Tona, what I don't want to do is bless something unworthy of the Emperor's grace. I've only got a limited amount of spirituality inside me, you see, so I don't want to waste any. The Archenemy, damn his hide, the Archenemy brought plants with him, you see. Crops and spores and other alien things.'

'Yes, I know,' said Criid.

'They've infested the whole place. Parched the soil. Choked off the local crops. Filthy things. The tall fellow's helping me to identify those and root them out so I don't go blessing them by mistake.'

'Are you going to weed the entire planet?' she asked.

'Don't be stupid, woman, I'm not an idiot. It's just if I see them, they offend me and I pluck them out. The tall fellow, he calls them… what is it you call them?'

'Unkynde,' said Eszrah.

'Unkynde. That's it. Means sort of alien. Not of this place. Not from round here. An outsider. A–'

'I understand,' said Criid. 'Father, I came here because the colonel-commissar needs Eszrah for a while.'

'But I'm still working here.'

'I know, but it's important.'

'Well, I'm not going to get to trees this afternoon at all now, am I?'

'It's a shame, certainly,' she agreed. She looked up at the Nihtgane. 'Gaunt,' she said. Without a word or another sign of notice, Eszrah turned and headed down the field towards the town.

Zweil puffed out a tired, disappointed breath and sat down on the bank of the ditch. He pulled up his skirts and fiddled with his large army-issue boots.

'My boots are too big,' he said. Then he complained, 'What am I going to do until the tall fellow gets back?'

Criid hesitated. 'Father, there was something.'

Zweil looked her in the eye sharply. 'Dalin,' he said. 'I hadn't forgotten. You know, I mention his name at all the sacred hours.'

'I think it's me,' she said. 'I need more than this morning's regimental prayers.'

He took her by the hand and knelt her down amongst the weeds. 'Here?' she asked.

'As good a place as any,' he replied. 'He's somewhere on this dirt, and so this dirt connects us. Mr Vadim?' Zweil held up his bony hand and gestured to Vadim to fetch the stole and rood and antiphonal that he had left on the edge of the ditch to go rooting in the weeds.

'Now then,' Zweil said, turning the pages of the old book. 'The prayer of a mother, for her offspring, under the eyes of the God-Emperor...'

* * *

II

'Ears on,' Gaunt said as he strode into the middle of the group assembled in the town square. The senior officers came to attention.

'I'll make this brief, because we've all got work waiting,' Gaunt said. 'Item one, remind the men in your commands that daily shots are essential. Dorden tells me there were quite a few who forgot to report to him this morning for anti-ague. No excuses. Let's get into a habit. Item two, Cantible's going to be our operational base for the next few days at least. For our own security we need to move ahead with the search patterns. Street by street, hab by hab, thorough flush searches. I don't want to find enemy scum holed up amongst us, and I certainly don't want reprisal cells managing to stay hidden. Basements, cellars, attics. Got it?'

There was an affirmative chorus.

'Any sign of glyfs or wirewolves yet?' Gaunt asked.

'No, sir,' replied Mkoll.

'Well, that's a part I don't understand,' Gaunt said. 'Anyway, remain vigilant. Anything strange, anything, vox it in. Make sure your men understand. Those are things they simply will not be ready for, or be able to deal with. That's why we brought tanks.' He glanced politely at the Dev Hetra officer present, who made a respectful nod.

'Indigenous survivors?' Gaunt asked.

'We've found about two hundred and seventy humans who appear to have been enslaved townsfolk,' said Hark. 'All of them are seriously sick, malnourished, and implanted with a thing in their arms. What did you say that was called? Consented? Some refuse to talk, or are unable to talk. Those that can, affirm their allegiance to the Emperor and bless us for rescuing them.'

'Which could just be them saying what they think we want to hear,' said Faragut. 'We will, of course, have to keep them interned. Envoys of the Inquisition will be arriving in the next few days.'

Gaunt frowned. He didn't like it, but he understood that there was no other way.

'After examination by the Inquisition, and the appropriate medical treatments, they have every reason to expect to be freed,' Faragut said. 'They may be exactly what they seem to be. Slaves. There is, after all, a precedent,' he added pointedly, 'for Imperial subjects surviving on this world for some time without becoming tainted.'

'But we've only located two hundred odd?' asked Cirk.

'Two-seventy,' said Hark.

'Out of a population of what? Thirty thousand?'

'About that.'

'What in the name of the Throne happened to the rest of them?' Cirk asked.

'I doubt we will ever know,' replied Faragut. 'Or want to know.'

'Item three,' Gaunt said, before the meeting lost its way, 'we seem to have made initial contact, which was our primary objective, so I'll be leaving this site shortly to pursue that. Mkoll will lead my escort detail. Is that drawn up?'

'Ready to go, sir,' Mkoll said.

'Good. In my absence, Major Rawne has the baton. Any questions?'

THEY SET OUT on foot about an hour later, a section of thirty men along with Gaunt, Cirk, Faragut and Eszrah, and moved north. Their route followed a farm road up through the devastated agricultural zones of Lowensa Province in the direction of a smaller town called Vanvier.

The day was warm and still, the sun climbing slowly behind a blanket of hazy white. Deep, scraping, doom-laden sounds reached their ears as if from vast distances, suggesting they could hear echoes of the main conflicts across the continents, although Faragut dismissed this as wishful thinking and blamed a trick of the wind.

'There is no wind,' Larkin said to Brostin.

Another trick of the wind, perhaps, was the sizzling static crackles that blistered the air from time to time, and appeared to be associated with the glare of the sun.

The rolling landscape was shrivelled and dead. It had once been a lush arable region, similar to the part of the country around Ineuron Town where Cirk had grown up and where her family had owned agricultural land. Her own lands, already plundered and razed before she left them, probably resembled this now: a dust bowl, where only the roughest, coarsest grasses and vile, imported fungi still grew, where homesteads and lonely farms stood empty and dead, and the dry bones of livestock littered the cracked earth.

It was a distressing sight. Cirk said little as she walked along, but Gaunt could empathise with the grief she was hiding. It hadn't been that long since he'd lived on this world, and it had been suffering then. The land, the climate, the plant and animal life had all begun to suffer, as if diseased, and natural cycles had begun to fall apart. It was nothing compared to this. Gereon was no longer a place afflicted with the brutal early onset of a disease or an infection. This was the terminal phase of waste and corruption.

As they marched, Gaunt checked with Beltayn. The vox officer, using the new codes that Bonin had found, had finally managed to raise Daystar early that morning. Daystar was code for one of the few underground contacts the Navy had managed to establish prior to the liberation. Gaunt's force had been meant to join up with them at the temple at Cantible. Plans had evidently changed.

'The resistance only survived by being as secretive as it could,' Cirk said. 'Unlocking it may be slow going. Even though we're not the enemy, getting them to let go of their secretive habits might be tough.'

'We'll manage. It's the task High Command has set for us, after all. It doesn't matter how much hot metal we throw at the main theatres, we can't properly take Gereon back until we open it up from the inside. For that to happen, the underground is vital.'

Cirk nodded, but it was a strange expression, as if she was trying to convince herself. Faragut, by her side, smiled. He looked as if he was about to say something.

'What is it?' Gaunt asked.

'Nothing, sir,' said Faragut.

Up ahead, Criid suddenly shouted, 'Down! Off the road!'

The section dropped off the roadway immediately and took cover in the low roadside ditch. The land around was rolling flat, and covered with a thick expanse of pinkish grass that grew to the height of cereal crops.

Gaunt crawled along to Criid and Mkoll.

'What did you see?'

'Something out there in the grass, about half a kilometre off. Something big, prowling low.'

'What sort of something?' Gaunt asked.

'A big animal. A predator. Just a shape, really, too low in the vegetation for me to make it out. It was like it was stalking us. As if we were a herd of game.'

Mkoll and the other scouts in the section crept out to sweep. When they came back reporting no traces, Gaunt moved the section on again.

'Must've been my imagination,' Criid said, not sounding as if she believed it. She was thinking of the hideous stalkers, the wrought ones of Ancreon Sextus, which had come and gone, thanks to the twisting influence of Chaos, in ways that a mortal man could not.

THEY CAME IN sight of their destination, a small farming hamlet called Cayfer. It was a ramshackle collection of stone buildings set on a low hill amid the pink, invader grasses, in an area studded with the dead remnants of talix and keltre trees. Several kilometres beyond the hamlet, a thicker belt of sickly woodland began.

There was no sign of life. The hamlet seemed dead, and turned over to the elements. Through his scope, Gaunt could see that stone walls were broken down, and habs and outhouses were missing their roofs. The bones of dead livestock spotted the stony ground amongst the rusting farm machinery. The ruin of an air-mill sat in the centre of the place, its still vanes like tattered wings. Air-mills were common in the agri-provinces. They'd seen several ruined mills during their march. Gaunt remembered a row of giant air-mills marking the border of Edrian Province, a place where Brostin had once performed a particularly spectacular stunt with a tanker load of promethium. That seemed like an awfully long time ago.

'Try the link,' he said to Beltayn.

Beltayn knelt down and set the dials of his nonstandard voxcaster. 'Daystar, Daystar, this is Skyclad. Please respond.' He sent the message as a verbal signal and a simultaneous non-verbal code pulse, tapped out by hand on the transmitter's key bar.

Nothing came back.

'What the feth is wrong with them?' Gaunt muttered.

'They weren't exactly chatting this morning, sir,' Beltayn said. It was true. The sum total of the previous message, aside from the verification ciphers, had been 'Cayfer mill, by tonight.'

'They could be watching us,' Cirk said. 'Making sure we're who we say we are.'

'I'd know it,' said Mkoll.

'Or maybe you wouldn't,' Cirk told the scout.

'They could be lying low,' said Beltayn. 'I mean, if something had spooked them. Maybe they think something's awry and they don't want to come out until it's safe.'

Gaunt was panning his scope around, taking in the hamlet and the surrounding vista of the countryside. He stopped suddenly.

'What, sir?' Criid asked.

'I think Bel's right. I think something is awry.'

'How do you mean?'

'You know you thought you saw something stalking us?'

'Yeah?'

'I think I just saw it too.'

III

THE BUILDING HAD once been a college or a hospital, and it stood in the south-west corner of Cantible. Early patrols had reported it to be empty, but now Kolea had charge of the search pattern in that part of the streets and he wanted to make sure.

'Something that big's going to have a basement,' he told Varl. 'Storerooms, cellars, vaults. We'll check it room by room.'

The squads moved in.

The sky had turned a fulminous yellow hue. Despite their care, the Ghosts' footsteps clattered noisily through the wreck-strewn courts and cloisters of the old place.

'Sir?'

Kolea crossed a quadrangle to an open door where Domor and Chiria were standing.

'What have you got, Shoggy?'

'Just a hall,' Domor said. Kolea peered inside. It was indeed a large assembly hall or congregation room. The walls had been defaced, and the floor was covered with broken glass and shattered wooden stalls. At the far end, large, smeary lancet windows were backlit by daylight, and showed the fuzzy shapes of trees outside.

'Any hatches here? Doors?'

'No, sir,' Chiria told Kolea.

'All right, then,' Kolea said, stepping back out into the quad. 'Carry on.'

His link pipped. It was Meryn.

'Yes, captain?'

'The habs are clear to the end of the street, sir. We found some bodies in one. Old kills. Nothing else. Shall I move on into the next row?'

'No, stay put. We'll be there presently. I want to keep the sweeps overlapping.'

'Understood.'

Varl trudged towards him across the quad followed by half a dozen other Ghosts.

'What's that way?' Kolea asked.

'An undercroft,' said Varl. 'It's derelict. There's a few storerooms, but they've been trashed.'

'And what's behind that wall?' Kolea asked him. The far side of the quad was enclosed by a tall stone wall.

'The street,' said Varl.

Kolea nodded and then paused. 'No,' he said, 'it can't be.'

'I'm sure it is,' said Varl.

'Were there any trees in the street?' asked Kolea. 'Do you remember any trees?'

'No,' said Varl.

Kolea thumbed his micro-bead. 'Uh, Meryn? You still in the street?'

'Yes, sir. Covering from the north end.'

'You see any trees?'

'Say again?'

'Trees, Meryn? You see any trees?'

A pause. 'Negative on trees, major.'

'What's going on?' asked Varl. Kolea pointed at the end wall. 'It can't be the street behind that. The street runs further over to the left. If there was any doubt, that wall screens off whatever this hall backs onto. You can see trees through the hall windows.'

They walked over to the high wall. The stones were dirty and black, as if soot had been baked on and then varnished. Kolea felt his way along, followed by Varl and some of the other squad members.

'Door,' Kolea announced.

'Feth,' said Varl. 'Who missed that?'

'Doesn't matter,' Kolea replied. 'I don't think this place wants us to know its secrets.'

The door, narrow and wooden, was painted black and set flush into the stonework. Even close to, it was virtually invisible.

'Ready weapons,' Varl started to say to the others. 'We're going to hop through and–'

But Kolea had already opened the door.

'Feth!' Varl said, and followed him.

There was a yard beyond, a small, dark courtyard bordered on all sides by high, black walls except for where the hall adjoined.

The ground was covered with human bones. Thickly covered. The bones were loose and jumbled, stacked deep in places, piled against the walls. There was a smell of old rot, and mould growth caked the inner walls. It was like an ossuary, or a foul, anatomical rubbish tip.

'Gak,' Kolea sighed. 'I think we found out where all the people went.'

Beside him, Varl stared in bleak horror at the disarticulated relics of the dead, the staring sockets, the gaping mouths, the brown ribs. The other troopers, no strangers to death, were similarly transfixed.

'Trees,' Kolea mused suddenly, swallowing hard and trying to get his brain moving again. 'Why could I see trees?'

He looked up and saw the three, tall, slender gibbets in front of the hall windows. The wood that they were made from was dark, as if stained with blood. Skeletal metal mannequins hung from steel strings, silent and empty and stark.

Varl saw what Kolea was looking at. The shock lingering on his face melted into fear.

'Gol,' he whispered, backing away very slowly and trying to make the others come with him. 'Gol, for Throne's sake... those are wirewolves.'

IV

THEY ADVANCED UP through the tousled pink grasses and tumbled stones towards the boundaries of Cayfer. Mkoll lingered at the back, watching the grasslands for signs of the thing stalking them.

'It was low down in the grass,' Gaunt had said, 'gone before I could see it.'

'A beast?'

'A hunting beast,' Gaunt had nodded. He refused to speak the word *daemon*, but what else might be haunting the moorlands of a world embraced by the Ruinous Powers?

The slopes approaching the hamlet were melancholy. Pink grass and violet lichens clung to the low stone walls and withered gates, and the trees were dead and desiccated like the bones of giant hands. Within the sagging walls, amongst the collapsing farm machinery and scattered animal bones were tiny shreds of human evidence: a tin bucket full of wooden clothes pegs, bleached by the sunlight; a row of odd boots and shoes, the leather cracked and worn like old flesh, mysteriously lined up along the top of a stone wall; a broken trumpet, lying in the weeds; a rag doll with one button eye; mismatched pots and drinking cups and other receptacles, laid out in a curious pattern in the grass, each one half-full of stagnant rainwater; a chopping block for splitting firewood, and a pile of cut wood beside it, but no axe.

The sky had darkened, and a low wind had got up, brushing the grasslands like an invisible hand and making the dead trees creak. A door banged somewhere. Cloth strung to the air-mill's ragged vanes began to flap.

They were closing on the main hamlet now. Gaunt drew his bolt pistol and waved everyone down. The section, spread wide, got down in cover around walls and outbuildings.

'Bel?'

Beltayn tried the vox again. This time the answer to his send was squealing distortion.

'Atmospherics,' he said. Gaunt nodded. No surprise. It felt as if there were a storm coming. The colour of the sky said as much, and the change in the light. The rising wind was cold, as if it was air displaced from some polar latitude. The warm stillness that had surrounded them since the drop was blown away.

Gaunt was about to move forwards again when they all heard a long, purring growl. It came from a distance away, and travelled on the wind, which suggested it had been loud to begin with. Eszrah started and raised his reynbow.

Gaunt looked back at Mkoll. The scout pointed. The sound, as far as he was concerned, had come from the swaying grassland.

'Criid,' Gaunt said. 'Hold the position here. Larks, Mktass, Garond... with me and Mkoll.'

The designated troopers picked themselves up and scurried down the slope after Gaunt.

'It's moving like a felid,' Mkoll whispered as they got into cover with him. 'Belly down, ears flat.'

'It's got ears?' Larkin asked.

'I haven't even seen it,' Mkoll confessed, 'but I can feel it. I can feel it watching us and getting closer.'

Another purring growl came up on them in the wind. It was almost a coughing, hacking sound.

'And we can hear it,' Mkoll added.

'Keep that loaded,' Gaunt told Larkin, pointing to his longlas. 'If it's big and fast, we're going to need to be able to put it down hard.'

'If I can see it, I'll blow its fething head off,' Larkin assured them.

'Right,' said Gaunt. 'Garond and Mkoll, split left. Mktass with me to the right. Larks, you move forwards from here, and we'll see if we can't pincer it.'

'Were there big predators on Gereon?' Garond asked.

'No,' said Gaunt. 'In the Untill, maybe, but not out in a place like this. This is trouble. This is something the enemy brought. Let's go.'

The two prongs hurried off, heads and backs low, through the nodding grasses. As he ran, Gaunt thought he heard the growl again, but realised it was the rumble of thunder approaching. He waved Mktass low, and they crept forwards. Gaunt felt for the grip of his sheathed power sword. It would be cumbersome to draw, in cover, but the time might come. It had a taste for warp-beasts.

Seventy metres away across the shivering pink crop, Mkoll and Garond slithered on their bellies to the base of one of the dead trees.

'Smell that?' Garond whispered.

Mkoll nodded. 'Blood. Dried blood.'

'What the gak is this thing?' Garond hissed.

'It's dead, that's what it is,' Mkoll whispered back. 'I don't care how big and ugly you are, you don't ghost the Ghosts.'

Mkoll peered out. There was still nothing visible. The coughing growl came again, a little surging purr. Then it was gone.

'Where are you?' Mkoll murmured.

LARKIN EDGED FORWARDS, nursing the long las. He'd got a tingle, the sniper's tingle that divined the location of a target when it still couldn't be eyeballed. Eighty, ninety strides ahead, in the downroll of the long grass, between the two forked trees. Larkin would have put money on it if Varl had been around. It was a gut thing, and Larkin had been a hunter for a long time. He snuggled his rifle up to his cheek.

'In that dip, between the trees,' he voxed quietly.

'Specify,' Gaunt replied.

'Make the two trees to your left. Tall skinny one with no branches, curved like a swan-neck? And the ragged one like a woman bending in a high wind and her skirts going up?'

'Got them.'

'Ground dips away there, pretty deep. Down there.'

'You certain?' Mkoll voxed in.

'My gut is.'

'Good enough for me,' Mkoll noted.

Larkin settled his aim. Through his scope, he tightened in on the nodding grasses. For the first time, he thought he could see a shape, a dark shape. He was lined up.

There was another growl, a sputter, a snorting sound, and the thing moved. It began to come up out of the grass, as if it was rising to pounce. Larkin saw its eyes, bright, yellow and glowing. His aim was set directly between them. Headshot. He took it.

The hot-shot round sizzled across the pink grass and struck between the beast's eyes. There was a scorching, metallic crack.

With a further hacking, coughing roar, as if goaded by pain, the beast rose up out of the dip in a sudden, violent surge. Now they could see it.

Now they could see what kind of beast it was.

'Oh feth,' said Mkoll.

V

'MOVE!' GAUNT BELLOWED. 'Stay low!'

They scattered. Roaring and snorting, the beast reared out of the dip, flattening the long grass in its path. Chugging geysers of black smoke streamed from its hindquarters straight up into the air as it exerted itself to move forwards. Its enormous engine revved. It was a machine, but it was a beast and a daemon too. It was an enemy tank.

The battered, wounded armour was crimson, the paint flaking off to bare grey metal in places. Twisted sheet plating and skeins of rusted barbed wire reinforced its skirts. Rivets covered it like barnacles. Strung trophies knocked and clattered against its flanks. On its turret side was a single painted mark, a runic symbol of cosmic malevolence. Yellow headlamp eyes glowed from the front of the hull.

The beast came up out of the dip with alarming speed, and set off across the flat ground with a steady clatter of tracks. It was heading directly for Larkin's position.

Gaunt was still moving. He looked back.

'Larkin?'

The autocannon hard point built into the left-hand side of the beast's forward hull began firing. Large calibre rounds wasped across the swishing grass. Clumps of earth sprayed up into the air. A small, dead tree splintered into dry kindling.

'Larkin!'

There was no sign of the master sniper.

The beast abruptly slewed around to its left, one set of tracks braking as the other raced on. Dirt and soil sprayed out behind it as it dug in. Bouncing, it rolled around in the direction of Gaunt and Mktass.

As if it had heard his voice.

The beast's main gun, lolling with its motion like a slack limb, was angled down steeply, slightly below the horizontal. The turret clamp squealed out above the brute thunder of the engine as the turret began to traverse.

Gaunt and Mktass were already down in the grass. Gaunt turned his head to the side and glimpsed Mktass a few metres away through the grass stalks, scurrying forwards on his hands and knees.

'Stay still–' he was about to say.

The beast spoke.

The sound of its main gun firing was painfully loud, like a sledgehammer striking an anvil. The range was so short that there was no space to hear the whistle of the shell. Twenty metres ahead of Gaunt, a large lump of moorland disintegrated in a cone of smoke and flame. The blast shook the ground.

The beast lurched to a halt, and another metal-on-metal squeal sounded as the turret traversed back in the other direction. It stopped.

Gaunt wrapped his arms over his head and clenched his teeth, waiting for the–

Again, the beast spoke. Another volcano of dirt and fire erupted out of the moorland.

Gaunt had heard tankfire hundreds of times before, both close to and from far away, and it wasn't just the proximity of the threat that made the beast's voice particularly monstrous.

It was the fact that it *was* a voice. It was the boom of a heavy gun, but in that boom, in that sledgehammer on anvil clash of main gun mechanism and shellfire, there was an organic note. A howl. A roar of lust and rage and glee. A rumble of hunger.

The engine revved again, and the beast swung about, track links rattling. It began to rock and bounce in the direction of Mkoll's position.

Its behaviour was extraordinary. Gaunt knew the use and value of armoured weapons, for power and strength, for psychological force. Tanks were a vital tool of warfare as unsubtle monsters that could roll in and deliver stupendous firepower.

This beast wasn't behaving like a tank. It wasn't just advancing inexorably towards them, firing its weapons. It was hunting them, and it had been hunting them since they'd first become aware of it earlier in the day. Since before that, most probably. They'd become convinced there was a big predatory animal shadowing them on the moors, and there had been. When the beast first emerged, it was all Gaunt could do to remember that it had been hull down in the dip and the long grasses, and not *belly* down.

Since when did tanks act like wolves or felids?

The beast trundled towards the area where Gaunt had last seen Mkoll. Its hard point spat out a few lazy shots, and then it lurched to a sudden halt. Braking hard, its hull rocked nose to tail on its suspension. The trophies decorating its flanks – mostly human skulls and Guard helmets strung on wire like beads – swung and clattered for a moment. The big turbine throbbed, idling. Little gusts of black smoke dribbled up out of the exhaust pipes.

What was it doing? What was it waiting for?

The turret began to traverse again, turning slowly to the beast's left. The metal turret collar made a laborious screech of unoiled joints, like a stone slab being dragged off a tomb. The turret stopped, facing the hill slope where the hamlet sat. There was an electric whine and the tank barrel elevated slowly until it was twenty-five degrees off the horizontal, aiming directly at Cayfer.

Not aiming. Gaunt raised his head out of the grass and risked a look. The beast sat thirty metres away, its heavy back end towards him. The main gun wasn't aiming at Cayfer, Gaunt thought. It was… sniffing, scenting the hamlet. Scenting the wind, like a cat.

Slowly, Gaunt drew his power sword. While it was occupied, maybe he could crawl towards its hindquarters and get in really close at its blind sp^t Armour plating or no armour plating, the pa^r blade of Heironymo Sondar could stab in thr^ne. vent grille or an exhaust slot and cripple the^

Providing someone was smiling down on him from a golden throne…

He edged forwards. He didn't activate the blade, for fear that the energised hum might give him away… for fear that the tank might hear it. The idea would be funny if it weren't so horribly real. To his right, he saw Mktass, still down in the grass, signalling frantically that Gaunt shouldn't try it. *Too much of a crazy risk*, said Mktass's gestures and wide, staring eyes. *You'll get yourself killed. You'll get us all killed.*

Gaunt kept going. He flexed his fingers around the grip of the power sword, down low beside his thigh. His nostrils were assaulted by the exhaust wash of the idling beast, the rank oil and soot, the smell of dried blood from the grisly battle trophies strung about it.

He was ten metres from the beast's rear when things changed. He saw a little flurry of sparks light up on the slope directly below the ruined hamlet, coming from behind one of the tumbled pasture walls. From a distance, it looked like tinderbox sparks. In a second, las bolts sang overhead. Someone on the slope was firing a lasrifle at the beast on full auto.

The range was poor, and even point blank, a lasrifle couldn't penetrate tank armour. Gaunt knew what it was. It was somebody's attempt at distraction. It was somebody's attempt to draw the tank off them. Gaunt recognised this with a mixture of warmth and annoyance. Someone in the section was risking their life to distract the tank, and that selfless. In the section, Trooper Gonry had been ng a tread fether and, presumably, whoever was shooting was hoping to lure the beast into range for a rocket kill.

Gaunt was very close, however, and this was spoiling his chance.

He broke cover and began to run, igniting the power sword in the hope that he could get a crippling thrust into the beast-machine before it moved.

The engine blitzed into life, pumping out a torrent of black exhaust, and the beast spoke again.

It spoke three times. Sledgehammer-anvil-howl. In dismay, Gaunt saw the three shells land in the slopes below Cayfer, shredding a wall line into a rain of stones, demolishing a pair of dead trees, and blasting a raw scab of earth out of the grass.

The beast started to surge forwards, tracks chattering like fast percussion. Dirt and stones and tufts of grass like small scalps spattered up and out from its rear as it moved, and Gaunt had to shield his face. He couldn't reach it. It was pulling away.

'No!' he spat.

The beast heard him.

VI

THE BEAST SWUNG right around, chewing the ground as it dragged its dark tonnage about. Exhaust smoke farted upwards in a sudden blurt of effort as it turned. It turned to face Gaunt. Its staring headlamps pulsed with yellow light.

Gaunt was gone. There was no one behind it.

The beast revved its engine, sounding like an angry growl. The hard point clattered and let off a burst of shells that raked the grasses ahead, and caused a cloud of shredded plant fibre to waft into the wind.

The beast sped forwards, grinding back across the track of flattened stems that it had left in its wake.

Something had knocked Gaunt flat just as the beast began to turn. Where Mkoll had come from, Gaunt wasn't sure. *Stay flat*, Mkoll had signed.

They lay on their backs in the deep grass, hearing the snorting, growling frustration of the beast nearby. They heard it fire its hard point, and heard the close whip and slice of the shells. Then they heard it start forward, coming closer.

Gaunt twitched involuntarily, but Mkoll put a firm hand flat on his chest. *Stay flat. Don't move.*

The din of engine and treads got louder and closer. It was increasing speed.

Don't move.

The beast passed by less than three metres from Gaunt's left side. Its noise receded behind them. They waited for what seemed like an eternity for the noise to change, for the beast to make its next turn, but the noise simply faded away.

Mkoll and Gaunt lifted themselves slowly and took a look across the nodding grass.

There was no sign of the beast. No sound. No smoke.

They rose to their feet. Garond and Mktass appeared, from different points in the weed cover.

'Where the feth did it go?' Gaunt asked.

'That way,' Garond pointed. A trampled path of pink grass led away down the slope, following the base curve of the hill on which Cayfer stood. Already,

the stiff pink grass stalks were beginning to spring
back up.

Mkoll ran forwards a short way and leapt up into
the lower branches of one of the dead trees. He
pulled himself up to get a good view.

'It's gone,' Larkin said.

Mkoll looked down. Larkin was curled up against
the bole of the tree, sheltering behind its withered
trunk. The sniper pointed down the slope. 'Last I saw
it, it was rolling down into cover again. Past that
cairn of stones into the small valley.'

Mkoll leapt down out of the tree. 'I'll go after it.
Track it,' he said.

'And do what when you find it?' Gaunt asked. 'No,
we regroup. We know it's out here and we know how
it moves. We'll keep watch, and when it shows itself
again, we'll be ready.'

THEY WORKED THEIR way back up the hill to the
fringes of Cayfer, past the three still-burning shell
pits that the beast had scarred the slopes with. Criid
appeared to meet them.

'That you shooting?' Gaunt asked.

She nodded.

'Brave. Maybe foolish, but thanks.'

'I wanted to pull it close so Gonry could slag it with
the fether,' she said, pretending her actions had had
nothing to do with pulling Gaunt's skin out of the
fire.

'Decent idea.'

'Where did it go?' Criid asked, following him up
the slope.

'It didn't,' said Gaunt. 'It's still out there. Post a watch. Fetlı, what's this?'

They had rejoined the main group, which had been sheltering in the dusty yard behind a row of outbuildings. Faragut was bolt upright against a pen wall, his pistol at his feet. Eszrah was patiently aiming his reynbow at him. The rest were grouped in, watching, many amused at the commissar's discomfort.

'There was an incident,' Criid said lightly.

Gaunt walk up to Eszrah and gave a nod. The Nihtgane raised his bow and stepped back. Gaunt looked at Faragut.

'What happened?' he asked.

'The bastard was going to shoot Criid,' Beltayn snapped.

'Yes, that's right,' Faragut snorted. 'Hear them tell it. That'll make for an accurate picture.'

'You tell me then,' said Gaunt. 'Did you threaten my sergeant with your weapon?'

'I drew my pistol for emphasis because she refused a direct order.'

'Your order?'

'A direct order. I told her I would be forced to shoot her if she persisted in insubordination, as per the *Instrument of Order*, paragraph–'

'Oh, please don't, Faragut,' Gaunt said. 'What was the order?'

'She intended to fire upon that tank. I told her not to. I ordered the section to hold fire and stay in cover.'

Gaunt nodded. 'I see. You had the tank rocket up here, and Criid wanted to bring the enemy in range, but you saw it differently?'

'I saw it realistically!' Faragut replied. 'The chances of us taking a tank were slim. Very slim. The chances of that tank destroying this team before it could achieve its mission objectives were greater, in my judgement. Contacting the resistance is vital. I could not permit anything to prejudice our chances.'

'Even if it meant leaving me and the others to die?' Gaunt asked.

'Even that. You know the stakes, Gaunt. You know what necessary sacrifice is.'

'You fired anyway?' Gaunt asked Criid.

'With you and Mkoll down there, I had section command at that point. The tank needed to die, in my judgement.'

'She fired. I went to reprove her,' Faragut said. 'I may have had my gun in my hand at that time. Then your partisan aimed his weapon in my face.'

'Eszrah's only got a few friends in the whole universe, Faragut,' Gaunt said. 'Aiming your gun at one of them is a bad idea. Let's get on. Pick up your damn gun.'

'Watchposts!' Mkoll called. 'I want a lookout spread along the rise in case that tread shows again!'

'Gonry, get the tube ready,' said Criid. 'Someone stand by to load him.'

Everyone was moving. Gaunt walked up through the farm buildings towards the air-mill. He realised that Cirk was walking with him.

'Gaunt?'

'Yes?'

'Faragut is–' she began.

'Faragut is what?' he asked.

'There is a broad agenda,' she said. Her voice trailed off.

He stopped walking and turned to look at her. 'I don't know quite what you're trying to tell me,' he said.

Cirk shook her head sadly. 'I don't know either. I haven't been told anything. You haven't been told. They don't have to tell us. We're just pawns.'

'Who are "they"?' Gaunt asked.

She shrugged. 'I don't know that either.'

Gaunt snorted. 'You're not doing much except sound terribly paranoid, Cirk.'

She smiled. She had hugged her arms around her thin body, as if she was cold. 'I know. Listen, have you ever wanted something so much you'd give everything to have it? Have you ever prayed for something that much?'

'I don't know.'

'You'd know if you had. You want something so much it hurts. You give everything, *everything*, away just to have it. Only… when you gave up everything, you gave it away too and so there's nothing.'

The wind caught her hair, and she screwed up her eyes while she brushed it aside and wiped her nose on her sleeve.

'Cirk? What can't you tell me?'

'It cost the resistance dear to get us off Gereon.'

'I remember.'

'A lot of time, a lot of materiel and a lot of lives, but it was worth it, because we swore that if we got away, if we got back to Imperial space, we'd return. We'd bring liberation back with us. That was the deal.'

'That's right. That's what we've done.'

'Just remember that's all I'm saying. Just remember that's how it's supposed to work.'

Gaunt frowned, and was framing another question when he heard Beltayn shouting. He looked round. His adjutant was standing at the top of the yard beside Criid and some other troopers. He was pointing, pointing up over the low, broken roofs of the hamlet, towards the air-mill.

In the rising wind, the vanes were beginning to turn.

VII

RAWNE STROLLED BACK across the quad to join Kolea and Varl. He looked back at the high wall, and the small black door that he'd just emerged from.

'I think they're dead,' he said. 'Just junk hanging there.'

'But–' Kolea began.

'Last time we were here,' Rawne said smoothly. 'Those things would go live at the slightest provocation.'

'I know. You briefed us,' Kolea replied.

'Well, they didn't wake up when we hit this place, and they haven't woken up yet. I don't know why they're dead, but that's what they are.'

Varl scratched his scalp behind his left ear. 'Yeah, but given they're not actually alive, there's a chance that's not a permanent state.'

'There's a chance,' Rawne agreed. 'For now, we cordon this whole area, put a round the clock watch on it, and level it with everything we have if something so much as twitches. There's been another signal from the Inquisition forces. They're on their way. They can deal with it when they get here.'

Rawne turned and looked up at the dark clouds chasing across the pearly sky. There was a wind in the air. Gaunt was overdue signalling, although the old blight of Gereon's atmospherics could explain that. 'For what it's worth,' Rawne said, 'I think they are dead. I think they're dead for the same reason that there are no glyfs around. Set up a cordon here and let's get on with the sweeps.'

Rawne left the quad to rejoin his party. Varl put Chiria's section in charge of watching the grim, walled secret.

Kolea had something on his mind. He stayed apart, sitting on a chunk of fallen masonry in the corner of the quad, musing and turning something over in his hand.

'Ready to move?' Varl asked once the place was secure.

'I suppose so.'

'What?'

'That was dumb,' said Kolea.

'What was?'

'What I just did. I just walked in there. We found the door and I just walked in there. You were getting a cover team ready, but I didn't wait. I just walked in.'

'No harm done,' said Varl.

Kolea looked up at him. 'No actual harm, but there could have been. It was real enough. The wire-wolves were there. We've been briefed. We'd been told what to look for and how careful we had to be, and I just walked in. I might as well have been whistling.'

Varl grinned. 'And your point? 'Cause I know if I stand here long enough, you'll eventually make one.'

Kolea stood up and brushed off the dusty legs of his battledress pants. 'We take a lot of risks,' he said.

Varl pursed his lips as if stifling amusement. 'We're soldiers. We're the Emperor's Guardsmen, true and faithful. Risks are the job.'

'I know. I just don't think sometimes. I charge in. I take the plunge…'

'That's your style,' said Varl. 'You led from the front, which is why you're a major and I'm not. At the moment.'

'It's going to get me killed. That's what I'm saying. Nearly has more than once.'

'Life's going to get you killed,' said Varl. 'Come the feth on with you.'

They wandered back across the dusty quad to where Domor had the search team waiting in the street archway. A dry wind chased eddies of soot and sand around the quad flagstones.

They started to head down the street, past the derelict faces of burned-out habs and slopes of rubble dotted with nodding weeds. Meryn's section was ahead of them, leading the way into the tattered produce barns of the old town commercia.

'Know what I've been doing since we started on this?' Kolea asked Varl as they walked along in the breeze-stirred quiet.

'Getting on my wick?'

'I'm serious.'

'So am I.'

'Since we dropped, all I've thought about is the lad, how he is, if he's safe, how gakking unfair it is that he isn't with us. He must be scared, wherever the gak he is. The big zones must be bad.'

'That's natural enough.'

'I've never once wondered… is he alive still?'

'Well, you can't think that way.'

'I know.' They had reached the gates of the produce area. Kolea fanned the section out in support of Meryn's advancing Ghosts.

'It just occurred to me, there's something else I should think about.'

'What?' Varl asked.

'When we're all done with this place, maybe I'll see the lad again, and that will be fine, but what if I die? What if I do something dumb and just die? How will that be for him?'

Varl shrugged.

'I left it too late before this started. My fear was, I'd left it too late full stop. Because the lad might die, I'd never get the chance to put things right. Never occurred to me it might work the other way around.'

IT WAS ANYONE'S guess how long the excubitor had been holed up in the outhouses behind the silent, boarded habs. The area was a maze of small yards and narrow alleys, dotted with store huts and privies, and it stretched all the way down to a row of market gardens inside the town wall.

Osket, Wheln and Harjeon had just shifted left, and Kalen, Leclan and Raess to the right. Caffran moved his fingers and gestured Leyr and Neskon up behind him.

'We'll go through that way,' he said, pointing to a dingy alley.

Neskon shifted his flamer tanks higher onto his shoulder. 'This is a waste of time.'

'I'll tell you when it's a waste of time,' Caffran advised. 'Now stay sharp.'

The whole place was too enclosed and too dirty to be anything but oppressive. They jumped at shadows, or shrank back from tiny pieces of horror. Bones were common, and so were the daubings and scratchings of the enemy. Glass pots of blood had been left in various locations as offerings, and their contents were starting to putrefy and separate. Not for the first time, Caffran saw evidence of vermin eating vermin. That was a testament, if one was needed, of how low Gereon had slipped. It was so spent and exhausted that the only thing left for the rats to eat was other rats.

They'd gone about ten metres along the narrow alley when the sound of a las-lock boomed to their right and the shouting started. There were several bursts of las fire.

'Report!' Caffran yelled into the link.

'Man down!' Leclan crackled back. 'Hostile came out of hiding. He's coming your way!'

Leyr and Neskon immediately raised their weapons. Caffran ran forwards a little way and looked around. He could hear footsteps echoing in all directions, but the alley walls and the sides of the outbuildings were too steep to see over.

'Get me up!' he said to Leyr.

Leyr cupped his hands and boosted Caffran up a wall. He scrambled onto the roof of an outbuilding, ran along it and leapt onto an adjacent roof. He saw a figure darting along the crookback alleys to his left.

Caffran turned and shouted down to Neskon, 'Fire up the left-hand turn!'

Neskon hurried forwards, nursed his coughing flamer for a moment, and then sent a spear of fire down the left-hand path of the alley junction. The boiling flames filled five metres of alleyway for several seconds. There was a stifled cry. Driven back by the surging flames, the excubitor reappeared, running back the way he'd come.

Standing on the flat roof, legs braced firmly, Caffran fired from the chest. Two shots and the vile figure dropped.

'Hostile is down,' Caffran said. 'Pull this place apart and make sure he was alone.'

CAFFRAN SAT DOWN on a kerbstone and pulled off his left boot. The dust and grit got into everything. He ached. His limbs were sore. The sky over the town was turning to evening and looked like marble.

Nearby, the rest of his section was resting. Leclan was checking the dressing on the grazing wound Kalen had taken from the excubitor.

Caffran leaned back against a wall and closed his eyes. He scooped out the silver aquila he wore on a chain around his neck and said a silent prayer. Two prayers. One for each of them, wherever they were.

'Caff?'

He opened his eyes and looked up. It was Kolea.

'Major?' he said, rising.

'Bask said I'd find you here. Busy afternoon?'

'Yeah. The work of the Emperor never ends.'

'Praise be to that.'

'Can I help you?'

Kolea nodded. He fished something out of his pocket. It was a Tanith cap badge. 'I'll make this simple. I was going to give this to the lad when he finished RIP, and I never got the chance. My mistake. I'd like him to have it.'

Caffran nodded. 'That'd be good.'

Kolea held it out. 'Please, could you give it to him? When you see him?'

'You can do that,' Caffran said.

'I just got this feeling, Caff. Like I'm tempting fate by hoping on this. His fate and mine. All the while I'm hoping I can give him this, I'm daring fate to stop it happening. So here's an end to it. I don't have to think about it any more. If you don't mind?'

Caffran smiled and took the cap badge. 'I don't mind,' he said.

'Thanks.' Kolea managed a smile too. 'Thanks. That's a relief. Feels like it... improves our chances a bit.'

'MAJOR?'

At Baskevyl's call, Rawne left the map tent and hurried over to the entrenchment that the Ghosts had built across the ruins of Cantible's main gate.

'What it it?'

Baskevyl pointed. 'They're here,' he said.

Out across the moors, three black landers were speeding in towards the town, riding low, hugging the rolling terrain in formation.

As they came closer, Rawne could see the insignia on the hull of each one.

The stylised 'I' of the Inquisition.

VIII

THE AIR-MILL smelled of old dust and starch. The slowly turning vanes made a low creaking that came and went with a dying fall. The shadow of the vanes passed over them at each sweep, like clouds across the sun.

Gaunt held off for a second. Mktass and Fiko appeared from around the side of the mill and Fiko nodded. Burone and Posetine held cover from across the dry yard in front of the mill.

Gaunt went inside. Mkoll followed, and then Derin and Nirriam. The floor was well-laid stone, but the structure was wood. The turning gears of the mill system made a painful, heavy rhythm through the floor above, like solid furniture being moved. Violet mould had infested the plasterwork and bleached some of the exposed beams. The place had been stripped, and nothing had been left except for some pieces of sacking and a litter of rope scraps. Mkoll crossed to the turning post of the mill.

'Deliberate,' he said. The mill's vanes weren't just rotating because the wind had picked up. Mkoll pointed to a heavy iron handle that had been thrown to release the bearings. Gaunt nodded, and walked slowly around, looking upwards. Through slots and

grooves in the plank flooring, he glimpsed the cob-
webbed upper spaces of the mill: shadows and shafts
of thin sunlight.

'Check upstairs,' he told Mkoll and Nirriam. He
turned to Derin. 'Bring Cirk in.'

'Sir,' said Derin, and ducked out.

'Nothing upstairs,' Mkoll voxed. 'Unless you're
interested in seeing more dust.'

'Sweep the nearby buildings,' Gaunt voxed back.
'Whoever set this going can't be long gone. They may
be watching us.'

'They're gone,' said Cirk, stepping in through the
door. Faragut came in behind her.

'They're gone?' Gaunt asked.

'They wouldn't stay around to be followed or discovered. Far too cautious for that.'

'But this is a sign? A... signal?'

Cirk started looking around. What clues or evidence she was searching for was beyond Gaunt. She
had far more experience than he did of the esoteric
practices of the Gereon resistance.

'It's got to look accidental so the enemy won't
notice it, but it will also be very precise. There–'

She pointed to a part of the floor where several
handfuls of rope off-cuts lay in the dust.

'I don't see,' said Gaunt.

'Compare,' she said, raising her pointing finger and
aiming it at a part of the mould-covered wall. Random marks had been scratched in the mould. Gaunt
would never have noticed it, but now she showed
him, he saw that the pattern of scratches matched
exactly the pattern of the scattered rope strands.

'They repeat the pattern so we know it's not random,' she said. She crouched down beside the rope strands and began to examine them, turning her head to one side, and then the other. Mkoll and Nirriam returned from the floor above.

'It's a map,' she said at last.

'Of what?' Faragut asked.

'This area, I would imagine, but it's encrypted.'

'Encrypted?' laughed Faragut. 'It's just bits of string…'

'It's encrypted. We're not meant to use all of it. Some of the rope used has a blueish fleck in the weave. The rest has red. Please look around. Can you find more examples of either?'

'Here,' said Mkoll immediately. He indicated the heavy iron handle. There was a short tuft of rope tied around the metal spoke. It had a red fleck to it.

Cirk smiled. She reached down and quickly picked up all the blue-flecked strands and threw them to one side.

'There. The red is all that matters. There's our map.'

'I still don't see…' Faragut began. Gaunt shushed him and took out his pocket book. He quickly copied the lines and shapes down.

'The aspect will be accurate, won't it?' he asked Cirk as he drew.

'I would think so. This is aligned the way it is in the real world.'

Gaunt finished drawing and put his stylus away. He hurried up the creaking wooden steps onto the boarded first floor, and then up a quivering ladder into the second, a dusty loft in the narrower upper part of the structure. Ducking under part of the noisy, rotating vane assembly, he found another ladder and clambered up. Cirk, Mkoll and Faragut were following him.

The third storey was a very cramped space, and there was a real danger of being snagged by the turning wheels, and dragged into the crushing embrace of the mill's machinery. Gaunt poked around cautiously until he located some metal rungs bolted to the wall. The rungs led up to a small trapdoor in the roof.

He climbed out onto the roof. It was a precarious, small space, a rough platform of pitch-treated wood with no guard rail. The air-mill seemed very much taller outside than in. Gaunt had a good head for heights, but he steadied himself. The sloping sides of the mill dropped away, and below them, the roofs of the hamlet, the sides of the hill and the spread of the countryside beyond. He had a commanding view of the area, and that was deliberate. This vantage point was why the resistance had led him to the mill and left the map there.

Cirk and Mkoll clambered out beside him. Both showed no alarm at the height, and moved about casually. The wind was quite considerable now, and buffeted at all three of them. Every few seconds, another of the mill's vanes would swish past like a scything blade, which Gaunt found disconcerting. He took his hurried sketch out of his pocket and tried to align himself.

'About... so?' he asked, holding the map out and orienting his body. Mkoll nodded, and took out his scope. He began to play it over the distances.

The sky was blotchy and very threatening. The thunder that had been grumbling ever closer was now a regular rumble, and the clouds along the western skyline had an underbelly full of hazy, ugly light.

Cirk stood by Gaunt's shoulder, comparing the map lines with the landscape. 'That's the line of the hill, and that's the large escarpment,' she said, her pointing finger moving between map and distance. 'That's the stand of trees to the right, and that's got to be the line of the watercourse.'

Mkoll agreed. He didn't seem to need to look at Gaunt's sketch. The lines of the map were already imprinted on his mind. 'I think the intention is to get us to head north-east. About three kilometres takes us to the edge of that woodland. Whatever is marked by that cross would seem to be about another kilometre further on.'

'Would they expect us to make that by nightfall?' Gaunt asked.

Cirk shook her head. 'I doubt it. The original message told us to be here by tonight.'

'But this fits with our expectations,' Gaunt mused. Mkoll knelt down and slid his copy of the mission chart from his thigh pocket. He unfolded it enough to study the section covering their location. The Departmento Tacticae had produced their charts using orbital scans, supplemented by detailed governance surveys of Gereon held on file by the Administratum.

'Yeah, it does. Untill,' he said, looking up at Gaunt. 'Eszrah will be pleased.'

'I'm sure he will,' Gaunt replied. During his time on Gereon, and thanks to his efforts, the partisans of the Untill had linked with the struggling underground resistance, and the fathomless wastes of the Untill itself had been a vital hiding place. Even the Archenemy found it difficult to penetrate those untillable swamps and marshes. 'So we're really that close?' he asked Mkoll.

'Well, the main tracts of the Untill are two, three hundred kilometres further east, but the limits of it extend out this far. That woodland we can see is the borderland. A day's march beyond it, you get into Sleepwalker territory.'

Mkoll got up and put the chart away. 'What do you think? Stay here overnight, or move–'

He cut off. Gaunt had raised his hand for quiet, and Mkoll knew that sign. Gaunt was staring west, down across the hamlet of Cayfer, down the hillside, onto the rippling pink moorland.

'We're about to have a problem,' he said.

'What?' Cirk asked.

Down below, half a kilometre from the hamlet at the base of the hill, the beast was back.

IX

GAUNT WAS ABOUT to trigger his link when the vox net came alive. Three of the troopers left on look out – Larkin, Brostin and Spakus – had spotted the tank and called it in.

'Hold your positions,' Gaunt sent back. 'Keep your eyes on it. Criid, get Gonry front and centre, and for feth's sake, keep him covered and safe.'

'Understood.'

Gaunt, Mkoll and Cirk scurried back down the ladders into the mill.

WITH GONRY RUNNING, head down, behind her, Criid crossed the inner yards of the hamlet and moved down through the derelict outbuildings. A sagging length of old wall fenced the sloping backfield from the rest of the hillside. Larkin was snuggled up there, long las resting on the lip of the wall. He was calmly watching the tank through his scope. Brostin was nearby, smoking a lho-stick as if he was waiting for his discharge papers. His flamer and its tanks lay on the grass next to him.

Brostin was a phlegmatic type. He knew when his area of expertise wasn't going to be called on. A flamer was no weapon to use against armour. Even the 'airburst special', a little party trick he and Larkin had improvised during their previous stay on Gereon, had no application here.

Criid dropped in beside Larkin. Gonry, a scrawny little Belladon, fell over beside her. 'Load that tube,' Criid told him. 'I'll stand by with the spares for cut and come again.' The satchel Gonry was carrying contained five rockets. That was their lot. He nodded to Criid and set to work setting the launcher and slipping the first rocket into place. Gonry was a sweet sort, and she knew he had a little bit of a crush on her. That helped. He did everything she told him as quickly as he could.

'Larks?'

'Just taking the evening air,' he replied.

'What?'

'Not me, lady. The tank,' Larkin snorted. He passed her the scope. 'Take a look.'

She swung up and panned the scope, being careful not to knock it against the wall top. This was Larkin's scope, after all. The master sniper had trusted her with a lend of his precious instrument.

She looked down the hill slope, past two runs of wall and several dead trees, skeletal-white in the changing light. The tank was down in the vale bottom, close to the place where it had played cat and mouse with Gaunt and the others earlier in the day. It was entirely visible to them, but it had decided to go hull-down in the grass, gun lowered, headlamps off. This attitude seemed insouciant to her. Something that big couldn't hide in open landscape, but it seemed to be pretending to do just that, as if all that really mattered was if the wind changed and its prey caught its scent and scattered.

She could hear its idling engine throbbing. No... panting.

'Two fifty metres,' she said, slipping back into cover and giving Larkin back his scope.

'Two sixty-two, with crosswind making the effective range three plus,' Larkin replied.

'Too far for a rocket either way,' Gonry said. 'I wouldn't waste anything over a hundred.'

He was right, but cautious. Criid bridled. 'Caff would smack it at three,' she said. She was boasting, but not much. Caffran was the best rocket lobber in the regiment.

'Caff's not here,' Gonry said. He said it with a smile that made Criid understand that he was happy about that fact.

'More's the fething pity,' she said, letting him know the score. She touched her link. 'Boss? We need to buy a little range to kill that gakker. Permission to sting it?'

'Refused,' Gaunt came back. 'Keep holding.'

'But sir–'

'Tona, that big thing on its topside is a high-calibre cannon. If it decides to start firing, it has the range and force to wipe us out. Don't go taunting it.'

'Understood.'

There was a repeated clicking sound. Larkin, Criid and Gonry looked around.

Brostin was playing with his igniter. 'Feth,' he said blithely, shaking it. 'Anyone got a light?'

GAUNT, CIRK AND MKOLL emerged from the mill.

'Shall I issue orders to retreat?' Faragut asked.

'Retreat?'

'We are overcome by armour,' Faragut said. 'We should withdraw and regroup. For the good of the mission.'

'Throne, you're scared,' Gaunt said, turning from his path to look at the young commissar. He stepped up until they were face to face.

'I'm not. How dare y–'

'Before with Criid, and now… it makes sense. Faragut, how much action have you actually seen?'

'I served on Ancreon Sextus and–'

'Yes, but how much?'

'Sir, I–'

'How much?' Gaunt snarled. 'Nothing? You haven't seen any real combat, have you? Not like this. Not in the thick of it?'

Faragut stared at Gaunt, so angry he was trembling slightly. 'How dare you question my courage, Gaunt.'

Gaunt took a step back. 'Holy Terra, I'm not. That's not what I'm doing. I'm questioning your humanity, Faragut. If this is new to you, tell me! I need to know. It's all right to be scared, but I need to know!'

Hadrian Faragut blinked. 'I... I've not yet... I mean...'

Gaunt took hold of Faragut's upper arm tightly and stared into his eyes. 'Faragut. Get down and get ready. Believe in yourself, and, for the sake of us all, believe in me. I'll keep you alive. Do you believe me?'

'Yes, sir.'

Gaunt slapped him on the upper arm and turned away, running. 'Larks?' he voxed. 'What's it doing?'

THE BEAST HAD been still for a good ten minutes. Dug down in the shuffling grass, it had grumbled its engines and kicked up the occasional spurt of noisy exhaust, as if clearing its throat.

Thunder stomped in the distance, and then a spear of lightning stabbed at a nearby hilltop for one brilliant second.

With an grinding whir, the main gun came up, and then the turret traversed, the raised gun chasing the source of the sudden sound. The turret almost turned back on itself before returning to face front.

The engine revved. Once, twice, three times.

'Feth on a stick,' Larkin whispered.

The yellow headlamps flicked on like eyes opening wide. The beast engaged drive and thundered forwards. It came out of its scrape like a hunting dog, and began to charge up the slope. Black smoke squirted out of its exhaust pipes as it made the surge.

'Here it comes,' Criid said to Gonry. 'You're about to get your range.'

The beast came up the hillside, driving a wake through the long, pink grass. It reached a wall, and the wall went over under its clattering treads.

'I would like to be somewhere else,' Brostin remarked, lighting another smoke.

'Relax,' Criid said. 'Gonry's got the bastard. Haven't you, Gon?'

Gonry hefted the tube up onto his shoulder and grinned at Criid.

The beast came on. The second stone wall collapsed beneath it, and a tree folded over as it was sideswiped by the machine's track guard.

'I think now might be a great time...' Larkin said.

'Almost,' said Gonry, aiming carefully. 'Ease!'

The enemy tank filled his sights. Gonry squeezed the trigger spoon.

Trailing a fat wake of white smoke, the rocket barked off from his launcher and missed the advancing tank entirely. It went off so wild, anyone would have thought Gonry was working for the enemy.

'What the feth was that?' Criid screamed.

'I'm sorry! I'm sorry!' Gonry exclaimed. 'I thought– I wanted– I–'

'Down!' Larkin snapped.

A banging, rattling noise cut the stormy air. The charging tank was firing its hard point cannon.

Gonry reached down for his satchel of rockets and his head vanished. Criid was facing him as it happened, and it seemed like one of Varl's conjuring tricks. A puff of red, and bang, no head. Gonry's headless body slowly fell away and hit the ground.

Something hard hit her in the mouth and also in the right cheek. Criid fell over. Larkin grabbed her and picked her up.

'Was I hit?' she slurred through split and bleeding lips.

'You're all right.' Larkin said. 'You'll live. Skull shrapnel.'

Pieces of Gonry's exploded skull had struck her. She shook her head, grateful that Larkin was holding her upright, and looked down at Gonry. A high-calibre shell had atomised his head and painted blood on everything in a five metre radius.

Dazed, unsteady, she bent down and dragged the tread fether off Gonry's corpse. The strap caught and Larkin had to help her.

'Load me,' she said.

'Tona–'

'Load me!'

Larkin ripped open the satchel and slammed a fresh rocket home in the back of the tube.

'Go!'

She swung it up onto her shoulder.

'Ease!' she yelled.

The beast was just ten metres away, thundering on. Caff had taught her all the tricks. Aim low, because the rocket will lift on its initial burst of propellant. Keep steady, because a tube doesn't aim like a rifle. Aim for seams, like the turret/body seam. Maximize that piercing shell head, and all the spalling you can get.

It was as if he was standing beside her, coaching her.

She fired.

The swishing rocket struck the top of the beast's turret, spun off and exploded in the air.

Criid suddenly forgave Gonry entirely. This wasn't half as easy as it seemed, or as Caffran made it look.

'Load me!'

'Feth, Tona!' Larkin replied. 'I want to be running. Bros has the right idea.'

Criid looked around. Brostin, tanks slung over his wide shoulders, was thumping up the hill into the hamlet.

'Just load me!' she said.

Larkin slotted another shell into the tube.

'Ease!'

Criid fired. A wide blossom of hot fire ripped across the beast's hull. It jerked to a halt. Flames rippled and flickered off its bodywork. A strange, mewling, sobbing sound came up from its engines. It began to roll backwards.

Then its main gun fired. The first shell it lobbed went right over Cayfer. The second hit the top of the mill and disintegrated it. The spinning vanes tore out of the structure and crashed down into the yard, turning and fragmenting as they rolled like a giant wheel into the outbuildings. The third round blew out the lower stages of the mill tower.

Wounded, hurt, the beast sat back and fired on the hamlet of Cayfer until it was reduced to smoking rubble.

* * *

X

IN THE DISTANCE behind them, in the failing daylight, the beast's gun was demolishing Cayfer. Gaunt's section scurried away through the grasslands towards the woods.

As they closed on their destination, they saw how scabby and thin the trees were. Poisons had stunted the wood. The Ghosts advanced, spread wide and moving slow, into a wasteland of parched, twisted trees and invader grass.

Behind them, a bright fire lit the encroaching night as the hamlet died.

The daylight was really fading when they reached the rendezvous point. They waited for an hour, and suddenly Mkoll rose, his gun aimed.

Two figures detached themselves from the enclosing darkness and came forward. They were thin, scrawny, dressed in rags, bearing las weapons strapped together with tape and cord.

'Gaunt,' Gaunt said. 'Daystar?'

The men stopped and stared at him. They lowered their rifles.

'My name is Dacre,' said one, extending his hand.

Gaunt took it. He could feel the bones. He could feel how thin it was.

'Gereon resists.'

'Just about,' said Dacre. 'Is this really it?'

'Yes,' said Gaunt.

Dacre nodded, and other figures emerged from the shadows. Some of them were Sleepwalkers.

Eszrah stepped forwards to greet them eagerly. They pulled back, reluctant.

'Unkynde,' announced one of them. Gaunt winced.

'Follow us,' Dacre said. 'There's something you have to see.'

In silence, the section followed Dacre for two hours through the dimming woodland. Behind them, thunder rumbled and the funeral pyre of Cayfer lit the sky.

They entered a dark tract of woodland. The trees there were especially bent and deformed. Dead leaves covered the dark ground.

'I was told you should see this,' Dacre said simply.

'Told by whom?' Gaunt asked.

Dacre didn't answer. He was pointing towards a cairn of rocks.

Gaunt stepped towards it. Mkoll was beside him.

The stones had been piled up in a makeshift manner, but the purpose was clear, even in the dying light. It was a tomb, a barrow for the fallen.

'Oh, great Throne above me,' Mkoll whispered.

He had seen the inscription. It was cut into a block in the middle of the heap.

'Feth,' Gaunt murmured as he read what Mkoll had seen.

The inscription was simple.

MkVenner.

GRINDER

I

'THE THING IS about nightmares,' Fourbox said, 'the thing is, is that they end. Sooner or later, eventually, they end. But this doesn't, you see? So I don't see how you can keep saying this is a nightmare, because it's nothing like a nightmare. When you wake up from a nightmare, the nightmare's over, and there's a whole rush of relief, but not here. There's no relief here. It's just non-stop.'

'Perhaps we haven't woken up yet,' said Lovely.

Fourbox seized on this. 'Now that's a good point!' he exclaimed. He was almost, as if this was possible, cheery. 'Maybe we haven't. Maybe the waking up is yet to happen.'

Dalin was pretty convinced he knew what was yet to happen. The river of meat was going to strike the

271

wall of iron for the third time in ten hours. Something would give. If the last two occasions were anything to go by, it would be the meat.

'Perhaps we haven't…' Fourbox said, significantly. War changed men, so it was said. It had changed Fourbox into a philosopher, just not a terribly good one. Dalin wanted to tell him, frankly, what an idiot he was, but his voice was wedged up inside him like a jammed round, unable to clear.

The thing about nightmares, in Dalin's opinion, was neither the unpleasantness nor the relief of waking, though both were component parts. The thing about nightmares for him were the tiny, little bits of surreal or mundane nonsense that laced through them and rendered the horror all the more horrible. He'd once had a nightmare where he and his sister were being chased by a chair that was going to eat them. He'd been very young at the time, and very scared of the chair and its shuffling legs. But what had made the nightmare truly terrifying was that, all the way through, Aleksa, a nice woman from the followers on the strength who looked after them sometimes, kept appearing, smiling, and asking, 'Have you tied your shoelaces?' She'd had a drowsy, fidgeting hen tucked under her right arm.

If his current situation could be properly called a nightmare, the elements were certainly in place. They were assaulting the giant bulwark in the company of hundreds of thousands of Guardsmen. They were moving forwards, under a sky of flame, under increasing fire, in a flood of bodies, across the bridges and up the trench approaches, towards the gates.

They were running, without cover, into death, with only the flimsy odds of their great numbers to protect them.

Fourbox, all the while, was having a conversation about whether or not the circumstances were like a nightmare.

On the first two assaults at the mighty bulwark, AT 137 hadn't even come close to the front of the charge. Carried along in the midst of the press, they had surged towards the gateways and then been drawn back by the tidal retreat. Many of the dead came back with them, held upright by the density of bodies, and only falling, hundreds of metres from where they had died, once the pressure eased and the spacing increased.

The great surge was building momentum to rush forwards for the third time. They were beginning to press together. A tangle of shouts rose from the moving troops and became one loud, commingled howl.

The whole scene was lit by flames. As they came out onto one of the great bridges, Dalin saw the thousands of faces around him tinged with gold, and down below them, another wide bridge crossing at a deeper level, streaming with golden faces. Other bridges stood to his left and right, heaving with moving troops. Far beneath, in the approach trenches, thousands more. Aircraft and lancing rockets swept in over his head, jewelled with light.

The bulwark wall rose up hundreds of metres above them. Its flamer towers were the main source of the blazing orange light, but the wall was dotted with gunloops and emplacements that were crackling with gunfire. It looked as if the giant wall was ablaze in a million places, but it was the fire that the wall was sending at them. Blue and white las bolts showered like sparks. Tracer fire wound and clung like climbing ivy. Shells airburst in flowers of smoke that trailed fingers of burning debris beneath them like the strings of jellyfish. The exhaust trails of rockets left arcs from ground to wall, or wall to ground, each lingering trace describing some aspiration of ascent, like the diagram of a proposed attack drawn in smoke. The great structure of the wall itself glowed amber, and looked as if its heavy battlements and bas-relief emblems had been plated in copper and bronze.

A nightmare was something you woke up from, but this was a horror he was waking up to. Every minute since the drop ship had launched had been a minute too long, every horror a horror too much, every effort an effort too far. This, this senseless mass effort to dash bodies against a solid wall, over and over again, exceeded everything.

He heard Sobile shouting, 'Forwards!'

Sobile said it as if it were obvious, as if there was no choice. Logic screamed that forwards was the last way they should be going.

II

SHOTS SEARED DOWN into their ranks almost vertically from high above. Teaser died. So did Bugears and Trask. Mumbles caught fire, became a screaming torch, and ignited the men around him in his thrashing despair. A Binar close beside Dalin had the top two-thirds of his head demolished, right down to the lower lip and jaw, and then stayed beside him, lolling back and forth, propped up by the crush around them. Ledderman died slowly, shot twice, unable to drop back. Boots, and then Frisky, both disappeared under foot. Corporal Traben was hit in the eye and died with smoke coming out of his half-open mouth.

The great gates were looming ahead, as heavy and immovable as a dwarf star. The front of the streaming charge was striking them, breaking around them like a wave against a quayside. Cascades of fire poured down from upper crenellations: wide, spattering torrents of burning promethium.

The Guardsmen were struggling uphill. They were stumbling and struggling up a ramp that was built out of corpses. Its steep slope, stacked against the gates by those that had come before and died already. It was so ridiculous, that Dalin wanted to scream and laugh. This was not the proud warfare his parents had raised him to admire and expect. This was nonsensical behaviour, quite without merit or point. Dalin felt a huge hatred for Sobile, in as much as Sobile embodied the insane Guard mindset that had brought them all to this astonishing futility. *Climb a mountain of bodies under heavy fire to a dead end.*

Why would we do that, sir?

Because the Emperor tells you to.

Dalin's foot slipped on a leg or an arm. He clawed at those jostling around him to stay upright, as they in turn clawed at him. Clothing tore. Bruises overlaid

bruises which overlaid bruises. Elbows and gun-
stocks and knees and helmet rims knocked into him.
There was a stink of fear-sweat, bile-breath, dirt and
offal, and ordure.

Because the Emperor tells you to.

Dalin wondered, in a moment of sacrilegious
epiphany, if he was the first Guardsman ever to wish
the God-Emperor dead. It wasn't Sobile he felt
hatred for, or the commanders, it was the lord above
all others that they served. He wanted to kill the
Emperor for this. He wanted to slay the God-
Emperor for driving humanity out across this
bloodstained galaxy.

It was a liberating thought. Pain and fear helped
him to slough off a lifetime of loyalty and condi-
tioning, and think the unthinkable. War had carried
him past the end of all that was rational and showed
him the empty imbecility of the stars.

Unless…

Dalin slipped, and rose again, and slipped once
more.

Unless…

Unless he'd been made to think that way by this
place. Perhaps it was no epiphany, but rather the
malign touch of the Ruinous Powers. He had been
steeped in Gereon's taint for some time. Perhaps he
had been led astray.

The idea made him gag in self-doubt and revul-
sion. Out loud – though no one could hear him over
the outrage of war – he begged and prayed to be for-
given. The pain and the anger of his ordeal had made
him wish harm on the God-Emperor, nothing more!

A moment's weakness, not a taint. Not a taint. Please, Golden Throne, not a taint!

He threw himself forwards, galvanised by some overriding impulse to purge himself and prove his loyalty.

'The Emperor protects! The Emperor protects!' Dalin yelled at the churning bodies packed in around him. The man beside him smiled, and seemed to agree, but the man beside him had no arms nor any back to his head.

Dalin turned, looking back across the faces, trying to see anyone from his unit. He glimpsed Fourbox, Ganiel, and Trenchfoot, although Trenchfoot was gone a second later in a flash of light. He saw Lovely and several others, further back, swept close to the side of the bridge.

'Come on! Forwards! Forwards!' he yelled.

A rocket or mortar bomb from the wall above hit the side of the bridge, shaking the entire structure. The limbs of some unfortunates caught directly in the blast flew through the air. A large section of the bridge's guard wall collapsed, taking part of the roadway with it. Dozens of Guardsmen fell into space, tumbling down amongst burning fragments of stone. Dalin saw some land on the bustling bridge below, or rebound brokenly off that bridge's rail and continue down into the abyss of the trench.

The pressure of bodies forced those on the outside off the side like a leak in a hose. Some tried to stop themselves falling by grabbing the troopers beside them. As the bridge crumbled further, groups of figures, clinging together, fell away, the first to fall dragging the last.

Dalin saw Lovely. She was screaming, reaching out to grab someone or something as she was dragged backwards by the frantic hands of those behind her.

He lost sight of her in the smoke, and never saw her again.

The press of the charge wrenched him forwards again, close into the killing zone of the gates where the flamers swept and washed, and the las bolts fell like torrential rain.

The world went white.

III

SOUND RETURNED FIRST. A voice was yelling above a background world of noise. Then light and colour came back to him too.

'Get up and get forwards! Get up and get forwards, dogs! You morons! Get up and fight on in the Emperor's name!'

Commissar Sobile was bellowing at the top of his lungs, his face flushed, his neck thick with veins, phlegm specking the corners of his mouth.

'Get up, you laggards! You wastrels! Fight on! Get up and repay the God-Emperor what you owe Him! Fight on!'

Dalin heard the lash crack. He got up, his head swimming, one of several men struggling to their feet from a smoking slope of dead and injured. He glanced around, unable to concentrate, unable to focus. What was different? What was–

They were inside the gate.

The immense bulk of the wall rose up over him, but the gates themselves had gone. What great force or accident had destroyed them, he had no idea. The impact had surely cast him down, and scattered his senses. The gates had fallen and, with them gone, the awful spoil heap of bodies that had built up against them had been released, and had gone tumbling and sliding forwards into the gatehouse like water from a broken dam, carrying the injured and unconscious alike with it. Dead men had borne him into the heart of K'ethdrac'att Shet Magir.

Storm parties of Guardsmen, most of them Krassian, were pouring in over the slumped heap of the dead. Dalin checked the load of his lasrifle and began to move ahead with them. Someone grabbed him by the arm.

'Fix your blade, scalp!' Kexie snarled at him, before releasing Dalin's arm and rushing on. 'Fix blades! Fix blades!'

Dalin drew his combat blade and attached it to the bayonet lug of his lasrifle. He ran forward with the rest. Visibility was hazy in the gatehouse, but greater radiance beckoned ahead of them.

They were running as they came out into the open. Some men were yelling unintelligible warcries. They burst from the smoky gloom onto a vast public square overlooked by threatening towers and skeletal steeples. The enemy awaited them in force.

Momentum carried him forwards, moving with the pack, but suddenly there were impacts all around: heavy, meaty thumps as men ran into obstacles. Bodies crashed into bodies as the charging Imperial line met with the surging rows of the enemy. Men tumbled and fell, slammed clean off their feet, crunched into the air by body-to-body blows. There were grunts and exhalations of effort, and grunts of pain. Shots fired, point blank, and, one by one, the men in the assaulting tide were halted by jarring collisions and crippling bodychecks. Shields and body-armour met. Bayonets jabbed and trench axes flashed. Dalin slammed into a figure in green, and punctured it with his bayonet, and the pressure of bodies behind him pushed him on. His bayonet tore free, and the enemy soldier disappeared underneath him. He was immediately into the next one.

More jarring impacts. Near to Dalin, a man was struck so hard that his helmet flew into the air. Sprays of arterial blood feathered across their faces. Dalin was shoved face to face with some feral thing with augmetics plugging its eyes and mouth. Yelling, he lunged with his blade, and fired for good measure. The thing fell backwards and then was knocked limply forwards into Dalin again by the swell of the mob. The Krassian beside him cried out as a bayonet slashed his arm guard. The man's own bayonet was lodged in the chest armour of the enemy soldier facing him, a diseased wretch in decaying black wargear. Dalin desperately hooked round with his own weapon, tearing out the enemy soldier's throat with the tip of his bayonet. The Krassian grinned at Dalin in gratitude. Ten seconds later, a bullet from somewhere had felled the Krassian with a solid *www-spakk!*

Dalin felt adrift in the stormy sea of bodies. Above their heads, out over the seething mass, banners and flags swayed and flourished. Las rounds zipped. Half

a kilometre away, one of the other huge gateways on
the bulwark trembled and blew out in a gargantuan
sheet of flame. From the raging fire, through the
breach, a titan strode forwards, its armour scorched
black by the fireball. A vast cheer went up from the
men.

The tide moved forwards with renewed vigour. The
resistance ahead gave way, and they advanced with
greater speed, free to move apart and spread out, free
to find breathing space. The flagstones underfoot
were cracked by weight and impact, and stained
brown with blood. Bodies lay everywhere, amongst a
litter of debris and pieces of equipment.

Dalin ran. He found an enemy trooper in his path,
a man with copper armour plates on his green cloth
battledress. Dalin charged into him, and they grap-
pled. Dalin swung the butt of his rifle up, brought
the man to his knees, and delivered the death stroke
with his bayonet.

Raising his weapon, he saw another man running
at him with a sword. He fired two shots from the hip,
and the man turned around as he fell, spun by
torque. Small explosions blew stones and grit into
the air nearby. He met another warrior face to face,
and they locked bayonets. The enemy, a grotesque
mutant beast with sunken features, screeched at him
as it struggled. Dalin couldn't wrest his blade free. A
passing bolter round blew out the warrior's midriff,
and Dalin tore clear.

As far as he could see, the Guard was engaging
hand-to-hand in furious skirmish fights right across
the city square. The enemy warriors they were

fighting were things he would spend the rest of his life trying to forget: bizarre things, some armoured and ugly and brutal, some strange and almost beautiful in their weird forms. Some seemed diseased, and so dependent upon their armour and augmetics that they were fused, flesh and metal, into one whole. Others were resplendent in bright wargear, flying banners from long spears on which the ignominy of Chaos was spelled out.

An entire catalogue of corruption, decay, mortification, mutation, mutilation and decoration was on display. The Archenemy faced mankind's assault armed with lasweapons, cleavers, autoguns, swords, talons and teeth. Dalin saw a man with a festoon of thin, barbed tentacles billowing from his open mouth. He saw a cyclops woman with a single jagged tooth curving down over her deformed lip. He saw bat-faced things, wailing and chirruping as they hacked with chain blades. He saw horned ogres, and men with the backwards legs of giant birds. He saw gleaming black flesh like sharkskin; bone fingernails worn on engraved metal hands; slitted eyes the colour of embers; grossly distended, encephalitic heads supported on sagging shoulders; cloaks of beaded, winking eyes; secondary faces blinking and mewling through gaps in garments and cloaks.

Shells landed with a woosh of fractured air and Dalin ducked instinctively. Heavy rounds fell across the square, hurling bodies off the ground in explosive swirls.

'Holy!'

Fourbox appeared. He had been drenched in blood and then dusted with fine stone powder.

'You're alive!' Fourbox cried, as if telling Dalin something he didn't know. 'We've got to move!' he cried, over the din. 'The armour's coming!'

The wide body of Guardsmen pouring into the square was parting and separating. Snorting plumes of smoke, Imperial tanks clattered forward from the sundered gates, firing their raised main weapons up into the towers and spires of the malevolent city. The first tanks were Leman Russes of the Rothberg division, puzzle-painted in beige and brown scales. Soot and dust jumped off their hulls every time they fired their main guns. Guardsmen ran along beside them, cheering and whooping at every tank round shot off.

The skirts of the city ahead were burning. Incendiary shells had created blistering firestorms that wrapped up the nearest towers and gutted their structures. The assaulting tanks moved out ahead of the expanding infantry line.

One tank rolled right past Fourbox and Dalin. They cheered as if it was a passing carnival float.

'Come on,' Dalin said, and they ran along behind it, joining others following the armour in. When its main gun fired, the sound was so loud and close that it made them all jump and then laugh. Dalin saw the mangled corpse of a commissar laying on the rubble. He wondered if it was Sobile. He hoped it was.

'Look!' he said to Fourbox. Nearby, the bodies of several Krassians lay around their fallen banner, a tattered aquila on a cross-spar square.

'Help me!' Dalin said, running towards it. Fourbox followed, along with two Krassian privates from the mob following the tank.

Together, they gathered the banner up and raised it. It took a moment to straighten the main flag and make it hang properly. Then they hustled it back to the file of men jogging after the tank. More cheers went up. The tank up ahead sounded its horn.

The smoke wafting in from the towers was getting thicker, draping across the square like a fog. Dalin suddenly spotted Merrt amongst the advancing lines.

'You made it!'

Merrt nodded and moved in to join them. His fight up from the gatehouse had been tough. The lasrifle he had ended up with, having swapped with Dalin, was poor: an unreliable old unit marked with a half-faded yellow Munitorum stencil on the butt. It had misfired twice, and each time that had almost got him killed. It was in poor condition, mechanically, and Merrt had a nasty feeling it was an old weapon recaptured from the enemy.

With Merrt were Amasec, Spader, Effort and Wash, four other members of AT 137. All of them were in a dirty, dishevelled state. Then Pinzer, the company pardoner, appeared. Dalin had assumed he'd been killed hours before. Pinzer held a laspistol in one hand and an open prayer book in the other, reading aloud as he walked along. The members of AT 137 cheered him as if he was a long lost relative. Pinzer looked up vaguely, but didn't seem to recognise them.

Wash spat on the ground and made the sign of the aquila. He'd seen something else. He nodded across the square.

Amid the advancing Guard ranks, Dalin could see gnarled dark figures coming forwards. Some were clad in stormcoats, and walked with the aid of long staffs. Others were bent, hunched forms in shackles who waddled along, linked to pairs of Commissariat guards by chain leads.

High Command had sent the sanctioned psykers forwards.

'Filthy bloody things,' Wash said, and spat again.

Dalin peered at the distant figures curiously. The daylight, admittedly sheened with smoke and dust, seemed especially murky around them, as if the air had been stained brown like the fingers of an old lho smoker. There was a slight flicker to the walking figures too, so they looked like an old pict recording, running slightly fast, with jerks and jumps on the file.

He felt his skin crawl, and imagined powerful, inhuman minds glaring at him, glaring at them all, and seeing inside them. He wondered how the psykers perceived the world. Were they looking into his mind? Where they seeing through his flesh to his weary bones? Did they even notice him?

Could they see into his head and read how scared he was of them?

He felt a touch, like light fingertips on his skin, and he jumped, and then reassured himself that it was his own imagination.

The sound of a fierce blow came out of the smoke ahead of them. The sound had been very loud, and expressed some considerable collision, like a wrecking ball striking a blast hatch. It was followed immediately by an impact that quaked the ground, and then by a long, drawn-out shrieking, scraping sound of metal on stone that grew louder.

A Leman Russ tank appeared out of the smoke. It was one of the Rothberg units, in beige and brown, part of the vanguard that had plunged ahead into the burning city.

It was half overturned, turret towards them and tracks away from them. The uppermost track section had been broken, and the loose tread segments trailed down like a lizard's loose scales. The hull armour on the raised flank was deeply dented, by some colossal force.

Sparks and scraping squeals came out from under it. On its side, the tank was sliding across the flagstones towards them.

IV

SEDATELY, ITS HULL still grinding on the ground, the tank slid past them and the Leman Russ they were following, and slowed to a halt. As it stopped, two heavy tread sections fell lumpenly onto the ground. There was almost a moment of silence.

'What in the name of hell could–' Fourbox started to say.

There was something in the smoke, something that had met the tank and struck it such a blow that it had knocked it over and sent it sliding across the square. The something was tall, the height of a two-storey hab, and it was barely moving. They could see it in the smoke, a grey shadow in the paler cloud. They saw it take a single, slow step. They heard a long, wet, rasping purr.

The advancing infantry lines had stopped. Banners flapping in the wind, they were staring at the bank of smoke and shadow inside it. The tanks had stopped too.

Another deep, wet purr came out of the smoke.

Along the line, officers and commissars were shouting orders and encouragement.

'Present your weapons! Firing ranks!'

'Hold order, hold order!

An officer that Dalin didn't know ran past them down the line. 'Steady guns! Two files!'

'What is it?' Wash murmured. 'What is it?'

The shadow moved again. It began to have a form. Dalin almost swallowed his tongue in terror as he gazed up at the two giant horns that topped the wedge-shaped skull. A vast cloven hoof clopped the flagstones as it took a step. There was a stench of burned sugar and volcanic gas, thunderstorms and shit.

'Daemon…' said the pardoner, looking up. 'D-daemon…'

Several men fainted. The Guard line broke and fled like a stampede of timid veldt grazers. Voices suddenly rose in a hubbub as men turned and scrambled for their lives. Banners fell, forgotten. Commissars yelled and threatened, and were knocked down. Hatches clanged open and tank crews leapt out, abandoning their vehicles in an effort to flee with the rest.

The daemon came for them. Though he stared, and was one of the last to run, Dalin didn't really see it. He glimpsed the tusk-like horns, the massive, quasi-humanoid shape, the back-jointed legs, and a mouth full of ragged teeth inside a mouth full of ragged teeth inside a gaping, fang-fringed maw. He glimpsed the round, black, glossy eyes.

He wanted to see the daemon. He wanted to steel himself and witness his greatest fear made flesh, and bear the sight and be stronger for it, or die. But the daemon possessed a quality beyond all those enumerated in the Ecclesiarchy's texts and warning sermons.

It was fast.

Its speed was as unnatural as all of its other ghastly aspects. It was not fast like a man or animal might be fast. When it moved, reality folded around it and allowed it to pass from place to place in an eye-blink. There was a sound like screaming, gale-force winds. Dozens of fleeing Guardsmen were suddenly hurled upwards into the air, as if thrown aside by a violent wake. The crew had only just abandoned the tank in front of Dalin when it flipped up sharply into the sky like a toy, turned over, and came crashing down thirty metres away with an impact that jarred Dalin off his feet.

He struggled onto his hands and knees. Dismembered dead lay everywhere. Bodies, stripped and flayed in a second of fury, sprawled in lakes of blood. Dalin screamed in helpless rage and terror. Wash sat on the ground near to him, hands in his lap, weeping and sobbing. Fourbox was still standing behind them, staring at the place where the tank had been. Pinzer wandered past. Dalin looked up at the pardoner. The man was gazing at the crumbling Imperial lines around them, at the great, horned blur of smoke and stinking air that ripped through them, casting bodies into the sky.

Pinzer looked away. He turned his back on the slaughter and sat down on the ground beside Dalin. His prayer book fell from his hand and landed on the gritty flagstones.

'There's no ham here,' he said quickly, his voice thin and perplexed. 'None at all. I checked. Bad eggs. You ran too fast for me to count. Preposition.'

'What?' asked Dalin.

Pinzer put his pistol in his mouth and pulled the trigger. His body flopped back from the waist onto the ground.

'Get up!'

Dalin turned. 'Get up!' Merrt told him. He looked at Wash. 'Get him on his feet.'

'We're all dead!' Wash moaned through his sobs.

A flicker of light caught the corner of Dalin's vision. It made his teeth itch, and he felt a nasty liquid pulse in his gut. He thought he was going to lose control of his bowels. Fourbox felt it too, and Merrt. The sensation made Wash, hard man Wash, squeal like a girl.

'What was that?' Fourbox complained, apparently unaware or unwilling to acknowledge the full extent of what was happening.

'The psyks,' growled Merrt. 'They've engaged the gn... gn... that fething thing.'

They could all feel it, like someone was squeezing their internal organs. Wash dry-heaved. Tears streamed down all their cheeks, unbidden. Dalin felt the mother of all headaches gnawing at him, and tasted the iron tang of blood in his mouth. All the cuts and gashes he had taken since landing spontaneously reopened.

Filthy yellow light spread out across the vast, disputed city square. The haze was like a rainstorm vapour, and obscured the bulwark and the distant skyline. Forking traceries of energy lit up the frothing darkness like veins. Some of the larger flagstones under their feet spontaneously cracked, as if exposed to cosmically low temperatures.

Merrt put a hand to the side of his head. 'Let's move,' he said. 'Let's move before it kills us.'

V

FOR TWO HOURS, some form of combat rolled around the darkened square. A foul mist, busy with flies, breathed into the side streets, and screams echoed from the noisome dark. There were strange, inexplicable crashes and thumps.

The streets nearby were burning. Some Guardsmen from the advancing line had fled forward into the ruins, and this had probably saved them, from the daemon and the telepathic conflict at least.

Dalin, Merrt, Fourbox and Wash fled that way. Two Krassians, one called Firik, the other Bonbort, ran with them. Firik had lost his left hand. He either didn't know how he'd lost it, or was too traumatised to remember. Merrt bound up the stump, and Firik sat alone, making little gagging sobs of pain every now and then.

They had taken shelter in the bombed-out shell of a building. Nearby, one of the grotesque city towers, a monstrous thing of spiked architecture and insectile buttresses, burned, long into the night.

They sat in silence in the flickering shadows, flinching at every howl or crash. They were too tired and numb to speak. Fourbox took out a ration pack, but his fingers were too stiff and trembling to tear it open. Merrt seemed content to sit and check his weapon, examining it carefully as if trying to correct some fault with the foresight.

Dalin sat still for as long as he could, knowing he needed the rest, but there was a ticking impatience inside him. They weren't out of this, and every step seemed, triumphantly and incredibly, to be worse than the last. He got up and paced the ruin, peering out of the broken windows. The street to one side was full of dead enemy vehicles that looked as if they had been burned out in one flash firestorm while in procession. White ash covered their hulls like snow.

'Eat something.'

He glanced around and saw Merrt. He shook his head.

'You need food,' Merrt said. 'It's a miracle any of us are still functioning after the last few hours. Lack of food's the last thing you're noticing right now, but you're gn… gn… gonna know it when the crash comes. Eat something and you might stay useful for a little while longer.'

Dalin took a ration pack out and picked at it. Merrt helped Fourbox to tear open his pack, and then gave the others the same advice.

Sucking reconstituted broth through a straw, Merrt rejoined Dalin.

'Worst thing you've ever seen, right?'

Dalin wondered which particular aspect of the last day Merrt was referring to. He simply nodded.

'Actually, there was a chair once,' Dalin said.

'What?'

'I had a nightmare when I was a kid,' Dalin said. 'Me and my sister were being chased by a chair that was going to eat us. Aleksa from the strength was there, with a chicken under her arm, asking me if I'd tied my bootlaces.'

Merrt raised his eyebrows. 'Why'd you tell me that?'

Dalin shrugged. 'Because I honestly can't think of a single fething subject for sane conversation just at the moment.'

'That's the truth,' Merrt agreed, and turned to look out at the ash-covered street. 'Probably symbolic,' he said.

'What?'

'Your dream.'

'How so?'

Merrt glanced back at Dalin. 'A chair? That's gn... gn... got to be a symbol, right? Of the Imperium. The Throne. No matter how hard you try to prolong it, sooner or later the Imperium's going to eat you and your sister up, like it eats everyone up. The Imperium gn... gn... gets us all in the end. It consumes us all.'

Dalin frowned. 'If you say so. What about Aleksa and the hen?'

'That part's the Imperium too. Feeding you and clothing you and looking out for you for as long as it can.'

'Does everything in your scheme of interpretation represent the Imperium?' Dalin asked.

'Usually,' said Merrt. 'The Imperium or sex. It makes it easier.'

'You have no idea what you're talking about, have you?' Dalin smiled.

'Not a single fething notion.'

They both ducked back from the window as someone, just a dark ragged shadow, ran up the street and vanished into the ruins at the top of the road.

'You know,' said Dalin., 'I can't believe I've spent my entire life wishing to be here.'

Merrt snorted.

'So, you going to tell me?' Dalin asked, looking around.

'What?'

'We know how I wound up here. I was so gakking desperate to be a Ghost. What about you? Don't give me some shit answer this time.'

'Because I was stupid, and desperate,' Merrt said quietly, 'because I had it all and it was taken from me and I wanted it back. Oh, and there was a girl involved.'

He turned to face Dalin. 'Look at me,' he said. 'Take a good luck. I was a gn... gn... good looking bastard once. Maybe not a stud like some, but I did all right. Plus, I had that eye on me! Marksman's lanyard. That was something. Then I got the wound.'

He looked away. 'Took my face off. Took my voice. Took my skill away. I got a shake in the hand I can't steady, and I just can't settle to aim with this jaw. I ended up at the bottom of life.'

Dalin wasn't sure what to say.

'A drink helped. No girl'd go near me, though. I worked out that if I could maybe get my hands on some cash, I could fix things. Not completely, you know, but make them better. Gn... gn... get a better prosthetic than this furnace box. Maybe a graft. On the hive worlds, they say you can buy a whole new you, if you've got the cash.'

'They do say that,' Dalin agreed.

'But where was I going to get cash? Earn it? No, sir. Steal it? I'm no crook. Only way I could think was to win it. So I started to play the tables.'

'Yeah?'

Merrt made a sound that Dalin realised was a laugh. 'Turned out I had the same sort of luck there. I've played the tables for years, lost much more than I've won. Sooner or later, that swallows you up.'

'What happened?'

'I got in over my head. Got caught in a fight. The commissar saved my life–'

'Gaunt?'

'No, I mean Hark. He saved my life, the merit of which is debatable. But I got a charge. Gambling, affray, disreputable conduct. Six weeks RIP. That's how I got here.'

Dalin nodded.

'Didn't you see where you were going?' he asked after a while.

'You see where we're gn... gn... going now?' Merrt asked.

'No.'

'But you know how bad it's going to be, don't you?'

Dalin nodded.

'And you can't stop it. That's how it was for me. Oh, and there was a gn... gn... girl.'

'A girl?'

'She worked in the gambling parlour I used. A place on the swelter decks. Her name was Sarat. Prettiest thing. Since I took the wound, I've looked at girls, of course, but she was the only one ever looked back at me. This face didn't scare her. She'd talk to me, and see how I was doing. We weren't together, you understand. She was just... I don't know, maybe she was doing her job. Pavver paid them to act nice to the gn... gn... punters. She seemed genuine. Got so I'd go there as much to see her as play cards. I started thinking I could make that big killing, raise the cash to get my face fixed up, and she'd–'

He shrugged. 'That's where I thought I was going. Somewhere where I'd have the guts to ask her to be mine, and she wouldn't laugh at my face.'

VI

A FEW HOURS later, night ended and day crept out.

They'd lost all track of time. Since the psyk-flare on the city square, their chrons had been dead or spinning wildly. They couldn't tell if it was real dawn, or just a change in the wind, clearing the smoke-cover that had been making the world nocturnal.

Dalin had been hoping for light. Wishing for light. Light would make things better.

It didn't. It just made things different.

The night, real or artificial, had been hard to bear. After the noises in the dark, there had been laughter, high and manic, that had come and gone like the wind in the eaves, and echoed out of empty stairwells and broken plumbing. More than once, they heard shuffling in the street and found no one there. No one visible.

Bonbort, one of the Krassians, ran off in the night. No one saw him go. No one knew why he ran.

The light, when it came, was white and flat. It made the sky over the city appear to hang low, like the ceiling of a theatre not yet dressed with a scene. The light was as thick and lazy as it was colourless. There was a fogginess to the visibility at street level. White dust and ash lay everywhere and, once a breeze had picked up, the dust began to mist the air like smoke.

Dalin and Merrt went outside. The war was still raging, because they could hear its roar, blunt and muffled, from all directions. Fat pillars of black smoke rose into the sky over the rooftops from parts of the inner city still ablaze.

There was a smell in the air of spun sugar.

They ate a little more and drank the last of their water. Firik, the other Krassian, was running a fever from the infections that had set into his amputation. There was nothing they could do to help him.

When they heard whistles blowing in the nearby streets, they gathered Firik with them and moved out. Within a few minutes, they had found a column of

Krassians moving up through the fire-blackened streets, collecting up the infantry remnants they encountered. The Krassians took Firik into their care. The officer could tell Dalin and the rest little of what was going on. They'd just been sent into the area to retake control.

The four of them trudged on through the ashy city. Sporadic gunfire coughed and chattered from nearby streets. They found a crashed Imperial Thunderbolt, its matted, crumbled fuselage embedded at the end of a long gouge in the ground. It had died with one wing raised to the sky, like a swimmer breaking the water with a stroking arm.

Then they found Hamir. They didn't know it was Hamir at first. They saw a lone figure in filthy battle-dress wandering along an empty street, looking up at the flakes of ash floating from the eaves like snowfall.

Wash raised his lasrifle at once, and so did Merrt, but Fourbox suddenly said, 'It's Scholam! Look, it's Scholam!'

Wash frowned. Dalin saw that Merrt was still ready to fire and knocked his gun muzzle aside. Merrt blinked and looked at him.

'What?'

'You nearly shot him!'

'I didn't. Gn. I...' Merrt looked down at the old rifle in his dirty hands, his brow furrowed.

Hamir heard them shout and stopped walking. He stared at them as they jogged to him. A dusting of white ash had settled on his shoulders and scalp like icing sugar.

'Hamir!' Dalin called as he came up to him.

Hamir smiled slightly, but acted dazed. He kept blinking as if he was having trouble focusing.

'Holy,' he said. 'Holy. There you are. Oh, that's good. Fourbox too.'

'How did you get here?' Merrt asked him.

Hamir sniffed and thought about it. He turned around, hesitated, and then turned back again. He put a grubby finger to his lips pensively.

'I don't– I don't remember. I don't remember which way–' Hamir glanced about again. 'The streets look the same. They all look the same.'

Dalin peered at Hamir. There was a crust of dried blood behind his right ear, below an ugly dent in the rim of his helmet. Hamir kept blinking. One of his pupils was a pinprick, the other dilated and black. Dalin wondered if he should take Hamir's helmet off. He decided he really didn't want to.

'Sobile sent me,' Hamir said suddenly.

'That bastard?' growled Wash.

'Sobile sent me,' Hamir repeated.

'Where is he?' asked Merrt.

'He'd gathered up some of the section. With the sergeant. He'd gathered up some of the section, what was left of the section, what he could find of the section–'

'Hamir? Where is he?' Dalin asked.

'Close by,' Hamir nodded. 'He told us to sweep the streets and see if we could find any other stragglers.'

'He sent you out?' Dalin asked.

'He sent me out to sweep the streets and–'

'He sent you out?' Dalin repeated. 'He didn't get you to a medicae or a corpsman?'

'We should try and find him,' Dalin said.

'Why?' Wash asked contemptuously.

'You got a better idea?' asked Merrt.

'Plenty,' Wash replied.

HOWEVER HE DIDN'T share any of them, and seemed content to fall into step as they started walking again. Dalin had hoped Hamir might be able to guide them, but it became clear he was following them.

Except, that was, for the many occasions when he stopped dead and looked up at the falling flakes of ash and soot as they descended silently.

'Hamir? Keep up.'

'Yed.'

'You all right?'

'Yed.'

He would start walking again obediently enough, but his words were becoming slurred, as if he had a blocked nose, or all his 'd's and 's's had become interposed. He remained standing in the middle of a street when a terrible, increasing rumble sent the rest of them scurrying for cover. The droning volume grew steadily, until they could feel the quiver of it.

'Scholam!' Fourbox hissed from cover. 'Scholam, get in here!'

There, in the middle of the road, Hamir stared up at the sky. He raised an arm and pointed.

Warplanes went over. They were the source of the deafening drone. Imperial warplanes, Marauder fighter-bombers. They were flying in mass formation at a height of about a thousand metres. Row upon row of their cruciform silhouettes passed overhead, chasing their shadows across the ash-whitened streets, darkening the sky like an immense travelling flock of slowly migrating wildfowl. The combined noise of their engines was so great, the men couldn't hear one another shout for the duration of the flypast.

It lasted ten minutes. Dalin couldn't even estimate the number of planes involved. The formation was heading north, coming in over the infamous bulwark and heading for the inner city, the central wards and high-hive of K'ethdrac'att Shet Magir. It was quite a spectacle, all in all, but during his brief yet intense career as a Guardsman, Dalin Criid had witnessed plenty more extraordinary sights.

They came out of cover while the warplanes were still roaring overhead and started walking again. Dalin took Hamir by the sleeve and led him along. Hamir was fascinated by the planes. He kept tripping because he was looking upwards instead of where he was going.

They started moving south, Merrt reasoning that direction was more likely to bring them into Imperial controlled zones, or at least some form of safety. Their boots sifted quietly through the deep, white dust.

They came along a particular street flanked on either side by blackened ruins. Half a dozen men appeared at the far end and turned their way.

'It's Sobile! It's Sobile and the others!' Hamir exclaimed, and started to run towards them, waving his hand and calling out.

It wasn't Sobile. The half-dozen men were big fellows, swathed in ochre clothing and black iron armour. They saw Hamir running towards them, calling cheerfully.

'Hamir! No, no! Hamir!' Dalin cried.

The enemy troopers opened fire.

VII

THEY FIRED QUICK bursts of lasfire. Hamir was still running towards them when they hit him. He crumbled and fell, face down, in the street, one waving arm still outstretched. His body looked especially forlorn, his blood splattered out across the white dust around him.

'Hamir!' Dalin cried. His voice was hoarse. He had unshipped his weapon. By his side, Merrt was taking aim.

The enemy was still firing. They began to advance too, apparently unfazed by the sight of four armed Guardsmen.

'Throne save us,' Fourbox yelped.

Each one of the enemy warriors was massive. Their upper bodies, shoulders and arms were thick with muscle, making them look slightly comical and top heavy. There was nothing comical about the speed or determination with which they were advancing. The bright yellow hue of their battledress contrasted, with an aposematic punch, against the gloss black of their body armour. Emblems of Ruin were welded to their chest plates, and long strings of beads and amulets rattled around them. Their heads were shaved and bare, and stained or dressed with a white pigment over which delicate black designs had been inscribed across the cranium and the brow. Their body armour rose up onto a broad neck guard which concealed their mouths behind a lip fashioned from black iron to resemble a cupping hand, as if they each had a hand placed over their mouths.

There had been enough briefings in the past year for even a no-gooder like Wash to know what they were. There was no doubt at all in Dalin's mind. These were Sons of Sek.

Las rounds zipped past the four Imperials. Dalin and Fourbox began to fire. Merrt cursed as his gun jammed again. 'Get to cover! Cover!' he boomed. Wash was already running.

The notorious Sons of Sek, the briefings said, were a fighting cadre raised by a local Archenemy warlord. They had started out as just a rumour, based on descriptions and warnings brought back from Gereon by Gaunt's team. Few Imperial forces had yet engaged them in the Sabbat Worlds, but they already possessed the same menacing reputation as the vicious Blood Pact.

Dalin wasn't sure if he'd managed to hit anything. He hadn't seen any of the hostiles go down, but the range had been good. He blamed himself. In his panic, he'd been snatching his shots. He, Merrt and Fourbox started to run, breaking off the dusty street through the ruins. Las shots struck the charred doorway and facade of the ruin behind them.

The interior was dark and jumbled with wreckage and charred objects. Everything was black with fire damage and there was no relief with which to judge distances. Merrt and Dalin both tripped and almost fell. They sprinted forwards, crunching over the debris. Wash was well ahead of them, a darting shadow between the heavy pillars.

The first of the Sons of Sek crashed into the building behind them, clawing in through window holes and sections of collapsed wall. They were moving fast too, clambering in and leaping down. Dalin could hear their guttural voices calling to one another. Renewed gunfire tore through the ruin, chasing their heels.

The three Imperial troops came out of the far side of the ruin onto another street where the remains of an iron portico stood. They'd lost sight of Wash. Two burned-out troop carriers sat on one side of the thoroughfare. A large part of the road was covered in rubble from a hab that had been flattened by a bunker-buster bomb. The running footsteps of the enemy came closer, through the ruin behind them. Several more shots whined past.

Lasrifle in hand, Dalin swung back to face the doorway they had emerged from.

'Go!' he said to Merrt and Fourbox. 'Go!'

GEREON RESISTS

I

THE STORM BLEW up into the night, and they struggled through it into the deep, dead woods.

The storm cured the sky a kind of dark, reptilian green, almost the colour of the world when seen through night scopes. The wind, which had turned the vanes of the mill at Cayfer, grew stronger, and lashed the stands of tall, mummified trees. The brittle branches swished and rattled like bone beads in a shaker. Dry leaf litter and dust swirled up from the soil.

The lightning chased them. White and thready, it sizzled in the sky, leaving brief, fragile traces like the filaments of light bulbs. There was no real thunder, just a pressure of air and a crackling, fizzling hiss of radiation.

Gaunt's section trudged along, wrapped in their camo-cloaks, following the resistance fighters into the strobing dark. It was hard going, but Dacre showed no inclination to stop and ride the storm out. Besides, any camp would have been swept away by the gale. They struggled on through blizzards of fossil leaves strewn by the wind.

The storm loaded their weapons and metal kit with static charge. Men jumped and baulked as guns tingled in their hands. Brostin spread a huge grin as he watched a crackling blue thread of electricity wander around the sooty muzzle of his flamer. He turned the torch in his hands slowly, watching the charge dance and jump, as if he was allowing a large insect to crawl around his weapon.

'Move up!' Criid scolded him.

Lambent curds of bright corposant lit distant trees, fuming and glowing, and making closer trees into skeletal silhouettes. The lightning also struck into the woods around them, and split ancient tree trunks like a forester's axe. Dry boles caught alight, husk branches burned. Sparks billowed up and were carried by the knifing wind.

At the tomb, two hours before, Dacre had refused to be drawn.

'Mkvenner? This is Mkvenner?' Gaunt had demanded. Dacre had shrugged.

'How did he die?' Mkoll had asked.

'I don't know. I didn't know him. He fought with the local cell and the Lectica cell. They thought highly of him. They said whoever came would want to see this, so I did as I was instructed and brought you here.'

'Who told you to?' Gaunt had asked Dacre.

'I'm not going to tell you that,' Dacre had replied. 'I don't even know who you are.'

'I'm Gaunt!'

'So you said. I don't know that.'

THEY'D BEEN TREKKING for three hours when the rains came. There was no warning, just a sudden assault of fast, fat raindrops. Within seconds, they were drenched. Within minutes, the deluge had killed off the dust and the skittering leaves. The thirsty earth became a quagmire. The white, dead trunks of the murdered woodland washed black.

The rain provoked the first emotional reaction they'd seen from Dacre and his men. The resistance fighters gazed up into the pelt, or took off their hats to bask in the streaming water.

'First rain this area's seen in two years,' Dacre said, brushing the running droplets off his face with a calloused hand.

Gaunt nodded. He knew it was the invasion that had triggered the storm. You didn't dump such a catastrophic amount of mass and energy into an atmosphere without the weather patterns flying apart. He remembered Balhaut, Fortis Binary and, most recently, Ancreon Sextus. It wasn't just the heat exchange of weapons use, it was ship drives in low orbit, gravity generators, overpressure and atmospheric insertions. This rainstorm in Lowensa Province was due, in part, to the null fields of capital ships squeezing the air over the ocean at Gereon's tropics, to the global warming of orbital barrage, to the rapid air displacement of a hundred thousand drop ships.

They squelched onwards, water pouring off their weatherproofs and capes. Dacre led them down the line of a valley, and then took them across a stream swollen by the sudden rain. They moved upland after that, to a crest, and then sharply down, into a wet hinterland of dead and partially fallen trees. The rain showed no sign of letting up. Cascades of flash-flood water boiled down the slopes around them.

They arrived at a platform made of dressed stone. It extended out into the bend of a suddenly fast-flowing river. There was no explanation for the platform except that it might have once been the foundation of a building no longer in existence.

Dacre bade them all sit down.

'What now?' Gaunt asked.

'We wait,' said Dacre.

Gaunt moved through the settling figures of his section and found Beltayn.

'Can you raise Cantible?' he asked.

Beltayn shook his head.

'Keep trying. Try and get a signal to Rawne that we're all right.'

'I will, sir.'

Gaunt sat down and drew his cloak around his throat against the fierce rain. It was cold and clammy.

He looked out across the platform, and the surging, dark river, at the trees. Rain seasons usually brought life back to woodland and forest, but here it was too late. This forest had perished and dried, and the rain was simply washing the corpse.

* * *

II

TIME BEGAN TO lose its meaning. Every wrist chron in the section started to misbehave during the night, all except, as Gaunt believed, his own: the battered, junk timepiece he'd brought through Gereon once already. It continued to tick steadily when everyone else's was stopping, or spinning their hands like the vanes of an air-mill in a gale.

The storm subsided in the slow hours before dawn. For a long time, in the enclosing dark, the only sounds were the gurgle of the swollen river and the *plick-plack* of water dripping from the dead trees. The sky became pale before sunrise, and the light turned grey and turgid. When true daylight came, it suddenly became darker. The sky was a lowering roof of gunmetal clouds, knotted like brain tissue.

A hand touched Gaunt's arm and he started, realising he had fallen asleep. He'd been dreaming. He'd been in a house at the lonely edge of some world. Tanith pipes had been playing. Tona Criid had come up to him from some dim hallway and punched his chest. Her face had been stained with tears. 'You're dead! You're dead! You're dead!' she wailed, beating at him. He'd tried to embrace her and calm her, but she'd pulled away.

There had been a repetitive clicking. Gaunt had looked around and seen Viktor Hark sitting by a window, racking the slide of a bolt pistol.

'Look, I'm sorry,' Hark had said, rising to his feet. 'I really am, but you're dead and I can't let this go on. You're killing my men with your ghosts.' Hark had raised the bolt pistol towards Gaunt's face and–

The hand touched his arm. He woke with a snap. It was Eszrah.

The Nihtgane was standing over him, his reynbow tucked under his arm. Gaunt noticed immediately that the weapon was loaded.

'Hwat seyathee?' he whispered.

'Gonn thesshaff,' Eszrah whispered.

Gaunt looked around and rose to his feet from his cross-legged stance. He reached for his weapon. Dacre and the resistance fighters had vanished. The Ghosts of his section sat hunched and slumbering on the platform around them.

'Feth!' Gaunt hissed.

'Seyathee feth?' Eszrah whispered back, sweeping the woods on the far side of the river with his reynbow.

'Yes I fething well do seyathee feth!' Gaunt spat. 'Oan?'

'Already awake,' Mkoll replied, materialising suddenly at Gaunt's elbow. 'Dacre's gone.'

'No, really?'

Mkoll gazed at Gaunt steadily to diffuse the colonel-commissar's anger and sarcasm.

'I was awake,' he said, 'although they didn't realise it. They were talking. I listened. They were worried about us. They don't trust us, and the storm overnight spooked them.'

'Why?'

'Oh, come on. You remember what it was like here. We mistrusted everything. They haven't seen rain in two years, so that freaked them out. The whole idea of liberation–'

'What about it?'

'Well, I don't think they believe in it. It's what they've been praying for. Now it's here...'

'Now it's here what?'

'It's too good to be true.' Mkoll looked up at Gaunt. 'That's what they were saying. Anyway, they left, about an hour ago.'

'Why didn't you wake me?'

'Because we've been under observation ever since.'

'We have?'

Mkoll nodded. 'Besides, you could use the sleep.'

'Who's watching us?' Gaunt asked.

'Dunno,' said Mkoll, 'but they're out there.' He nodded in the direction of the trees on the far bank of the swirling, peaty river. 'They're safe enough.'

'How can you tell?'

Mkoll shrugged. 'We're not dead yet.'

'Get everybody up,' Gaunt said.

Mkoll and Eszrah roused the section. They woke and stood up, groaning and bemused. Larkin roused so suddenly, his long-las fell on the ground with a clatter that echoed through the dripping glade.

'Sorry, sir,' he said. 'Bad dream.'

Gaunt smiled. He knew about such things. His own recent dream still hadn't left his memory. He was especially locked on the image of Tona Criid, thumping at him. She'd had a dream too, he remembered, on the transport just before they'd come in. She'd dreamed that he had died. Gaunt believed in the power of dreams. They'd spoken the truth to him more than once. He'd fobbed Tona off, but now it troubled him. On Gereon, last time out, she'd dreamed so accurately of Lucien Wilder, Throne bless his memory. She'd dreamed of Lucien Wilder long before she'd known any man of that name actually existed.

'What was your dream, Larks?' Gaunt asked.

'Cuu,' Larkin said. They both laughed, for although Cuu was a true nightmare, he was a nightmare long gone.

'Sir,' Mkoll whispered, touching Gaunt's arm.

Gaunt turned to look.

A skinny figure had emerged from the treeline on the far bank of the river, stumping forwards through the silt and mire. He was tall and scruffy, rake thin from malnourishment.

Gaunt knew him at once.

Gaunt hurried to the end of the platform and leapt down into the gurgling river with a splash. He waded across to the far side and came up the muddy shore to greet the man standing there.

'Gereon resists,' he said.

The skeletal man nodded. 'So it does, Ibram. Shit, it's good to see you.'

They embraced. Although drawn and haggard, there was no mistaking the man.

His name was Gerome Landerson.

III

'You CAME BACK,' said Landerson.

'I swore I would.'

'And you brought…' Landerson didn't finish the sentence. He made a nod with his head. He didn't mean the combat section on the platform behind

Gaunt. He meant the invasion forces rolling into Gereon half the world away.

'I swore that too. As well as I could.'

Landerson smiled. His skin was like old leather, and a poor diet had lost him several teeth. 'When I first met you, Ibram, you broke my heart. I thought I was going to meet salvation itself, and you told me you had just come to silence some rogue high brass.'

'I remember.'

'But you *were* salvation. Eventually. You've got them on the back foot.'

'It's only been a couple of days.'

'We have lines of information,' Landerson said. 'Two, maybe three main strongholds have fallen. The south is yours. Unholy fights are going on at Brovisia, Phatima, Zarcus, K'ethdrac, a dozen other zones. We know the Plenipotentiary fled the planet two hours before the first drop, presumably forewarned by pre-translation patterning. And the power's gone.'

'What?'

'In all the outlying regions. No wolves, no glyfs, no sorcelment barriers. It's like they've sucked every shred of power they have back into the main fights.'

Gaunt nodded. 'It's a start. But this isn't settled by a long way. Even given the military strength Crusade Command has unloaded on Gereon, we could be weeks, months from liberation. Maybe even longer. We don't know what the enemy has up its sleeve.'

'I understand.'

'I need you to know that. Even if the end is coming, there may be a lot more days of pain to come.'

'I understand, Ibram.'

'That's why we needed to broker proper contact with the resistance as quickly as possible, to speed the process.'

Landerson spread his hands. 'Well, here we are. I guess we should group up and start sharing data.'

'That'd be good.'

'Look,' Landerson said, 'I want you to know... I stand here in simple gratitude. What you've done for me. What you've done for my world. I–'

Gaunt held up a hand. 'Don't, Landerson. I know what you want to say, and I don't deserve it. I fought for Gereon while I was here, and I fought for it when I got back. I don't know what it was I said that made High Command decide to resource this liberation and commit to it. Maybe it had nothing to do with me at all. Maybe they just decided it was time.'

'I don't–'

'Whatever the reason, I'm glad it's happening and I believe it's a crime that it has taken so long to begin this effort. If anybody should be thanked for ensuring Gereon's survival, it's men like you.'

Gaunt's section crossed the river, and Landerson brought his own team of cell fighters out of the trees to meet them. They were all in as poor a state as Landerson himself. Gaunt actually knew three of the men from his time with the resistance, but he had difficulty recognising them.

Landerson and his men greeted Cirk, and Larkin, Brostin, Beltayn, Criid and Mkoll, who had all been members of that original mission team. Landerson had been resistance even back then, and had guided them loyally through the entire hunt for Sturm. Effectively stranded on Gereon after the mission's completion, Gaunt and his team had put all their efforts into building the resistance to wage an underground war against the forces of the Occupation. Together, they had taken risks and faced horrors that were difficult to frame into words. Gaunt was a career soldier, and had served on some of the bloodiest battlefields of the Crusade. In terms of personal danger, privation and extremity, none of them compared to his time in the resistance war for Gereon.

But they had made their mark. Under the leadership of Landerson and the Ghosts, the resistance had become a strong, supple thing that defied the occupying forces. They had built a pact with the partisans of the Untill, Eszrah's people, and learned to use both the Nihtganes' stealth talents and their impenetrable territories. Mkoll, Bonin and Mkvenner had schooled them in covert actions. Varl, Rawne and Criid had taught the resistance fighters, many of them civilians, how to live and operate as soldiers. Beltayn had engineered their communication network. Feygor had taught them the tricks of explosives, Brostin had taught them how to use fire, and Larkin had taught them how to shoot. Gaunt had instructed them in fluid principles of leadership. They had personally destroyed eighteen garrisons, seven power stations, thirty-six communication hubs, seven airfields and a large number of daemonic machineries, including several of the abominable jehgenesh. And the Plenipotentiary that Landerson had reported fleeing Gereon just prior to the invasion was not the same being who had held that office when Gaunt's mission team had first arrived. Assassination was not beyond them.

As they travelled together into the deep woodlands, under the grey sky, the Ghosts and the resistance fighters said little to one another. Both, for different reasons, were used to being silent.

Landerson walked with Gaunt.

'I'm sorry about all the precautions,' he said.

'You don't have to be sorry. I understand.'

'We have to be wary, even now. These last few months, the Archenemy's become more skilful at infiltration. Face changers. Mind swaps. Remote psychic control. We've had losses. Just last week they cremated an entire cell in Edrian, deep in the Untill. Eighty dead, most of them Nihtgane families.'

Gaunt shook his head.

'It happens that way,' said Landerson. 'But you remember Carook?'

'Carook the Butcher?'

'The very same.'

'Feth, the time we spent trying to sanction him. The ambush outside Phatima. The bombs in his palace.'

Landerson nodded. 'We got him. Last month. Finally. We got word he was going to observe worship at the ahenum in Fruslind, but an insider source, a palace servant, leaked he was going to stop en route and oversee some Son training at the Peshpal Garrison. Diggerson took a four-man team in three days before. Hid themselves behind the rostrum, and laid low for sixty hours. When Carook sat down to observe the display, they sprung him.'

'Clean kill?' Gaunt asked.

'We were low on firearms anyway, but Peshpal was warded, so nothing metal could be slipped in. Diggerson and his men tunnelled under the wire, naked. They were armed with slivers of glass. I don't believe it was a clean kill, Ibram. But it was a definite kill.'

'And a long time coming. I'd like to shake Diggerson by the hand.'

'So would I. None of them came back. Carook's life-ward slaughtered them.'

Gaunt didn't reply. Such was the desperate nature of resistance war. Missions, especially those aimed to assassinate high-ranking monsters, were regularly suicide.

'Diggerson was a good man,' Landerson said. 'He would have liked today. Anyway, I'm sorry we strung you along.'

'I understand.'

'We were observing you.'

'I know. Since Cayfer.'

'Since before that, my friend. The coded exchanges with Navy Intelligence seemed solid enough, but we had to be certain. The code said it was you that was coming, to establish contact, but it would say that, wouldn't it?'

'So you sent Dacre?'

'I sent Dacre, so I could look at you, and make sure you were on the level, and make sure you weren't being followed. You'll forgive me for being over careful.'

'Rawne will be sad to hear Diggerson's dead,' Gaunt said. 'They worked well together.'

'Rawne's here, is he?'

'Back at Cantible.'

Landerson nodded, as if this small fact made his world a better place. He asked after the others, Bonin and Varl and Feygor.

'Murt Feygor's the only one who hasn't come back with me. We lost him, on Ancreon Sextus.'

'I'm sorry to hear that,' said Landerson. 'He was a good man.'

'You know,' said Gaunt, 'he really wasn't. He and Rawne were black-hearted devils when I first met them. Gereon changed them both. I still take a pause to think that Rawne's a friend of mine now. My best friend, to be honest. Time was, we'd have happily killed one another. I still hate him and he still hates me, but the necessity of Gereon bound us tight. Feygor too. Not a model soldier, but after Gereon, I'd have sold my soul for him and vice versa. He died well, Landerson. He died in combat, at the front. He died like Diggerson did, selfless, heroic.'

'Murt Feygor?' Landerson laughed.

'I will count him amongst the heroes I've known,' said Gaunt. 'Thank the God-Emperor, I now don't have fingers enough. Now, you tell me about Ven.'

'Ven?'

'You had Dacre show me his tomb.'

Landerson nodded. They were slipping their way down a deep slope, surrounded by tall, dark trees and thickets of lichen brush. Gaunt didn't have to be told that they were entering the edges of the Untill.

'Ven was a giant,' Landerson said, reaching out to steady Gaunt as they slithered down the rain-mushed earth. 'I mean, peerless. We owe him as much as we owe the Nihtgane. Shit, it always seemed like he was a Nihtgane. I've never known a man move so quiet and kill so hard. Before you'd even left us, he was making a reputation for himself, you remember. The Archenemy wanted him. After you went, he came into his own. He wasn't shy. He knew that word-of-mouth was as important a weapon as blowing shit up. He started to–'

'To what?'

'Take credit. Spread the myth. Scare the enemy. He was supernatural, unkillable. A ghost in the woods. An avenging phantom. He became a figurehead for the resistance. Just like you told him to.'

'I did,' said Gaunt, remembering his final conversation with Mkvenner.

'Ven did you proud, Ibram. He did what you told him to do. He became a legend. Everything the resistance did was attributed to Ven. Sabotage, assassinations, bombings. He became their bogeyman. When they got him, it was our blackest day.'

'How did they get him?'

Landerson shook his head. 'It was one of those things. He was operating out of the deep Untill with a hand-picked team of Nihtgane. They called themselves the Nalsheen. That mean anything to you?'

Gaunt nodded.

'They'd done three raids in three days. A Sons garrison, a vox hub, and a provincial governor. I was in contact, via the network. I sent to Ven he'd done too much and that he should burrow down for a week or two. He responded he would, said he was taking the

Nalsheen west into the coastal Untill. I can only presume they were intercepted. A few days later, I got word that the Nalsheen had been slaughtered in an ambush by enemy killteams.'

'Confirmed?'

'Yes, confirmed. So we built the cairn.'

'You recovered his body?'

'No. We just built the cairn. That was the point. After Ven's death, we kept attributing kills to him, as if he couldn't die. That's why we built the tomb up in enemy territory, so they'd know about it. The man they'd finally killed was still hurting them. It was propaganda. They became more afraid of Ven dead than they had been when he was alive.'

'He would have appreciated that,' Gaunt said. 'The irony. The economy. The–'

He stopped short. They were advancing through a glade where the trees had been stripped of their branches and rendered into stakes. The rotting heads of Nihtgane sat transfixed on the tops of the spikes.

'What the feth is this?' Gaunt asked.

'This is the edge of the real Untill,' Landerson replied. 'This is the boundary the enemy makes. A warning... to us, to stay in, and to them, to stay out.'

Solemnly, respectfully, Gaunt walked past the first stake. 'You never thought to take them down?' he asked.

'Why? They'd only want to put up more.'

There was a sudden commotion in the file behind them. Ghosts and partisans alike raised their weapons. A figure appeared, stumbling through the ruined woodland.

It was Dacre. At some point since they'd last seen him, he'd lost his right arm. He was clutching the shattered splinters of the limb's bone and meat to his chest, his jacket soaked in blood.

'Feth!' Gaunt exclaimed.

'They were followed!' Dacre gasped, falling to his knees in front of Landerson. 'They were bloody well followed!'

Landerson looked sharply at Gaunt.

'We were clean when we came in,' Gaunt said firmly. 'By the God-Emperor, man, you watched us.'

'Dacre?'

'They brought something with them,' Dacre moaned. 'I swear to you. Despite all our efforts, they were followed. Nine of my men are dead. And I–'

He stared down at his shredded arm and fainted.

'Pick him up!' Landerson yelled.

From a distance away, through the trees, there came a snort of exhaust.

Gaunt knew what that meant.

The beast still had their scent.

IV

'CROPPER!' LANDERSON CALLED out to one of his men. 'Take the party forwards to Mothlamp. We're doubling back–'

'No,' said Gaunt firmly.

'I'm not arguing about this,' said Landerson.

'Good,' said Gaunt, 'neither am I. Take the main party on, and link Cirk and Mr Faragut with your people. Beltayn has unit command. I'll take the rest and double back.'

'But–'

'This is my problem. We led it in here.'

'Ibram, let the Nihtgane–'

'You got a rocket tube, Landerson? The partisans still packing kit like that?'

'No.'

'Then do as I tell you. The mission is more important than any of us. We'll deal with this and then swing back around. Post a watch to look for us and pick us up.'

Landerson looked at Gaunt for a moment, then saluted quickly.

Gaunt looked around. 'Short straws… Criid, Larkin, Mkoll, Posetine, Derin. Let's go!'

The selected Ghosts followed Gaunt back up the trackway. The soil was sticky and black from the overnight rain, and the grey sky above the perished trees was threatening a further downpour. By the time they had passed the grotesque markers of the staked skulls, the rest of the party had vanished behind them.

Except for Eszrah.

'Go with the others,' Gaunt told him.

Eszrah shook his head. Gaunt wanted to argue. Having a fluent native speaker with the contact party would be useful. But when Eszrah became so tight-lipped he didn't even use his own language, there was no point debating with him. Gaunt knew he'd been dismayed at his sour treatment by the other Nihtgane, though such behaviour was hardly unexpected. Eszrah had been cut free of his roots, and had gone to places further away than any Nihtgane had ever gone. It wasn't a matter of cruelty or prejudice, he was genuinely 'unkynde' to them now. But it left him stranded and disenfranchised, adrift between worlds. The only place left for him was the place his chieftain father had given him: standing at Gaunt's side.

They spread out, off the trail they had followed into the Untill, hoping to lure the beast around in a wide loop. There had been no further sign of it since Dacre's appearance. They travelled silently, following the lines of ridges and the cover of stands of trees. It began to rain again, a fine, heavy torrent that twinkled in the sidelong light. Pungent odours of mud, mould, and woodrot were reawakened by the sudden rain. The air scent was cold and clear, and organic.

At last they heard sounds. From far away, the splash and spatter of movement in wet mud, the grumble of an engine revving to cope with mire. In the enclosed box made by the rain, the sound suddenly travelled much further than before.

Gaunt ranged them out in a wide line. Criid carried the tube. Gaunt signalled Mkoll and Larkin forwards to sweep and locate.

They had crossed about three kilometres of woodland since separating from Landerson's party. The area they now slipped through was dense, dead forest that had been punctured in several places by artillery fire. They passed the charred wreck of a troop truck in one clearing. It had been there a long time, possibly since the original invasion. Further on lay the rusted shell of a light armoured car. Fallen tree trunks were rotting back into the mulch around the wrecks. Pieces of kit – buckles and buttons and the occasional gorget or helmet – showed up in the mud, all that remained of the bodies that had fallen in that place years before.

There was a signal tap on the micro-bead, and everybody got down. Gaunt waited a moment in a stillness where there was only the chirring of the drizzle. He heard a grumble up ahead, a wet purr. He smelled a hint of oil, a whiff of exhaust.

Larkin reappeared and ran back to Gaunt, head low, long las like a spear at his side. He dropped into cover beside the colonel-commissar.

'Other side of that mound,' he whispered. 'We caught sight of it, just for a moment. Fething thing is stalking us again.'

'Which way?'

Larkin pointed.

'Spot for Tona, Larks,' Gaunt said and signalled through the rain to Criid. Criid and Larkin immediately got up and took off, weaving in and out of the dead trees as they made their way up the slope, past the rusty chassis of another troop truck.

Criid ducked down behind some fallen logs just over the top of the slope. The rain was getting heavier. She could see down through a depression, thickly wooded, and into a clearing beyond. Larkin came up level with her, and she nodded. They took off again, heading down the slope and into the trees, slowing and crouching as they came through the black husks of ground vegetation.

Criid knelt down. Past the rot-black trunks of trees ahead, she saw into the clearing. The beast was partly masked by the woods behind it, a black shape against black shapes. She could just make it out through the rain, hull down, side on, as if it was waiting.

She glanced at Larkin. He had his scope raised, but the rain kept spattering the lens. He rubbed at it with a vizzy cloth and looked again. The view was poor, even with his optics. It was just a dark shape, but he could get a decent range for her. He had no wish to get any closer for a clearer look.

Thirty-two metres, he signed to Criid. She nodded, carefully loading one of the last two rockets into the tube.

The target wasn't moving. Through the streaming veil of rain, she lined up on its shadow through the cross hairs of the tube's aiming reticule.

Braced, she squeezed the trigger spoon. On a noisy streamer of smoke, the rocket arced across the clearing. It struck the tank in the side armour, detonated, and penetrated, flooding the interior of the hull with superhot gas.

Direct hit. Killing hit.

Even so, it was the worst mistake of her career.

V

CRIID AND LARKIN rose up out of cover, staring at the burning wreck.

'Good kill,' he murmured.

'Made a strange sound,' she said, taking a step forwards.

'What?'

'It made a strange sound, when it hit.' She was walking towards her kill across the clearing. The sound of the impact had been dull and hollow, like a gong, like a hammer on scrap metal. Rain streamed off her as she closed on the blazing machine. She could hear the rainfall hissing and spitting off flames and hot metal. Steam and white smoke pumped out across the black mud of the clearing.

The tank was dead. The tank had been dead for years.

In the poor light, she had killed a rusted ruin.

'Of feth–' she began. She turned, and started to run. She saw Larkin's face, wide eyed, mystified, wondering why she was breaking towards him so suddenly.

'Go! Larks, go!' she yelled.

The beast came through the trees to her left. The sudden howl of its raging engine shattered the rain-drenched quiet. Its treads were kicking up divots of mud and wet soil. The forward mantle of its hull shattered through the boles of the dead wood in its path. Entire trees folded and collapsed, ripping down through the relic canopy of the extinct forest. One crashed down across the beast itself, and fractured as it rolled off the moving armour. Another toppled away and fell into the burning wreck, where the lacy branches began to smoulder.

The beast left stumps, fallen timber and wood-debris in its wake. It hit some standing trunks so hard they disintegrated into flurries of rotten wood fibres. Bouncing, it thundered after the fleeing Criid. Larkin was finally running, plunging through the wet under-growth and rot.

'Move! Move!' he voxed, his voice high with panic and jarred by the violence of his motion. 'It's on us!'

Plumes of angry smoke snorted out of the beast's rear end as it clattered after Criid. It seemed intent on running her down, on crushing her into the forest floor. At some point since they had last seen it, it had lost one of its front lamps. Only one baleful yellow light shone from its hull. The other had been smashed and mangled, most likely by the rocket that Criid had smacked into it at Cayfer.

It moved like a half-blind thing. Did it know Criid was the one that had hurt it the night before? Was that why it was hunting her so intently?

She snapped right suddenly, turning faster than it could, leaping and sprinting into another break of trees.

Larkin was running parallel with her about fifty metres off. He could see the beast through the trees, and he could see her running, dodging between the decomposing trunks. Over the link, he heard the urgent voices of Gaunt and the rest of the squad, demanding information as they closed in.

'It's ignoring me!' he yelled. 'It just wants Criid!'

'Have we got a tank shell left?' Gaunt demanded, his voice close to incoherence over the micro-bead.

'One,' Larkin answered. 'But Criid's got it. She's got the tube too.'

Larkin slithered to a halt and looked down the slope. He could barely see Criid. She was bounding through the dense wood, moving away from him. The beast had come to a halt. She was putting some decent distance between herself and it.

The tank gun boomed. Larkin fell to the ground even though he knew the shell wasn't coming his

way. The beast had fired its turret weapon at zero ele-
vation. The tank round sliced through the woodland
like a giant bullet, leaving a trail of atomised
branches and pulverised boles behind it. It went off
against a heavy, ancient tree five metres to the left of
Criid. The blast smashed her off her feet. She went
rolling over and over in the black mire.

'Tona!' Larkin yelled. 'Keep running!'

He saw her get up, and head off to the left. She
seemed all right. She was running as fast as ever.

The beast fired again. Larkin glimpsed the hissing,
fibre-spraying track of the shell as it passed through
the trees. There was a big blast of impact, big enough
to tear down several small trees nearby. When the
flash died and the smoke began to melt away, Tona
Criid was gone.

'Oh no,' murmured Larkin. 'Oh no no no.' He took
a step forwards and began to slither back down the
slope towards the beast. He was filled with an urge to
do something, to obtain revenge, yet had no idea
what that might be. He raised his long las, aiming it
at the tank as he skidded down the muddy bank.

With a surge of engine revolutions and an acrid
belch of smoke, the beast began to roll again, and
turned to meet him.

VI

LARKIN SAW THE single yellow lamp swing round to
regard him. He stumbled backwards, lowering his
weapon for a moment. The beast came for him,
spraying black mud out on either side as it ham-
mered across the clearing. Larkin raised his long las

again and fired directly at it. The shot blew out the remaining lamp.

The beast shuddered to a halt, slewing around slightly. A high, strangled note rose from the thrashing engine, which sounded to Larkin like a gurgle of pain and rage. Had he blinded it, or was that just his imagination?

The beast lurched forwards once more, swinging the front of its hull from left to right. Its main gun came up above horizontal and the turret traversed back and forth. Larkin started to run.

The hard point cannon began to fire. Heavy gauge shots chopped the air behind the Tanith sniper. Dead vegetation was chewed up and disintegrated like mist. Larkin heard the shells smack into the mud behind him. He'd chosen to run back up the slope, and that was foolish.

Eszrah appeared from behind a tree trunk and dragged Larkin to the ground. Down low, they bellied through the leaf mould and dead branches. Eszrah put a finger to his lips so Larkin would be in no doubt. The beast came up the slope behind them, felling more decomposing timber. They crawled quickly between the trees, heading for the top of the rise.

They reached the ridge top about ten seconds in front of the lurching, squirming beast. With line of sight cover provided by the terrain, they both leapt up and started to run down the far bank towards the rusting troop truck.

They both felt the wet ground quiver beneath them as the beast reared up over the rise at their heels. It came at speed, angry, hungry. As soon as its huge bulk had flopped over the crest, its treads dug in and it slalomed down the muddy slope after them. Larkin and Eszrah had just passed the rotting truck when the beast fired its main gun at them.

Liquid mud fountained into the air in a gout like a hot spring. Larkin felt himself lifted into the air by the shockwave. He landed hard, with dazing force, and in the blurry moments that followed, registered a terrible pain in his left leg.

He tried to snap awake. He felt the rain hitting his face and the ooze squelching beneath him. The snorting of the approaching beast was in his ears.

'Eszrah?' he called out, hoarse and choked by fumes. The blast had thrown Eszrah four or five metres away into the treeline. Larkin could see the sleepwalker, sprawled unconscious in the dead bracken. Larkin tried to get up and run to him. He wanted to drag Eszrah into better cover.

He couldn't. Pain flared through his left foot and leg. Larkin struggled round to identify the source of the pain.

The blast that had knocked him flat and cast Eszrah across the glade had thrown the shell of the rusting truck too. The scabby metal bulk had rolled over and pinned Larkin's left foot beneath it.

He tried to pull free, but the weight of the wreck was far to great. All he got for his efforts was a sear of agony from his damaged foot. He began to scrabble feverishly.

The beast was thundering down on him, in a direct line that would bring the truck wreck, and Larkin himself, under its crushing tracks.

* * *

MKOLL COULD HEAR the beast's growling engine through the rain from the far side of the slope. He and Derin had cut around to the east as soon as Larkin's urgent call had reached them. Mkoll knew they had nothing to kill a tank with, unless the last rocket Criid had been carrying had survived.

'Look around!' he cried to Derin as they struggled through the brittle undergrowth. One of the tank rounds had punched clean through the dead trees, leaving kindling and rotting fibre strewn in a path. Mkoll located the half-cup of a shell hole bored into the black soil. He saw part of a Tanith issue sleeve hanging from a branch. A boot.

'Feth!' he cursed to himself. The tank had hit her so squarely, she–

'Chief!' Derin called.

Mkoll ran across to him. Derin was dragging back some of the black, tangled ground cover. He'd found Criid.

She was alive. Her battledress was torn, and burned in places, and she had suffered several deep gashes from zipping wood splinters. The force of the blast that had thrown her and left her unconscious in the undergrowth had torn one of her boots off and buckled her lasrifle.

Mkoll checked her throat for a pulse. 'Dress her wounds,' he told Derin. 'Stay with her and get her ready to move as soon as she comes round.'

'What are you doing?' Derin asked.

Mkoll was rummaging through the undergrowth for the fallen rocket tube and the remaining shell. He found the shell quickly, half-spilled from its torn satchel. Then he found the rocket tube. It was twisted and useless.

From up the ridge, the boom of a tank gun rolled.

LARKIN CRIED OUT as he dragged at his leg again. The pain from the crushed foot was immense, but it was eclipsed by his desperate desire to get clear. There weren't many ways Larkin fancied dying, but crushed under the treads of a predatory battle tank wasn't one of them.

His pinned foot wouldn't budge. He yowled again.

Running full tilt, Gaunt and Posetine slammed against the wreck beside him and immediately put their shoulders into moving it. The beast was almost on them, the roar of its engine quivering the air.

Gaunt grunted in effort. The truck wreck weighed several tonnes. They weren't even going to rock it far enough to yank Larkin free.

The old sniper was frantic. 'Don't let it crush me!' he stammered. 'Don't let it! Please, sir! Finish me quick! Finish me quick, I'm begging you! For the time we've served together, I'm begging you for this!'

Posetine's mud-spattered face was pale with fear. He glanced at the oncoming beast. 'Sir!'

'Please! Please!' Larkin was wailing.

'Oh feth,' Gaunt snarled. He wrenched out his power sword, activated it, and slashed down in a single stroke.

Larkin screamed. Gaunt and Posetine grabbed him under the armpits and hurled themselves towards the trees, dragging him between them. Not even a full second later, the beast went through, flattening the truck wreck like wet flakboard.

Gaunt and Posetine fell over into the wet undergrowth. Larkin had passed out. Gaunt scrambled
around, his power sword still ignited. He stripped the
remains of the boot and sock off Larkin's truncated
leg and quickly pressed the flat of the blade against
the stump to cauterise it. Larkin woke with a cry and
then passed out again.

'Oh shit,' said Posetine.

The beast had overshot them, but now it was coming about, ripping through the weeds and stringy
brambles.

'Carry him!' Gaunt said. Posetine nodded and
hoisted Larkin up in a shoulder lift. 'Go that way!
Into the trees!' Gaunt ordered. Posetine started to
run, hauling Larkin's loose body into the darkness of
the deep wood.

Gaunt ran to where Eszrah lay. The Nihtgane woke
as Gaunt dragged him up.

'Come on!' Gaunt hissed. They struggled a few
metres, and dropped into cover behind a pair of
fungus-caked trees.

The beast had turned. It stood its ground, its
engine throbbing. With an electric whine, the main
gun rose slightly, and then the turret traversed slowly
to the left with a dry squeal. It stopped, and traversed
slowly back to the right. Rainwater streamed back
down the raised gun.

Curled in cover, Eszrah looked around for his
reynbow, but he'd lost hold of it when the blast
overtook him. It was lying in the mud in the middle of the rain-dimpled clearing. Not far away
from it, beside the flattened truck chassis, was

Larkin's long-las, bent almost in half by the weight of grinding tracks.

Neither weapon would have done them any good anyway. The only chance they had lay with the power sword. Gaunt realised he had to kill the beast's engine the way he had tried to do on the moor land outside Cayfer.

Gaunt signed for Eszrah to stay put, and then began to crawl along the tree line. He was partly obscured by the truck wreck. The beast continued to sit where it was, rumbling and panting.

Gaunt had got about five metres. It was going to be a long, arduous crawl to get himself behind the thing. His left boot caught against something, a stone or a piece of bark, and made a slight sound.

The beast's turret tracked in his direction instantly and fired.

Gaunt dropped flat. He felt the air-burn and the shock of the round as it went over his position, heard it zip and punch and slice through the canopy. The round struck the exposed root-ball of a tree further up the slope and exploded. Debris pattered down in the fine rain.

The beast's gun tracked to and fro, edgy, wary. Its engine flared with revs and it jumped forwards a metre or two before it slammed to a halt again, rocking on its springs. The hissing rain steamed off its engine cover. Grey smoke lifted from the muzzle brake. It started forwards again violently, slewing slightly to its left, and then stopped once more, engine chuntering.

A small noise sounded off to its right, and the beast swung around, turret tracking, both sets of tracks driving in opposite directions to turn it around on its own body-length. The main gun swung slowly to cover the area of trees where the offending noise had come from.

Gaunt peered out. Eszrah was where Gaunt had left him, well hidden. He'd scooped some iron quarrels from his pouch, and was hurling them one by one into the trees behind the beast. It had already half-turned to face the sound. He was trying to make it turn right around.

Eszrah threw another dart. It thunked off a tree stump. With a snort of exhaust, the beast lurched around further, and swung its weapon. It fired. Water droplets jumped off its armour as the gun thumped. A large fireball burst through the trees on the far side of the clearing. Gaunt was already moving. He knew he wouldn't be able to reach the rear of the tank in one go, but he was sure he could get as far as the truck wreck, which now lay behind the beast.

He flopped into cover as the echo of the gun's blast rippled away. Eszrah threw another quarrel, but this time the beast did not respond to the lure. Slowly, it began to track its turret around to the left, gun raised, as if it was cocking its ear to listen to something behind it. Gaunt couldn't help anthropomorphising the machine's behaviour. It had behaved like a wild animal from the very start of their conflict. Blinded, it was hunting by sound, and by smell.

It had his scent. He was close to it, and it had his scent, or else it could hear him breathing, or simply feel his presence. Eszrah tried another dart, but it wasn't interested at all. Gaunt wondered if he had the time to break and run, or if it was simply toying with him, waiting for him to make a move.

He decided to try it. He tightened his grip on the power sword.

The beast's engine roared and it lurched backwards at speed to crush the truck wreck a second time.

VII

GAUNT THREW HIMSELF headlong to the side as the beast ploughed into his cover. Already mangled, the wrecked truck twisted and sheared under the tank's weight, the metal screeching and pinging as it deformed. Gaunt rolled, praying that he would have time to manoeuvre back behind the enemy vehicle before it swung at him again.

It was already moving. Slipping in the ooze, Gaunt tried to get a footing and dash in close beside it. He reignited his power sword and plunged forwards. The tank bellowed and wheeled around on him. He had to dive and roll again to avoid its swinging track guard.

There was a clang. Gaunt looked up. Mkoll was perched on top of the tank, right on top of the turret. Gaunt didn't know if the scout had dropped out of a tree or had run up the beast's back while it had been busy with him. Mkoll clung on tight, his left hand clamped to a hand rail. The last tank rocket was in his right hand. He tapped the side of the rocket two or three times against the top hatch cover, as if he was knocking on a door.

The beast halted sharply, rocking on its springs once more. Mkoll fought to cling on and rapped again. The turret traversed one way then the other, with increasing vigour, like a man trying to turn his head to see something pinned to his back. The main gun came up. The muzzle of the hard point weapon jerked around blindly like a mole clawing up from the ground.

Mkoll rapped with the shell again. The beast's top hatches were armoured and locked. There was no way in, but there was no way it could get him off its back without one of the crew coming outside. He rapped again, deliberately goading it.

Gaunt got up, circling, waiting for a chance to lunge closer. The beast lurched forwards, stopped sharply, and then did it again, braking so hard the second time, it almost threw Mkoll forwards and off the hull.

He held on.

The tank abruptly powered backwards, spraying up mud, throwing Mkoll's footing the other way. He kept his grip and knocked again.

As if demented, the beast braked, and then threw itself forwards, picking up speed. Gaunt ran out of its path. The sudden acceleration threw Mkoll onto his chest, but he looped his elbow around the hand rail.

He clung on as the tank left the clearing and tore into the woods, demolishing a path as it went. Twigs and boughs raked and clawed at Mkoll as he was carried along. It was trying to scrape him off its topside.

Gaunt and Eszrah ran after it, following the trail of splintered stumps and exploded logs into the dead forest. Black leaf matter and wood fibres swirled down in the rain around them.

Deep in the tract of dark trees, the beast slewed to the left and scraped its starboard side against the mass of a big, old tree, like a hound scraping its flank against a post. The tree, soft and corrupted, folded over and crashed down onto the tank. Mkoll saw it coming down at him, and let go of the hand rail. He rolled sideways off the turret and landed on the top of the engine compartment as the dead tree broke like brittle honeycomb across the tank's topside.

The beast took off again, dropping nose-first into a hollow that bounced the rear end up and bucked Mkoll into the air. He grabbed the edge of an armour plate as he landed, and barely avoided a tumble off the side.

The enemy tank was nose in, gouging up the far side of the hollow in a spattering sheet of mud. It lurched to the left to find a better path, and churned through the undergrowth ahead of it, taking down another lifeless tree. Mkoll clambered back up onto the rocking turret top, and rapped the side of the missile against the hatch.

The beast thumped to a violent halt, unable to shake off its tormentor. Gaunt came sprinting out of the trees behind it, Eszrah close at his heels. Gaunt didn't break stride, but simply leapt up onto the tail plates of the big machine, clambered from there onto the engine compartment, and ran on up the engine cover to the turret.

Without hesitation, Gaunt sliced the power sword around and cut through the armoured lock and hinges of the top hatch. Sparks, a billow of steam, and a stench of burning metal accompanied the blow. Beside him, Mkoll kicked the severed hatch away with the heel of his right foot, jerked the detonation tape out of the rocket, and lobbed it in through the open hatchway.

Neither of them ever saw what was inside the beast. They got a quick impression of a lurid, infernal gloom, and a smell like an abattoir.

They leapt off the beast into the air, side by side, arms outstretched as the fireball gutted the tank and rushed up out of the hatch to chase them.

VIII

THEY TREKKED BACK into the Untill to the north-east, past the defining, warding line of partisan skulls on stakes. Criid had recovered well enough to limp, but she was battered and dazed. Posetine and Derin supported Larkin, who faded in and out of shock and consciousness.

'I'm sorry,' Gaunt told him. 'It was the only way.'

Larkin muttered something, but he was too woozy on the field kit shots Posetine had stuck him with to be coherent.

The rain cleared, and then came back with driving force. The sky darkened like wet cloth. Behind them, a ragged trickle of black smoke marked the beast's grave in the deep forest.

About two hours after the brawl with the tank had ended, they were met by partisan scouts in a glade at the edges of the marsh. Nightfall was beginning to add to the storm's darkness.

Silently, the Nihtgane led them on, into the swamp groves, along tracks and trails between the root masses and the filthy water, into a darkness that was darkness no matter the time of day or the weather.

In there, in the true Untill, Gaunt at last saw some remnant of Gereon as he had known it. The Untill, that most inhospitable and treacherous part of the world was now the only part that showed any sign of life. There were insects, small animals, some fish and lizards. The trees, and matting frond plants and climbers, were alive. The moths fluttered. It did not look so green and fecund as he remembered it – it was greyer and paler, and life was less abundant – but the Ruinous Powers had not encroached enough to kill it yet.

They trudged on into the green darkness, clouds of moths trailing them like confetti at some great triumph. Birds called in the canopy, and amphibians croaked and splashed in the marsh ways.

Mkoll paused at one spot, listening.

'What?' Gaunt asked him.

Mkoll was staring into the twilight distance of the Untill glades beyond them. 'I could have sworn,' he began. 'Something familiar, like...' he shook his head. 'No, there's nothing there.'

SOME TIME LATER, THEY arrived at the partisan encampment that Landerson had chosen for the operation. It was a large place, partly a Nihtgane village, partly a prefab camp, populated by underground soldiers and partisans alike. All told, some sixty people lived in the huts and habitents raised in clusters around a small island in the middle of the swamp, its limits extended by platforms and walkways. The division between Nihtgane and Gereonite, already eroding in Gaunt's time on the planet, had vanished. This was simply the resistance.

Landerson had brought the rest of Gaunt's section to the camp. Faragut, it seemed, had already begun discussions about shared tactical data. Cirk was present, helping to smooth the conversation between the commissar and the wary underground.

Landerson greeted Gaunt's party.

'We'd almost given up on you,' Landerson said.

'I thought you'd have learned not to by now,' Gaunt replied. He helped Criid onto the camp platform, and then made way for the two men carrying Larkin.

'It wasn't easy,' Gaunt said. 'It would be good to get a medic for Larkin. Do you have a medic?'

'Of course they have a medic,' said a voice from further up the platform. Ana Curth pushed her way down to reach Larkin.

'Ana?' Gaunt blinked.

'What did this?' Curth asked, examining Larkin. She was dressed in rags and scraps like all of Landerson's people, and was so thin that he barely recognised her.

'My power sword,' Gaunt said, staring at her.

'What?'

'His leg was pinned.'

Curth glanced at him. Whatever else had changed in her, changed or faded or perished, the fierce look in the eyes had not.

'Throne, Ana–' he began, taking a step forwards.

'Talk to me later,' she snapped. 'I've got to patch him up. Criid too, by the look of it. Talk to me later when I've finished.'

She gestured, and Posetine and Derin hoisted Larkin up and carried him after her into the camp.

'Ana Curth…' Gaunt murmured. 'I always hoped she'd make it and always feared she wouldn't.'

'She was always tough,' said Mkoll. 'A Ghost after all.'

And looking more like a Ghost now than ever, Gaunt thought. He followed Landerson into the camp.

'This Faragut's keen,' Landerson remarked.

'Cut him some slack,' Gaunt said. 'He doesn't know any better. Where's Beltayn?'

Landerson glanced around. 'I told him you had caught up. I don't know where he's got to.'

'Over in the hut there, sir,' said Garond.

Gaunt hastened over to the dwelling that Garond had indicated. It was a makeshift comms room and repair shop for weapons. By the light of a small prom lamp, Gaunt saw cannibalised rifles and two or three battered vox sets. Beltayn had his own, customised voxcaster up on a bench and was studying it.

'Bel?'

'Sorry, sir. I was about to come and meet you when I noticed something.'

'Something?' Gaunt asked, joining him.

'Yes, sir. Something's awry. I've been trying to raise Cantible or Command on the vox, but the conditions are as bad as ever. My guess is it's because of the storms kicked off by the invasion.'

He was fiddling with the back plate of his vox unit, using a dirty screwdriver to prise off the cover of the enhanced aerial.

'What are you doing, Bel?' Gaunt asked, peering closer.

'Well, last time I tried the set, I noticed there was a slight power drain, as if I'd left the channel booster on, which I hadn't.'

'So?'

'So there's a little power light here, at the base, that wasn't on before. There's some kind of system hidden in my caster that I didn't know about, and it's been switched on for about the last hour or so.'

'Wait a minute,' said Gaunt. 'Are you talking about sabotage?'

'I don't think so,' Beltayn replied. 'I hope not,' he added with a grin, 'or poking around with this screwdriver is going to be a bad idea.'

The backplate came away, and Beltayn pulled out some acoustic padding. They both stared into the small cavity. The device was about the size of a tube-charge, with activation lights glowing around its top end.

'Throne!' Gaunt spat. He wrenched the device out of Beltayn's caster and carried it outside.

'What is this?' he yelled. Underground fighters and members of the section alike looked around at the raised voice.

'What the hell is this?' he yelled again.

'Gaunt?' Landerson said, coming over.

'What's the matter with you?' asked Faragut as he strode in across the boards.

'This is what's the matter with me,' Gaunt said, holding the device out.

'That's a locator,' said Mkoll. 'That's a damn locator. High power, pulse-beam beacon. Feth, it's on. How long has it been on?'

'Since I switched it on,' Faragut said.

'What the feth have you done?' Gaunt snarled at the younger commissar.

There was a sudden, glittering blue light around them, and it expanded to fill the entire glade. Many of the underground, especially the Nihtgane, cried out in alarm. Long shadows fell across the camp and the waters of the swamp, cast by the sudden radiance.

The flare of the mass teleport beam died away. Gaunt stared at the squads of armed personnel ringing the camp. They wore black and gold armour, and the symbol of the Inquisition.

'My job,' Faragut replied.

RIP

I

About half an hour after Caff spoke to him the second time, the Imperium loosed another deluge of wrath on Gereon.

It happened a long way away from Dalin, but he saw the flashes. Long-distance blinks of white light lit the sky, and he felt the hot wind pick up and brush his face a few moments later. A forest grew along the eastern horizon, a glade of giant, dark trees composed of smoke.

They had tall trunks and crowning caps of black vapour. They were evidently huge, because they were hundreds of kilometres away, and they stayed there for hours, unsmudged by the wind. Two other giant mushroom clouds elevated themselves in the far north-west.

Lost in the heart of K'ethdrac, he stumbled through the ash-white streets alone. The city skyline was smouldering, and to the south-east of him, several huge spires were burning up, consumed by extraordinarily ferocious fires that seemed to blaze with unnatural power. The silent, sentinel mushroom clouds formed a backdrop to these intense combustions.

Near at hand, the city was dry and still and empty, so caked in ash it looked like a town after a snowstorm. The bones of buildings rose above him like old, dry coral.

Dalin had killed the Sons of Sek. This thought alone contented him. He had killed three of them, single-handed. He had no idea what had happened to the rest of them.

He'd shot down the first two as they emerged from the building. They had been running, not expecting their quarry to turn and fight. He'd put three shots into each one, spilling them flat on the ground. The vaunted soldiers, the dreaded Sons, brought down so easily! Dalin felt elated. He felt as if he had passed some advanced test. Not only had he tasted battle and killed the enemy, he had killed the *best* of the enemy.

That was when Caff had spoken to him again. 'Watch yourself,' was all he had said. Immediately, Dalin got a picture in his head of the other Sons of Sek inside the ruin. He saw them hearing the shots outside, and coming to a halt. He imagined how they would sneak out of the building, now that they had been forewarned, and get the drop on him.

He stepped back into the cover of the old iron portico, and got down, panning his weapon around. Little zephyrs of ash were dancing through the rubble, conjured by the ragged wind. Shredded plasterwork flapped in the breeze. Dalin remembered his breathing and his visual checking.

Sly and well-trained, the third of the Sons of Sek emerged from a window-hole twenty metres along the face of the building from the doorway, and slipped down into the shadows and the rubble. Dalin watched him for a minute or two, admiring the man's noise discipline and use of cover. The Son was moving around to flank any shooter covering the doorway.

Dalin watched and waited. He waited until the Son of Sek had drawn in close and entered a very reliable range band. Then he shot him through the forehead.

The enemy warrior grunted and fell face down onto the rubble. Dalin waited a while longer, but nothing else stirred.

He withdrew. He moved silently for a while, but after the flashes of light announced the crop of mushroom clouds in the sky, he relaxed. There was no sign of anybody around. He'd given Merrt, Fourbox and Wash enough time to get clear of pursuit. They were long gone. He called out a few times, shouting their names across the rubble and demolished lots.

His voice echoed, but the echoes were the only answers he got.

* * *

II

HE WONDERED WHY it was Caff's voice he had heard.

Obviously, it wasn't really Caff's voice. Dalin understood that well enough, and though he was as superstitious as the next Guardsman, he didn't believe in phantom voices or clairaudience. It was all in his own mind, and he was content with that fact. He'd been through a sensory onslaught in the past days, and he was exhausted, and stretched to the edges of his nerves. His combat instincts were pulled as taut as they could go. In the thick of the moment, his own mind had sent him subconscious warnings, and he had heard them as if they'd been spoken by Caff.

It was no big deal – men went an awful lot madder than that on the battlefield – and it was no mystery.

What vaguely puzzled Dalin wasn't that he heard a voice, but that it happened to be Caffran's.

He sat down to rest for a while, and thought about it a little longer. The light over the city had gone an odd, glazed colour, and the wind was chasing clouds across the sky, so that a rapidly moving pattern of shade and light dappled the landscape.

Why had his imagination chosen Caffran's voice? Why not his ma's, or his real father's? Technically, they were both more important to him. Dalin wished he had some water to drink. His throat was dry and he had a headache. He tried sucking on a small piece of one of his last ration bricks, but it didn't help.

He decided that his relationship with Caff was a particular thing. He had a bond with Tona of course, as close a bond as a real mother and son, as close as the harsh life of the Guard permitted. He and his sibling had come into her care on Verghast years before. Chance had thrown them together. He'd always assumed she'd never had much choice in the matter. They were small children, Yoncy a babe in arms, in the middle of a hive war, and she'd taken care of them. Without her, or someone like her, they would have died.

She hadn't been that old, probably not much older than he was now. She'd simply coped.

Sitting there, in the ruins, under the racing sky, he realised, properly for the first time in his life, how selfless her decision had been. Fate had given them into her care, and she hadn't hesitated. She hadn't hesitated in the rubble of Vervunhive, and she hadn't hesitated since. Perhaps it hadn't been fate. Throne, he saw that now. Perhaps it had been the strange ministry of the God-Emperor. Watching the chasing clouds, he felt a strong, unbidden sensation of the divine, stronger than he'd ever known it in temple worship, or daily blessing, or even during one of old Zweil's sermons. For a few minutes in that desolate place, he had an oddly intense feeling that the God-Emperor was watching over him.

He wondered if Tona had ever resented the responsibility she'd been landed with at Vervunhive. Certainly, she'd become a proxy parent for him and his sister, because there was no other option. Necessity had manufactured their relationship. She'd looked after them as fiercely as a she-wolf protecting her young.

His father, his real father, was different. Gol Kolea had believed his children dead for a long time until chance had revealed the strange twist of fortune that had kept them close to him. Kolea had never tried to remake his relationship with Dalin or Yoncy. Tona had explained on several occasions that Kolea had decided it best, for the children's' sake, not to upset their lives any further by stepping back into them. Dalin had little patience for this excuse. It felt like Kolea was washing his hands of them. He didn't understand it, and he'd never approached Kolea directly about it, because it made him angry. It wasn't as if you could have too many parents, especially in an odd social structure like the regiment. Plenty of Ghosts had been surrogate fathers and uncles and mothers and aunts over the years – Varl, Domor, Larkin, Aleksa, Bonin, Curth. His real blood father taking a role wouldn't have fethed up anything worse than it was already fethed up.

But Caff… Caff had chosen, where Tona had been offered no choice, and Kolea had backed off. Caffran had chosen to be a father figure to Dalin. Caffran could have stepped back at any time, the way Kolea had stepped back, and, unlike Kolea, no one would have thought badly of him for it. For the last eight years or so, Caffran had raised him. Caffran had been there.

This was why it was Caff's voice he had heard, he decided. He had been the one who had chosen, without duress, to care.

Caffran said, 'Don't be a fool, Dal. It's not a big deal. I wanted to be with Tona. It's not a thing. In the

Guard, you just get on and you do it. You play it as it lays, that's what Varl says, am I right? If we don't look out for one another, what's the point?'

'Who's "we"?' Dalin asked.

'People,' said Caffran. His uniform was tightly pressed and funny looking, like he'd had an accident with the starch. He looked awkward, as if he was gussied up for dress review. He sat down beside Dalin in the dust and leant back against the wall.

'Clouds are fast,' he said.

'Really running by,' Dalin agreed. 'See how they paint the city. Like sunlight on running water.'

Caffran nodded.

'I'm thirsty,' Dalin said.

Caffran reached down and unhooked his water bottle. He passed it to Dalin.

The bottle felt light. Dalin unstoppered it. Something tugged at his right foot.

'Stop that,' Dalin said.

'What?' Caffran asked.

'Stop it with my foot.'

Caffran didn't answer. The water bottle was empty.

III

THE WATER BOTTLE was empty. It was his own water bottle. He let go of it and it fell off his chest.

The light had gone. The sky was petrochemical black. Cloaked by it, the half-seen sun glowed like a dirty lamp. His lips were dry and cracked, and his throat was like dry vizzy cloth.

He wondered how long he had been dead, and then realised he had only been asleep. He'd known little sleep since the drop, little of quality anyway. Just stopping for a moment, resting, it had stormed him and conquered him, like a drop ship invasion. He'd been unable to resist.

He wiped his parched mouth, but the back of his hand was as rough as sandpaper from the ash. His lips bled. He sucked at the hot moisture. He looked around in the darkness for Caffran, but there was no Caffran, and there never had been any Caffran. Fatigue hallucinations had segued into dreams.

He was alone. Even the presence of the God-Emperor had withdrawn. Something tugged at his right foot.

That was no hallucination.

The dogs were big things. Scrawny dark shapes in the enveloping night, they closed their jaws around his right boot and worried. They were vermin dogs, scavengers loose in the ruins.

'Get off. Get away,' he said.

They looked at him reproachfully and whined.

'Get away!' he snapped, reaching for his rifle.

'Looking for this?' a third dog asked. It was sitting close by him, his rifle clamped under its paws.

'Give me my gun,' he said.

The dogs laughed. They rolled him over and started to search his pockets.

HE FELT HANDS on him. He was face down in the ash dust.

'Nothing. Just some food,' a voice said.

'His flask's empty,' someone replied.

Dalin groaned and rolled over.

'Shit! He's alive!'

Dalin opened his eyes. Three dirt-caked Krassians bent over him. They'd been stripping his body. Night had fallen when he hadn't been paying attention. The black sky was rimmed with orange fires around the horizon.

'What are you doing?' Dalin mumbled, but the words came out as another groan.

'He's bloody alive!' one of the Krassians said, and pushed Dalin back down.

'Croak him then, for Throne's sake,' said another.

Dalin saw the first Krassian reach for a long sword bayonet and draw it.

'Imperial Guard!' Dalin cried in alarm.

'Yeah, yeah,' said the Krassian. 'Welcome to the bloody war.'

The sword bayonet stabbed down at him, and Dalin rolled. The blade almost missed him. He felt the slick, hot pain of it as it sliced through the meat of his left hip.

'Bastard!' he cried.

'Hold the little shit!' exclaimed the Krassian with the knife.

Dalin kicked the man's legs out from under him, and the Krassian fell with a curse. Dalin's right boot, half undone, flew off with the effort. The other two Krassians pounced on him.

'What are you doing? What are you doing to me?' Dalin wailed. They struck at him. He felt their knuckles batter at his ribcage. He rolled the way Caff had taught him when they practised hand-to-hand on the billet decks. He broke free from one, and planted his fist in the other man's face. The Krassian lurched backwards, blood and mucus spraying from his crunched nose. He set up a loud cursing.

Dalin sprang up. The Krassian with the sword bayonet came at him. Dalin dipped to one side, caught the man's wrist, and broke it. Taking hold of the long blade, he slid it across the man's throat in a single, unsentimental sweep. Arterial blood squirted out and covered one of the others in such quantities that the man began yowling and spitting in disgust.

Dalin dropped the twitching corpse and slammed the sword bayonet down between the shoulders of the gasping spitter. Impaled, the man fell on his face.

'You little bastard,' sputtered the one with the broken nose. He was standing again, and aiming his lasrifle at Dalin with shaking hands.

A las round hit him square in the back with such force that it cannoned his body into Dalin. Their heads struck hard with a crack, and they both went down.

Dazed, unable to move, Dalin watched as a fireteam of Sons of Sek approached out of the gloom to inspect the bodies.

The ochre clad figures moved slowly, stopping to check and examine each corpse in turn.

One of them got hold of Dalin's shoulder and rolled him. Dalin could smell the mysterious perfumes and oils that the Son had anointed his body with.

'A'vas shet voi shenj,' the Son said.

* * *

IV

'PLEASE, GET UP.'

Dalin played dead.

'Get up, Holy. Get up, get up, get up…'

It was Fourbox.

Dalin opened his eyes.

It was still dark, and the only illumination came from the burning towers in the distance.

'There you go! Come on, Holy!'

'Fourbox?'

'We were looking for you.'

'Fourbox?'

'Yes, wake up.'

Dalin sat upright. There was a stinging pain in his left hip, and he felt a damp warmth around the side of his fatigue breeches and the side of his body.

'He all right?' Merrt asked from nearby.

'He's fine. Aren't you, Holy?' Fourbox said.

'But the Sons of Sek…'

'No Sons of Sek around here,' said Fourbox. He helped Dalin up. Dalin felt more bruises and pains that seemed fresh.

'But…?' he said.

'We gn… gn… gn… got to move,' said Merrt.

'Where's my boot?' Dalin asked. He looked down. His right boot was missing.

'Here,' said Merrt, tossing it to him.

Dalin sat back down, wincing from the pain in his left hip, and started to lace his boot on.

'Hurry it up,' said Merrt.

Dalin stopped lacing. He slowly looked around and saw the three dead Krassians crumpled in the white dust around him.

'What the feth is–?' he began, pointing.

'Deserters. They were trying to loot your body,' said Merrt. 'You'd stiffed two of them by the time we arrived.'

'What… what time is it?'

Fourbox waggled his chron. 'Who knows?'

'He's blowing for us,' Wash said, looming into vision. Dalin could hear whistles in the distance.

'Who is?' he asked.

'Sobile,' said Merrt. 'We found Sobile. Now get your boot on.'

SOBILE WAS WAITING with AT 137 in a neighbouring street. There were about ten men left, all told, all of them wounded or scraped in some minor way. They looked like beggars, like lepers in some underhive commercia. Kexie, more stringy and raw than ever, was blowing his confounded whistle.

Sobile stood on his own away from the huddle of exhausted men. His clothes were dirty, and there were tear stains on his soot-caked face where the dust had made his eyes run. He looked like the tragic clown prince in the Imperial mystery plays. His face was utterly without expression. He slouched. He seemed bored, or dismissively weary. Most of the men had lash marks on their scalps or shoulders. The cord of Sobile's whip was caked in blood.

Sobile stared at Dalin as he rejoined the section with Merrt, Wash and Fourbox. There was not a hint of recognition. There wasn't even a spark to show that Sobile was pleased to see that another of his charges had survived.

'Get in line, you moron,' he said. It was as if Dalin had only been out of the commissar's sight for a few minutes. The whole world had ended around them, but Sobile was acting like they were on routine manoeuvres. He was acting like there were more important things on his mind.

He glared at Dalin, but Dalin made no effort to hurry. Sobile let the cord of the whip flop free into the dust on the ground, its length played out to crack. Dalin held Sobile's gaze as he got in line. He stared back, defiantly. He knew that if Sobile used his whip on him now, he would shoot Sobile. He was sure of this fact, and quite reconciled to it.

Sobile rewound his whip and looked away. Perhaps he had seen the look in Dalin's eyes. Perhaps it was a particular look that he always watched for. *When a trooper glares back so hard you know he will shoot you if you strike him, then the trooper is ready and needs no further beating.* Maybe that rule was somewhere in the odious fething book the Commissariat worked from. Watch for the look of a beaten dog, then refrain from punishment.

'Check your loads,' Kexie said, walking down the line. 'Anyone choking?'

One of the men raised a hand.

'Share him some clips, you others. Anyone thirsty?'

Dalin raised his hand.

'Share him a bottle.'

Brickmaker passed Dalin a half-empty canteen.

'Ech, fit and square,' sad Kexie. He turned to look at Sobile. 'Fit and square, commissar. Awaiting yours.'

Screwing the cap back on Brickmaker's canteen, Dalin braced himself for Sobile's next utterance. It was as wholly inevitable as it was insane.

'Forwards,' the commissar said.

UNKYNDE

I

'START YOUR EXPLANATION now,' Gaunt growled. He had shouldered his way past several Inquisition troopers to reach Faragut. The troopers, visored and quiet, were rounding everybody up, partisans and Ghosts alike.

'Nobody do anything provocative until I've got to the heart of this,' Gaunt had told Mkoll.

'Once you have, it'll be too late,' Mkoll replied. They had looked at one another, and both had known Mkoll's words to be an untruth. Despite the reputation of the Inquisition's soldiery, the Gereon partisans were never to be underestimated, even when disarmed and 'restrained'.

'Faragut!'

Faragut was talking to a couple of the senior Inquisition officers. Cirk was nearby. She was looking washed out and not a little taken aback. The sight of armoured Imperial troopers herding members of the resistance was a hard thing for someone like her to see.

She caught Gaunt's eye and shook her head.

'Faragut!'

Faragut turned. 'I'm too busy to deal with you now,' he said. Gaunt grabbed him by the lapels.

'No, you're not.'

'Get off me!' Faragut snorted. Inquisition troopers nearby had stepped back and were suddenly aiming their guns at Gaunt.

'Get off me, now!' said Faragut. Gaunt slowly released Faragut's jacket. 'It's all right,' Faragut said to the guards. 'Lower your weapons.'

'What the hell is this?' Gaunt asked, his voice a whisper.

'This is the business of the Inquisition,' replied Faragut, who clearly seemed to be enjoying the situation. He reached into his jacket pocket and pulled out an identity module. When he activated it, it displayed the rosette of the Inquisition. 'I have been seconded to ordo operation with the permission of Commissar-General Balshin.'

'Of course you have,' said Gaunt. 'That bitch tricked me. I'm a fool. I should have known she had a deeper agenda.'

Faragut clicked off his module and put it away. 'Gaunt, you are a regimental officer. In almost every respect, you're disposable. There's no reason at all that you should have been kept in the loop on this.

You didn't need to know, and you're not important enough to have an opinion.'

'My men were ordered to stage at Cantible, and then exploit our prior knowledge of the Untill and the resistance to establish a line of contact with the Gereon underground,' Gaunt said, 'so as to develop cooperation, and hasten the liberation effort. You've used us.'

'You're a soldier,' Faragut said, with a light, mocking laugh. 'What the hell did you expect, except that you were going to be used? You're such an idiot, Gaunt. You're far too liberal and highly principled for the Imperial Guard.'

Gaunt pulled back a little. 'I'll take that as a compliment. Now explain this. I will not stand by and watch these men and women manhandled like prisoners of war.'

'No, you'll not stand by. You'll stand down. Your job is done. Contact with the resistance is established. We'll take it from here. In fact, as soon as I've got clearance, you and your Ghosts can ship out back to Cantible.'

'No,' said Gaunt. 'You'll have to do better than that. I'm not going anywhere all the while it looks like I've sold these people out.'

Faragut smiled and leaned in close to Gaunt's face. 'You know, I used to quite admire you. High minded, strong, always with the right, brave turn of phrase ready to dish out for the benefit of the common dog-soldiers. But now I see it for what it is. It's just hot air, isn't it? What in the name of the Throne can you do about this? Have a tantrum?'

'He might kill you,' said a voice from behind them.

Gaunt and Faragut both looked around. Inquisitor Lornas Welt walked up the camp decking to join them.

'I thought you commissars were trained to read body language, Faragut?' Welt said. 'To know when to goad a man and when to refrain? Isn't that in your *Instrument of Order*?'

'Yes, lord,' said Faragut.

'I don't think you're reading Gaunt very well, Faragut. I think you were about twenty seconds away from a field execution. Wasn't he, Gaunt?'

'More like sixty. But, yes.'

'Hello, Gaunt,' said Welt. He smiled. 'Let's have a conversation.'

II

'LET'S BE CLEAR about this,' said Welt. 'Let's be clear so there is no misunderstanding. The Inquisition can be very heavy handed. The Inquisition *will* be very heavy handed. Here, in the next few weeks, the agents of the ordos will not be gentle. Which is unfortunate, because these brave people deserve better. However, don't expect me to apologise, and don't expect me to order restraint. What we are engaged in here is vital work. It's potentially the most important thing I've undertaken in my career.'

Gaunt blinked. 'What?' he replied.

'I'm not joking, Gaunt,' Welt said.

They had withdrawn to one of the upper habitat platforms, suspended in the tree canopy over the green waters. Down below, Welt's soldiers were securing the camp and watching over the bewildered partisans. Troopers with flamers were moving out into the swamp to fell trees and clear the canopy wide enough to form a landing zone.

'Why do you think the Crusade moved on Gereon, Gaunt?' Welt asked.

'Because the Second Front needed to start winning back territory to bolster its legitimacy. Because we could not suffer to have the Archenemy bedded in amongst us. Because individuals like Cirk and me have been petitioning for a liberation effort since we returned.'

'All valid reasons,' said Welt. He was a short, broad man with receding grey hair and a black goatee beard on his boxer's jaw. The pupils of his eyes were so large, the blue of the iris filled his lids to the edges, showing no white. He wore a brown leather storm coat, and the rosette of his office was strung across his breast on a pectoral. Like all the inquisitors Ibram Gaunt had ever known, Welt was frustratingly ambiguous. Commanding, authoritative, appealing in his great intelligence and polymath learning, yet treacherous and untrustworthy in that nothing was too precious to be sacrificed if it served his ends. Lilith had been like that. So had Heldane.

'But?' asked Gaunt, weighting the word.

'There is one other, better reason. The most compelling reason of all.'

'Which is?'

'You, Gaunt. You are the reason. The fact that you came back.'

Gaunt shook his head in disbelief and turned away. He walked to the edge of the platform and leant on the rope rail, staring down. The first time he'd ever been up on a camp platform like this, he'd been fighting for his life against the monster Uexkull. This conversation seemed somehow far darker and more dangerous.

'You still obsess with this?' Gaunt asked. 'I thought we'd laid it to rest. The tribunal–'

'Was just a formality.' Welt walked over to join him. He had a habit of looking people in the eye and not wavering. 'You and your mission team came here, to an enemy occupied world, and were here for sixteen times the recommended length of exposure. You were changed, of course. Such an ordeal would change anyone. But you were not tainted. You came away uncorrupted. This is a remarkable thing, Ibram. A remarkable thing.'

'So you have told me, inquisitor. I supposed I might have been dissected by now.'

Welt smiled. 'This isn't the Dark Ages,' he said.

'Oh,' said Gaunt, 'I rather think it is.'

'Your own theory was that you had survived corruption because you had been blessed by the beati herself,' said Welt. 'As theories go, it's reasonable. And not without precedent, historically. But there are other ways of looking at it. Ways that my colleagues and savants believe may repay examination.'

'You mean that this place is the reason?' asked Gaunt. 'That this place has some property that counters the touch of Chaos?'

The inquisitor nodded. 'Gereon... and, most specifically, the famously impenetrable Untill. You've spoken to me of this, and I've read your reports carefully. Cirk has also divulged a great deal. In the case of every single one of you, and especially in the case of Trooper Feygor, organic extracts derived from the Untill's singular, toxic biology appeared to combat the effects of taint.'

'Feygor died on Ancreon Sextus,' said Gaunt.

'I know. And his body was not recovered. If anyone should have been dissected, it was him. Alas, we never got the chance.'

'Are you saying the Imperial Guard and allied Crusade forces... millions of men and vast quantities of material... have been committed to the invasion of Gereon... because Murt Feygor died in battle?'

'That's an over-simplification.'

Gaunt laughed. 'Murt would have loved that. Say what you like about him, he appreciated good irony even if he couldn't voice it.'

He looked back at Welt. 'So you haven't come back for Gereon? You've done all this on the long shot that the Untill might be hiding something?'

'If the Untill has what we're after, it will change the course of history. It will change the destiny of the Imperium and mankind. It will liberate us from our greatest enemy.'

'A cure for Chaos?'

'Too trite. But yes. I suppose that's how it will be seen.'

'There's no such thing here,' said Gaunt. 'I could have saved you a great deal of effort. It's not here. It never has been. The Nihtgane may know of some extracts with strong medicinal properties, but not the miracle you're looking for. Mkvenner, one of my original team, had a notion. He reckoned Chaos didn't destroy us. It didn't taint and infect like a disease. It didn't work like that at all, which is why there could be no cure.'

'He believed in force of will, I presume,' said Welt.

'Precisely. Chaos isn't evil. It simply unlocks and lets out our propensities for evil and desecration. That is why it is so pernicious. It brings out our flaws. Force of will, determination, loyalty... these are the qualities that combat Chaos taint. If a man can remain true to the Throne, Chaos can't touch him. A hatred and rejection of Chaos becomes a weapon against it.'

'The armour of contempt,' said Welt. 'I am familiar with Inquisitor Ravenor's writings. The idea was not original to him.'

He stepped back from the rope rail. 'You may be right. It is an enobling notion. We might save mankind by strength of character, rather than by an extracted tincture of moth venom. History will like the former better.'

He looked back at Gaunt. 'But you'll forgive me for testing the moth venom.'

III

'IT WAS A cellar,' Caffran told Rawne. 'Under the habs over that way. Street eighteen, I think.'

Leclan nodded as he took a swig from his canteen. 'Street eighteen.'

'I went in first, Leclan behind me,' Caffran continued. 'Black as pitch. I could smell something.'

'I said there was something,' Leclan put in.

'He said there was. I could smell it. I was pretty sure we'd run another excubitor to ground. I was all for lobbing a tube-charge in and sorting the bodies after.'

'You said that. You did,' Leclan agreed.

'But, you know, orders,' Caffran said. He scratched his chin and squinted up at the sun.

'Go on,' said Rawne.

'I almost shot him,' said Caffran. 'I had a lamp on, sweeping, and I saw movement. I just reacted. I almost put a las bolt through his head.'

'But you didn't,' said Rawne.

'I almost did. His face. He was so fething scared.' Caffran nodded across the ruined street to a nearby aid station. Under the close scrutiny of Inquisition troopers, Dorden and his corpsmen were treating the latest batch of emaciated civilians that the sweeps had flushed out of Cantible's hidden corners. The head count, according to Hark's tally, was now five hundred and fifty-eight survivors, all of them in a terrible condition. Dorden was treating a child, a boy of about ten standard, whose shrunken frame looked more like that of a five year old. The child was dazed, bewildered, in shock. That much was obvious, even from across the street.

'I don't know how long he'd been down there,' said Caffran. 'But he was too scared to come out.'

'This is happening a lot,' said Baskevyl. 'The survivors have been living in terror for too long. Most of them have been reduced to the level of animals. We're just men with guns, Rawne. They're too messed up to realise we've come to save them.'

'We have to finish the sweeps. We have to clear the entire town,' said Rawne.

'I know,' said Baskevyl.

'There's no other way.'

'I know,' Baskevyl nodded. 'But nobody wants to be the first to shoot one of these poor wretches by mistake.'

'Those fellows aren't helping much,' said Zweil. They all looked around. The old ayatani had squatted down nearby, resting his feet. He indicated the agents of the Inquisition nearby. 'We promise them they're safe, and we bring them out of hiding, and then those fellows take over.'

Some of the Inquisition soldiers were leading a troop of liberated souls away down the street towards the pens that had been erected in the town's main square. Under the direction of Interrogator Sydona, the agent in charge of the Inquisitorial forces that had arrived the day before, Cantible was being turned into a processing camp for the dispossessed. Sydona had made it clear to Rawne that the Ghosts were expected to act as security for the camp, and several sections had been seconded to help raise the wooden palisade fences of the pens. Sydona had also made it clear that Cantible would be expecting a further influx of survivors from the outlying districts over the coming weeks.

Rawne didn't like it much, and he knew none of the Ghosts did either. They were picking their way through the most miserable waste of a town, seeing small horrors everywhere they looked. The few people they found were dragged off for interrogation and internment. Rawne understood it had to be this way. No one who had lived on Gereon through the Occupation could be trusted. They had to be processed, and examined for taint or corruption. Many were likely to be executed. Quite properly, the Inquisition would take no chances whatsoever with taint. But it made the Ghosts feel as if they were staffing a concentration camp for Imperial citizens. It made Rawne wonder why they'd ever bothered with a liberation effort if this was all they could offer the people of Gereon.

'I'll speak to Sydona,' Rawne said. 'But I think this is how it's going to be. This is Imperial policy, and even if we did suddenly find ourselves in a topsy turvy world where the Inquisition listened to the opinion of the Imperial Guard, I'm not sure they're not right anyway. The Archenemy has held this place for too long. What was it Gaunt said? There's nothing left to save.'

'I don't think that attitude does much for morale,' said Baskevyl.

'Feth take morale,' snapped Rawne. 'I'd give most of all I have to help Gereon. This last year or so, I've dreamed of coming back and bringing the relief they begged us for. Now, I wish we'd never come.'

'Because they're not flocking out of their houses and cheering us, and crowning us with victory garlands for liberating them?' Zweil asked.

Rawne's face darkened. 'Because this is no more than a death bed vigil.' He strode away to find the interrogator. A couple of minutes later, the noise of a small explosion – a grenade or a tube-charge – rolled in from a neighbouring street, and Baskevyl set off to investigate.

Caffran remained where he was, staring across the street at the boy he'd almost shot.

'He's about the age Dalin was,' Caffran said.

'What?' asked Zweil.

'That boy. He's about the age Dalin was when Tona found him and Yoncy in the ruins of the hive. And I found all three of them a few days later. They were feral. Scared. Hiding. Just like him. I could have shot them by mistake. Like I nearly shot him.'

Zweil had been fiddling with his ill-fitting boots. He stood up, leaning on Leclan for support. 'Are you due off on another sweep?' he asked.

'Streets twenty-six and twenty-seven,' said Leclan. 'Another ten minutes, once the section has rested.'

'I'm coming with you,' Zweil said.

'I don't think so,' said Caffran.

'Well, I am. If you're just men with guns to them, maybe having a priest with you will help. I'd like to believe I can help diffuse their fears. Maybe coax them out of hiding a little less traumatically.'

'Father, there are still things hiding in this place,' said Leclan.

'So?'

'So you'll be in the line of fire,' said Caffran.

'And about time too,' Zweil replied. 'Do you know how old I am, Dermon Caffran?'

'No, father.'

'Neither do I. But it's high time I did something more useful than catalogue plants.'

Caffran and Leclan exchanged wide-eyed glances.

'This is why I came along,' Zweil said. 'To do real good. It's been a long time since I did any real good.'

'Whatever you like, father,' said Caffran. 'In truth, I could use the help. But if you get yourself killed, don't be blaming me.'

'I wouldn't dream of it,' Zweil grinned. 'If I'm killed, I'll just take the matter up with a higher authority.'

'JUST DO YOUR job, major,' said Interrogator Sydona. He was a tall, slender man in red and black garments, robed like royalty. He had a thin face and a thinner mouth.

'I assumed you'd say that,' Rawne replied, 'but for the sake of my own conscience, I had to ask.'

Sydona shrugged. 'I commiserate, major. Sometimes our holy duty is painful and ugly. But it must be done. Those we find who are still true, bless their courageous souls, will thank us one day.'

'I'm sure,' said Rawne, not sure at all.

'If I might say so,' said Sydona, signing a data-slate one of his aides held out for him, 'I find your concerns quaint. In a good way. I have had many dealings with the Imperial Guard. I have, most usually, found the soldiers of the Guard to be base and soulless. Your attitude does you credit.'

'I've kept good company over the years,' said Rawne.

'You mean Gaunt? I'm looking forward to meeting him. I've heard so much about him from my inquisitor. A rare creature, as I understand it. Honourable and highly principled. A total misfit, of course. They say when Warmaster Macaroth dines with his senior staff, he always asks to hear the latest stories of Gaunt and his ways. They amuse him so very much. Gaunt is a throwback to another era.'

'Which era would that be, sir?' Rawne asked.

Sydona laughed out loud. 'I have no idea. A better one, perhaps. One that progress has left behind. He is atavistic. Noble, yes, but atavistic. We may enjoy the luxury of admiring him, but his breed is dying out. There's no place for sentiment in the Imperium. No place for his kind of nobility either. If you're career minded, major, you might consider a transfer to a unit with a more rational commander. Gaunt's wearisome honour will get you killed.'

'I am an Imperial Guardsman, sir,' Rawne said. 'War will get me killed. That is a matter of fact.'

'But Gaunt will get you killed worthlessly, over some idiotic point of morality.'

'I spent a long time wanting to kill him myself,' said Rawne. 'Dying along with him over some idiotic point of morality sounds like a death I would be happy to choose.'

He turned to go, then paused. 'You speak of my commander as if you expect to hear from him,' he said.

'Contact has been made with his section,' Sydona said, matter-of-factly.

'I wasn't informed. I've been trying to reach him for hours.'

'The weather has impaired vox traffic,' replied the interrogator. 'But I have it as a fact that my inquisitor has made contact with him in the Untill.'

'Who is your inquisitor?' Rawne asked.

'My lord Welt,' said Sydona.

'Ah,' said Rawne, nodding. 'Him.'

IV

STREET TWENTY-SIX was a commercial thoroughfare that began at the north end of Cantible's main market square and ran west around the lower edge of the town's central hill. The roadway was cobbled, though many of the cobblestones had been displaced. A main sewer had been ruptured by a tank shell, and the gutters had become stinking channels of waste.

The habs on either side were washed out and grey. Flamer teams had been along already, burning off the worst of the heathen scrawl that the enemy had written on the walls. Most of the windows had been broken or blown out years before. Several buildings had been flattened by shelling from the Dev Hetra armour in the last two days. On the street corner, a pyre had been made of the bodies of the enemy recovered from that stretch of street. It burned lazily, as if the immolation was some kind of cruel torture, or as if the intention had been to slow burn charcoal from the corpses. Caffran's section pulled their capes up around their noses as they went by.

They passed Domor and his squad, heading in to one of the habs, and wished them luck. Then, a few buildings down, they encountered Kolea and Varl with a ten-man unit.

Kolea nodded to Caffran.

'We're going to take the buildings at the end of the road,' Caffran told him.

'Watch how you go,' Varl advised. 'We've smoked three excubitors out of the basements along here already this morning.'

'One was wired. Packet bombs,' said Kolea, lightly.

'What did you do?' asked Caffran.

'Shot him before he could detonate. Why, what would you have done?'

Caffran smiled.

'What's the priest for?' asked Varl.

'Decoration,' replied Zweil.

'This is no place for a–' Kolea began.

'I've read him the rules,' Caffran interrupted.

'All right then,' said Kolea. 'Good luck.'

'The Emperor protects,' said Zweil.

Caffran moved his section on. He had eight men, plus the priest. Osket, Wheln, Harjeon, Leyr, Neskon, Raess, Leclan and Vadim. They spread out through the weed-engulfed rubble. Caffran kept having to stop to help the aged priest. He already regretted allowing the old man to come along.

They entered the portico of an abandoned hab. Someone had been using it as a latrine. The doors were broken, and all the tiles on the atrium floor had been prised up as if they were something someone wanted to collect. The word *PLEASE* had been written on one wall in whitewash. For some reason, Caffran found that especially chilling.

'Let me go first,' Zweil suggested.

Leclan and Leyr glanced at Caffran. Caffran paused and then nodded. Zweil limped along ahead of them, down the hallway. The building had skylights, but the shutters were broken and swinging limply in the wind, making the light in the hallway come and go, as if clouds were racing by overhead. Patches of grey and white light shifted uneasily around one another across the scabby walls and the ruined floor. Halfway down the hallway, they found a human collar bone lying on its own,

'Don't touch it!' hissed Caffran, seeing Zweil about to stoop.

'Poor soul,' whispered Zweil, recoiling.

'Poor soul my fething foot,' muttered Leyr.

Something banged somewhere far off in the empty hab. A loose door on its hinges, tugged by the wind, Caffran guessed. It banged again, and they jumped a second time.

'Hello?' Zweil called.

'Don't fething speak!' Wheln exploded. 'They'll know we're coming!'

'I want them to know we're coming,' said Zweil, tapping his nose. 'Trust me.' There was virtually nothing about the ragged old priest that seemed remotely trustworthy.

'Please be careful, father,' Caffran whispered, fiddling with his rifle. The word *PLEASE* on the wall behind him echoed uncomfortably in his mind.

Osket and Neskon pushed open some doors and found hab apartments in terrible states of ruin. The stink was appalling. There was debris on the floors that might have once been body parts. The skeleton of a large grox had been patiently and carefully reassembled in one hab room, the bones threaded onto wire.

'Why?' asked Leclan.

'If I knew why,' Caffran replied, 'I'd be insane.'

'Hello!' Zweil shouted. 'I am an ayatani of the Holy Creed. I've come here to help you. Show yourselves. Everything will be all right.'

'As if,' murmured Neskon.

Raess suddenly raised his long las and aimed it, sweeping.

'What?' Caffran barked.

'Saw something. Down the end.' Raess kept his aim steady. 'Something moved.'

They moved on slowly.

'I am an ayatani of the Holy Creed–' Zweil began to repeat.

Something moved. Caffran saw it this time. Something skittered through the shadows twenty metres ahead.

'Feth!' Raess exclaimed.

'Did you see that?' asked Caffran quickly. 'What do you th–'

Distantly, they all heard the *crack-crack-crack* of a lasrifle firing. They all tensed.

'What–' Zweil started.

'Shhhh!' Caffran hissed.

The link pipped. They could all hear a voice in their ear-pieces.

'–love of the Throne, feth… he just came at me… for the goodly love of the Throne–'

The channel went dead.

'That was Varl,' said Vadim. 'Shit, that was Varl.'

'Section eight, this is section five,' Caffran sent. 'Signal back. Kolea? Varl?'

There was a long pause.

Caffran waited and then began again. 'Section eight, this is–'

'Caff, it's Kolea,' the link suddenly crackled. 'The priest with you still?'

'Yes.'

'Feth's sake, Caff. Bring him here, would you?'

V

CAFFRAN'S SECTION LEFT the hab and hurried back to the block that Kolea's squad had been sweeping. Zweil, old and infirm, moved so slowly that Neskon finally stopped in frustration and, with Leclan, made a chair of their arms to carry him.

Kolea and several of his men were waiting in the atrium of the hab block.

'Down here,' Kolea said bluntly.

The rest of his section was thirty metres down inside the desolate shell, grouped around something on the floor. Varl was nearby, standing alone, clearly very angry or upset.

'He just came out of nowhere,' Varl growled. 'Out of the shadows. Feth. Feth! The stupid bastard!'

Caffran pushed his way through the huddle of Kolea's men. A man lay on the tiles, bleeding out from a ghastly las wound through the gut. He'd once been a fine figure of a man, an agricultural worker or a smith, some trade that had put bulk into his shoulders. He was dressed in rags, and weighed no more than half his proper bodyweight.

He was still alive.

'Black cross,' said Kolea simply. 'Varl got caught out. It's a bad thing.'

'The stupid fether came out of nowhere!' Varl yelled behind them.

'It's okay,' Kolea told him. 'It's not your fault.'

'Except I shot him!'

'It's not your fault, Ceg,' Kolea murmured. 'It's just a bad thing.'

Leclan had dropped to his knees beside the man, binding the bloody wounds, entry and exit. He worked fast, with a corpsman's practiced skill, struggling to stop the man's life from leaking away. He threw aside three or four field dressing packs as they became saturated with blood. The sodden bundles of lint packing splatted into the pond of blood on the floor and pattered drops up the wall.

His hands red and wet, Leclan looked up at Caffran and shook his head.

'Father?' Caffran called.

Zweil stepped forwards and touched Leclan on the shoulder, signalling him to step out. He knelt in the blood pooling around the civilian that Varl had accidentally killed, and cradled the man's head.

'I am an ayatani of the Holy Creed,' he said softly. 'Be calm now, my friend, for the God-Emperor of Mankind is rushing here to present you with the gift of peace you crave. Is there anything you wish to confess at this hour?'

The man made a gurgling noise. Blood bubbled around his drawn lips.

'I hear and understand those sins as you have confessed them to me,' Zweil said, 'and I absolve you of them, as I absolve you of all other sins you cannot enumerate. It is in my power to do this thing, for I am an ayatani of the Holy Creed. The winds have blown your sins away, and the beati has blessed you and, though there is pain, it will end, as all pain ends, and you will ascend without the pain of the mortal world to the place the God-Emperor of Mankind has set aside for you at the train of the Golden Throne of Terra. These last rites I give you freely and in good faith. Be at peace, Imperial soul, and may–'

Zweil stopped. Very slowly, he let the man's head rest back onto the tiled floor.

'He's gone,' he said.

VI

WELT'S FORCES CLEARED the partisan camp. Drawn by signal buoys, drop ships landed in the clearing that the soldiers of the Inquisition had made in the canopy. More troops dismounted: troops, and inter-rogators, and sundry other agents of the Holy Inquisition.

Perched in the branches of a tree across from the camp, Mkoll watched. The order and authority of the Imperium was being restored. He understood that the process of that restoration would be fraught and uncomfortable, but this was a curious triumph. It felt as if some honourable compact had been betrayed. He could hear Landerson shouting, protesting.

He looked away.

A white moth fluttered around him, and came to rest on the back of his right hand. It stayed there for a moment, lifting and closing its furry wings.

'Gereon resists,' he whispered.

It flew away at the touch of his breath.

Mkoll waited a few minutes more, putting off returning to the camp. His senses were sharp. The sharpest. Only Bonin and Caober came close to his degree of skill in stealthing. Only one man had ever bettered it.

And that man was dead.

Mkoll looked around. Something had stirred, some slight sound, off to his right. He made no sound himself, but turned slowly in the crook of the branch.

The undergrowth of the Untill behind him was immobile and secret. The only movement was the flutter of the moths. He caught a scent, a very faint trace. He knew it, nevertheless.

'You're there, aren't you?' he called.

There was no reply.

'I don't expect you to answer. But you're there. You're out there, aren't you?'

There was still no answer. The scent had gone. Perhaps he had imagined it.

Mkoll dropped out of the tree and waded back towards the camp.

'CIRK?' GAUNT SAID.

'Ibram.'

He sat down beside her on the edge of the platform stage. Cirk had picked the most faraway part of the camp to sit, all alone in the edges of the swamp dark.

'Are you all right?' he asked.

She nodded. He could see that she had been weeping.

'You're not all right,' he said.

'I never meant this to happen.'

'This?'

'All of this. I cut a deal with Balshin and Welt.'

'When?'

Cirk shrugged. 'When we got back. On Ancreon Sextus, after the tribunal. I did it for your sake.'

'Oh, don't give me that.'

Cirk stared at him. 'You bastard. I did. I really did. You and the others had done so much for us and you were facing execution. I stepped up, and sold what little I had.'

'What exactly did you sell, Cirk?'

'The myth of our survival,' she replied with a sad smile. 'I told them that they had to liberate Gereon, because they'd find a way to proof themselves against Chaos. They found the idea deeply attractive. The mystery of how you came out of Gereon without taint infuriated them. And now, here we all are.'

'Here we all are,' Gaunt nodded. 'This isn't the way you thought it would go, though, is it?'

'Throne, not at all.'

She drew her feet up onto the edge of the platform stage and hugged her knees. 'Gereon's going to keep suffering. We suffered under the Archenemy, and now we'll suffer under the Imperium, as they take the planet apart looking for something that isn't there.'

'I take it you don't believe?'

Cirk began to laugh so hard that Gaunt almost had to steady her to prevent her from falling off the platform's edge.

'Sorry, sorry...' she sighed at length. 'I believe all right. I mean, we came through unscathed. But I think it's in here–'

She tapped her temple with a finger.

'It's in here. It's not something you can analyse and manufacture and stick in a pot. The very idea is so funny. But Welt and Balshin just seized on it. Those bastards. Such simple minds.'

She stared at her boots. 'It's such a bloody mess, isn't it, Ibram?'

'It's not exactly as I imagined it. I thought I'd be proud. I'm not proud of this. High Command didn't initiate this operation for the benefit of the people of Gereon. They're only bothering with Gereon because they think there's something valuable here.'

'I wanted them to rescue my world so much, I'd have told them anything. I never thought what the consequences might be.'

'Me neither,' Gaunt admitted. 'Be careful what you wish for... that's the lesson, isn't it?'

Cirk nodded.

'It's ironic, don't you think?' she asked, 'to want to save your world so much you end up killing it?'

BROSTIN TOOK OUT a crumpled pack of lho-sticks and wedged one in Larkin's mouth. He took one himself. He lit them both off his flamer.

Larkin sat back in the small cot. He was the only patient in the camp's small, makeshift infirmary.

'It's not so bad,' Brostin said. 'You could have been dead. The colonel did you a favour.'

'Cut my fething foot off.'

'Well, there is that.'

Curth appeared through a tent drape. She was carrying something bundled in rags.

'That's bad for your health,' she said, taking the lho-stick out of Larkin's mouth and clamping it between her own lips.

'Throne, it's been a long time,' she sighed, exhaling.

'I thought you said it's bad for your health?' said Larkin.

'It is.'

'So are power swords, I've discovered,' Larkin scowled.

'Not as bad for you as being killed by a tank, so shut up,' said Brostin.

'I've got something,' said Curth, putting the bundle down on the cot.

'What?' Larkin asked.

'Good medicine. It'll make you feel better.' Inside the rags, broken down into its component parts, was Larkin's old long-las, the nalwood-stocked rifle that Larkin had brought all the way from Tanith and had finally abandoned on Gereon for lack of ammo.

'Holy fething Throne...' Larkin whispered. 'You kept it.'

'I knew you'd need a reason to come back,' said Curth. She watched as Larkin began to fit the weapon back together.

'Get me some gun oil, Bros,' he said. Brostin nodded and got up. He passed Gaunt on his way out of the infirmary.

'Ana?'

She turned away from Larkin, who was lost in the act of rebuilding his precious gun, and walked with Gaunt into a small side room.

'How is he?'

'I think I've taken his mind off the injury.'

'That's good. I wish there had been some other way.'

She started cleaning some medical instruments.

'Ana,' he began, 'if I'd known the Inquisition–'

'Were you about to apologise?' she asked, glancing at him. 'There's no need. I've been expecting this.'

'You have?'

'Living and working with the resistance, you do tend to dream about the day of liberation. A reassuring fantasy. I happened to imagine what the reality would be like. Gereon will never be the same. It will continue to suffer. That's the way of things. The Imperium is a blunt instrument, Ibram, and Chaos is too dangerous a quality to take chances with.'

'The Inquisition believes there is a… a secret here in the Untill. That's why they moved in with such speed.'

'What secret would that be?' she asked.

'When I and the others got out, no one could understand why we hadn't been tainted. They think there's something here that protects against taint.'

'Something in the Untill?' she asked. 'Is that what this is all about? They'd have left us to rot, except there's something in it for them?'

'I'm afraid I think that's exactly what's happened. I think they're going to spend years, decades maybe, picking over Gereon, taking it apart, trying to find this secret thing.'

'I could save them some time,' Curth said, 'if they spoke to me. I'm a trained medicae, and I've been working here under these conditions for a long time. Various toxic compounds derived from natural sources here in the swamp habitat have remarkable properties that could benefit the Imperium. Anti-coagulants, counterseptics, and several extracts that have particular efficacy in dealing with agues and xenos-derived infections. But that's it. There's no secret here. No miracle protection against taint. You resist the touch of Chaos by resisting it. You resisted. I resisted. And Gereon resists.'

She stopped her cleaning work and faced Gaunt. She was so thin and so ill he found her painful to behold.

'You did a noble thing, Ana,' he said, 'staying here to help these people. I'm not leaving you behind again.'

'Good,' she said. 'I think I'm done. I think I'm worn out. I've prayed you would come back, Ibram. I know you promised, but there were no guarantees. It's just something that kept me going. But I've entertained no romantic follies of a happy ending. Just an ending, that's all I want now. An end to this. This place has nearly killed me.'

She sighed. 'Is Dorden with you? Is he still alive? I'd like to see him. It would be good to see him.'

'He's at Cantible.'

She nodded. 'Turns out, I have a limit,' she said. 'I've devoted my life to helping people, as a medicae. I left Vervunhive to serve the Guard, and left the Guard to serve the people here. They say that good works and selfless effort are their own reward. But this has been horror, without relief. It has taken me beyond a limit for selflessness I didn't know I had. I am not rewarded by what I have done. I do not feel a better servant of the God-Emperor for it. I hate this, Ibram.'

'It's over,' he said.

VII

BELTAYN REPORTED THAT the transports he'd signalled were inbound. A flight of Valkyries would be on station within a few minutes. Gaunt nodded, and went over to Criid and Mkoll.

'Is the section ready?'

'We're ready to go,' said Criid, her face bandaged. 'I'll be glad to leave.'

'Make sure Curth gets on board,' Gaunt said to Mkoll. He walked through the waiting Ghosts, speaking briefly to some, and reached Eszrah.

'Are you coming with us?' he asked.

The Nihtgane nodded. 'I am unkynde,' he said after a moment, struggling slightly to form his Low Gothic words, 'and this world is ending.'

'Geryun, itte persist longe, foereffer,' said Gaunt.

Eszrah shook his head, and walked away down the platform walkway, heading out of the camp.

'Ten minutes!' Gaunt called after him. 'If you are coming with us, you've got ten minutes!'

Eszrah looked back and nodded. Then he carried on his way, along the path into the swamp woods.

* * *

'WITH YOUR PERMISSION,' said Gaunt, 'I'm moving my force out and returning to Cantible.'

Welt was in one of the large habitents that the Inquisition had erected, reading through data-slates. Envoys, analysts and Inquisition troopers came and went. The place was well lit, and insect repellent devices hummed and crackled around the roof posts.

'The Emperor protect you,' the inquisitor replied. 'Thank you for your contribution.'

Gaunt shrugged.

'I believe the work here will take some time,' Welt said, still distracted by the documents. 'A grand undertaking, but a worthy one. Early results seem to confirm what we suspected.'

'Which is?'

'The resistance fighters, especially the Sleepwalkers, are the key. Their knowledge of the Untill's biology is a vital tool. That's why we needed you to make contact with them, of course. I'm sorry you felt used, Gaunt, but we needed to bring them out, and that meant utilising someone they would trust. I can't imagine how long it would have taken to locate them in this wilderness otherwise.'

'For the record,' Gaunt said, 'you're wasting your time.'

'I know your feelings, Gaunt,' Welt replied. 'If there's even a chance, a hint of a chance, I must pursue it. It would be a crime against the Throne if I didn't. Can't you see that?'

'I suppose so.'

'The liberation of Gereon was always going to be painful, Gaunt. A place that has suffered like this doesn't just pick itself up, dust itself down and get back on with it. It will take years. Centuries, perhaps. Gereon may never be what it was. But you must look at the positives. At least there has been a liberation. High Command regarded Gereon as an entirely lost cause until we presented good reasons for coming here. And if I find what I am looking for, the future of mankind will be more secure. Don't bother yourself with the whys and wherefores, colonel-commissar. You got the liberation you wanted.'

'I'm not sure what I wanted anymore.'

Welt sniffed. 'Carry on, then.'

Gaunt made the sign of the aquila, and left the habitent.

AWAY FROM THE illuminated camp, and the light falling through the canopy space cleared by the Inquisition, the Untill was dark and green and quiet. Amphibians called and plopped in the algae-surfaced water. Moths billowed in the mist-threaded air. Insects crawled on the dark root balls and gnarled branches.

Eszrah carefully collected bark samples into one of his old gourd pots. His jars of wode, moth venom and other tinctures were now almost full again. This, he knew, was his last chance ever to replenish them. What he collected now would have to last a lifetime.

He heard a splash, and looked around. Sabbatine Cirk was walking towards him, shin deep in the green water. He stood up and watched her coming closer.

She came to a halt facing him, and looked up at his face, his eyes screened by Varl's old sunshades. Eszrah had trouble reading people's expressions, but it seemed to him that she wanted to say something and apparently couldn't. After a moment, she reached out her hand, slipped it into his leather satchel, and drew out a single reynbow quarrel. It was a short iron dart, the point caked in venom paste.

She looked back up at Eszrah's face, and half smiled. Then she turned and walked away into the swamp.

Eszrah watched her until she was out of sight. He heard the sound of jets from the landing clearing, and knew he was running out of time. He crouched down to collect the last few things he wanted: a particular herb, a particular snail, a beetle with a red diamond on its wing cases.

He was busy sealing the last gourd flask when he realised he was being watched. There had been no sound, but he felt eyes upon him. He looked up.

The man was standing amongst the trees facing Eszrah, so still and green and quiet that he seemed to be a tree himself, or a hanging bough. He was very tall, and slender, and clad in the wode of a Nihtgane, but he was no Nihtgane that Eszrah knew. He held a fighting staff in one hand, and the filthy remains of a camo-cape were wrapped around his shoulders.

He was staring straight at Eszrah.

'Histye, soule,' Eszrah said, rising.

The man calmly raised one hand and put a finger to his lips. Eszrah nodded. The man was looking past Eszrah now, looking in the direction of the camp.

Eszrah turned his head to see what the man was looking at in particular.

When he turned back, the man had vanished, as if he had never been there.

IN THE PALE light of the clearing, the Ghosts splashed out to board the waiting Valkyries. The noise of the fliers' engines was shrill, and shook the glade. The water shivered. Brostin and Derin helped Larkin cross to the vehicles. Gaunt saw Criid escorting Curth. Inquisition officers with light batons were marshalling the Valkyries, and directing them to their take-off point. Lamp beacons had been bolted to the trunks of trees around the clearing.

Gaunt had wanted to speak to Landerson before he left, but the entire partisan contingent had been interned prior to interview. The Inquisition was keeping them in a series of huts, under guard, and Gaunt didn't want to jeopardise walking out with Curth by making a fuss.

'Eszrah?' he yelled over the jet noise. Mkoll shook his head.

'I told him we were going,' Gaunt shouted.

'There!' Mkoll yelled back. Eszrah had materialised in the trees, and was jogging to join them.

'Come on!' Gaunt called. 'We nearly had to extract without you!'

The three of them hurried to the nearest Valkyrie, where the Ghosts already on board reached down to pull them up through the hatch.

'What were you doing out there?' Mkoll yelled to Eszrah.

Eszrah calmly raised one hand and put a finger to his lips.

SHE HEARD THE rising echo of the jet engines as the Valkyries climbed out of the landing clearing. The din faded, and the quiet of the Untill re-established itself.

The camp was a smudge of light in the distance, like a swamp light flickering beyond the trees. Where she was, it was so black the trees were like anthracite and the air like oil. Tiny white moths fluttered in the air like blossom. There had been white blossom like that in her family orchards once, all those years ago.

Sabbatine Cirk took out the reynbow quarrel. She held it in her hand for a while, and then pressed the venomed tip against the palm of her left hand until the skin broke.

With no splash, no murmur, and hardly any ripple at all, she slid down beneath the glossy surface of the lightless water.

VIII

SQUALLY RAIN WAS beating down on Cantible when they arrived. The sky billowed with fat grey rain-clouds, and seemed soiled and dirty. There was a smell of thunder in the wet air.

The Valkyries came in over the town and dropped into a paddock west of the walls. The downpour made the battered buildings of the town seem more drab and lifeless than before. The paddock, and the neighbouring fields were soaking into an unhealthy mire.

Gaunt jumped out of the flier onto a field covered in puddles that were splashed and rippled by the rain. From the air, he'd seen the changes that had occurred in Cantible since he'd left. Repaired defences, the extensive facilities of the camp, the habitents and vehicles of the Inquisition. As the other Ghosts dismounted, he hurried with Mkoll to the edge of the paddock where Rawne, Baskevyl and Daur were waiting.

'Welcome back,' said Rawne.

'Anything to report?'

'Business as usual, sir,' said Baskevyl.

'Not our show any more, anyway,' said Rawne. 'The Inquisition's in charge.'

'Speak of the devil,' said Daur quietly.

Interrogator Sydona was approaching, flanked by his aides.

'This one's in charge?' asked Gaunt.

'His name's Sydona,' said Rawne.

'Does he always look so pissed off?' Gaunt asked.

'Now you come to mention it, no,' Rawne admitted.

Sydona came to a halt in front of Gaunt. Both men made the sign of the aquila.

'Gaunt?'

'Colonel-Commissar Gaunt, yes.'

'I am Interrogator Sydona. You have come directly from the Untill site?'

'You know I have.'

Sydona paused. 'There have been urgent vox transmissions from the Untill site while you were in the air. My inquisitor, the Lord Welt, demands to know if

you or any of your detail know anything about the
events that have just taken place.'

'What events?' Gaunt asked.

Sydona looked a little awkward. 'As I understand
it,' he said, 'at some time in the last hour, all the partisans detained at the Untill site for interview have
gone.'

'Gone?'

'Yes. They have all disappeared. Despite the fact
that the area where they were being kept was secure
and under guard. Can you shed any light on this?'

Gaunt looked at Mkoll, who frowned and shook
his head.

'I don't believe I can,' said Gaunt. He started to
walk away with his officers, but hesitated and looked
back at the interrogator. 'Tell your Lord Welt, I'm not
finding them for him this time.'

IX

THE NEXT HAB in the line was just like all the others.
Halfway down street twenty-seven, it was a four
storey residential made of rockcrete and grey stone.
The driving rain made the flaking rockcrete look like
putty. A litter of broken furniture and discarded
household possessions lay on the rubble in front of
the property. Inside, the rain had brought out a dank
smell.

The stairways and halls ran the depth of the building. Rain ran in through the skylights high in the roof
space, and pattered down into pools along the tiled
hall. Caffran watched the drips falling like tracer
rounds, bright and silver in the gloom.

'Hello?' Zweil called out.

They were getting tired and cold. 'Lamp packs,' Caffran instructed. 'You three sweep that way. You three, up there. Stay in contact.'

The section divided up. Harjeon, Wheln and Osket moved up the stairs. Neskon, Raess and Leyr went off to the right. Caffran continued on down the hallway with Leclan, Vadim and the old priest.

'Hello? Hello? I am an ayatani of the Holy Creed. I've come here to help you. Show yourselves. Everything will be all right.'

The rain dripped down around them out of the invisible roof. Their moving lamp beams wobbled and danced across the floor and the stained walls. In the corner of one room, they found a nest of old blankets and torn clothes that looked as if someone had been sleeping in it. In the next room, a dead man sat in a chair at a table, the corpse untouched for months, mummified.

They moved on.

'You feel that?' Vadim asked.

'What?'

'Really feels like we're being watched.'

'Go slow,' said Caffran. Leclan crossed the hall to another doorway and his lamp flickered round to illuminate more debris and filth.

'Careful,' Vadim hissed.

Zweil shuffled forwards and cleared his throat. 'Hello? Hello? Is there anyone there? I am an ayatani of the Holy Creed and I've come to help you.'

They waited. Caffran held up a hand for quiet. They all heard the tiny scurry from beyond the doorway.

Caffran slipped through the door into the chamber beyond. The floor was covered with broken glass and torn paper scraps. The remains of a bed or couch rotted under a broken window. There was a door on the far side of the room, half closed.

Vadim swept in behind Caffran, panning his weapon.

'You smell that?' he whispered.

Caffran nodded. There was a slight scent of burning.

He moved across the room, and found something near the collapsed remains of the bed by the window. It was a small fire, made of twigs, still warm although the flames had been put out. A shrivelled Imperial Guard ration pack, stolen from somewhere, lay amongst the heaped twigs. Someone had been trying to warm up a meal.

Caffran was about to call Vadim over when something he had taken to be a heap of litter beside the bed moved and fled towards the other door. Caffran cried out, and tried to follow it with his lamp beam. Vadim raised his weapon.

'Don't shoot!' Caffran called out.

Leclan and Zweil had entered the room. With Caffran leading, they moved towards the second door. It led into a storeroom, a small chamber of rockcrete with shelves along one wall and an old cold store pantry beside them. There were no other doors, and the window lights were just slits high up near the ceiling. There was a powerful reek of human waste. Caffran saw there was nothing on any of the shelves, except a collection of buttons and bottle caps, laid out in rows in deliberate order of increasing size.

There was no sign of anybody. Caffran moved his lamp beam around. Leclan came in beside him.

'Pantry?' he whispered.

Caffran nodded. The pantry door was pulled to, but it was large, a walk-in larder where meat could be hung. They began to approach it.

'Feth!' Caffran exclaimed suddenly. Something moved under the lowest shelf. He swung around and aimed his rifle and his torch beam down at the floor.

The child was very small, twisted with starvation and disease. He was dressed in rags and his skin was brown with dirt. His eyes seemed fantastically big and wild, and he shielded them, whining, when the lamp found him.

'Feth! It's just a child!' Caffran said, bending down to get closer.

'Father!' Leclan called. Zweil and Vadim followed them into the storeroom. The child tried to climb deeper and deeper into the shadows under the shelving, making animal mews of fear.

'It's all right, it's all right,' Caffran called, reaching out his hand.

'Everything will be fine,' Zweil said. 'You come out of there, my young friend, and we'll look after you. Hello? Are you hungry? Do you want some food?'

Zweil glanced at the others. 'Anyone got a ration pack? Dried biscuit rations? A sugar stick?'

'I have,' said Leclan. He leant his lasrifle against his leg as he opened his breast pocket and fished around.

The pantry door opened.

The excubitor who had been hiding inside had a las-lock. When it went off, the noise in the confined space was huge. Zweil screamed in surprise and shock. The las-round hit Leclan, and took off the side of his head. He rotated slightly as he fell, and broke some of the shelves under him.

Caffran opened fire and cut the excubitor down with a flurry of close range shots. The impact threw the servant of the Anarch backwards into the pantry.

After the brief, furious gunfire, the silence was shocking.

Vadim went to the pantry, checked it was empty, and put an extra shot into the excubitor's head to be sure.

'Oh, feth... feth, feth, feth...' said Caffran. He crouched over Leclan's body.

'Is he–?' Zweil asked over his shoulder.

'Vadim! Get the others! Go and get the others!' Caffran yelled.

Vadim nodded and ran out of the room. A moment later they could hear him shouting.

'It's no good,' Caffran said. He sat back from Leclan. 'He didn't stand a chance.'

Caffran rose to his feet and looked at Zweil.

'What a mess.'

Zweil didn't answer him.

'Father?'

Zweil nodded, indicating something over Caffran's shoulder. Caffran turned.

The child, a boy of about nine or ten, had come out from under the shelves. Although it was much too big for him, he had picked up Leclan's lasrifle and was pointing it at Caffran and the priest.

'Get back, father,' Caffran breathed. He looked at the child and smiled encouragingly. 'Come on, little man, give me that.'

The boy fired three shots, the weight and discharge staggering him. Then he threw the weapon aside and ran.

'Caffran? Caffran!' Zweil yelled. He bent down and cradled the Ghost in his arms. There was blood everywhere, pumping from a huge, messy wound in Caffran's chest. 'Medicae!' Zweil shouted. 'Medicae!'

Caffran gasped.

'Hold on, you hear me,' Zweil demanded, trying to support Caffran and staunch the bleeding at the same time. 'You hold on. Help's coming.'

Caffran's eyelids fluttered. He looked up at Zweil for a moment. He tried to speak, but he couldn't. His left hand clawed at the vest pocket of his battledress tunic, trying to unbutton it.

'Medicae! Medicae!' Zweil yelled over his shoulder. 'Someone!'

He looked back at Caffran. He swallowed hard as he saw the distant look in Caffran's eyes, the receding light. As a priest in war, he had seen it before, too many times. Caffran's bloody left hand still fumbled with the pocket fastening. Zweil reached over and undid the pocket for him, and took out what was inside. It was a Tanith cap badge. Caffran's mouth tried to form words.

'I am an ayatani of the Holy Creed,' Zweil said softly. 'Be calm now, my friend, for the God-Emperor of Mankind is rushing here to present you with the gift of peace you crave. Is there anything you wish to confess at this hour?'

Caffran didn't respond. Zweil continued to hold him up, his hands and arms wet with Caffran's blood.

'I hear and understand those sins as you have confessed them to me,' Zweil said, his voice hoarse, 'and I absolve you of them, as I absolve you of all other sins you cannot enumerate. It is in my power to do this thing, for I am an ayatani of the Holy Creed. The winds have blown your sins away, and the beati has blessed you and, though there is pain, it will end, as all pain ends, and you will ascend without the pain of the mortal world to the place the God-Emperor of Mankind has set aside for you at the train of the Golden Throne of Terra. These last rites I give you freely and in good faith...'

PROPER BLOODY GUARDSMEN

I

TWENTY DAYS EXACTLY after the initial wave of assaults had hit Gereon, the first retirement orders were sent through. Front-line units who had been on the ground since day one were drawn back, or switched out for fresh brigades from the carrier fleet. A quarter of a million new Guardsmen were dropped into the field. The exhausted soldiers they were relieving filtered slowly back along lines of transport to base camps, and then back to the fleet.

AT 137 was retired just before noon on the twentieth day, and moved back along the line with a Krassian division. The Krassians had taken especially heavy losses during the citadel war that had raged in the heart of K'ethdrac'att Shet Magir between days six and fourteen of the liberation.

In a single afternoon, AT 137 walked back the fourteen kilometres they had covered in the previous twenty days, through the gutted city, under a sky full of smoke, passing the newcomers marching in.

Brigade bands were playing, and colours were being carried high. The new arrivals they passed looked clean and healthy. They cheered and applauded the retiring troopers when they saw them. The retiring troopers tried to muster the effort to return the salutes.

Dalin wondered if the new blood knew what they were walking into. He wondered if he ought to stop and talk to them about the things he'd seen and the things he knew. There was a hell of fight left to be fought.

He decided to keep walking, because he believed Sobile might shoot him if he started telling people about the shit ahead. Bad for morale. Besides, no one had ever bothered to warn him.

They reached a dispersal point on the coast, and waited three more, leaden days in the Munitorum camp for extraction. Conditions were hot and dusty, but there was fresh food and clean water at least. Munitorum staffers processed each man in turn, and filled out forms and audits. Each man got a paper tag with his destination and redeployment details written on it riveted to his collar.

Dalin slept for a while in the grubby shared tents pitched along the shore behind the sea wall, lying in a bed roll that had been used by fifty men before him. It was hard to sleep, because he was wound up so tight, and though he tried, his mind and body would not unclench. He wondered if the tension would ever ease. It didn't feel like it would. He felt he would be two heartbeats from ducking and firing for the rest of his life. The instinct had been ground into him. Every sound from outside the tent made him reach for his weapon.

When he did sleep, it was a troubled slumber. Dreams plagued him, though on waking, he couldn't remember the details. The wounded were being processed through the area and, at night, he could hear their moans and screams coming from the hospital stations.

On the third day, they were directed to a row of drop ships waiting on the hillside above the shore.

THE DROP SHIP took them up out over the bay. Through the heavy armoured ports, Dalin saw the sea far below, like a sheet of chipped plate glass. He saw the city behind them, receding. The enemy city. The corpse of a city. Then it was gone in the haze, and it seemed as if Gereon had been entirely reduced to a realm of dust and smoke where nothing solid remained.

He fell asleep in his restraint seat, his head knocking and rolling limply against the backrest as the ship jolted. This time he didn't dream. This time his mind slid off the edge of some precipice and dropped into nothingness.

THEY RODE THE hydraulic platforms up through the decks of the carrier from the drop hangar. Most of them sat on the metal decking, their kit and weapons clutched to their chests, cold weather ponchos draped around their shoulders. The climate on the carrier was a good eight degrees colder than the surface, and the air had a metallic, chemical flavour.

Sobile stood on his own at the edge of the rising platform, hands clasped behind his back, watching the thick cross-sections of deck slide past. Downdraft air gusted down the riser shaft. There was a lot of noise from the repair decks: voices, machine tools, metal on metal. Dalin saw a row of fifty Leman Russ battle tanks drawn up ready for transportation. Twenty-three days earlier, he would have been thrilled by such a sight. He tried to remember what his twenty-three day younger self had been like, but all he could imagine was another young corpse face down in the white dust of K'ethdrac.

On the fifth deck level, they climbed down into the dispersal area. Munitorum officials mobbed around, sorting men and checking them off. The chamber was milling with personnel and ringing with chatter. Steam billowed up from under-deck vents.

'What does this mean?' Dalin asked, holding out the tag pinned to his collar. 'What does this mean?' The Munitorum staffers passing by ignored him.

'Company, form up!' Kexie yelled. 'Quick time, now!'

All that remained of AT 137 gathered in a row in the middle of the deck. It wasn't an impressive sight. Every one of them was dirtier than Dalin thought it was possible to be. They stank. Their kit was shredded.

'Stand to, stand to, ech,' Kexie said, walking the pitifully short line. He looked no better than they did.

Sobile had been talking to some Munitorum officials. He wandered over to face them.

He held up a data-slate and read from it.

'Attention. Hereby order given this day of 777.M41 that reserve activation has now been suspended. This detail, afforded the name Activated Tactical 137, that is AT 137, now stands deactivated, and the individuals here should report to their original regiments or divisions. So, you're free to return to your units. All obligation to RIP details is done with.'

Sobile lowered the data-slate and regarded them with a blank, humourless look. 'I can't see the good of that. You all started out morons and you're morons still. The likes of you give the proud tradition of the Imperial Guard a bad smell. I have never gone to war with such inadequate soldiers. In my opinion, you should be on RIP for the rest of your bloody lives. You're shit. I'm glad to wash my hands of you.'

He looked at Kexie. 'That's all. Sergeant, carry on.'

'Salute!' Kexie thundered.

They saluted. Sobile looked at them for a moment longer, and then turned and walked away.

They lowered their hands.

Kexie stood in front of them for a moment, chewing the inside of his cheek. His hands clenched and unclenched, as if imagining Saroo. Saroo was in a locker somewhere, waiting for him, waiting to greet the next RIP detail.

He looked at them, his eyes moving from one man to the next. Dalin hadn't realised that Kexie was quite so old. Perhaps it was the dirt caking his lined face.

With a final, diffident sigh, he saluted them.

The salute was straight backed and firm. They all returned it instinctively. Dalin felt something hot on his face, and realised that tears were rolling down his cheeks.

'Ech,' said Kexie, with a half smile. 'Proper bloody Guardsmen.'

He dropped the salute and walked away.

LEFT ALONE, THE row of them slowly disintegrated. Some of them sat down on the deck. Others wandered away. Fourbox was one of the ones who sat down. He dropped his kit and weapon beside him, and bowed his head, drawing his hands up over his scalp. Dalin saw that his hair was growing back in. The hard edges of his scalp cut were gone.

'Screw all this,' Wash said. Brickmaker sniggered. 'Screw all this and all of you,' Wash continued. 'I'll see you in the Basement.' He picked up his kit and walked off.

Dalin picked up his rifle and rested it across his left shoulder. He scooped up his filthy kit bag in his right hand.

'See you, Fourbox,' he said.

Fourbox looked up at him. 'Yeah, I'll see you.'

He called out as Dalin turned. 'Holy?'

'Yes?'

'We did it,' Fourbox said.

'Did what?'

'Whatever that was. We did it. We lived.'

'You say that,' Dalin replied, 'like it's a good thing.'

Dalin crossed the deck, looking for an exit. He'd gone quite a way before something occurred to him and he turned back. By then, Fourbox had disappeared.

'What are you looking for?'

Dalin looked around. Merrt was there, watching him.

'I was looking for Fourbox,' Dalin said.

'Why?'

'Because I suddenly realised I have no idea what his real name is.'

Merrt shook his head, amused.

'You know what?' Dalin said to him. 'All of this, all of this, and I don't think any of us have learned a single fething thing.'

'You have,' said Merrt. 'You just don't know it yet. Come on.'

'Where to?'

'We're supposed to report to our units,' said Merrt. 'I think you should follow me.'

'Why?'

'Where else are you gn… gn… gn… gonna go?'

Dalin walked alongside the Tanith soldier across the bustling deck.

'Hey,' said Merrt, pointing. 'Isn't that–?'

Through the press of bodies ahead of them, Dalin could see a figure waiting. A woman, tall and slender, wearing dark combat gear and the pins of a sergeant.

'Yeah,' said Dalin.

'Count yourself lucky,' said Merrt. 'My mother never waited on any dispersal deck to meet me.'

Dalin nodded, but he didn't feel especially lucky. As he walked towards Tona Criid, she spotted him and moved forwards to meet him. He saw the look in his ma's eyes, and felt even less lucky than before.

'Ma?' he whispered. His throat was dry and he dearly wished his canteen wasn't empty.

She had something in her hand.

It was a Tanith cap badge.

ABOUT THE AUTHOR

Dan Abnett lives and works in Maidstone, Kent, in England. Well known for his comic work, he has written everything from the *Mr Men* to the *X-Men*.

His work for the Black Library includes the best-selling Gaunt's Ghosts novels, the Inquisitor Eisenhorn and Ravenor trilogies, and the acclaimed Horus Heresy novel, *Horus Rising*. He's also worked on the popular strips *Titan* and *Darkblade*, and, together with Mike Lee, the Darkblade novel series.